Carol Smith, formerly a leading London literary agent, now concentrates full-time on her writing career. She is the author of the highly successful *Darkening Echoes*, *Kensington Court*, *Double Exposure*, *Family Reunion* and *Unfinished Business*, all published by Time Warner Books UK.

Praise for Carol Smith

Family Reunion
'. . . a humdinger of a story . . . all the ingredients of a top-class mystery novel. It is very well written, has bags of atmosphere and truly believable characters' *Publishing News*

'A gripping read' *Family Circle*

'Full of action, twists and surprises, this intricate suspense story offers a fascinating new take on the nature of family ties' *Good Housekeeping*

Double Exposure
'Totally fascinating' *Express on Sunday*

'A hugely enjoyable book' *Woman & Home*

Kensington Court
'A rattling thriller' *Daily Express*

'*Kensington Court* . . . will have you racing through the final pages for the brilliant, twisting climax' *Company*

Darkening Echoes
'A witty, hugely enjoyable and confident debut' *The Times*

'It's skilfully plotted, has well-drawn characters and a blood-thirsty climax' *Daily Express*

Also by Carol Smith

DARKENING ECHOES
KENSINGTON COURT
DOUBLE EXPOSURE
FAMILY REUNION
UNFINISHED BUSINESS

Grandmother's Footsteps

CAROL SMITH

A *Time Warner* Paperback

First published in Great Britain in 2002
by Little, Brown and Company
This edition published by Time Warner Paperbacks in 2003

A CIP catalogue record for this book
is available from the British Library.

ISBN 0 7515 3250 9

Typeset in Berkeley by
Palimpsest Book Production Limited,
Polmont, Stirlingshire
Printed and bound in Great Britain by
Clays Ltd, St Ives plc

Time Warner Paperbacks
An imprint of
Time Warner Books UK
Brettenham House
Lancaster Place
London WC2E 7EN

www.TimeWarnerBooks.co.uk

Acknowledgements

Special thanks to Roger Anson of Oxford Brookes University for so patiently explaining to me the rudiments of cartography, to Andrew Puckett for clueing me in about blood, and to Dr Paul Mapleston Smith for correcting my punctuation and casting a fraternal eye over the medical bits.

Thanks, too, to my agent, Jonathan Lloyd; my editor, Tara Lawrence, and Rebecca Kerby whose expertise on small children has helped to make those details accurate.

As always, I am indebted to the wonderful sales and marketing teams who do such a tireless job.

Prologue

It was lambing season and fresh new leaf time but the Urquhart family were oblivious. They were quarrelling.

'Mum,' wailed India from somewhere in the back. 'Make him stop playing with my Game Boy.' She had saved for weeks to afford this coveted toy. It was typical of her brother to try to spoil things.

'Give it back,' rapped out Annabel distractedly, most of her attention still glued to the pages of *Vanity Fair*. She was sick and tired of these family expeditions, not least when the old trout, Adrian's mother, came along.

'It's kid's stuff anyhow,' snorted fourteen-year-old Hugo dismissively, withdrawing back into his football magazine. Annabel sighed. These days it seemed they couldn't go anywhere together without perpetual bickering. And not just between the kids.

'Can we please have a pit stop soon?' moaned Adrian's mother testily. She always claimed car sickness and bagged the best seat. Stuck in the front with her tweeds and silly felt hat, she looked like the Lady Muck she purported to be. There were times, like today, when Annabel would gladly have crowned her. If only she wouldn't keep suck-ing those disgusting mints, a smell as unpleasantly perva-sive as gum. Though she did have a bit of a point, it was quarter to one. They could all do with stretching their legs, and it might help defuse the growing tension in the car. The kids must surely be starving by now. It wasn't like them at all not to have mentioned it yet.

'Pull over at the next service station,' Annabel instructed, but Adrian, now in one of his snits, drove doggedly on. He adored this car but preferred it empty. Alone on the road as in his youth, with just a snatch of Verdi for company. He longed for his bachelor days and the open Jag. The BMW was highly enviable but still just a company car.

'Watch out for that caravan,' his mother said sharply. She made him edgy with her persistent commands. 'All over the road, they ought not to be allowed.' *Hoi polloi*, he could sense her thinking. God, but she'd grown into such a snob.

'Don't drive too close!' She grabbed for his wrist. Careful, she'd have them all in the ditch. He shook her off. *Who's driving this goddamn car?* he wanted to snarl, but knew it wasn't worth the hassle. If he put on some speed they'd be there in half an hour. He glanced at his watch.

His mother was right, the caravan was swaying, a road hazard waiting to happen. He couldn't see the driver as it swung and bounced all over the place but it was clearly overloaded and not entirely under control. This Sunday expedition to Salisbury Cathedral was turning out worse

2

than even he had expected. They had missed morning service but the kids didn't care, they were right little heathens, and his mother was well on his wick.

'Watch out!' she screamed urgently as he pulled out past the caravan, then froze into stunned silence, like a rabbit caught in headlights, as the dreadful inevitability loomed ahead.

'Didn't stand a chance, poor bastards,' said the first cop on to the scene. 'Not even in hardware like this.' He kicked the buckled German-built fender, envious but also respectful. But then this stretch of the A303 was notoriously treacherous. The other car, a lightweight sports car, was infinitely more damaged, crushed like a beer can in a hooligan's fist. Yet, despite its shattered glass and the blood, it was the Urquhart family who were dead. There was still the flicker of a failing pulse in the other driver, trapped like a rat in the wreckage. Sirens and flashing lights isolated the accident scene, and a traffic policeman in fluorescent yellow stood in the centre of the highway, importantly waving people on. Two ambulances arrived at breakneck speed, weaving their way through the crawling traffic, with a pair of wailing fire engines right behind them. It was touch and go whether they'd get the poor blighter out in time. And that was quite apart from the petrol danger.

The cop was pacing, his radio on the go. 'They're sending an air ambulance,' he assured the horrified bystanders. The cars immediately following had all pulled over, their

drivers keen to do anything to help. Looked pretty hopeless but you never could tell, and at least the emergency
services were doing their stuff. The immediate witnesses
were kept back for questioning; the others, mainly rubber-
neckers, were asked politely to move on. The fewer vehi-
cles that clustered, the clearer the road would be, and
they needed space around them for the airlift.

'Jesus,' breathed a second, younger cop, wiping his
sweaty face. One glance inside the BMW was more than
his stomach could take. Those kids and that pulverised
old lady, with her head right through the windscreen,
virtually severed. At least the other guy had had more
luck – the paramedics seemed to think he might still have
a fighting chance. Though from the look of him and all
that blood . . . The policeman's head was swimming again.
He was obliged to withdraw for a quiet puke. They didn't
cover this sort of eventuality at training college.

Nobody's fault, was the consensus of opinion, though
a formal investigation was bound to follow. They came at
each other on a blind dip in the road. No one could have
foreseen it, just one of those tragic black spots. The driver
of the caravan was fortunate to have escaped. He had
witnessed the collision as they raced towards each other,
powerless to do anything more than swerve. The usual
tests would have to be done, of course, to check if either
driver had been drinking. Though at this time on a Sunday
morning the odds against it were great. The driver of the
BMW had, after all, the family along. It might have
happened to anyone at any time. And these expensive

4

sporty models had more power to them than was healthy. If anyone was likely to be at fault, it was the dreadfully injured victim in the wreckage. And he had surely suffered enough, poor sod.

'Move along now,' said the policeman, back on the job. Then the jarring noise of the helicopter landing drowned out all further speech.

'The trouble with these flimsy foreign cars,' said the coroner carefully as he scanned all available facts, 'is they look good and move fast but crumple like sodden cardboard the minute they meet any resistance on the road.' And yet it was this chancer in his dashing sports car who had managed to pull through, at least for the time being. The reports from the hospital were tenuous. He had taken such a bashing, his life was still in the balance. Resuscitative on-the-spot surgery plus an urgent complete blood transfusion. He was lucky to have kept all his limbs, not to mention his life.

The coroner thumbed through his notes, then raised an eyebrow.

'Survivors?' he asked. 'Anyone else involved?' Someone they could interview who might be able to throw light on what had actually happened. Going like the clappers, they said the sports car had been, though to mention speeding at this stage would be heartless in the circumstances.

'One,' said the clerk, consulting his own papers, 'who seems miraculously to have stepped out of the wreckage and walked away unhurt. Wouldn't stay around for more than a cursory check-up or even some professional counselling, which we usually recommend. No doubt in shock. I hope there were no repercussions.' But they couldn't hold anyone against their will when no one had broken the law. And the accident scene had been so grim, all attention had been focused on saving the trapped driver.

'Inquest adjourned then.' The coroner signed the document. He was keen to get back to his golf.

Part One

1

I came to Alton Coombe under cover of fog, as befitted the clandestine nature of my mission. The trees were blanched and skeletal after a tougher than usual winter, their branches glazed with ice like brittle glass. I got off the train at Kemble around mid-morning and found the station deserted and banked with snow. This was something I had not expected. It looked as if it had not been in use for months. I stood in the empty forecourt, figuring out what I should do. Luckily I had little luggage with me for I always make a habit of travelling light. A taxi service's toll-free number was conveniently posted on the door of the booking hall, but I, not wishing to herald my arrival, preferred the hour-long wait for the local bus. I came in stealth, in the footsteps of my prey. For I had serious business on my mind. Murder.

The village, when I eventually got there, was all that the guidebooks had led me to expect. Steep, winding streets, studded with antiques shops. Yellow Cotswold stone and dry crumbling walls. Rows of handsome, protected houses dating back several centuries, and, in the centre, the original covered meeting place, once the focus of local commerce but now the Saturday flea *market. A pale disc, like a phantom moon, hung low in the sky as the sun burned its way through the vapour, and groups of locals emerged from behind stout doors to get on with the business of the day. There was a pervasive smell of woodsmoke in the air and the distant promise of spring. An enchanting place which I fell for at once. In any other circumstances, I think I would have wanted to stay on.*

At this time of year, before the tourist invasion, finding suitable lodgings presented no problem. I took a couple of decent-sized rooms in a winding lane close to the church, explaining to the landlady (as if she would care) that I had some urgent business to attend to. And would not be staying very long, though I couldn't yet give her a definite departure date. For I had plotted and lain in wait and tediously followed up false trails all these years until my brain was practically numb. Had I known what I was taking on, I might never have got started, but now there could be no turning back. The amount of research I had put in already might have earned me a doctorate in sniffing out the truth. I was proud of how much I had achieved so far, and now was all set for the next stage. God knows, it had taken me long enough. Three years to complete my list. It was time for the fun and games to start. And number one was a certain Miss Jane Fairchild.

I saw her first in the parish church that Sunday when, with my landlady, I attended morning service. All unknowingly, she obligingly pointed her out without my having to ask, which was just as well. In a village this small, a cesspool of gossip, Jane Fairchild was a prominent fixture and, to my mind at least, fair game. She stood self-importantly in front of the altar, making minor adjustments to the flowers, while the organist practised his opening chords and the choirboys giggled in the vestry as they robed. We had come deliberately early. I had explained that I wanted to look at the graveyard because of my interest in tombstones but we also had a good wander around the church. The windows were fairly impressive, though the stained glass nothing very special. Not one of the finer examples of its kind, but then, you could say I've been spoiled. I made some suitably enthusiastic noises and my landlady beamed her approval.

Jane Fairchild, however, was no disappointment and I studied her with total fascination. There's a bossy type of woman, quintessentially British, who manages always to set my teeth on edge. Exuding an innate aura of virtue that smacks every time of crass hypocrisy. As though she possessed her own hotline to heaven and was confident that God was on her side. Well, not any more He wasn't, as she'd shortly be discovering. My heart started quickening at the prospect and I wondered if I'd have the guts to see it through.

I watched her, spellbound, throughout the service, keen to pick up every little detail. She was tall and spare, in a velvet hat and serviceable brown suit, and boomed her responses loudly from the front pew. Local aristocracy, as I'm sure she would like to pretend, though I knew enough of her former life to know that wasn't actually the case. A retired headmistress, she'd been raised in Luton with an elder brother, acclaimed as an academic. Throughout her life, no doubt to her chagrin, she had had to live in the shadow of his brilliance. Until here, in

11

Alton Coombe, she had settled on her retirement and finally achieved the lifestyle she'd always desired. Her cottage, close to the duck pond, was quaint and pretty and well kept. She had obviously put a lot of effort into its maintenance. The paintwork was fresh, the thatch in excellent trim. The garden, even in winter, freshly turned over. It was plain Miss Fairchild was something of a perfectionist, which fitted exactly the profile I had drawn.

She took her parochial duties extremely seriously and ran a regular charity stall in the flea market. Proceeds to the Haemophilia Society, which she'd been helping to fund since she'd first put down roots in the village. I checked it all out the following Saturday and boldly loitered in front of her, fingering the bric-à-brac. Lace doilies, Victorian knife-rests, the usual sort of clutter – stuff accumulated over the years that no one could conceivably actually want. Brooches and pill-boxes and garish glass bowls. It was amazing quite how much of it there was. I paused to examine a slightly chipped Toby jug, while listening unashamedly as she gabbled away to the woman on the adjoining stall. Her shoes were sturdy brogues, her stockings thorn-proof lisle. No doubt, tossed into the back of her car would be the requisite Barbour and green wellies. At her feet, half hidden by the tablecloth, shivered her silly little dog. White curly hair freshly laundered, and decked with a blue satin bow. Jane Fairchild had recreated herself as a bit of a country cliché. Village Lady Bountiful and doer of good works, still with that attitude that was holier-than-thou. Fake upper crust and quite insufferable with it. I itched to wipe the smugness from her face.

'My brother this' and 'my brother that' snobbishly punctuated the ceaseless flow. It was clear the other woman was well used to her and took the condescension in her stride.

'Anything I can help you with?' At last I had her attention.

'Thank you but no,' I said with an amiable grin, replacing the jug and casually strolling away. Her spectacle frames were tortoiseshell, a few sparse whiskers sprouted from her chin. Around her withered throat she wore a fine gold chain with some sort of number engraved upon a disc. Whether she'd know me again I couldn't be sure, but even if she did, it would be too late. I experienced an adrenalin surge so powerful I went across the road for an early drink. I had laboured so long and hard to reach this point. Nothing in the world could stop me now.

My most immediate need was a job to tide me over, something to keep body and soul together while I perfected my careful plans. Bar work was usually the simplest thing and, by chance, The Snooty Fox had posted a vacancy. Casual labour, cash in hand. Few questions asked, my luck was certainly in. I started that evening, pulling pints in the public bar, my ears wide open for any fresh snippets of gossip. Not that the lady in question was likely to venture in here. A gin and orange would be her wildest tipple, and even then she would drink it discreetly in the privacy of her home. I knew the type.

They were a friendly bunch in Alton Coombe and I found it very easy to fit in. By constantly smiling and keeping my mouth shut, I was able to draw no attention to myself. I saw very little of my landlady, too, other than at breakfast when she liked to

13

discuss the weather. The place was ideal and suited all my requirements – a hearty breakfast to set me up for the day, plain but comfortable rooms that were clean and warm. And time on my hands just to wander and observe and recall past memories, now long gone. Right on the edge of the Cotswolds, too. The scenery was sensational. A vast improvement on Milton Keynes but that, of course, went without saying. I would have liked to go riding but hadn't the proper clobber; in any case, I wouldn't be there long enough to make it worthwhile. Besides, this was no time for splashing out, not with my list still to work through. I had only my meagre earnings to keep me going, in addition to the joint savings we had carefully put aside to provide for a glorious future that never came. So instead I trawled the antiques shops and wandered around the village, enjoying the rawness of country life and patiently biding my time.

I stalked my prey discreetly and soon had a fair idea of her fussy routines. You could practically set your watch by her, her movements were so predictable. It was easy to imagine what she must have been like at school. Thursdays at ten to the hairdresser, to have the greying curls spruced up, with a manicure thrown in once a fortnight. Tuesdays a.m. to help with the Red Cross, in which, I soon discovered, she was a general. Saturdays, the flea market followed by lunch at the vicarage. She was very pally with both the vicar and his wife, who must have been veritable saints. Just the sound of that trumpeting, affected voice jarred me to the core. Plus I never could forgive her for the terrible thing she had done. Part of my reason for being here in the first place.

She regularly walked the dog in the early mornings and again last thing at night before turning in. A woman much set in her ways was our Miss Fairchild, which made her the perfect target for a hit, particularly for a beginner. After all those solitary years of dreary research, the time for action was finally here. All I needed now was to pick the right spot, after which I would be able to move on. I narrowed it at last to the church, where she did the flowers on every third Friday, according to the rota. From ten until twelve, as part of a regular team. Convenient that they left details like that in the porch. But in these country villages folk are still trusting.

The weather was fast improving and the flowers she had brought were impressive. Hothouse blooms, not fresh from the garden, but all the more showy for that. They were heaped around her as she worked on the altarpiece while her dog was tethered whimpering outside. An elderly verger pottered nearby, stacking hassocks and sorting piles of hymnals. While he was still there, there was little I could do, so I simply lurked tourist-like in the shadows of the lady chapel. Eventually, however, he finished and shuffled away. The time had suddenly come for swift action before I lost my nerve. I nodded to him cordially as I passed him in the nave, then stopped beside her to admire her work, at which she was amply proficient.

'Beautiful flowers,' I said with unfeigned sincerity.

'Aren't they just,' she replied with her customary satisfied smirk. She scarcely bothered to glance at me as she secured each sturdy stem with green picture wire. She had a mass of mixed foliage arranged in a marble urn into which she was

skilfully weaving each separate stalk. Bronze and gold chrysanthemums, spiked with a deep russet red. A veritable cornucopia of winter glory.

'Are you from around these parts?' she asked idly as she snipped, hacking away at the stems with lethal-looking secateurs. I told her I was but I doubt she took it in; she certainly showed no sign of remembering my face. The coil of wire lay tantalisingly close. One swift, sharp movement and I would be able to reach it.

Just then the church clock struck noon and I realised, with a sudden chill, how little time there was left. Five minutes, at most, before the lunchtime influx or else I would have to put it on further hold. Which, having finally plucked up my nerve, I wasn't prepared to do. And she might well know who I was another time. So I took a chance and grabbed for the wire, then looped it over her head and wrenched it tight. She was a big, strong woman but I had the advantage of surprise. As well as being less than half her age. She struggled and tried to scream, and knocked over the flowers, but I garrotted her until I felt her choke. Then took the secateurs which she'd dropped on the floor and swiftly completed the job. I needed the world to know that this was no accident. Simply the visible start of my bloody campaign.

I left the church as discreetly as I'd entered, pausing only to deal with the dog on the way out. Well, Miss Fairchild, it was interesting to make your acquaintance. One down, only seven left to go.

16

2

'Don't bother waiting supper for me,' said Edwina Huxley as she rushed through.

William, patiently coaxing Morwenna to finish her eggs before they got cold, looked up mildly. He was used to his wife's erratic timetable, also her fanatical dedication to her work. In recent weeks she'd been coming home later and later. She rarely explained why, just blamed it all on the job.

'Something exciting?' He was always politely receptive, found the crazy whirl in which she lived oddly invigorating just as long as he wasn't obliged to join in. Edwina was driven to an extent he could only admire. At times it seemed that her feet barely touched the ground.

'Meeting with possible investors. One of the big German banks.' Since she'd embarked on this crazy dotcom scheme of hers, she lived, breathed the internet, scarcely taking time off to eat. In fact, she was telling only half an untruth. They really did have a big investment session at five, but if she mentioned the aerobics class too, he might just take exception. And not without cause. But it was imperative

17

she worked off those few extra pounds or she'd soon be heading down the slippery slope. And that wouldn't do at all, not with all she currently had at stake.

Edwina returned in her coat and grabbed a slice of the buttered toast her husband had cut into neat soldiers. That way went her figure, but today she couldn't resist it. Nursery food was perfect when her nerves were so much on edge. The new company was teetering on the brink of a yawning abyss, but now was not the time to be talking about that. Not that William would understand or was even likely to care much. He had long ago left it to her to act the adult role.

'Remember to ring the plumber,' she said. 'His number is there on the pad.' The bathroom tap still persistently dripped and was etching a stain into the porcelain. Other people's husbands would have fixed it long ago, it was probably only a question of a new washer, but Edwina had given up complaining. At least he would be there to let the fellow in. For such small mercies she knew she should feel blessed. She stooped to kiss her child's small egg-stained face.

'Bye, bye, precious. Mummy has to go.' She glanced at the clock. It was heading towards half past. Any second now and the taxi would be here, ready to brave the horrors of the rush hour.

'Have a good day,' said William placidly, pouring himself another cup of tea and switching on the regional news to check out the weather forecast. Days for him were all much the same since he'd quit work. Or, rather, since the

18

job had let him go. *Instead of just sitting there* . . . Edwina itched to scream, but instead just bit her lip and pocketed her keys. There was no point in getting at him now, not while the child was having breakfast. A horn sounded sharply from the street.

'Must go.' She pecked his cheek and ruffled his hair and was off up the basement steps in her ultra smart boots. Well, rather her than him, thought William contentedly as he flicked out the pages of *The Times*.

It was Mrs P's morning so he cleared things into the sink and made a desultory attempt at tidying up. He scrubbed his daughter's face with a damp corner of her bib and lifted her down from her high chair. It was this time of day he had grown to love best, while the rest of the civilised world was still fighting its way to work. He didn't miss the rat-race one bit, had let it all go with relief. Morwenna was asking for cartoons so he carried her into the playroom and switched on her favourite *Cobbleywobs* series, all that was ever on at this time of day. Then settled back comfortably at the kitchen table for a bit of well-earned peace and quiet.

'Lord,' said Mrs P as she bustled in at nine. 'Talk about lovely weather for ducks. It's teeming.' She was wearing her old trench coat, which had seen better days, the usual fag sticking out of her mouth and a colourful headscarf tied low over her forehead in obvious imitation of the Queen. She shook out her coat and hung it on a peg, then coughed her way over to the kettle.

'Another cuppa?' she asked as she fluffed out her platinum curls. She was a cliché copy of the old-fashioned daily, straight out of Andy Capp. William found her an endless source of amusement. She always enlivened his day.

He glanced at his empty mug. 'Please.'

Mrs P did for them a couple of times a week and they started off most mornings in just this way. While William sorted the laundry and tackled the dishes, she set to work with a hoover and duster, trying to bring order to their chaos. Twice a week wasn't really enough, with the child to keep clearing up after, but since they'd had only the one salary coming in, they had tried to make a few basic economies. At least, Edwina had. William really wasn't bothered. Left to his own devices, he'd have been content to do it all, provided he didn't have to hurry or be too meticulous. He genuinely enjoyed this new role of house husband, did not miss the workplace one bit.

First, however, they had to review the week and catch up on the gossip, to which both were increasingly addicted. Soap operas, scandal and the ghoulish stories the papers were so satisfyingly full of. Even *The Times* was going more and more down-market and had started to carry stories formerly found only in the tabloids. Mrs P carried two full mugs over to where he was sitting, took the weight off her feet and lit up again.

'Awful about that Paula Yates.' It had been all over the weekend papers. William, who sometimes struggled to keep up with Mrs P, for once knew what she was talking about. Even *The Times* had carried the story, the tragically premature death of a high-profile celebrity. 'That's what fame does,' added Mrs P, the arbiter of popular culture. She shook her head as she blew out the match and flicked it into the sink. Edwina would have tutted but William didn't care. He enjoyed these cosy twice-weekly sessions, had grown to look forward to them.

Mrs P lived down by the viaduct, on the far side of Westbourne Grove. He couldn't even begin to guess her age but suspected she might be far younger than she looked. She had raised a motley collection of kids and was full of funny stories about them. She particularly doted on Morwenna, a surefire way to William's heart.

'Come here, duck,' she called through the playroom door, and Morwenna, instantly distracted from the cute little woodland folk, came running to her obediently with open arms. Mrs P stooped and hoisted the sturdy child on to her lap, where she settled benignly, thumb in mouth, to listen to the grown-ups' conversation. Edwina would also have clucked at the thumb but again William didn't care. Sucking a thumb was a natural way to seek comfort; there had even been occasions when he felt like doing it himself. She'd grow out of it soon enough as normal children do. No point in fussing over what was perfectly natural.

Mrs P dunked a biscuit in her tea then gave half of it to the child to suck. She kicked off the short fur boots that she wore in all weathers and got stuck into her chat. Plenty of time later to get some order into the house. She savoured these sessions with William as much as he did.

'Did you see there's been another nasty murder?' She stretched across to her shopping bag and pulled out the *Daily Mail*. No, William hadn't. *The Times* was concerned with the Chancellor of the Exchequer, who had just been voted the most unpopular ever. The *Mail* had a far more sensational front page. He took it from her hand.

Family murdered on picnic, the headline shouted, above a collage of heart-rending photographs. Appalled, William read on. A housewife in Northampton, with her two small daughters, had been attacked and killed while picnicking in a meadow. In the act of making daisy-chains, it said. The smudgy photos showed a sweet-faced young woman, probably no more than her middle twenties, with two cute replicas of herself. Lauren Marsh with Melanie and Sadie, aged seven and four. They'd been bludgeoned with a pick-axe, then savagely chopped to pieces. Reading the gruesome details made William want to throw up.

'Shocking, ain't it,' said Mrs P with relish, breaking into her racking cough which seemed to be getting worse. She loved nothing more than a juicy bit of drama, could take as much blood and guts as she could get. She continued to puff, filling the kitchen with smoke, apparently oblivious of the health hazards. William felt it wasn't his place to warn her. Wordlessly he reached across and shifted his daughter to the cleaner environment of his own lap. No point in risking her health at this young age. Rain or not, Edwina would have made Mrs P stand outside.

William scanned the inner pages where more of the

story was detailed. The husband, a chartered surveyor, looked rather distinguished and was currently helping the police with their inquiries. Poor bastard.

'It's nearly always the husband that did it,' said Mrs P knowledgeably, reluctantly rising to her feet. 'You mark my words, I bet they arrest him. Terrible, really, to think of the things that go on.' She burrowed inside her capacious bag and produced a flowered pinafore that had seen better days. Her nails, fairly ludicrously, were painted a dashing damson and looked as though they were fresh from the beauty salon. One of the daughters was a stylist, William knew, so perhaps Ma's upkeep was all part of the package. Mrs P shuffled across to the sink and rinsed the mugs under hot running water.

'There seems to be a lot of it about,' she remarked.

'What?' asked William abstractedly.

'Murder,' said Mrs P cheerfully as she started to do her work. Playroom first then the stairs and upper floors. With a good long clean down here before she was through.

William went on sitting there, studying the details in the *Mail*. *The Times* had dismissed it in a single paragraph, their minds still on loftier matters. Though no doubt when the case came to trial, they'd exact their four pennyworth along with the rest. *If* it came to trial. He wasn't at all convinced that the father was the culprit, he looked too responsible and honourable for that. Arresting the closest male relative was fairly routine; however innocent he might appear, statistically he had to be checked out. But what kind of monster would slaughter his own children, not to mention their mother, his wife? William looked down tenderly at his own beloved infant, slumbering now in the crook of his arm, thumb firmly back in her mouth. He gently kissed the nape of her delicate neck. He loved Morwenna more than anything else in the world, and that, he was bound to admit, included Edwina. He would do anything in his power to shelter her from harm. Part of the privilege of having full-time care of her.

'More likely some kind of nutter,' he said, folding the paper and returning it to the bag. He really ought to get going himself. There was the plumber still to phone and other assorted chores which Edwina would not be pleased to find left undone. The murders in the meadow had really caught his attention. The bodies were brutalised and drenched in their own blood. The details rang an uncomfortable bell; it took him just a few moments to connect. Edwina's Aunt Jane had met with a similarly gruesome death, an apparently motiveless murder, her dog hacked to pieces nearby. That had happened four years ago, before Morwenna was even a twinkle in his eye. He'd still had a proper job in those days, but had taken time off to go down to the Cotswolds to find out more. She had, after all, left them her cottage. A little family involvement was the least the poor woman might expect.

Northampton was not that far from the Cotswolds. Maybe a coincidence, for the actual locations were still some distance apart. Nevertheless. That trail had petered out almost immediately though the ghastly state of the body had made William gag. She had been garrotted with

picture wire, her throat gouged out with her own secateurs. Slashed almost through to the spinal cord, the altar-
cloth drenched in her blood. And her poor little Bichon
Frise outside, impaled on the railings like a macabre sacri-
fice. It was hard to imagine a mind as sick as that. Almost
as disgusting as those poor kids. Aunt Jane herself had
been something of a handful, yet respected in Alton
Coombe for her charitable works. William had never
particularly warmed to her, but could not imagine anyone
bearing such a terrible grudge. These atrocities made no
sense to the sane mind but the world was growing sicker
by the minute. As Mrs P would be the first to point out.

'Right, then,' he said, making a reluctant move and
peering out of the window to check the weather. The rain
had stopped and pale sunshine flooded the basement
steps. He'd sort the laundry for Mrs P then take Morwenna
off to the swings before it started again.

'It's not that I don't love him any more, it's just that he's
started to drive me slightly potty.' Never one to beat about
the bush, Edwina had finally come to the end of her tether.
She sat in the crowded bar of the Oxo Tower, sipping her
Seabreeze and confiding in her friends. Sue and Meryl,
devoted allies and staunchest of confidantes through many
a shared tribulation. She felt at ease with them; they spoke
the same language and understood the stresses of her life,
especially now with all this dotcom business. The aerobics class was over and done with, the trio felt stretched
to the limit, virtuous too. Not, however, to the extent of

cutting out alcohol. A girl had to draw the line some-where. Meryl was even smoking.

'So go on,' she said now, through a haze of smoke. 'Give us a for instance.' She had to lean forward to hear through the babble. This trendy watering-hole was filling up fast.

'It's not just one thing or another,' said Edwina. 'He seems to have given up looking for proper work.' That was the real drag. He no longer seemed to care.

'There can't be a lot of call for his sort of expertise.' William was a cartographer. He had been axed with the Nicholsons merger two years before.

'But there are other avenues he could explore. He really is awfully gifted.' Despite her frustration, she remained quite proud of him. It was his expert draughtsmanship that had attracted her in the first place. That and his amaz-ing imagination. Edwina, ever the high-flyer, was impressed by anyone creative. The left side of the brain, and all that. A brilliance she entirely lacked herself. For no matter how formidable her business skills might be, in no way could she ever be described as creative. Practical, maybe, and certainly go-getting. Determined and stubborn and impos-sibly exacting, though without a single original thought in her head. She couldn't even tell a bedtime story. Yet it hadn't stopped her getting on in life. Look what she was on the brink of right now. Success beyond imagination. A glittering dotcom career.

Meryl exhaled a thin stream of smoke. Secretly she'd always rather fancied William, while aware that he was also a bit of a dope. Charming, though one of life's losers. Sooner Edwina than her. Meryl preferred a man with a bit of financial substance. She had long been on the hunt for one but was lately beginning to lose hope. Thirty-four was pushing it a bit and the rules were growing dirtier by the minute. She glanced around the trendy bar – two-thirds women and most of them on the pull. She sucked in her stomach and smoothed her streaked blonde hair. Upkeep at this age was becoming increasingly costly, and once past thirty there was no looking back.

'Well,' said Sue briskly in her usual no-nonsense way. 'I think you should insist that he get out there and look.' Everyone knew that Edwina was on to a winner but it wasn't entirely right that a man should permit himself to be kept. Letting down the side somehow. Not enough of the stiff upper lip.

'Not quite that easy,' said Edwina. 'He actually enjoys being home during the day. Seems not to get bored at all. Can you imagine?' She certainly couldn't, all those tedious hours of mind-blowing boredom, chatting inanely to a two-year-old and having constantly to pick up after her. Potty training, marmalade in his hair. That terrible television series. He certainly was a marvellous father, she couldn't deny him that, and secretly she envied the special relationship he was forging with their child. But someone had to bring home the bacon and lately she'd been doing that on her own. She was honest about the fact that she wasn't by nature maternal. In that way their union was proving a perfect fit. Though they had not envisaged a situation like this when they'd first tied the knot four years ago.

'How does he spend his time?' asked Meryl. It was wet in the extreme for a man to be little more than a nanny.

'The usual sort of domestic things. Shops and tidies and takes Morwenna to the park. Messes about on the patio while she's napping. Does the crossword puzzle, watches tennis. And *Neighbours*, he confesses, when he can. As well as old movies in the afternoon. It really is the life of Riley for him.' The bitterness was evident in her voice. She wished now she hadn't raised the subject, regretting them knowing too much. Edwina's marriage had always been something of a fairytale. She hated to reveal her underlying discontent. Though that's what close friendships were all about. And a good old moan did nobody any harm as long as they kept it within the group, which was not always easy.

'What happens when Morwenna goes to school?' With a family of her own, Sue saw herself as an expert.

'That's not for at least a couple more years. Though I'm not entirely sure I can hang on that long.'

As bad as that. So now they were getting to the real nitty gritty. All three of them shuffled their stools a little closer and Sue signalled to the bargirl for another round. Although they genuinely were dyed-in-the-wool best mates, there was a secret thrill to be had from another's misery. Made Sue feel smug and Meryl less insecure. Edwina, with her slightly superior beauty, rarely showed even a chink in her outward calm. She always appeared to have conquered the world, what with the job and the man and now the baby. And recently she'd been cresting the wave of unimaginable success so shortly wouldn't have any financial worries either. It was therefore refreshing to discover that all was not necessarily roses. Of course, they both wished her well, they did sincerely, but it wouldn't be quite human not to feel the teeniest frisson of smug delight. They were keen to sniff out every tiny detail. That, after all, is what girl talk is all about.

'So what are you going to do?' Meryl held her breath.

'Don't know exactly,' Edwina admitted. 'In some ways the situation works ideally for us both.' If only he'd not be quite so humdrum, had some sort of stimulus in his own life so they'd at least have something to talk about at night. Other than domestic issues which bored the pants off Edwina. 'Morwenna really loves her daddy and it means we save money on the nanny.' Not that that was going to matter any more if things worked out the way they looked. But a full-time nanny was something she preferred to be without. Having one underfoot in those first few months had driven her virtually to snapping point. She recalled the rows and petty irritations, the invasion of her territory by a stranger perpetually there. It also meant they didn't need to run a second car. All these considerations added up. And it gave her space for girls' nights out like this, away from the grinding monotony of her home. Most other mothers of a two-year-old would be guiltily racing home the minute the whistle blew. It was eight o'clock already. Her husband must be a saint. It would never even occur to him to ask what she had been up to. He'd be ready waiting with a meal prepared and a welcoming drink already poured. But that only added to what was really troubling her. There were times when she wondered if he still loved her.

'Gotta go,' she said reluctantly, picking up her things. Fortunately, by this time in the evening, taxis were easily found. Blackfriars to Notting Hill would take less than half an hour. She certainly did have blessings though these days rarely found the time to count them. As long as he hadn't left the kitchen in too much of a mess.

William sat in front of the evening news, finishing the crossword puzzle. The sensational slaughter of the Marsh family came only second to the petrol crisis, though with fewer details than in that morning's *Mail*. The injuries had been horrendous, said an obviously shaken policeman. They had a man in custody who was helping them with inquiries, and would probably be holding him overnight.

Poor devil, thought William again, glancing up. First, to lose his family like that, then to have to face such a barrage of publicity. The two little girls looked like miniatures of their mother, bambi-eyed and similarly sweetly smiling. Just looking at their images brought spontaneous tears to his eyes. Children were so vulnerable. How could anyone possibly harm them? There was an interview with a distraught neighbour who spoke of what darlings the three of them had been.

'Find this killer!' she implored on camera, tears gushing

down her stricken face. Yet Mrs P was right and statistics went against the husband. William knew that in the majority of cases the trigger was invariably domestic.

The programme changed and he popped upstairs to check that Morwenna was sleeping. She had had her bath and he'd read her a story and had not heard a peep from her since. He wondered idly when Edwina would be home, had baked a shepherd's pie which was still keeping warm in the oven. She certainly put in long hours, bless her heart, but he was scarcely in a position to complain. The only thing that mattered was that one of them was earning real money, or this house, for starters, would almost certainly have to go. And after they'd spent so much time finding it and fixing it up, he knew that would for certain break her heart.

Morwenna lay on her front in her cot, her beloved Eeyore tucked protectively under one arm, her thumb as usual in her mouth. He tiptoed over and straightened the covers then stroked her glossy little conker-like head with the softest of angel touches. People often laughed when they saw father and daughter together, for there could be no doubting her parentage. Same dark hair and extravagant lashes, same rosy cheeks and impish grin. Edwina complained that he had the dominant genes but they had worked out very nicely in their daughter. He kissed her gently then crept back downstairs. Edwina had told him not to wait supper and he was starting to get slightly peckish. First, though, he'd open a bottle of wine to breathe and then fill in the last of the crossword clues. Edwina

31

was often quite edgy when she got home; he tried to smooth things out as much as he could. One of these days, sooner rather than later, he knew he would really have to look for a job. He was just reluctant to give it all up now, the full-time parenting that had become so all-engrossing. He was proud of all he had achieved so far, helping this lively infant to develop.

Then he remembered he had forgotten about the plumber. Oh Lord. Yet another black mark.

3

Edwina's workplace could not have been further removed in character from the cosy domesticity of her husband's. A stark high-rise building close to Blackfriars Bridge, it had mirrored windows, round-the-clock security and electronic sensors all over the place. She and her partner had rented space on the eleventh floor, in which they were developing their brand new internet company, Dotcom-Whatever – they hadn't yet decided on the name. It was designed to help small-time punters invest their savings safely without being messed around by the high-street banks. Gareth was supposedly working on the package while she got on with the financial under-pinning. Which of their different roles was more crucial to the project, she hadn't yet had the time to think about.

She sat in an open-plan office, surrounded by banks of computer screens. All she could hear were endlessly ringing phones with an undercurrent of the heavy thrum of state-of-the-art technology. Soulless and lacking in creature comforts, it was nonetheless a paradise to Edwina and where, these days, she increasingly felt most at home. Working on her own behalf, with the promise of making a killing. With a long-term future stretching ahead, devoid of financial stresses. Provided they got the fine-tuning right and the market didn't subside.

It was after seven on the following evening, and again she was in no great hurry to get home.

'Still at it?' Gareth Prendergast, once just a compatible colleague but now her business partner, halted as he wandered by and propped himself nonchalantly against the wall. He was wearing one of his chic designer suits with a black silk open-necked shirt. His greying fair hair was clipped severely short to disguise a receding hairline. But he still had the looks of a sixties rock idol, something of which he was very much aware. Edwina stretched and tilted back her chair, wearily massaging her neck.

'I'm just running over these costings one last time.' What the Germans had proposed had been close to miraculous. They had loved the simple concept, spotted its vast potential and seemed extremely keen to come aboard. All that remained now was the paperwork and then they could probably go public. Fruit of several months' hard planning, the pinnacle of their dreams. She could hardly believe they had got this far. Was scared that something might still go wrong.

Gareth glanced at his watch. 'Well, I'm off over to the Ivy to meet up with some chums.' He sighed and stretched and adjusted his collar. Wow, but the man had some front. He admired Edwina's extreme dedication, but had a far more casual attitude to work himself. This potential money-spinner had originally been his inspiration, but he needed her grounded common sense to make it work.

Once a boy wonder of the investment world, Gareth, at forty-something, had shifted to e-commerce, shrewdly foreseeing that that way lay the future. They had worked together as market traders and always hit it off remarkably well. He admired her style and the way she looked as much as her formidable intelligence. He also found her sexy but that was by the way. One of these days, when he felt in the mood, he rather fancied seducing her, just for fun. Today she was wearing a black leather skirt with knee-high, spike-heeled crocodile boots, which he found disturbingly erotic. Her thick dark hair was tied severely back and she frowned with concentration as she stared into her screen. One classy chick, well worth a bit of effort. A cut above his usual mindless dollies. He knew she was no pushover, respected her for that. Which would make the eventual chase that much more exciting.

'You can join us if you like,' he said casually, but still hoping.

'Can't,' said Edwina abruptly. She was already unforgivably late.

'Ah yes, the husband,' said Gareth mockingly. 'Marital bliss in trendy Notting Hill.'

Edwina glanced up with rising irritation, then laughed when she saw his pained expression.

'You're just jealous,' she said, 'because you've got no one of your own.' Nobody waiting for him at home with a hot meal ready to be served. No enchanting toddler clambering on to his knee, begging him for a favourite bedtime story. No bathtime frolics or innocent night-night games or the moving sight of an exhausted child falling gently asleep in her father's protective arms. No one to carry upstairs to bed, not, at least, to a nursery. Gareth had none of the traditional appendages of his age and position in society.

And yet there certainly was no shortage in his life of gorgeous willing aspirants for the job. Very often desperate, always over-compliant, she knew his life patterns so well. Women, some of them pretty remarkable, prepared to abase themselves at the snap of his world-weary fingers. Gareth Prendergast was, in short, a louse, little more than a traditional old-fashioned bounder. He ran them in droves, paid them minimal attention and usually ended up breaking their silly hearts. Not hers, however; she was far too clued up and considered his obvious charm too fake to be effective. But she did find his company in the workplace stimulating, enjoyed his caustic wit and weary cynicism. Also she liked being seen out with him at functions. Face it, there weren't too many men like him around.

Yet William really was extremely long-suffering. She had to concede him that when she finally walked in and found her gin and tonic already poured because his sharp ears had heard the taxi. Devoted or what? All she felt was guilt and silently vowed to be nicer to him, if only he weren't such a doormat. The kitchen was a warm safe cavern with the most appetite-inducing aromas wafting from the stove. Tonight she couldn't fault him on a thing. He was there to give her a welcoming hug and help her off with her coat. The house, for once, was remarkably quiet, with only the muted strains of a Debussy nocturne drifting through the open living room door. He had even made something of an effort to clear up. The sink was stacked with the pans he'd used but the table, for once, was immaculate. A clean, crisp cloth already set for two, with a bottle of Merlot thoughtfully opened to breathe. Fresh flowers too, her favourite freesias. She stretched up impulsively and pecked him on the cheek.

She had married him after a string of unsatisfactory relationships, largely because of this same intrinsic thoughtfulness. At first he hadn't particularly made her knees tremble, but he had more important qualities than that. Like loyalty, steadfastness and a great sense of humour, with patience and honesty thrown in. Not to mention that remarkable artistic talent, if only he would put it to some real use. He always called when he said he would and had never been late for a date. People had married for far less, she reasoned. At least with William Huxley she had known she would always be safe.

'She in bed already?'

'Off like a lamb,' said William, beaming as he fished the iron casserole from the oven. 'We watched her *Bob the Builder* video and she went up good as gold.' The truth was she'd grown so used to an absent mother, she no longer kicked up a ruckus when bedtime came and still Edwina

37

wasn't home. These days they'd become almost like a single-parent family, though he wouldn't risk spoiling his wife's genial mood by drawing attention to her inadequacies. It was good she was currently so hyped-up about her work. Her cheeks were flushed and her eyes unnaturally bright. He found her, in this mood, quite irresistible. Once she'd relaxed and her adrenalin level was back to normal, he'd remember to ask for a general update. Sometimes she liked to talk about the job, at others she chose to shut him out completely. It all depended on her mercurial moods. He couldn't always foresee how she would react.

'How's Gareth?' he asked casually as he served the stew.

'Coping,' was all she said.

The two men met only rarely, on official occasions; she preferred to keep it that way. She sensed the disdain in Gareth's eyes, knew also that William couldn't abide him. Found him phoney and unnecessarily acerbic, disliked his pseudo-intellectual pose. He might have been a Balliol scholar but had done very little with his first-class degree, had always been something of a wastrel. Until he'd teamed up with the focused Edwina and produced that vital spark of inspiration. Gareth might take credit for the seed of the big idea but any success the new company might have would be due, almost totally, to her. Of that William had no doubt, he was a fan. Regardless of his unvoiced disapproval of her somewhat suspect business partner.

Chalk and cheese were these two main men in Edwina's life. William, with his ingenuous charm; Gareth the calculating sophisticate. Both of them clever and attractive in

38

their way yet light years apart in their approach. And she had to admit, if only to herself, that Gareth was the one currently making her tingle, though she tried her level best not to let it show. Four years with William had somewhat dimmed her ardour, especially since the arrival of Morwenna. Broken nights and relentless domesticity were surefire suppressers of sexual passion. Ideally, right now they should be trying for a second child so there wouldn't be too much of an age gap. But the mere thought of a new pregnancy filled Edwina with horror. She wasn't a natural mother, had not been raised in that way. Her own mother, now in her seventies, still worked full-time with no thought of retiring. Her Highgate practice was always fully booked, her text-books still widely available. Helge Dorfman was a giant in her field, a Jungian psychiatrist, originally from Vienna. And married to Arnold Fairchild, the famous economist.

'Think how our grandmothers fought to get the vote.' That was the mantra with which Helge had raised Edwina, who had no intention of dropping out now, on the threshold of such a glitzy future.

When supper was over, Edwina wiped her mouth and folded her napkin. There was still a little wine left in the bottle but she'd leave it for William to finish. With all that was going on in her life, she needed to keep a clear head.

'I'm off upstairs for an hour or so's work,' she said. 'We have to sort out the German deal and still have a fair way to go.'

* * *

She was doing it again, thought William despondently, excluding him from the most important part of her life. He was actually keenly interested in the progress of her company, but she always kept him waiting till she felt like opening up. Edwina, all over, self-absorbed, unaware of just how much she sometimes hurt him. One of the flaws that he blamed on her hothouse upbringing. When she went at something there was no deflecting her. Not even her own little daughter was permitted to get in her way. Which was one hundred per cent selfishness, and he knew that some day she'd regret it, once Morwenna was finally grown and had moved away. Luckily there was little chance of his daughter inheriting her chilliness, for she took after him in so many integral ways. His expression softened as he thought about his child. He would just give these pans a preliminary soak, then pop up to check on her. Edwina, engrossed in her financial calculations, was unlikely to have given her a thought. Morwenna could be missing when she sauntered home from work, yet he wasn't entirely convinced that she'd even notice.

While he was still pottering around at the sink, he switched on the television to catch the news. They were still banging on about those horrible murders. Stuff about the mother with her blameless, innocent life and the hard-working father who had provided for them so well. A model, middle-class family, or so it appeared on the surface. Not so much as a breath of scandal or hint of why it might have happened. Dishcloth in hand, William stood trans-fixed, soaking up every detail of the crime. Quite what it was that so engaged his attention, he hadn't yet been able to figure out. He wasn't by nature a True Crime enthusiast and rarely ever opened a detective novel, while even Morse on the box made him yawn. He could never get to care about the meandering plot.

But there was something so horrific about these real-life killings that he just couldn't shake their savagery from his mind. Perhaps it was this empty existence beginning to addle his brain, with all those hours of gossip with Mrs P. If he had a little more drive, like the lovely Edwina, he'd be up there now beside her, doing his stuff. Putting his talents to work on something worthwhile, finding himself a real man's job to earn back Edwina's respect. Earning a bit of hard cash for a change. No wonder she got fed up with him, what a drag he must be to come home to. Stand-in housewife, surrogate mother, general dogsbody incarnate. It was time to shake a leg and get a life. He'd enjoyed the last job, producing atlases. It was possible that he'd strike lucky like that again. But not if he didn't get up off his arse and start doing something about it. First thing tomorrow, or possibly the day after, he'd log on to the internet and see what he could find.

Yet the prospect of having to part from Morwenna, even for just a few hours a day, filled him with utter despair. To let some stranger put ideas into her head was almost too painful to contemplate. At two years old, she was already a fully formed person, his baby, his creation, his whole life. At the same time, he knew it made sense. He flicked his cloth round the sink and rinsed it out. Then

41

tiptoed up the stairs to say goodnight. He'd not risk disturbing Edwina at her work but he might, if he was lucky, get a cuddle from his daughter.

4

*C*hildren, and all they stand for, meant virtually nothing to me then. Life was far too exhilarating even to think of settling down, with mortgages and other shackles like that. Love, of course, in those heady far-off days, had barely even touched me. I was a green and ignorant fool with far more worldly matters on my mind. There was still so much I wanted to explore and far too little time in which to do it. Or so it appeared to me in my breathless youth. I suppose I was way too cocky and self-absorbed and left the serious business of living to others. While my friends were mellowing and beginning to pair off, I was still out there having a permanent fling. Of course, had I known then what I've had to learn the hard way . . . But that's how it is with life's ups and downs.

For through these recent monochrome years I have known more than my fair share of sorrow. And have consequently learned how to hit someone where it hurts most while also letting the world know it was me. No point in hiding your light beneath a bushel. I intended to leave my signature on each crime.

* * *

Next on the hit list was a man called Robert Marsh, apparently yet another exemplary citizen. He lived, conveniently, on the fringes of Northampton, a relatively easy ride from Milton Keynes. Which meant I was able to operate from home and save myself both money and anxiety. I had kept on the flat, and the mortgage was fully paid up. Marina could well have wanted it but she didn't. She was actually terribly reasonable when it came to dividing the spoils. She was ever the lady; I will always respect her for that. She had ample reason to hate me, but amazingly appeared not to do so. Believed, so they tell me, with unusual compassion, that I'd already been punished enough.

So here I was now, with no need to look for new digs and run the constant risk of recognition. I could do the next one at my leisure and give it all the time that it required. Also continue with the dreary little job which, though mind-numbingly dull, I could see was essential. As well as allowing me access to the files, it also provided me with the requisite cover.

Locating the right Robert Marsh had not been easy, for lots of Marshes were listed in the book. Also, it transpired, he had moved around quite a bit, so I wasted valuable months on futile trails. Eventually, however, I did strike lucky and managed to track him down. He was, by profession, a chartered surveyor. I'd established that fact early on. And worked from an office in his spacious home, popular, successful, much admired. Best of all, he appeared to have a perfect marriage with two little cute-as-pie kids. The ideal scenario, I couldn't have made it up. Matching little angels, miniatures of their mother. Enough to bring a lump to the throat.

I had found his name on the electoral roll after numerous fruitless searches. And the man who responded so politely to my call seemed to fit all the necessary criteria. He would, he told me courteously, be delighted to take on the job. At more or less any time convenient to me, he could come round and look the place over. I said I'd call back to arrange a definite meeting but that was no longer necessary, not now I'd established who he was. So instead I took the bike out for an early-evening spin and popped over to his neighbourhood for a recce.

The house was situated in a pleasant leafy lane with a handy public garden right alongside. The weather had turned quite balmy, ideal for an evening stroll, so I pushed the bike under the cover of some willows and continued my cautious investigation on foot. There was no point in taking unnecessary risks, not at this early stage. For this time my prey was Lauren Marsh and her daughters, three instead of one, a perfect hat trick.

For a while the papers had been full of the Fairchild murder and I still got a buzz whenever I saw it mentioned. I had got away with that one apparently scot free and these days was feeling considerably more confident. The police had made little progress with their fumbling inquiries and the story had inevitably died a natural death. The crucial thing was that we had met only that once. There was nothing else whatsoever to connect us. No mutual friends nor interests, no ties. It seemed that, beginner though I might be, I had pulled off the perfect crime. I was starting to feel quite good in this new profession. Killing was something that stretched me to the limit and gave back some feeling of purpose to my life.

Still, as a safety precaution, after the Fairchild murder I lay low for a few more years and allowed things to drift while I concentrated on my research. Every name on my list was important, for each had played their part in the destruction of my life. They had all of them, in one deadly swoop, harmed me irreversibly. So it was only right that now I should turn the tables. An eye for an eye and all that. It was, after all, the ethos on which I'd been raised.

It seems, looking back on my childhood, that the sun nearly always shone. Which can't have been true but that's the impression I have. I was always right there in the spotlight, never one to linger in the shadows, and might have had any person that I chose. Male or female, it made little difference but all came down to the same thing in the end. My power over others, call it charm if you will. I found very few who could resist me. I was bold, I was adventurous and had my fair share of looks. And was in there in the centre of things, wherever the action was. By the age of fourteen I had learned to drive a car and practised in the farmland round where we lived. My mother was dubious but Pa was okay and since he was very much king of his own back yard, what he said usually went. My brothers and I were allowed to run wild and I don't think it did us any harm. Certainly it made me confident, which has stood me ever since in excellent stead.

If you have faith in yourself, a priest once told me, then that's the largest part of winning life's battle. Stand up for what you believe in and never ever back down. No need to resort to fighting at all if you know in your heart you can win.

Provided, of course, you have right on your side, though he felt that that went without saying. Wise words on which I reflected now. My thinking might not be conventional, but I've always known what I wanted and gone after it.

From what I could glean from the local rag, Robert Marsh was soundly established in this town. He more than pulled his weight in local affairs, had even served his stint on the parish council. He was a governor of his children's school and a spirited member of the football club, was widely respected and considered a regular bloke; this last I found out by drinking in his local. He also sang tenor with the Gilbert & Sullivan Society and was currently in training for the marathon. A good all-rounder; by the time I'd completed his dossier I almost found room in my heart for mild regret. Except that it wasn't him I was planning to kill.

I couldn't help accosting him in the pub that Sunday morning. I have always been over-impetuous and inclined to take foolish risks. Which is how I landed myself in this mess, though I prefer not to think of that now. Certainly Marina used to cluck and shake her head, half admiring the madcap antics I got up to. That was in the early days when I think she still rather liked me. What happened later was to change all that, though, to be fair, it was not entirely of my doing.

Anyhow, Marsh was leaning on the bar when he spotted me drinking alone and included me in his next round. I was surprised.

'Just a half,' I insisted when he pointed to my glass, rewarding him with an enigmatic smile. Soon I was in there, the hub

of his intimate circle, and he introduced me around to all his cronies. He had clear blue eyes and well-kept teeth and you could see, beneath the grey jogging suit, how fit and muscular he was. Mid-forties or thereabouts, I would guess, though he'd certainly worn well. And the iron-grey hair didn't age him, just added distinction. When he finished his drink, he said regretfully he must go.

'They'll be waiting at home to start their lunch. Mustn't upset my little women.'

He touched me lightly on the shoulder as if he had known me for years and said he truly hoped we would meet again. Asked how long I was likely to stick around, and I smiled and told him I wasn't entirely sure. Then he was gone, at a loping trot, and those still left at the bar began to discuss him. The camaraderie of the public house. I shook hands all round, left my glass on the bar, muttered a bunch of platitudes and was off. I had accomplished what I'd come in for, a closer acquaintance with my prey. What I had in mind for him was far worse than any easy death. I wanted his suffering, like mine, to be infinite.

When I first saw London it nearly blew my mind. This was what I'd been waiting for all my life. At that time, in the eighties, life was one continuous party and I threw myself right into it up to my neck. I got a job in Sloane Street and a flat in Cadogan Gardens. I couldn't really afford it but had help. Restaurants and clubs and the whole busy drug scene. I couldn't get enough of it and burned all my candles at both ends. Who knows what might have happened to me, I would probably be dead by now. But something entirely unforeseen came out of a clear blue sky. A thunderbolt struck me when I wasn't paying attention, thus totally altering the course of my life. In one blind unthinking moment, I fell in love.

Marina has always put the blame on me, but that's actually not how it happened. The coup de foudre *at that crowded reception hit us both simultaneously. We couldn't have helped ourselves, it was written in the stars. And all the other clumsy clichés from popular songs. We stared transfixed, then fought our way through the throng, and stood there, smiling foolishly, in clumsy silence. And from that moment on, we never looked back, until death inevitably came along to divide us.*

Due to my other commitments, I was obliged to snatch time where I could. I even feigned the occasional bout of sickness in order to further my plan. Having tasted blood once, I was longing to do it again, but had to be sure that my plan was entirely foolproof. The more times I did it, the more they'd be watching out for me. Just one false move and my neck would be on the line. So in mid afternoon, as often as I was able, I biked over to Northampton and lay in wait. Regular as clockwork, just a little after three, Lauren would let herself out of the house and walk the few blocks to the school. There she would pick up the two little girls and take them off somewhere for a treat. I could see from just watching what a marvellous mother she was, pretty too and apparently permanently happy. I confess I watched her with something close to envy, though there wasn't room in my life right now for regret.

Where to do it was the problem, for I had to tread very

carefully in this town. My face had been clocked by Marsh and his gang and might well be recognised again. It would have to be somewhere outdoors, I decided; the house was far too difficult to breach. Besides, he worked from home, I now remembered. The local baths were one possibility but perhaps that bit too public for me to risk. Also, drowning was relatively tame, not the way I wanted to leave my mark.

I selected my tools with precision, having learned my mistake from the first time. Killing is a serious business. It was vital I should come already prepared. Close to where I lived was a builder's yard, so it took no more than a skilfully picked lock to collect the necessary essentials. I hesitated over the pickaxe, I confess, but this time there were three of them to dispatch. After a few trial swings, I made my decision. Never send a boy to do a man's job.

The rest, as they say, is now history. The media folk went to town. Talk about slaughter of the innocents, they just couldn't get enough. The most horrendous triple murder the world had seen in years. What kind of vile depravity could have led to such a thing? I watched my friend, Marsh, that evening on the news and saw, with satisfaction, the agony etched into his face. Precisely what I'd intended. Let the hurting continue for ever. Now he knew what it felt like too and would for the remainder of his life.

5

The *Express*, which William picked up on his way to the park, gave additional gruesome details of the murders. What some crazed, depraved animal had done to those poor little girls positively made his gorge rise. It was obscene. He glanced instinctively down at the stroller and pulled Morwenna closer. Soon they'd move on to the Princess Diana playground but only when he was good and ready. Here, in pale sunlight by the Italian fountains, he wallowed in every grisly detail. He had that sort of mindset, an attention to minutiae that regularly drove Edwina wild, usually not without cause. Despite the fact that he always knew most of the answers on most subjects and could probably have made it on to *Mastermind*.

'For heaven's sake,' she would shriek at him. 'Put that aside and get on. There are far more important things that need doing.' Things pertaining to the real world, was what she meant. She just couldn't stand all this constant aimless wool-gathering. And yet that was a main part of William's intrinsic charm. A refreshing change from the crashing city bores she'd been stuck with until she met him.

It was one of their fundamental differences; she was a pragmatist, he an unstructured dreamer. It still amazed him secretly that they'd ever got it together, but he'd admired her hugely from the moment of first meeting and when William wanted anything enough, nothing could stand in his way. It was all part of the paradox that made up his complex character and explained how he'd held her entranced all these years when some occasionally saw him as a wimp. Edwina always charged in with both feet while he was more inclined to think things through. His little Boadicea, he liked to call her, as he proudly stood on the sidelines and watched her conquer the world.

She had been astounded when he was suddenly without a job yet made no instant attempt to find another. He'd always been so happy with his topography and maps; the house was strewn with the evidence because he was constantly browsing. But he liked the leisure to look around and now had Morwenna to teach. What riches he would be able to pass on to her as soon as she was old enough to understand. It worried him not at all that his wife was the sole provider. He felt quietly confident there'd be work out there for him when the time was finally ripe. Talent like his did not come cheap, of that he had always been certain, and the distinguished vocation, of which he was a part, grew more specialist year by year.

What Edwina had never taken the time to comprehend was that the mapping industry was no longer what it had been. When William first came to it, with his brilliant degree, the profession was still very much based on dedicated graphics. He had had a ball in his first two jobs, experiencing a sense of real achievement. Not so now, however. In the past few years those perfidious purveyors of crap maps were increasingly taking over with their computers and IT skills. Cartography as a career choice was losing its aesthetic allure, William's principal reason for being in no particular rush to re-enter the fray.

Plus, of course, there was the advent of Morwenna which had brought him more joy than he could believe. He hadn't so much as dreamed he would feel this way about fatherhood, but now knew these precious hours with her could never be replicated. Unless they did have that longed-for second child, which he was starting to fear was unlikely. Not as things stood between them lately. There were too many broken bridges that needed fixing.

Some day, when she was old enough, he would pass on his delicate draughtsman skills to his daughter. She already showed signs of sharing his talent, which brought him immeasurable pleasure.

'Come along, cherub,' he said now briskly, binning the newspaper and rising to his feet. Time to head on towards the new playground, always a highlight of their day. The park just now was looking particularly luxuriant, touched as it was with a hint of autumn magic. If they made fast tracks, they'd be bound to catch up with some friends, regulars sharing the swings.

'Hi!' said several of the mothers, when William arrived and released Morwenna from her stroller to join the other children in the sandpit. William watched her crowing with delight as she toddled on sturdy legs from child to child.

'Morwenna's looking particularly bonny this morning,' remarked a mother he encountered occasionally at the doctor's. She was plump, bland and comfortable, intent on crocheting something small and white. She lived quite near him in Hillgate Village; he couldn't for the moment recall her name. William smiled. He was a favourite among this particular klatch, a rarity by virtue of his sex. Not many fathers ever ventured into this territory, certainly not during weekday working hours. He made appropriate comments about her own pallid child and then they briefly got on to things like the weather. After that, for a painful few moments, he found himself utterly stumped. His mind was absorbed with the details of the murders, but that was hardly a subject for idle chat. How did other people fare when they knew each other only slightly? Women were so much better at handling these things. Small-talk for beginners, it ought to be on the curriculum. He thought very hard while he racked his brains. Then inspiration struck.

'I don't suppose,' he said brightly, pretty confident he was on the right track, 'that you have a really good recipe for orange marmalade?' Then was able safely to return to his morbid thoughts, pretending all the while to be absorbed.

William came to his vocation in a slightly roundabout way. At school in Devon he had excelled at art, though not quite enough, his teachers felt, to make it a viable career choice. Also his family wasn't keen. All you heard about art students in those days were their bawdy rags and the Chelsea Arts Ball, and William's parents were far too grounded to take such a chance with his future. As was he. With two good As in Maths and Geography, he was headed for something more mundane until he chanced to take a holiday job in Exeter. In a shop that dealt exclusively in old maps, where he found himself instantly seduced by their musty appeal. He had long been a crossword addict and loved the challenge of working things out. So the study of how the land once lay immediately sucked him in. He was a genius at jigsaws and an early addict of Rubik's Cube, which he cracked, when it first came out, at the age of eleven. He would gnaw at a problem with dogged persistence until he had got it solved. He was, in short, a natural lateral thinker. So he took a course at Oxford Polytechnic and ended up with a joint honours degree in Computer Studies and Cartography.

From there he landed a job with *Reader's Digest* and after that moved on to Nicholsons for what he perceived as more scope and additional prestige. A mistake, as it turned out, for soon they were gobbled up and were forced to streamline their staff, which meant having to let him go. A halt, for a while, to his glittering career and the start of his full-time nannying. Which, after the first hard jolt, no longer fazed him. There'd be time enough in the future for his maps. Right now he was overwhelmed with delight at just being Morwenna's dad.

* * *

On sudden impulse William decided to take a trip down to Alton Coombe, the pretty Gloucestershire village where Aunt Jane's cottage was situated. They hadn't been there for far too long and she had, after all, been good enough to leave it to them. The weather was bright and, for once, not raining. A bit of country air would do them good. They could stop off in Tetbury and look at antiques. Already the child was starting to appreciate quality. Edwina, predictably, thought he was off his rocker. All those dreary hours of driving with only a baby for company. And he was bound to hit the worst of the traffic on the long journey back. William, however, was undeterred. Aunt Jane had been neglected quite long enough. He still had nightmares when he thought about her death and that terrible confrontation in the mortuary. The least he could do now was help to cherish her memory. He hadn't cared much for her in life but could not get her out of his mind.

'What are you planning to do?' asked Edwina suspiciously. They had stopped their regular visits because of the domestic upheaval. Just transporting one child for a two-day weekend resembled an army on the move. They were both worn out by the time they even got there and then had to turn right round and reverse the process. Also, on a more practical level, she felt Aunt Jane's possessions were hardly the setting for a lively, destructive child. Among the general old-ladyish clutter were items of genuine value. It needed a thorough sorting out, which neither had the time to do right now.

'Oh, this and that,' said William, deliberately vague. He

hesitated to tell her he had murder on his mind, but since he'd become obsessed with the recent Marsh massacre, curiosity was getting the better of him. Alton Coombe was a fair distance from Northampton, yet some vague inner instinct was quietly starting to hum. 'We might even stay overnight? Would you like that, duckie?'

Any adventure with Morwenna along was bound, by definition, to turn out fun. She was so clued into everything at this age, he loved to see the wonder on her face. And it meant he needn't feel guilty, at least for today, at still not making a move towards finding real work. For despite his personal contentment on the domestic front, he sensed Edwina was growing increasingly testy. It wasn't natural, he could see it in her eyes, for a man to take such pleasure staying at home. And those supercilious girl friends, to whom she was constantly gabbing, were doubtless sowing dissension in her mind.

Of course she hmm-ed her disapproval as she sorted through her briefcase but couldn't stand in his way if he wanted to go. It would, at least, get him out of the house instead of just idling all day. Or distracting the cleaner with all that pointless chatter. Or doing one of his endless crossword puzzles.

'If you go you can tidy up the garden,' she said. 'After all this rain, it must be like a wilderness.'

But gardening was not on William's current list of priorities. There were far more important things he wanted to do.

* * *

The hedge needed trimming and the last of the roses dead-heading, but the cottage, on the whole, appeared to be still in good nick. It was a pity they had neglected it so much. The village was chocolate-box pretty and they ought really to make more use of it. Perhaps when Morwenna was slightly older it would finally come into its own. Or otherwise they should consider putting it on the market, though he doubted Edwina would agree. She felt they should honour her aunt's bequest and use it at least occasionally. William parked outside the white gate and released Morwenna from her car seat. She ran unsteadily on her fat little legs and cooed with delight at a neighbour's geese while William wrestled open the heavy front door.

There was a mass of junk mail scattered across the hall and a spider's web artfully veiling one window. Otherwise all seemed in apple pie order since Edwina's effective last onslaught. There was a slight smell of mildew around the kitchen sink and the bedclothes would need to be aired. He opened a few windows to let the breeze blow through, then scrambled eggs and tomatoes for their lunch. Aunt Jane had spent her last years here and her touch was still very much apparent. He could almost sense her presence around, with a strong whiff of her trademark lavender. It seemed, slightly eerily, like entering a time warp. He half expected her to come striding through the door.

They never did catch her murderer, just wrote it off as a random killing and doubtless closed the file out of lack of interest. But William couldn't forget her nor the horrible way she had died. That sad little lifeless dog of hers, pinioned like a rag doll on the churchyard railings. Whoever had done that had got to be seriously deranged. Suddenly William found he had lost his appetite.

'Come along, sweetheart, eat up,' he urged. 'Then Daddy will take you out for a nice walk.'

Their first port of call was the parish church, scene of poor Aunt Jane's untimely death. They lingered in the churchyard to check the state of her grave, and William felt a renewed pang of guilt when he saw how overgrown it was. For the first year or so they had paid for its upkeep but somehow that service seemed to have slipped by the wayside. Before he left he would try to come back and weed it, perhaps plant something lasting like a rosebush. He slowly pushed open the creaking door of the church and inhaled the aroma of candle wax and polish.

The vicar, already robed, was by the font, preparing for a christening. William introduced himself, reminding him of their sombre earlier meeting, and the vicar bowed his head in mute respect. Jane Fairchild might have been a bit of a thorn in his flesh but her passing had been truly shocking. It had brought reporters to the village in their hordes, but public memory was fickle and they had very soon faded away. Even the police inquiry had been closed these past two years. She was hardly ever even spoken of these days. And now this amiable stranger with the small enchanting child was asking questions to which there were no answers. The vicar, suddenly wary, was reluctant to get involved. The last thing he needed now was any more trouble.

'Are you living down here?' he asked. William shook his head. Explained they kept the cottage solely as a weekend retreat and regretted they couldn't make use of it any more often.

'I just wondered,' he said, after a suitable pause, 'if anything more had surfaced about Miss Fairchild?'

The vicar looked at him blankly, sudden panic in his eyes. He needed some space to compose himself before the christening.

'What kind of thing did you have in mind?' The whole world knew that her killer had never been caught, was almost certainly a vagrant passing through. They had combed the place in their cursory way then finally, when the heat went off, declared the whole matter closed. She was, after all, a woman on her own, never particularly liked. Until this minute the vicar had forgotten the existence of relatives at all.

'The thing is,' said William, suddenly confidential, 'I've been wondering about these latest beastly murders.'

'The Marshes?' asked the vicar, fully aware. The story was still on all the tabloid front pages. William nodded.

'Dreadful business,' said the vicar, shaking his head. Another horrible tragedy stirring up trouble. Though he couldn't, for the life of him, see any connection here. The Fairchild business had happened four years ago.

'I just have the strangest feeling the two cases might be connected. Both apparently motiveless and also excruciatingly bloody.'

Also two counties apart. It didn't add up. Compassionate though he tried to be, the vicar felt William was stretching things quite a bit. Having to do the identification must have unsettled the poor fellow's mind. The police had shown him all the relevant photos including the sad little carcass of the dog.

'Are you a reporter?' He was suddenly on his guard. The last thing they needed now was any more scandal.

'Just an amateur,' said William reassuringly. 'Wondering what I can do about my wife's aunt. I might look in at the police station,' he added, 'and see if they've managed to turn up anything new.'

'I'd do that,' said the vicar, relieved, glancing surreptitiously at his watch. 'Now, if you will excuse me, I have to get on.'

The village bobby could hardly have been less helpful, but that, William now recalled, was nothing new. An ungainly figure with a vacuous stare, he could barely contain his irritation at William's unwarranted questioning.

'So what's your interest?' he asked belligerently, looking as though he was ready to pick a fight. William patiently explained again the family connection, reminding him that they had met before at the time of the actual murder.

'I wondered,' he said, 'if you had come up with any more evidence. Surely she can't be forgotten just like that.' He thought of all her charity work, of the splendid floral arrangements in the church. This slob of a man had been unhelpful then, apparently taking as a personal slur any of William's questions. Even though, at that time, he'd had every right to ask them. And, to William's thinking now, still did.

'None whatsoever,' said the policeman without reflection. He had quite enough on his hands in this village without scraping up things from the past. The woman was dead and buried and that was that. He was surprised anyone even remembered her, let alone cared.

'Only these latest murders, the ones in Northampton, strike me as having similarities.' A blank stare. 'What with the very savagery of the crimes.'

'Northampton's a different area. Nothing to do with us here.' Go and pester them, he implied, and let me get on with my job.

'Thanks for your help,' said William blithely, determined more than ever to chase things up. He remembered this soulless bureaucracy well from four years ago. If they weren't going to help, he would damn well go it alone.

6

William's morbid interest in murder was something comparatively new. Edwina privately blamed it all on his current idle state, with not enough else to occupy his brain-cells. That was the way she'd been raised herself, never to waste a second of precious time. Instead of squandering whole days on end just bumming around with the baby, he ought by rights to be back there in the competitive world, doing something profitable as well as intellectually stimulating. Making his mark, as her father would say. Of course Edwina also made the connection with Aunt Jane's murder. Poor William had been the one coerced into having to identify the body. Her parents were travelling in South Africa at the time and had only got home for the funeral, which was anyhow delayed by the police for a couple of months, to fit in with their inquiries. Father had been shocked, of course, and had made the right sort of public mumbles, but, deep inside, he had always despised his sister and did not consider her shocking demise to be anything much more than a nuisance. Which might seem cold-blooded, but was how it was. Edwina hadn't liked to discuss it.

William, on the other hand, had been pretty nearly traumatised. He hadn't known Jane Fairchild well, but the very least she had been was a human being. Not to mention flesh and blood to his own wife. A single glimpse of the desecrated corpse had been sufficient to send him into shock. He had never seen anyone dead before, hoped not to have to do so again. Not for a good many years, at least. Old age was a different thing.

'I just can't get her out of my head,' he kept saying, snuggling close to Edwina in the night, trying to blank out the memory. She would pull him towards her and cradle him in her arms, whispering and soothing till he finally nodded off and she felt his rigid muscles start to relax.

'Poor baby,' she'd murmur as she rocked him gently to sleep, stroking back the glossy hair that was so touchingly like Morwenna's. Though Morwenna, at that time, was way in the future. They were then still in their honeymoon phase.

It was the first real break they had taken since the wedding and Alton Coombe in April was burgeoning with new life. The police investigation had been finally wrapped up and Jane Fairchild's defiled body laid to rest. It had all been the most horrendous trauma from which the Huxleys were trying to recover. The will had disclosed that she'd left them all her things, and now Edwina was suffering remorse for not having cared for her more.

'She wasn't the easiest person,' she explained. 'Forever on at me to do my prep.' Having a headmistress as an aunt was bad enough, but she'd also fawned upon Arnold all the time. Which, in Edwina's mind, was fairly yucky. She knew her father privately shared her opinion, though was too detached and absorbed in his own world to care about it one way or another.

'She really made me sick,' said Edwina with absolute candour. 'Acting as though my father's house were her own. I can't imagine why my mother ever put up with it. I suppose she just didn't care.'

There was something quaintly Victorian about Aunt Jane, who had behaved as though she had family rights which gave her automatic precedence over wife and daughter. She styled herself grandly 'Miss Fairchild' at all times, and took it for granted she was welcome to stay whenever she came to town. Which was more often than they wanted her, especially Edwina. She'd appropriated a bedroom as her own where she left a change of clothes and a cluster of possessions. Luckily the house was large so they still had several spares. Helge, with her mind on higher things, had managed to rise above it, but Edwina loathed coming home from school to find her aunt installed. She bossed around the long-suffering cook and interfered in the kitchen. Behaved as though the house were an entailed family property and not just the fruit of a lifetime's hard work. She took, as though by right, her place at the head of the table while Helge simply smiled grimly and shrugged it off. If it weren't so damned annoying, it would actually be quite funny. Arnold, as ever, didn't notice.

She was hot on Edwina doing her cello practice and scolded her if she ever cut it short. Also she insisted on checking her homework before she was allowed to go to bed, sometimes had even been known to make her redo it. Life with Aunt Jane on the premises was worse even than boarding-school. Why they'd allowed her to act in this way remained to Edwina a mystery, but both parents had always been so self-involved, it had probably suited them well. A handy babysitter as well as unpaid governess. They had had the child late deliberately and didn't want her constantly underfoot.

'She was always terribly stingy with presents,' said Edwina, still feeling guilty as she had a look around. 'And at meal times she bored us all to tears. Chewed every mouthful at least a hundred times and talked incessantly about the school. We'd be sitting there for hours, just waiting for her to finish. Father occasionally left her to it but even that didn't stop her flow. She was a proper horror, an archetypal old maid. And now I feel really dreadful that she's dead.'

She laid her head against William's chest and he saw that her eyes were brimming. He had just romantically carried her over the threshold and was still a little out of breath. He held her gently and tenderly kissed her hair, touched by this sudden emotional display.

'I expect she loved you really, it was just her way of expressing it. Why else do you think she would have left you all this?'

The cottage was slightly stuffy and smelt a little of mildew but otherwise was still in excellent repair. Even the thatch had recently been re-done, another major expense they were glad to avoid. It was years since Edwina had bothered to pay her a visit which only went to make her feel guiltier still.

'Only because she had no one else,' she sniffed. 'I am the sole remaining natural heir.'

They stripped off the faded old eiderdown and replaced it with an expensive goose-feather duvet, bought ceremoniously at Conran for just this purpose. Eventually the curtains would also have to go, as well as the antimacassars on the wing chairs. It was amazing that, in this day and age, she had still clung so resolutely to the past. But she had always been a traditionalist whose intrinsic taste could not be faulted. Each piece of furniture had been meticulously selected to fit the age and ambience of the room. The effect was homely and pleasing and stirred something basic in William's heart. He envisaged a future, after their as-yet-to-be-born children had left home, when the two of them could grow old together in this cosy little nest. Which brought him back neatly to the matter in hand.

'Let's try it out,' he said hopefully, closing the curtains. 'It's only right that we christen the place appropriately.'

Things had been so perfect then; where had it started to go wrong? Losing his job, of course, had not exactly helped and the withering scorn of her parents had made things worse. Arnold Fairchild, emeritus professor of economics, still worked long hours in his early eighties. He despised what he considered a shirker and made no bones about it. Whoever married his precious daughter needed to pull up his socks.

'What that young man needs is proper employment,' was one of his regular moans. He had no time at all for the concept of New Man, considered his son-in-law a bit of a sissy. In his day a woman's place had been firmly in the home, no matter that his own wife was a prominent feminist. Helge Dorfman had always had a voice and had ruthlessly raised her own daughter in her image. Which was a large part of Edwina's confusion now. She didn't know which way to turn.

When she'd first met William, in South Kensington, he was one of a group of spirited youths who had hung out together in the various winebars and contrived to have loads of fun. He was working then for the *Digest*, his first job. Edwina, fresh from a shattered involvement, was grateful to meet up with such a lively crowd. She had never had any problem with finding new admirers but was not yet nearly ready to settle down. William's ambivalent situation suited her down to the ground. And she found his boyish enthusiasms rather endearing.

He had bright dark eyes, like a questing robin, and thick shaggy hair, nearly always in need of a cut. He took an intelligent interest in practically any subject, in particular (at that time) astronomy and Egyptology. When he got on to one of his hobby-horses, he sparkled like a merry little elf. She liked the way he looked and his infectious zest for life and started to keep an eye out for him at parties. Her daughter, she was glad to see now, had inherited that bustling curiosity. It was one of the strong similarities she treasured most.

'I'm just going out to look at the stars,' was what had led to that first furtive kiss. She was astonished when she actually found him sexy. Take away the faux aura of school-boy nerd and there within lurked a man of genuine depth. Plus originality. He shared with her the wonders of the solar system and also started to teach her hieroglyphics.

Father was slightly sceptical when Edwina first brought William home but her parents were tired of the strings of Lotharios and felt it was definitely time she settled down. They still had mixed views on a woman's proper role but agreed they would dearly love a grandchild. All had gone well till he'd suddenly got the sack. Arnold Fairchild had disapproved of him ever since.

So what was she to do? She was still very much in awe of her parents, found it hard not to play for their approval. They doted on Morwenna, dropped hints about wanting another, yet let their basic disillusionment with William show through. Though they did allow, somewhat grudgingly, that he was an excellent father. On the other hand, they were proud of Edwina's career and showered her with praise as they watched it grow. Arnold, the economist, was particularly pleased with her progress. This latest collusion with Gareth seemed to him an excellent thing. He had met Gareth once and approved of his debonair manners but, then, Gareth had always known how to pile it on. Ever a bit of a star-fucker, he was impressed by the distinguished academic. The Fairchild name carried considerable clout, especially in financial circles.

'Perhaps we should offer him a directorship?' suggested Gareth, but Edwina was emphatic in her refusal. Father offstage, giving an approving nod, was good for her ego as well as reassuring. But Father hands-on would be a nightmare quite unthinkable. Apart from the obvious snub it would mean to her husband. She let him know the basic parameters of what they were doing, that was all. Possibly, at a later stage, she might also permit him to invest.

Now, as she worked on her abs in the gym, her thoughts were fully concentrated on Gareth. She would loathe him to see her hot and sweaty like this but was proud of the way she was toning up. She ran her hands appreciatively over her flat, taut midriff, then did fifty extra crunches just for luck. When you saw someone daily, you dared not ever slack off. Though she still remained outwardly haughty, inside she was definitely wavering. She was due very shortly to meet the girls for a meal in a Butler's Wharf bistro. Just time for a ten-minute sauna and shower and then she would have to get going.

'No William?' asked Meryl hopefully, as if it were even likely. Everyone smirked; they had been through it all before.

Edwina shook her head. 'What do you think? He's home playing happy families with the kid.' She knew as she said it she was being unfair. Just occasionally she couldn't help herself. They'd had the whole dialogue again that morning, just before her taxi arrived. Sue was hosting a 'family' get together; even the elusive Nick was rumoured to be turning up. And they'd promised to lay on something toothsome for Meryl. A cosy meeting of the six of them was something they didn't often do. But William, rot his socks, had failed to come through. Even though he had to be the least stressed of the lot. By quite a long chalk from her reckoning.

'You know we can't leave Morwenna,' he had said, as if she had suggested some depravity. Making Edwina, quite unfairly, feel uncomfortable. Not just for this once, to see her friends? It wasn't as if they couldn't afford it or did it all the time. He was turning into a seriously odd homebody, with definite views on childcare that she didn't necessarily share. Though Arnold and Helge, she knew, would approve which was probably why she wanted to rebel.

'Doesn't he ever get out on his own?' Sue, diplomatically, had cancelled the other two men. Nick, the rising Eurocrat, would be glad not to have to spare the time but at least, when it was necessary, was amenable. But then, for years, they'd had the backup of a round-the-clock nanny. Yes, it could be inconvenient, not to mention claustrophobic, but neither of them would change the arrangement for the world. It enabled Sue to hold down a high-flying banking job and still find time for these sessions with the girls. Which was really, if she were honest, what it was all about. Helped to keep the marriage harmonious and her sane. Nick, with his separate agenda, amiably went along with it. As a result they were popularly viewed as the perfect couple.

'Not very often,' said Edwina, answering honestly. 'But then, he's his own man, isn't he, during the day.' Bitchy again but she couldn't help resenting it. Somehow he'd managed to arrange a perfect lifestyle. Time to play with the kid and gossip with the cleaner. Now to chase murderers to his heart's content. But she didn't want to discuss this with her friends. She suspected they already thought him a bit of a wally.

'How's Gareth?' asked Meryl hopefully. She had only ever glimpsed him and had been angling ever since for an introduction. So far Edwina had succeeded in keeping them apart. Meryl was deceptively brassy but fragile underneath; a head to head collision could prove disastrous.

'Okay,' she said off-handedly, aiming to steer clear of the subject. But soon her resolution slipped and his name came creeping back in. Gareth, she told them with a fair degree of pride, was currently in New York. Raising the profile of their dotcom venture, hoping to rope in mammoth bucks.

'He really is a terrific schmoozer,' she said, the glint in her eye unknowingly blowing her cover.

William, if he were honest, was rocked to his socks by these latest murders. Aunt Jane's death had been quite

72

horrific enough; he still had the occasional nightmare. But this, by anyone's standards, was far worse, as well as being constantly in his face. Despite the fact that he hadn't ever known them, he felt a distinct affinity with the Marsh family, and found it hard to eclipse them from his thoughts. This time he didn't try talking to Edwina; she would only think he was losing it altogether. Instead he ran it past his most reliable supporter, Mrs P, who didn't have a lot to add to the equation. But at least she paid him the courtesy of listening to every detail, then giving it the benefit of her reasoning.

What these two disparate crimes had basically in common was the more than sheer brutality of the killings. In other words, the absolute *bloodiness*. Both had also included innocent extras: in Aunt Jane's case, the pathetic dog; in this, the duo of cute little under-age daughters. And both in broad daylight with nobody hearing their screams. Though things like that did occur all too frequently, most recently the snatching of schoolgirl Sarah Payne. The police confessed to being utterly in the dark about the Marsh case and had drafted additional manpower on to the job. What interested William most was the killer's motivation. Could it, perhaps, all be part of some private vendetta? Interestingly also it was trumpeted in the press that Robert Marsh had lived a blameless life. Like Aunt Jane. That faintly resounding bell just wouldn't stop ringing.

'I still think he did it,' said Mrs P dogmatically, though she did give thought to what William had to say. He had taken to following her around the house, shouting to be heard above the hoover. She smoked all the time, dropping ash as she progressed, then efficiently vacuuming it up before moving on.

'But why?' asked William. 'And why Aunt Jane?' Being a pain in the neck was just not enough. And to do it so gorily, it didn't make sense.

'Don't really know,' admitted Mrs P. 'It's just that it's nearly always someone in the family.' Which was true.

She was, as it happened, wrong in her supposition. Forty-eight hours after his apprehension, Marsh was released on police bail. The television cameras caught him returning to his home, an obviously broken man. William watched the newscast over and over, channel-hopping out of morbid fascination. Marsh had visibly shrunk since the ordeal and looked at least twenty years older. Mrs P might consider it a sign of his guilt but William remained far from convinced. This was a man clearly going through living hell and finding it hard to carry on. Not a kind of monster, just an ordinary guy who'd experienced the worst sort of depravity. The cameras lingered on the firmly closed front door and filmed him as he rapidly pulled down the blinds.

Leave the poor sod alone, thought William with real empathy, *and allow him to do his grieving in peace.*

7

I've always had a bit of a thing about graveyards. I'm not
quite certain why. Perhaps because the public affirmation of
our mortality serves as a reminder that we all end up the same.
Death, after all, is the great leveller. Whenever possible, I idle
among the graves, deciphering the inscriptions and thinking
about those who have gone before. Who now include among
their number the two I loved best in the world. It comforts me
to think they are up there together, waiting for me to arrive. I
like the vast, archaic, moss-covered tombs and the children's
scaled-down monuments, often quite moving in their very
mawkishness. The Victorians made an art of all this, but then
they were so much more at ease with death. Families in those
days were so much larger and infant mortality high. Losing
eight out of a total of fifteen must surely have put a different
spin on things. They may have swept sex beneath the carpet
in those days but they gloried in all the public trappings of
death. They wore full black for at least a year, presumably
finding it cathartic. Occasionally, when I have nothing much
else to do, I take a picnic to the cemetery and bathe my agony
in the timeless peace you find in that sort of place. Face it, the

75

dead won't ever desert you or let you down. But remain there eternally, unchanging. Watching. Or so I like to imagine.

I considered for a while attending the funeral, until reason luckily got the upper hand. You can't be too casual in this killing game and I couldn't rely one hundred per cent on the crass ineptitude of the police. I would like to have seen for myself those three matching coffins, each one covered with a mass of white daisies and followed by a crowd of stupefied mourners, outraged by such a brutal and senseless crime. The daisies, I suppose, were symbolic. They'd been making daisy-chains when it happened. Doubtful taste, I privately thought, though maybe somebody simply didn't think. I would have liked to have mingled among the bereaved and tasted their grief first-hand, but the fact I was a stranger might have drawn attention to me. And that was the last thing I wanted.

In the end I watched it on the news in the pub and enjoyed it vicariously when the ceremony was over and a handful of mourners came in. Everyone was so angry and outraged I think they might well have lynched me had they known. I slipped away with a feeling of quiet satisfaction. Do as you would be done by, I've always believed.

My next target was a schoolmaster, Alan Hargreaves, who lived in Dorset, quite a distance away. Which meant another tedious shift of lodgings, but by now I was fairly used to that. And it helped to cover my trail by moving on. All my possessions fit into two modest bags; I have grown adept at travelling light. Landladies invariably ask me what I do, and I spin them some *piece of nonsense about being in sales. Everyone these days seems to be some sort of salesperson; they are thicker on the ground than autumn leaves. Or else, depending where I've reached in my research, I attach myself to some government department and rely on ad-libbing from there. My story has never once been challenged so I'm gradually beginning to relax. Blind them with science; it never fails. They are invariably overworked and self-involved, absorbed by their narrow little lives. They rapidly lose interest and cease their prying so I reward them by being no trouble as a guest. Permanently smiling and polite, that's me, grateful for whatever might be on offer. The ideal lodger with no tiresome little ways. Plus I always tidy up and make my bed. Of course, they never get to know my real name or identity. I am certain they quickly forget me once I've gone. Total invisibility, that's my secret. I have learned, chameleon-like, to merge effectively with my background.*

I had spent a great deal of time on Mr Hargreaves and tracked him down at last to a minor boys' prep school. Forty-three and married, with a family of his own, he was active in the scout troop, and his hobbies included sailing and playing the saxophone. Definitely one of the boys, I would guess, and fitting the profile precisely. Gaining initial access is always the hardest part, but here, once again, I was lucky enough to strike gold. While trawling the local job ads in search of some casual work, I chanced upon a vacancy actually in the school. Someone up there was finally on my side; I couldn't have hoped for better had I planned it. They were in need of temporary assistance in the bursar's office, transferring data to their brand new computer system, stuff like that. Not quite my usual style but perfect for the advancement of my mission. The vacancy hit the spot; that was all that counted. The present incumbent was off on maternity leave; they were seeking a three-month stopgap, which was ideal. No tricky question of references or even a P45. Payment straight from the petty cash with no questions asked, I would wager. And even if they did ask, I would have an alibi ready. I had bluffed my way through trickier situations than this.

The thing about me is I can turn my hand to practically anything, have all the basic skills to back me up. That's one of the pluses of growing up on a farm. My brothers would laugh if they could see me today, polishing my keyboard skills while toning down my act. Not like those days when we kicked a ball around and vied to drink each other under the table. I doubt they would even recognise me now. Even the Armani suits have gone. Trouble has sobered me, at least for the time being, and totally quenched my desire to play the clown. Of course I had to rework my CV but no one was likely to give it more than a glance. I backed my application with the plain unvarnished truth. You can't go very far wrong if you stick to that. I had recently relocated, I explained, and hinted at family problems. Keen but not eager, respectful but not too much. I was doing them the favour; I wanted to make that clear. My luck was in and I landed the job. To start the following Monday.

Now I needed a plan. I had allowed myself only three months and so far still hadn't a clue. I had grown accustomed to lying in wait, but it was the time for swift action. Once inside that chaotic office, however, the pieces began to fall into place. My very first task was to transfer the personnel data, as a result of which I was able to filch Alan Hargreaves' file. I was aware of the bursar regarding me askew, suspicious and slightly resentful. He was obviously surprised I would want such a menial job. I was more than aware myself that my face didn't fit. I waited for him to make some sort of move but, since I was always punctual and polite, there wasn't really a lot he could say. He was a blustering, ruddy-faced bear of a man who instinctively I mistrusted on sight.

Maybe the fool thought I was after his job, he certainly had all sorts of delusions of grandeur. There is just no telling where paranoia will strike, and the poor fellow had been stuck there most of his life. Once he even asked me point blank why I'd wanted to work there in the first place. I stared back coolly and produced my standard reply, not that it was any of his business. I'd been recently travelling abroad, I explained, and needed a breather like this to get myself sorted. Family commitments, that sort of stuff. Problems with ageing relatives, I knew he'd understand. He did have the grace to look faintly uncomfortable, though it did nothing to deflect his curiosity.

'Married?' he asked and I mutely shook my head. If he fondly imagined we had anything in common, he couldn't have figured me more wrong. He was the absolute antithesis of all that I respect, the sort of guy I normally avoid. Almost certainly latently repressed and never, ever amounting to very much. Stuck in a timewarp from his middle teens with an appetite for beer and scatological humour. England's minor public schools abound in this sort of misfit, devoid of any savvy or the aptitude to cope. But as long as I had to work alongside him, I would make sure I kept things harmonious. So I kept out of his way as much as I was able and concentrated on maintaining a low profile. In spite of himself, I was clocking up points by acting the congenial spare pair of hands.

The schoolmaster, Hargreaves, I discovered from reading his file, had an unremarkable past. Redbrick university followed by teacher training. A model teacher, popular with pupils and staff. This last I got from the bursar in one of his rare expansive moods.

'Though the wife's a bit of a pill,' he added grudgingly. He gave all the signs of not much liking women which, given the way he lived his life, came as no big surprise. Not that it mattered to me either way. Each to his own and my tastes were more refined, though I'd not be trying to ram them down his throat. Internal politics were to be avoided at all costs, especially when my life could hang upon the merest slip. Right now I needed to keep my head well down and all my defences up. Should anything go wrong, it would be my neck on the block. That was what kept my adrenalin level high.

'I'll close up,' I'd occasionally offer, 'if you want to be heading off home.' Down to the boozer was closer to the truth, though of course I never let on how much I knew. The bursar's home was a rundown bungalow in the grounds, which meant he was, technically, permanently on duty. Only we in the office worked regular hours and were viewed by the school as civilians. I usually contrived to be out of there by six. With barely three months before I had to move on, there was still a huge amount to be got through.

*   *   *

Things finally fell into place when I sneaked a look at the teaching rosters and spotted that Alan Hargreaves had a wildlife field trip planned. Eight boys in a minibus on an outing to Portland Bill. Superbly rugged scenery with a conservation area thrown in. They would leave at the crack of dawn and take packed lunches and not return to the school until after dark. I bought myself an Ordnance Survey map and studied the terrain minutely. I wished now I'd paid more attention to geography; certainly no room here for careless errors. If he took, as I assumed he would, the scenic route, there were one or two obvious spots he was likely to stop. For this was more than just a jolly summer jaunt but also a serious wildlife lesson on wheels.

To strengthen my plan, I went out of my way in an effort to get to know him better. He wasn't exactly my usual cup of tea but it pays to know your prey, a golden rule. Also there was the additional motive of wanting to know what made him tick. He was a keen, fresh-faced enthusiast with thinning hair and a hearty laugh, inclined to wear long shorts and sandals with socks. Another overgrown schoolboy if ever I saw one but, nevertheless, kind-hearted and sincerely dedicated. The sort of born teacher I think I'd have liked for my own kids, though I tried not to dwell on that now.

We fell into an easy discussion about the beauties of the local countryside. He was only too willing, in his obliging way, to share with me the benefits of his knowledge. He had lived in these parts for most of his adult life and burbled with infectious enthusiasm. Even sketched, on the back of an old envelope, the basic route he thought he might take the boys. There were so many natural beauties he wanted to show them, he'd be hard-pressed to fit it all into one day.

'Come with us, if you like,' he added spontaneously. 'There's room inside for another one, just, if you don't mind squashing up.'

Caught completely off my guard, for a second I was lost for an excuse. So I pleaded pressure of work, which sounded wet and also made me look a touch ungrateful.

'Some other time . . .' I said vaguely, and he beamed and promised we'd make that a definite date.

'Any time that suits you,' he said. 'Provided, of course, that the weather holds up.'

He drove me home – he was going my way – and dropped me off outside my lodgings. I hadn't wanted anyone from the school to know where I was staying, but, at this advanced stage of the game, it no longer seemed to matter. For if everything went according to plan, he would soon no longer be there to blow the whistle.

It was always a bit of a family joke how much I liked to tinker with engines. They seemed to find it hilarious, though I really can't see why. We all learned to drive at an early age and there's not much under a bonnet I cannot fix. It didn't sit well, they said, with my clothes and lah-di-dah manners, all thought I was getting ideas above my station. Engine grease under my nails wasn't quite Armani. But I didn't care. Messing about with cars is a great way of relaxing, and I could often be found in a neighbour's barn of a weekend, doing something tricky to a tractor. Which was excellent experience for this latest little project. Odd how these things always seem to work out in the end.

I let Hargreaves play around with my bike and he, congenial fellow that he was, reciprocated by showing me his engine. Of which, I may say, he was justly proud. Even though the van was now ten years old, he had kept it in tiptop condition and fingered that lump of lifeless metal as though it were a prize animal on show. It was parked beside the playground and we lounged there as we chatted. So that by the time we were done with gabbing, I had every detail I needed off by heart. It should only be the work of seconds, providing I got my timing right. So far my most ambitious crime yet. I could hardly wait to get going.

Shame about the boys, of course, but the truth is you can't make an omelette without breaking eggs.

8

The shocking Hargreaves massacre made all the front pages. Plus headlines on the evening news: *van goes over a cliff. Nine dead*, with blood-curdling pictures of the accident scene, showing the horrifying skid-marks. At first they put it down to pure bad luck until they detected the skilfully sawn-through brake cable. And the fact that Hargreaves had had his throat sliced. *After* he went off the road.

One of the neighbours, Polly Graham, was giving a charity coffee morning. William and Morwenna went along. She lived just round the corner in Callcott Street, in a pretty blue-washed townhouse that had once been an artisan's cottage. The front door was open and the hall-way packed with prams. William folded his stroller and stowed it helpfully outside in the porch to allow extra room for latecomers.

'Children into the nursery,' called Polly over the buzz. She was wearing a fashionable long Indian skirt, with earrings that dangled to her collarbones. Her nanny, aided by three others, was holding court amid an array of cuddly toys. There was even a juggler, a fresh-faced young man who looked barely out of the cradle himself. William had grown to enjoy this kind of event. It was fun for Morwenna, meant that she met other children, and also took him out of his rut. It was one of Mrs P's mornings, but they'd still found a minute for their regular update.

'Imagine,' she had said, through an aureole of smoke, 'those poor innocent kiddies all smashed to smithereens.'

Excellent fodder for such a compatible pair of ghouls. They pulled up their chairs with unusual relish and settled down for a comfortable chinwag over a fresh pot of tea. In Mrs P's opinion, it was likely to be one of the parents. Out to bump off an unsatisfactory teacher, unaware that there would be children involved. William was doubtful. What kind of parent would consider going to such lengths when the problem could be solved simply by removing the child from the school? Or by launching a formal complaint through more regular channels.

There had recently been a case in America where a child beauty queen had been neatly dispatched by the overly ambitious mother of a circuit rival. Perhaps it was one of the boys who had been the actual target. The swot of the Lower Fourth or something like that.

'But someone slashed the master's throat.' No getting away from that gruesome fact. He had been savagely finished off, the papers said, by someone foolhardily slithering down the cliff and knifing him as he lay there, fatally injured. The van had dropped more than two hundred feet. There was blood all over the accident scene. Not one

85

of the boys had survived, poor little beggars.

Mrs P gave a delicious shudder. There was nothing she liked more than a catastrophe.

William was still pondering this topic as he took his place in Polly's designer kitchen. She had had the house completely gutted and walls knocked through for more space. Her husband was something impressive in insurance, no sign of a shortage of available income here. The walls were lemon with dark-blue fittings, with flagstones of polished granite on the floor. Edwina would be green with envy should she ever get to see it, though she wasn't part of Polly's social scene. Edwina was always dreaming of home improvements they might make. If only more cash were available day to day. But with just the single salary coming in, it was something that, for now, they couldn't afford. Certainly not till the fabled dotcom ship came in. William, for his part, felt not a twinge of guilt. He liked his own house just the way it was, perhaps a little down-at-heel but comfy and homey, in which he could go to ground. This house was more like a department-store showroom. Even the pristine tea towels were an exact match.

There were eight young mothers, including Polly, but William was, as usual, the token male. He really couldn't have cared less, was used by now to the imbalance of the sexes and rather enjoyed being in the limelight. He helpfully handed round plates and mugs and was useful for lifting things down from high shelves. The women all clucked and made little-girl jokes. Every housewife ought to have one, they all agreed. It did make him feel occasionally like a kissogram or male stripper, but he'd always been fundamentally at ease with his sexuality and some of these women were developing into real friends.

'Tell us what you've been up to lately, William.' One of Polly's girlfriends was ogling him without shame. He was wearing cords and a fisherman's jersey, and his hair, with its ragged fringe, could do with a cut. He looked, Polly thought, like a mischievous five-year-old who would soon have his hand in the cookie jar. Her own husband, Martin, was anal and tense. When he wasn't in his office, he was studying the financial pages. William beamed his beguiling smile and answered with considered seriousness.

'Not a lot,' he was obliged to admit. 'Domestic chores and stuff like that. Nothing much out of the ordinary.'

'Life's a bitch.' They all agreed, yet not a single one of them had a job. All had nannies and cleaners, some also a personal trainer yet, what with the tennis and the beauty parlour, there weren't enough hours in the day. They all complained how stressed they were. It made him want to poke fun. In these days of enlightenment, he privately thought, these women were an anachronism. At least he had the spirited Edwina crashing home at the end of a long trying day, full of news and energy and irritation, ready to be smoothed and fed and counselled. At which he had become rather an expert. He had certainly had enough practice.

* * *

Edwina couldn't have cared less about the murders, had far more important worries on her plate. *Grow up, William*, she thought testily, dropping her coat at the foot of the stairs and venturing up behind him to dip her finger into his cooking.

'Lay off.' He hated it when she disturbed him at the stove or, worse still, attempted to interfere. He squinted again at the list of ingredients, sheltering it firmly from her questioning eyes. He preferred to produce a *fait accompli*, not have her nosing through his recipe. If a man couldn't have a bit of privacy in his own kitchen, things were certainly come to a pretty pass. Tonight he was trying out something from Jamie Oliver which, at this stage, required his full attention.

'Go and put your feet up, love, and I'll pour us both a drink.' *Better still, get up dem stairs sharpish and have yourself a relaxing bath*. She was always better when she'd had a chance to unwind. A G and T should fill the bill once he'd got this thing safely into the oven.

'Hard day?' he asked sympathetically later, when calm was restored and Morwenna tucked up in bed. Edwina lay supine on the sofa, her bare feet cradled in his hands. She had delicate feet with neat little toes, immaculately garnished with frosted polish. She loved to have her feet rubbed, it was one of William's best treats, and purred like a jungle cat with real pleasure. William knew what he was up to. If the food was okay he might well be in luck tonight. Though these days nothing was ever quite that certain. Her mood could swing sharply like a weather-vane.

Things at the office were difficult, she told him, but was not yet prepared to go into much detail. She was worried about the German funding. Something didn't smell entirely right. William was great at analysing situations but also infuriatingly fair-minded. Which was something she really didn't need right now. She wanted Gareth to give her more support and not act quite so flippantly. They might be finding their way slowly out of the wood but had quite a distance still to go. And one false step at this precarious time could wipe out all they had achieved. But she didn't want William to start fussing about it now. Had had quite enough for one day.

Her colleagues were all great but needed to pull together, and Edwina had her work cut out just keeping them on their toes. Team spirit ought to be the name of the game, but whenever she nagged, Gareth turned a deaf ear and rapidly disappeared. He seemed to believe that his own contribution, conceiving the basic idea, had been enough. But without hard graft and full attention to detail, they could still find themselves in deep trouble. She longed to talk it all through with William but was reluctant to reveal too much of the true situation. Even though she knew he would back her up.

The fish pie was pronounced a success, and William started the coffee while Edwina switched on the news. This reversal of roles was quite natural to them by now;

neither ever commented any more. What they were was a team; he felt satisfied with that. And if he could manage to make his wife content, then he had achieved his main objective. Edwina removed the combs from her hair and let it sweep softly forward on to her shoulders. He was proud of her looks, her striking exotic beauty, glad she had never succumbed to having her hair cut. William trailed his fingers through the long luxuriant tresses, pulling her forward gently for a kiss. Slightly to his surprise, she didn't resist and snuggled into his shoulder, as trusting and warm as Morwenna. He kissed the top of her fragrant head and massaged the back of her neck. Soon, if he was lucky, she'd suggest an early night, a fitting finale to a pleasant and unstressed meal. And then he involuntarily stiffened and pushed her away as he took in precisely what the newscaster was saying.

The schoolboy massacre was still the principal item and occupied almost all of the news. There were moving shots of Hargreaves with his children, and film of the anguished widow being assisted back to her home. So far no one had come forward with information. They were appealing urgently for any first-hand eye-witness accounts. Or anything else that might be conceivably relevant. The police were obviously still in the dark and groping for any clues that they could find. The headland where it had happened was pretty much out of the way, far from even the most minor roads and cloaked by dense foliage and arid scrub.

'He was always so keen on nature,' sobbed his wife. He took a select group of boys from the school on this kind of field trip several times each year. Occasionally they even took sleeping-bags and camped out overnight. It was always a highlight of the year, one of the parents contributed. Hargreaves was such an inspiration to them all, almost like one of them himself.

'A dedicated teacher,' pronounced the Head. 'Popular with the boys and pulled his weight with the staff. Alan will be sorely missed.'

There followed details of his exemplary career, honed for the benefit of the viewers. Scoutmaster, chorister, almost too good to be true. Modest and self-effacing, devoted father. Something vital clicked in William's brain; it reminded him all of a sudden of Aunt Jane. Robert Marsh's family, too, seemed to fit a similar profile – genuine all-round good guys. Someone, it very much appeared, was bumping off the saintly and the good. The question to be answered now was, was there something sinister going on? Or were all these bloodthirsty crimes purely coincidence?

Edwina had quite lost her patience by the time she regained his attention and stomped up grumpily to bed. William shrugged. Slowly he cleared the dishes and stacked the machine. Left to his own devices, he would have allowed them to sit until morning, but Edwina was fanatical about tidiness and hygiene. He'd grown used to doing things her way. He shook out the cloth and brushed away the crumbs, then flicked a yellow duster over the table. Some of the petals from the roses had dropped so he scooped those up as well. He would one day make someone a perfect wife, his mother was constantly joking. But really he wasn't like this at all, just conditioned by this endless domesticity.

He could hear Edwina clumping around upstairs, expressing her displeasure by the banging of closet doors. By the time he got up there she'd be stiff and turned away, but he'd lost his own enthusiasm by now. After four years together, the edge had gone off their passion. He still, on occasion, found the old flame stirring, when just looking across a room at her could arouse him. But he had grown to expect and dislike her uncertain moods which he always found such a total turnoff.

He feared he was turning into a self-pitying ersatz hausfrau so went to the fridge and opened himself a beer. If that was the way she preferred to play it, it was all right with him. He would wait down here till he was certain she was asleep, thus avoiding another of their spats. Something was bugging her, he'd been aware of it for days, but if she didn't care to share it with him, he was damned if he was going to ask. Mutual support had always been one of their strengths and had kept their marriage alive through uncharted times. If they lost that intimacy, they'd be in serious trouble. And he dared not face serious bickering because of the child.

A small flicker of something unsubstantiated continued in William's brain, so he bolted the door and slipped on the chain, then carried his opened beer up to his study. Edwina had grabbed the attic for herself but this, the smallest bedroom, was his favourite. It overlooked the patio through a tangle of wisteria and remained his ultimate sanctuary whenever the heat was on. Of course he would have to forfeit it if they did expand their family, but right now it was an oasis of calm, filled with his books and maps. And his childhood collection of fossils, lovingly gathered on the Devon coast and arranged in a showcase on tiny wooden shelves that Mrs P always complained about having to dust.

Maps had been a feature of William's life since that fortuitous holiday job so long ago. He spent more money than he really ought to on them, was regularly under attack for being a spendthrift. It wasn't worth the argument but he had few other extravagances. Whereas Edwina's bank account was a faucet of gushing outlay, facials, massages, re-touched roots, exercise classes and clothes that she really didn't need. Whenever they planned economies, those were the last things to go. She needed them all, she explained to him patiently, since upkeep was so important to her career. If she failed to look smart and immaculately groomed, she wouldn't cut the mustard with the city. William didn't care, had never been preoccupied with money.

He did love his maps, however. Over the years they had become a bit of an addiction. At times when he was feeling particularly frazzled, a sortie up here always helped to calm him down. Also, he seemed to think better when engrossed in them; he liked their deft precision and the delicacy of execution. To think, a human hand had traced those lines while minutely recording the changing face of history. Edwina now seemed to think it all a great waste of time but, then, she hadn't the mindset to enjoy them. Hers was a more analytical sort of mind without the patience or dedication you really needed for maps.

Now he spread out an ancient map of the south west and compared it to a detailed modern road map. All those new roads that had sprung up over the years, webbing the whole of the country with faster transit. It wasn't the main arteries, though, that held his concentration, but the minor byways and winding lanes that plotted the earliest journeyings of man. He took a sheet of tracing paper and drew a freehand circle to encompass the murder sites. These he carefully shaded in with all the rapt absorption of Morwenna. There had to be some sort of connection, though what it might be continued to elude him. Aunt Jane, the Marshes and now this sad van load of kids. All that apparently linked them so far was the vileness and horror of their deaths. Blood shed profusely yet for no apparent reason. As though someone were killing them simply for the thrill of it.

9

Edwina was badly out of sorts, though not entirely sure why. She had spent a restless night, tense and huffy with her husband, yet knew in her heart she was being grossly unfair. For what was really troubling her had little to do with William. She was worried about their financial state, which was more precarious than she pretended. Being sole earner was a lonely burden, and she longed to be able to share with him just how scared she actually was. The idea was sound, as the Germans had endorsed, yet actually taking the company public was far more dicey than she'd imagined. Dotcom fortunes could be made overnight. Just as easily also lost. Setting up with Gareth had required a lot of guts, leaving a safe and well-salaried job to hitch herself to a shooting star that might very quickly burn out. She just didn't know. He was bright and charismatic yet lacked a basic gravitas, which was why he hadn't really made it until now. Though already in his forties, he still acted the feckless blade, without any adult responsibilities to weigh him down. She liked to grouch about William's lack of drive, yet secretly valued him more than he'd ever know. For she relied on his stability, the knowledge that he was there, but was often far too stiff-necked to let it show. In recent months they'd been bickering more than ever so that sometimes she feared for the survival of their marriage. Although he increasingly drove her wild, life without her husband was unthinkable. He was both her ballast and guiding light, not to mention her conscience. She needed him there to fall back on. And the thought of risking losing Morwenna froze her blood.

Edwina had never had a proper childhood, despite all the advantages showered upon her. Growing up in Highgate had been comfortable yet severe. Her parents, the academic and the fashionable shrink, willed her to pass every single exam before accelerating on to the next hurdle. She had never had dolls or a dressing-up kit. The presents they bought her were purely educational. And instead of watching television, they forced her to practise her cello, with extra Latin coaching on the side. Which was why, she now realised, she found it hard to relate to Morwenna. She lacked the basic instincts of a mother.

What worried her more, though, were the dreams she had lately been having over which she had no control. It was doubtless to do with her currently sexless state – the two of them hadn't made love in quite a while – so that now her eroticism was spilling out of her subconscious and waking her with embarrassingly graphic thoughts. All of which, disconcertingly, centred upon Gareth. She had always viewed him with a measure of suspicion, while liking the arrogant swagger of his lifestyle. He was so far removed from the man she had married that his very raw maleness excited her.

The dreams were crude and vivid to the extent that, on suddenly waking, she occasionally, for a second, believed them real. She would come to with a start with a dampness in her groin and the terrible fear she'd been having sex without any memory of the act. It felt about as frightening as society's latest fad, date rape, with some sort of mind-numbing drug slipped into her drink. She feared she was being unfaithful in her sleep, yet the sensations were seductive. She was sorry when she awoke to find William turned away from her, a solid, unyielding back. If she'd had less inhibition she might have made the first move, knowing that he would melt the instant she touched him. But her mother's constant telling her that women were very silly stopped her showing spontaneous love to the only two people who really mattered. William and Morwenna; at least they had each other. The fairies had been generous when Morwenna was born and the child had inherited her father's sunny nature.

When she got to the office, she found Gareth already installed there, leering at her in an all-knowing way as though he could read her guilty thoughts.

'You're looking particularly fetching this morning,' he said. 'Had an active night?' He was constantly taunting her with crude insinuations and she no longer knew how to respond.

'Mind your own business.' She tried to keep her cool,

97

scared that she'd blush and give the game away. If only he wasn't so damned attractive. She could sense the sexual fallout from across the room. She risked another cautious glance and he was still leaning back, watching her with obvious approval.

'I like the blouse; is it new?'

She had bought it yesterday lunchtime, an extravagant whim, and William, needless to say, had not even noticed. It was really more than she ought to have spent while their finances were so precarious. But the colour, deep violet, went well with her eyes and she'd wanted to wear it right away.

'Just some old thing I dug out of my closet,' she said stiffly, alarmed as she felt her cheeks beginning to glow. She wanted to tell him to leave her alone, that it wasn't fair to toy with her like this. She wasn't one of his pathetic trophy bimbos, hated herself for allowing him to rattle her.

Gareth walked over to where she was sitting and bent down with his hands on her desk. In a low soft murmur he looked her straight in the eye and told her just how much he'd like to fuck her.

William was at the kitchen table, hunched over the travel section, when Edwina came blustering through. It was Saturday morning and she was dressed for the supermarket: jeans and trainers and a smart navy Sloppy Joe, with her hair tied severely back in a bandanna. Later they had a tennis court booked; she didn't hold with wasting a single second.

'What's that?' she asked as she scribbled down a list, ignoring the fact that he was nominally in charge of the shopping. Even though, these days, he did most of the cooking, she was determined to keep in her hand. It made her feel more like a proper wife with chores of her own she had to do. With an element of wistfulness, she remembered the early days of their marriage when she'd still been allowed to be the star of the kitchen. Growing herbs along the windowsill, snipping interesting recipes from the supplements. All that had really intervened was a surplus of solid work, and Edwina had temporarily taken her eye off the ball. She would hijack Morwenna and balance her on the trolley and for once reap the kudos of having a really cute kid. They adored Morwenna in Sainsbury's and everywhere else, with her cherubic smile and merry eyes and questioning air of wonder.

'I'm thinking of taking off for a sailing weekend,' said William, stopping her dead in her tracks. It had always been a passion of his, the solitary thrill of battling with the elements, growing up as he had on the Devonshire coast. He still had a mooring in Falmouth harbour, though the boat had long been in dry dock. Among the small sacrifices he had made to this marriage had been his innate passion for the sea. But the drive was too long and he refused to compromise with the lesser thrill of an urban gravel pit. And then had come the advent of Morwenna and, quite simply, that was that. It was all far too complicated, he no longer had the time, so had hung up his oilskins for a while. He had never said so much as a word about it, but now this newspaper article had caught his eye. Two days away with only the north star for company. Even the most lowly employees were granted a break.

'You're insane!' said Edwina, with her usual delicate tact. As if he needed respite from just staying at home. There were loads of useful things he could do with any spare time: decorating the playroom, sanding the floors, finishing the bookshelves he had started in the attic, digging over the patio, planting shrubs. All of it seemed like a holiday when compared with her gruelling work-load. She couldn't believe he had even said it. Wanted to slap him in sudden rage.

'It was only a thought,' said William mildly. 'You lock up and I'll go and get the car.'

He left her to her glory once he'd dumped them off at Sainsbury's, and slumped in the car to wait for them, not feeling in the mood to trail behind. Too many couples came to serious blows over something as banal as Saturday shopping. And if she wouldn't even allow him to touch her, he knew when it was safest to back off. He'd brought the paper, so settled down to read. Quiet moments at the weekend were all too rare. Whoever was committing these truly horrific murders seemed to be systematically stepping things up. As yet more gory details of the schoolboys' deaths were revealed, William found his gorge beginning to rise. No one who had ever had a child of their own could possibly stomach such cold-blooded carnage. Whoever the perpetrator, he had to be out of his mind, though it still wasn't remotely clear why he was doing it. That tantalising link again; it nagged away at his mind and he ran the tape right through again to see what he might have missed. Somebody somewhere possessed a terrifying grudge and had to be stopped before he killed again.

What, wondered Edwina, as she wandered along the aisles, would happen to baby Morwenna if the marriage should come unstuck? Not that she'd ever allow it to, but Gareth's outrageous suggestion had certainly rocked her. He had never before gone quite that far and she sensed that he hadn't been joking. It was almost as if he were in on her salacious dreams and knew just how much he disturbed her. Which was really quite a lot, considering everything. After all these years, too, when she had thought she knew him so well.

Morwenna, like Cleopatra on her trolley, rode regally around the store, graciously acknowledging every passing acquaintance, ruthlessly taking hostages with her charm. She could certainly turn it on when she had a mind to, drama queen that she was. She was going to become a right little handful when she reached that difficult age. Edwina just hoped they'd still all be together. And quaked at the thought that they might not.

It was still very much on her mind that afternoon as they walked out on to the tennis court and William started practising his serve. Though not especially athletic, he was

101

still quite nifty at the net and gave her a really hard working out, exactly what she needed. She was aware, as she ran around in her short pleated skirt, of admiring glances from the adjoining court, where two young exhibitionists in matching tracksuits were battling each other to the death. Edwina smiled inwardly, vain as her daughter. She knew that in tennis whites she looked particularly fetching, with her well-toned body and impressive legs. Which brought her thoughts back to Gareth again with a shiver of half-fearful apprehension.

The attraction was certainly there and it was mutual. Now that she acknowledged that, it wouldn't go away. Gareth Prendergast, with his earthy allure, was a lot more exciting than the man she'd already got, altogether in a different league. She knew he was shallow, with the morals of a sewer rat, but also that she couldn't help herself. He was temptation and she was balanced on the edge. As she bashed away, returning William's serves, she tingled in anticipation of his touch. Would he – could she? What would it be like? The fantasy was beginning to make her crazy. Since she'd first met William, she had never considered straying, but four years was a very long time for her. She was a super-charged, sensuous woman on the brink of dazzling success. She had to go where fate led her, regardless of the consequences, for this was no dress-rehearsal, it was life. High on adrenalin, she played like a tornado, beating William easily in three short sets.

'Wow, old girl, what in the world has got into you?' He was half admiring, half a bit miffed that a slight little thing like Edwina could trounce him so soundly. But that was all part of her extra special magic, one of the reasons he had always found her so stimulating. Stubborn and dynamic with the tenacity of a bulldog. Whatever she went after she invariably got. He had a nasty suspicion her daughter might turn out the same. Which gave him the uncomfortable feeling of sadly lacking behind.

And succeeded in finally getting him up off his backside with renewed determination to continue with his quest. Why not? If the police in two counties could be so lethargic, what was there to prevent him going it alone? The least he could do for poor Aunt Jane's memory, more productive than planting a rosebush, was programme his intricate and highly trained brain in an attempt to discover the truth. He could certainly do with the mental stimulation. Lately he'd felt his mind was beginning to atrophy. It might also earn him bonus points from Edwina, who seemed to be drifting away. Something elusive still gnawed at his subconscious. He wouldn't be totally satisfied until he had worked out what.

All of a sudden he was hugely inspired and went upstairs to his study to look at his maps. They were like a mantra when he needed to concentrate, helped to stimulate his draughtsman's eye and focus his teeming brain. In his professional life they called it 'cartographer's reality', which meant building up an artist's impression as parallel as possible to the truth. Which, for now, was enough for him. He trusted his own instincts to work things through. He spread out his careful tracing of the older map and boldly pinpointed the murder sites in red. Then laid it alongside the up-to-date roadmap and slipped into almost a catatonic trance. If you took away the arterial roads it all became infinitely easier. His practised eye studied the topography of the land until, like an image from a Magic Eye book, a three-dimensional pattern began to emerge. After a long, long while he leaned back wearily in his chair, reflectively tapping his teeth. What he needed more than anything right now was someone with specialist knowledge to confide in. He didn't think the police would be persuaded by his theories but he had a sudden crazy notion that he knew of a man who might well be. At the very least, it was worth a shot. The worst that could occur would be a door slammed in his face.

Robert Marsh's house looked prosperous and well kept; also, from one rapid glance, deserted. William parked boldly right outside and studied it with open curiosity. It had clean paintwork, tidy lawns and a swing in the garden, legend of a family life now over. William thought of the poor man's dreadful suffering, facing a barren future on his own. He didn't know if the police still had tabs on him. The latest atrocity had driven him off the front pages. He opened the car door slowly and stepped out, still doubtful whether to pursue his outrageous plan. An authoritative voice from the next-door garden challenged him, stopping him dead in his tracks.

'There's nobody there,' said an elderly woman, rising

from where she was weeding behind the hedge. She looked him up and down suspiciously, hostility on her face. Not another of those intrusive reporters, she thought, though William, with his ingenuous smile, certainly looked harmless enough. He crossed to talk to her and she put down her trowel. The weather this morning was unseasonably mild. She seemed actually quite glad of the diversion.

'Don't know where he's gone to, poor man. Probably into hiding. The police let him go about a week ago which shows there is still some justice left in the world. What he's had to go through would drive most people mad. Hasn't begun to come to terms with it yet, poor fellow.'

William shuffled, embarrassed by his duplicity, and muttered about it being just a spontaneous visit because he'd been driving by.

'I ought to have called first to make an appointment,' he said and the woman agreed.

As he headed back to London, the plan wouldn't budge from his head. It might be grasping at straws and over the top but Robert Marsh, in a way, was the only survivor. And all the more relevant for that.

10

*C*ontrition hit me like a blow to the solar plexus. I was
infinitely shaken by the terrible thing I had done. Of
course, there was no denying it, I had known all along about
the children, yet still had gone ahead and acted regardless.
What kind of a monster was I turning into? Was I really as
sick as the papers were now saying? I had become as conscienceless as a terrorist lobbing grenades in a shopping mall, regardless of whom I might injure along the way. As I carefully picked
my way among all those sad little corpses, the pain in my
throat was threatening to choke me. For it summoned back
memories I had tried for so long to suppress, culminating in a
year in hospital under constant heavy sedation. For not even
one of those poor little blighters had survived the terrible crash.
Their frail little necks had snapped like twigs when the van
went over the cliff. I checked each body carefully to ensure I
was leaving no witnesses. One slip up now, and the game would
be over for me.

Hargreaves himself was still breathing shallowly, flung half
out of the driving seat, a great jagged gash in his head. I pulled
out the butcher's knife I had this time remembered to bring

and finished him off with one efficient stroke. Mission accomplished, though it lacked the customary high. I was sick to my stomach to acknowledge I had acted so vilely. Of all life's obscenities, surely the death of a child must be the worst. Innocence snuffed out before it has had a chance to develop. The Victorians took it more in their stride but we, more sophisticated but also thinner-skinned, have grown acutely more sensitised to such things. Even Hitler, when it came to it, could not face shooting his dog.

How I had grown so corrupt, I had no idea, for there had been a time when I too was a rational being. Nine lives lost and all through my own ruthless actions. I had given no thought to those faceless parents who tomorrow would wake up bereaved. Had I thought it through before I began, I might well have just walked away. Not even my mother could forgive me now, and her revulsion would not be misplaced. And as for my brothers, who had always looked up to me . . . I shied away from the thought. One wrong turning and I'd descended into the pit. For me now there could be no possible hope of salvation.

Lest I arouse suspicion, I resisted quitting the job ahead of time. A single false move and I risked giving myself away, and caution must be the byword of the killer. I went to ground and effaced myself so effectively I don't think anyone noticed me at all. Me, the lowest of the low; I have become adept at such psychological disguise. In recent years particularly it has stood me in excellent stead. The school and its grounds were swarming with police and reporters, keen to detect the perpetrator of such evil. It was, of course, my coup de grâce, the slashed throat, that gave it away, which had now become my signature, widely recognised. If even one of them had had the wit to spot it, that single tenuous link which connected the crimes. I got quite a buzz out of silently standing by, listening to their various theories, each one that much more fatuous than the last. Not a single one of them was remotely on my trail. I was tempted to encourage them by leaving some sort of a clue.

I suppose it was conscience that prompted me to do it, or else the old daredevil spirit which wasn't quite dead. Whatever it was, on a spur-of-the-moment decision, I carried a bunch of chrysanthemums round to the widow. I had never so much as glimpsed her before, except in a brief newsflash on television, but something deep in my heart refused to lie quiet. She had, like me, just lost someone very close. The least I felt I could do was show some solidarity. Also, I admit it, I was curious to talk to her and find out how effective my vengeance had been. I needed first-hand evidence that my action had not been in vain. For the dead, once dead, can unfortunately no longer suffer.

I rang her doorbell tentatively and she answered it after a while. An ungainly woman in a heather twinset that clashed unattractively with her high colour. She held a lace handkerchief up to her nose as though in the throes of a cold. And, when she saw the flowers I had brought, exploded in a burst of frantic weeping. For a moment I froze and didn't know what to say, then introduced myself clumsily as having come from the school.

'Come in,' she said, through a volley of violent weeping, and I had no choice but to follow her inside. This was slightly more than I'd actually bargained for, but I hesitated to offend her in any way. She clung to me hard in her narrow, dark hall and for a minute or two just let go. Told me what a paragon of a man he had been, perfect husband and father, loved by all. The thought of having to continue without him was something she had never even envisaged. It was, in fact, only the children that kept her going. I was moved, indeed awed, by such outpouring of grief, and all for that rather ordinary little man. I located a box of tissues and made appropriate noises, then led her into her sitting room and suggested she should sit down.

'I'll go and stick the kettle on,' I said, thrilled to the core at just being there. Talk about revisiting the scene of the crime. I could practically hear his footsteps on the stairs. I took a quick look round her kitchen while I rummaged for mugs. It had Ikea cabinets on plain whitewashed walls and a serviceable patterned lino on the floor. Certainly by no means an affluent home but one that was lovingly cared for. The plain pine furniture showed signs of wear but had been carefully cleaned and polished to look their best. I was touched to see standing, forlornly in a corner, a fishing-rod and a pair of ancient skis.

'He was always so keen on his sport,' she said, when she popped her head round the door to see what was keeping me. I had luckily just closed the larder door, having scrutinised her rows of immaculate shelves. Homemade jams and pickles, all kinds of preserves. Mrs Hargreaves was a modern-day Mrs Beeton. She bent, with some effort, and located a pewter teapot, which she lovingly warmed beneath the running tap. These household rituals would be what kept her sane. I had been sloppily searching for teabags to steep. But she even had a caddy and cosy that had seen better days. To my sudden alarm, I feared I might show some emotion. I grabbed the sugar bowl and a packet of digestives and rapidly preceded her from the room.

'Tell me,' I said softly, once we were seated again. I needed to know, to ensure it had all been worthwhile. So the poor woman told, and I think it made her feel better, as she listed his achievements and countless virtues.

'He meant the world to me,' she said at last simply, and again I found myself reaching for her hand. Careful now, I warned myself. Don't go giving things away. Best get out before she begins to suspect. I had done my bit, any more might be excessive. Word could seep out to that merry band and then I'd be really in the soup.

'I must be off,' I said, edging towards the door, and suffered another damp hug that left powder on my lapel.

'Please come again, you have been such a comfort.' And she meant every word of it too, foolish woman. I marvelled at, and envied, the love they had obviously shared. It is easy to mock, but her feelings came straight from the heart. And now she was having to face living with her loss. I knew how she felt. I had been there.

Love of that dimension, even homely love like theirs, is something almost humbling to behold. Laertes flinging himself into Ophelia's grave, Juliet snatching the dagger on Romeo's death. I, too, have suffered, though in a less dramatic way, and therefore could imagine how she felt. Those I hung out with in the casual, careless days would scarcely have credited I had a heart

110

at all. It had all come too easily, I was selfish and quickly bored. And no one who ever caught my eye had been beyond reach. Which was, I suppose, how the whole thing came to happen. Up till that point in my life I'd been utterly spoiled. Until, without warning, I met my Waterloo when I suddenly crashed unwittingly into love.

Love, there is nothing like it, worse than adult measles. The fever and inner turbulence I had never experienced before. A rapid, unthinking exchange of glances and my world was turned upside down. We fought our way to each other's side, abandoning any foolish attempt at pretence. We stood and smiled awkwardly, then cautiously touched hands, our fate in that single exchange irrevocably sealed. By late afternoon, we had made it into bed, by morning had plighted our troth. Despite agonising obstacles, we knew we had no other choice. Our roller-coaster ride was just beginning.

Later I did feel sad about Marina. But this was far more powerful than any of us.

These days I stand in the shadows, remembering how it once was. Our love was as strong as a forest fire, consuming all that stood in its way. We caused irreparable damage, I know, and shattered a number of lives. Yet all we could see in that selfish state was our passion and mutual need. We had five brief, beautiful, illicit years, a mere drop in the enormity of time. After which it all screeched to a catastrophic end, as happiness inevitably is bound to. We were wrenched apart forever and yet had done no real wrong. Only fallen in love, if that can be called a crime.

11

There was a man sitting near the swings when William got there, just outside the railings. He had seen him before. Thin with wispy hair, huddled in an ancient tweed overcoat, raw bony hands tucked between his knees to ward off the chill autumn wind. The weather just lately had been unremittingly dire and the forecasts warned of still worse to come. Floods in Yorkshire, a tornado in Bognor Regis. Gale-force winds, the most serious since the war, bringing down trees and disrupting traffic. The Channel tunnel was closed, the airports severely restricted and thirteen rivers were now on full flood alert. It seemed that the country was sinking like Atlantis. In a million years' time it would be little more than a legend. 'An island once known as Britannia,' future archaeologists would say. Assuming the human race survived at all.

William trundled the pushchair along a path that was inches deep in soggy leaves, brutally ripped from the trees. Morwenna had her hood up and was wearing scarlet mittens. When he leaned forward to look down at her,

112

almost all he could see was the tip of her tiny nose. And a red one at that.

'Don't worry, poppet, we'll not stay out too long. But a go on the swings will do you good.' He paused to blow on his own chapped fingers. Next time he'd risk looking like a wimp and wear gloves.

The stranger was watching the children in the play-ground, his eyes forlornly fixed on two little boys. On an impulse William went to sit beside him. For some unknown reason he was intrigued by the man and suddenly wanted to know more about him. Something about his behaviour seemed not quite right.

'Nippy this morning,' he said cheerfully, adjusting the blanket over his daughter's well-padded legs. The man nodded agreement and continued to hug his hands. His coat was threadbare, his scarf moth-eaten. His shoes looked like rejects from a charity shop. Morwenna, ever the party girl, looked up at him coyly through her gorgeous lashes and smiled in provocative greeting. She reached out one little scarlet paw and coyly touched his knee. The man responded surprisingly – looked uncomfortable for a fraction of a second, then shifted nervously further along the bench. Even though there was quite sufficient room, with inches of clear space remaining between them. This was no natural with little children, William could see that at a glance. Morwenna's presence clearly made him uneasy. William's suspicions were immediately aroused; there was something about this shiftiness he didn't like. Or trust, come to that; you could not be too careful, and strangers hanging around children were very often suspect.

So why bring Morwenna needlessly to the fellow's attention? Edwina would be quite sharp with him for taking unwarranted risks. But she was not part of this friendly morning routine, where almost every person they met was known to them. He looked across at the little boys playing on the slide, on whom the man's attention seemed fixed. He might be their father, though it didn't look much like it. If he was, he should be in there playing with them, not furtively skulking around out here.

'Those your kids?' asked William casually. The man appeared startled, then shook his head.

'I'm just out for a walk,' he said, as though it was any of William's business. But he made no immediate sign of moving away so William stayed firmly put. He knew it was nothing to do with him, but there was definitely something here he didn't quite like. He pulled out some peppermints, then offered the tube to his neighbour. At first the man hesitated, then gave in and accepted one.

'Thanks.'

'I don't think I've seen you around here before. Do you live locally?' asked William. Again the man paused before finally shaking his head. He came from over Paddington way, was simply out for some exercise and fresh air. William, remembering his own unemployed state, sternly chastised himself for jumping to unfair conclusions. And bothering the poor blighter with his intrusive prying. All that gossiping with Mrs P was obviously doing him no good. But a quarter past ten on a Thursday morning was an odd time to be loitering, especially in weather like this.

'Well,' he said cheerfully, rising at last to his feet. 'This won't get the baby bathed. Time to get on and do some work.' He grinned and nodded and wheeled Morwenna away.

When he turned at the swings to check, the man had gone.

'There was a slightly unsavoury cove this morning, hanging around at the playground.'

Edwina, doing her nails, showed her usual lack of interest. For once she'd managed to get home early and put Morwenna to bed herself, even taking time to read her a story. Normally she was too late and far too frazzled. Something must have nudged her, perhaps her conscience. She was wearing fetching brushed-cotton pyjamas and had braided her thick hair into a single plait. He loved her most when she looked like this, as guileless and unpainted as her daughter. Innocent, somehow, no more the hardened high-flyer. His heart suddenly melted towards her and he wanted to give her a hug. But he knew she was likely to push him away and whine that he'd only smudge her nails.

'Well it takes one to know one,' said Edwina eventually. 'Perhaps he was there with a kid.'

'No, he wasn't. I checked,' said William. 'There was something slightly furtive about him.' He refrained from mentioning his original theory, that the man was almost certainly unemployed; he knew the sort of biting rejoinder that sort of statement could provoke. Even at her most benign, Edwina could be a right bitch. He wondered now why he'd brought it up at all; it showed how little else of interest he had to tell her. But he did find it worrying when predators sniffed round kids. Fatherhood had altered his social awareness in a fundamental way.

The man was there again a few days later, smoking in the shadow of an enormous oak. The tree was so large and enveloping that if it weren't for the recent severe storm spoilage, he'd hardly be visible at all. This time he was in a different part of the park, but just as intent on his voyeurism. A group of small boys were kicking a ball around, apparently the focus of his attention. Or so it would appear from where William was walking, approaching the famous statue of Peter Pan.

'Fairies!' shouted Morwenna with her usual scream of delight, straining at the straps that held her in. She leaned forward with both little chubby arms, drumming her heels impatiently as he stooped to unfasten the buckles. This particular walk was one of their absolute favourites. William looked forward, before she was very much older, to taking her to see the show on the London stage. Magic was one of the most valuable gifts you could give to a child, especially at this age when they were still so receptive. They'd already embarked upon Beatrix Potter at bedtime, and William was hugely enjoying reliving so many happy memories from his childhood.

Poor Edwina was missing out on so much by being

such a regular glutton for work. She came home late and crotchety most nights, then raced around like a wild thing at weekends. She was constantly shifting furniture and turning out cupboards and had become a dab hand at doing home improvements. These days it seemed she could never sit still. If she'd only learn to let go a little she'd be that much easier to live with. And would also get to know her daughter better and realise what an individual she was becoming.

After Morwenna had gone through her ritual of fondly stroking the heads of Peter's animals, William persuaded her to get back into her chariot and allow him to push her home by way of the shops. The seedy man was still watching the football game, but when William raised his hand in casual greeting, he turned abruptly away. Maybe he was just short-sighted, but William wasn't convinced.

It was nearing Morwenna's bedtime and the Huxley kitchen was a warm, safe haven of contentment. The empty bowl from which she had eaten her eggs was in the sink and she sucked up her orange juice from a plastic beaker as she watched her daddy perform. *The Archers* was on the radio and Mummy would soon be home. She had to be in her pyjamas by then, washed and combed and all ready for bed. That was one of the rules. Then, if she was lucky and Mummy not too tired, Edwina would carry her up to her bed and read her another chapter of *Winnie the Pooh*. William, meantime, was hard at work, completing his Noah's Ark in chalk on the large slate blackboard they kept on the wall for reminders. He'd been at it now for much of the afternoon and was entirely absorbed in the task. Every now and then he would consult Morwenna as to what precise colour she favoured for each new animal, and an adult discussion of contrast would ensue as he tried to accommodate her demands. The table was strewn with his coloured chalks and an ancient, dog-eared copy of *Britannica* from which he was checking his sources. A harmonious scene. Outside the rain had started again and the ominous creaking and banging of shutters heralded yet another force-nine gale. Not a night for being outside. He hoped Edwina was all right and glanced at the clock. He'd be happier once she was home.

'Come along, sweetheart, and finish up your orange. And then we'll go upstairs and get you into your jim-jams.' The Bengal tiger was the *pièce de résistance* and Morwenna could hardly bear to tear herself away.

'More, Daddy,' she pleaded, rising up on her toes to finger it. 'Make another tiger for Morwenna.'

'Careful, lovey, or you'll rub out its whiskers.' With the corner of a duster he smoothed away the smudge. 'There's already a second baby one, look, down here.' He pointed to the corner where a miniature tiger cub was peeking out from behind an elephant, a mindlessly daft expression on its face. Edwina often chided him for wasting so much time doodling, but Morwenna adored it when her daddy drew for her, and could watch him, mesmerised, for contented hours on end. Secretly he hoped she'd inherited some of his talent. It was likely never to make her rich but should add to her feeling of fulfilment. Which was all that really mattered, part of the quality of life. People were far too driven these days. It was good, just occasionally, to stop and take a breather.

Edwina arrived home in a flurry of raindrops, her nose bright red and her mood sour. She shook her umbrella at the foot of the basement steps, then stuck it into the sink to dry, ignoring Morwenna's supper bowl.

'God, it's a terrible night,' she said. 'With more bloody storms on the way.' The forecasts had been full of nothing else for days. Once *The Archers* was over, William switched on the television news and they both watched scene after scene of devastation, with miserable people in waders attempting to salvage their homes. Yet everyone seemed still in remarkably good humour. The famous blitz spirit reborn.

'We're expecting another three inches of rain,' said the weatherman, 'with seven more rivers about to burst their banks.'

Edwina paused briefly to admire his ark but he could see that her heart wasn't in it. Then she bustled up to the bedroom to change her clothes. Their basement area was already inches deep; he hoped they were not going to have to shift the furniture upstairs. But this weather was exciting and gave him a secret buzz, a throwback, he supposed, to his rural childhood. Sudden snow made him whoop with glee and he'd rush Morwenna off to the park with her sledge. One day, when she was old enough, they'd all go to Austria for the skiing. They needed to spend more time together as a family.

Tonight Edwina seemed unusually subdued. She did her maternal duty and read Morwenna a chapter and the child went off to sleep without a struggle. William had poured Edwina a hefty gin and tonic, which she downed quite quickly as he set the kitchen table. He left his chalks in a jumble on the side and for once she was too out of it to make a fuss. Tonight he had cooked a pork and cider casserole with garlic mash as a special treat. She smiled and pushed back her heavy damp hair.

'You're turning into a really good chef,' she said. 'We ought to try getting you on the telly.' With all the practice he'd been getting at home lately, he was every bit as competent as the pros. Down to earth too, which was also a bonus. All he had learned about culinary matters was mainly just plain common sense.

'Far too disorganised,' said William with a grin. The potatoes were slightly lumpy but wonderful all the same, and the casserole was great. Edwina wolfed it all down with hearty appreciation. Just the job for a blustery, chilly night. He had even done leeks which he zapped in the microwave and had bought his favourite fudge ice cream for afters. He might be somewhat lacking in the ambition department, but certainly knew how to make a girl feel good. Not to mention pampered; she knew she didn't deserve it. She found herself fearing for her waistline, remembered Gareth and laid down her fork. All of a sudden her appetite was gone. She couldn't even touch the special ice cream. William cleared the plates without a word.

The flooding brought back memories of Aunt Jane. He hoped the cottage was all right. He would go straight down there again to check, only the roads were probably closed. Edwina, tearing her thoughts from Gareth, tried hard to be conversational.

'Any luck with the police?' she asked. She knew what a bugbear it had all become, to her mind wildly out of proportion.

William shook his head. 'Not a peep,' he said derisively. They didn't even care about the Marshes. For a second he thought of sharing it all with her, of telling her about his latest idea. She was shrewd and canny with a fast analytical brain; he would be very grateful for her input. Might even get her interested, that would be something of a turn-up. It was, after all, her relative who had died, and these days they seemed to have very little else they could share. He pulled out a chair and was about to unburden when he caught her surreptitiously checking the clock.

'More work tonight?'

''Fraid so,' she said. She needed to be alone to sort out her head.

Part Two

12

When Howard Pilkington was offered early retirement, he grabbed it gratefully with both hands. They had moved to Bournemouth several years before, in anticipation of just such an event. The bank had been gradually closing its branches. It was only a question of when. Joyce was delighted, since it upgraded her social life as the town had a certain cachet. The house was even nicer than the one they'd left behind, and through the bungalows opposite you could catch a glimpse of the sea. Joyce had her sewing bee and voluntary hospital work but her friends all worried about her having Howard under her feet. If only he'd take up golf, they said, but he'd never been one for much exercise.

'Don't worry,' he said airily, 'I've plenty of reading to do.' He'd rarely so much as opened a book so now was the time to catch up. But of course, in only a matter of weeks, he'd adjusted so effortlessly his days were already full. After a leisurely breakfast, he'd take a short stroll along the sea front. Or potter lightly in the garden, though they had a man in for the heavy stuff. He joined the library and thought about evening classes, but quickly discovered he hadn't the time. He committed his services two mornings a week to helping at the Citizens' Advice Bureau and occasionally lent his car and chauffeuring skills to collecting stuff for the local charity shop. And then, of course, there was the Rotary. Always a strong feature of his life.

'My,' said his sister when she came to stay. 'Howard is even busier than before.'

'Well, it keeps him out of the house,' said Joyce. And meant she didn't always have to cook. Her own social activities were soaring. She certainly didn't intend to be housebound again.

He found he enjoyed this cosy little world, smaller than in his banking days. No more meetings with anxious, supplicant customers nor dreary afternoons of endless meetings. For the first time in his life he was his own man and determined to enjoy every second. He also saw no reason now for costly holidays abroad. All he could need in the way of sun and sea was right here in his own back yard. He thought about renting a beach hut, but Joyce felt it wasn't really them. Smacked a little of common, she felt, remembering her own frugal childhood. Ham sandwiches on the front at Swanage and shivering in the brisk breeze. The English summer with its endless cloudy days. At least here in Bournemouth there were shops. Howard regarded her shopping with indulgence. They were far more comfortable now the kids were off their hands.

He had long been a Rotarian, since they'd unanimously

voted him in. One of the perks of working for the bank. And it gave him a feeling of worthiness, knowing he was giving something back to the community. He tried never to miss a single meeting and was always on tap to lend them a willing hand. They sponsored bazaars, raised money for the hospital and sent deprived children off to camp.

'Goodness,' said Joyce admiringly. 'You will soon be needing a break.'

Howard laughed and puffed himself up. He was a short, dapper man with thinning slicked-back hair and a new, slightly racy taste in ties. Now that he didn't have to dress up for the bank, he had taken to wearing a sports jacket most of the time. And the constant subjection to sun and sea air had burnished him with a perpetual tan. He would drop in at the Grosvenor Hotel for Rotary Club meetings on Thursdays and, if he should bump into a kindred spirit, would often arrange to meet them again for lunch. Game pie and salad or a spot of steak and kidney, with a slice of apple and Stilton to finish up. No point in stinting himself after all those years of solid graft. Howard Pilkington was a hugely self-satisfied man.

'Done my bit for society,' he would bluffly inform his cronies. 'Now it's my turn to sit back and relax, knowing that I have put something back.'

But nemesis stalks on deceptively silent feet. If only he might have been forewarned.

Joyce was off on a jaunt to Scarborough, for a long week-end in a spa with the ladies of the Inner Wheel. Howard was always quite easy about such things. She was such a support that he didn't begrudge her some fun. What they got up to he never did find out, but she laughed herself silly if he ever enquired and said it was all one huge giggle. Saunas and general pandering seemed to be the order of the day, plus quite a hefty bar bill at the end, which wasn't at all in character. At home she rarely drank more than just the one medium sherry with perhaps a glass of hock to go with lunch. But the light in her eye on her return from these sprees more than made up for the cost. Also he quite enjoyed being left on his own. Cooked himself sausages and the things he really liked without her beady eye on his cholesterol.

But he wasn't particularly handy in the kitchen so usually took himself out for a proper lunch. On this particular Sunday he thought he'd drop down to the Grosvenor, have a few noggins at the bar with his mates, followed by a leisurely meal. The menu was especially good at weekends: traditional roast beef with all the trimmings. And homemade apple pie to follow, topped by a sinful dollop of clotted cream. He would walk it off later by leaving the car at home, which meant he needn't worry about what he drank. A bracing stroll along the blustery promenade would be just the ticket to round off a perfect day. He fairly smacked his lips in anticipation.

He was either early or else a little late but the bar was unusually deserted. He peered around in its darker recesses but none of his friends seemed to be there. Was it, he wondered, one of those special Sundays, or perhaps there was an event on locally which somehow he'd failed to register. Fortunately he'd remembered to bring the paper so settled down in a half-barrel seat and ordered a whisky and soda.

A waiter glided up with a dish of *hors d'oeuvres* but Howard scarcely gave him a glance. The staff at the Grosvenor were constantly changing, not like the old days when he'd known each one by name. These days they even employed some foreign chappies. Women, too. There were some of those around.

'Put it there,' was all he said as he sorted out the paper, discarding the sport and appointments sections and turning straight to the hard news. Revolution had broken out in Serbia and the evil dictator Milosevic deposed. For a moment he found himself pondering the implications to the financial world, then recalled with relief that he was no longer in harness. It was somebody else's headache now and good luck to them. He'd drink to that. His whisky and soda arrived at record speed and was silently deposited on the table. At least the standards of discreet service had not slipped. There was nothing Howard disliked more than a chatty barman, unless it was a loquacious taxi driver.

He finished the drink and called for another, and still the room remained unnaturally quiet. Odd that. He turned to ask if there was anything he'd missed out on but now not even the barman was in sight.

'Hello,' he called, beginning to grow slightly alarmed. What in the world could be going on?

'Coming, sir,' called a distant voice, and he waited resignedly to be served.

Lunch was as good as he'd hoped it would be and he made quite a pig of himself. Seconds of everything, especially the Yorkshire pud, with a spicy spoonful of horseradish on the side. Recalling that Joyce was off spoiling herself, he even indulged in a particularly good claret that he wouldn't normally run to. Well, he'd done quite well from his deal with the bank. If he couldn't afford the occasional indulgence what a very dull dog he would be. The dining room was reassuringly filling up, which meant he was able to relax. Nothing worse than eating alone in silence. Even the children at a nearby table failed to encroach on his contentment. This was the apex of a lifetime's achievement. Howard was well at peace with himself and the world.

'Coffee, sir?'

He hadn't heard the waiter approach, the floor was so thickly carpeted.

'In the lounge,' said Howard decisively. He would crown this excellent meal with one of Fidel Castro's best. He scribbled his signature at the bottom of the bill and preceded the fellow into the next room, where saggy chintz-covered sofas beckoned and a corner television was silently showing the horse-racing. Just the place for a leisurely snooze. Today there was nothing to rush home for. And while he was at it, he might also have a brandy. Shame to begrudge himself that final ha'p'orth of contentment.

*   *   *

Howard had not led an adventurous life but was satisfied with what he'd achieved. Steady advancement in a respectable career. No real risks but an eye for the main chance. Adequate marriage without too many hiccups and children he actually quite liked. More than many of his contemporaries could boast. At a recent college reunion he'd been able to feel quietly smug. He didn't give handouts to beggars on the street but that was purely from social awareness. The more you doled out, the more they would ask for when they ought to be pulling their socks up and looking for work. Youth today was not what it had been. At least both his children had good, responsible jobs. Howard smiled and shifted his position. That lunch had really hit the spot, now enhanced by the brandy. He wondered hazily what his wife would be doing and actually looked forward to welcoming her back home soon. She was always far friskier after one of these all-girls breaks. As if her libido had been restored simply by getting out of the house.

Howard smiled fondly. She was a bit of a brick, was Joyce, and he had never regretted marrying her. Always neatly dressed, with her hair just so, she had never embarrassed him in any way. Young Conservatives both of them, and once he'd even stood for the council. He thought back over those years as his eyes flickered shut. He wondered where he might have got to by now had he persisted up the tree. Possibly in parliament or even higher still. One thing he could say, when he faced his Judgement Day, was that he'd lived a good and exemplary life of which he was justly proud.

He was dimly aware of somebody straightening his paper and then the chink of china as his coffee cup was quietly removed. Soon he'd have to bestir himself and trundle off back to his house, but his legs appeared to have turned to jelly and his determination was nil. There was nowhere at all that he needed to be or anything special he had to do. He could take that healthy sea walk he had planned or else remain slumped right here. No one was bothering him, he wasn't in anyone's way. The choice was his entirely. He would take forty winks and then make a decision. No one would ever be the wiser, provided he was home ahead of Joyce. He drifted back into a dreamless doze, floating in an apathy of languor. His legs felt weightless, his gullet beautifully relaxed. Slowly and melodiously, Howard began to snore.

The pain when it came was so sudden and incisive that his head snapped up and he attempted to struggle to his feet. Something appalling, like the sting of a giant bee, had assailed him in the throat close to his Adam's apple. *What the . . . ?* He clutched at his face and felt the strong pulsing of blood as it gushed out steadily from just below his chin, saturating the front of his shirt. He tried to call out but his throat was completely blocked and he felt himself drowning as he fell. *Help me*, he whispered, but already it was too late. Besides, there was no one close enough to hear him.

13

An icepick through the jugular, the latest news head-lines blared. Bled to death in a matter of seconds, poor fellow never even stood a chance.

'Gross!' said Mrs P, using her children's vernacular, for once in her life quite genuinely repelled. Just reading the gruesome details made her feel queasy. Newspapers were no longer what they once had been when such unsavoury matters remained discreetly veiled. Violent death might be one thing and, in principle, thrilled her vicariously, but there was still a line across which even she was not prepared to step. Blood all over the carpet came far too close to reality, as well as offending her housekeeping sensibilities. At least she hadn't had the job of clearing it up. Practical to her fingertips was Mrs P.

William sat in silent contemplation, slowly re-reading the lurid front page. Bournemouth was nowhere near the locations of the other murders, yet again he had that odd feeling that in some way they might be connected. He couldn't quite put his finger on it but the hunch refused to budge. He ran through the victim's details again and read them aloud to Mrs P.

'Rotary Club. Well thought of by the bank. Even the Citizens' Advice Bureau. The man's another bloody saint. What's going on?'

'Don't know, petal,' said Mrs P, lighting up, ready as ever to drop her duster and talk. She came and peered over his shoulder, shuddering theatrically. There was a list of Pilkington's other achievements, including the long and happy marriage. The police, it was stated, again had no leads.

'Now why doesn't that surprise me?' said William, laughing.

'Still, a bank manager's pretty fair game,' said Mrs P cynically. 'It's probably the open season. I've often been tempted to have a go at me own.'

'But this one's been retired for several years. And, according to this, not known to have had any enemies.'

No one at the Grosvenor Hotel had seen anything amiss that particular Sunday. The man had been pretty well known to them there, would often drop in for a meal. He had lunched alone, then taken a nap in the lounge, where his body had been discovered by the evening shift. Swimming in a pool of his own gore, choked by the blood in his lungs. Whoever had wielded the icepick had done an effective job. Skilful butchery by a practised hand like each of the other recent murders.

'Odd no one heard him scream,' said Mrs P.

'He must have been caught unawares.'

William went upstairs and got his map, then carefully

extended the radius of his circle to include the new murder site. It did still fit his topographical theory except that the area in question was now wider.

'What are you trying to prove?' asked Mrs P.

'That the same unknown killer had a motive to bump them all off.' And since the victims appeared to have no other obvious connection, geography would do as a start as well as the sheer bloodiness of the crimes.

If he concentrated hard on another matter entirely, the elusive something lurking on the periphery of William's mind was likely to come popping back into sight. He zipped Morwenna into her cosy fleece-lined playsuit and the two of them set off briskly down the hill. He had promised Edwina he would pick up some fish for tonight. Because her timekeeping was lately so erratic, he'd wait till he actually heard her key in the lock before popping it into the pan.

The fish shop, with its open front, was a paradise to Morwenna. Father and daughter solemnly examined the array of strange sea creatures displayed on a slab while white-coated men in wellingtons sluiced the floor. Nearly as good as a trip to the new aquarium, though handier by far, being just round the corner. And here you could actually touch them and inhale their briny smell. Morwenna, for purely visual reasons, hankered after the exotic-looking octopus, like a small deflated set of bagpipes waiting to be played. But a nice piece of turbot was what William had in mind, which he'd sear and serve with wild mushrooms and rice. He would also pick up a suitable bottle of wine to turn it into a bit of a feast. The child could make do with fish fingers, her favourite, with frozen chips and baked beans. Which meant, of course, another long detour, back over the hill to Safeway's on the High Street. Still, it wasn't as if his time was exactly pressured. Edwina would snort with impatience and tell him some people didn't know when they were well off. But she had a demanding and responsible job which caring for this beloved child, at least in the eyes of the rest of the world, was not. Certainly for a man.

Edwina and Gareth were seated at lunch in an unpretentious pizza place close to the office, which surprised her. It had been a last-minute invitation but she hadn't demurred. She knew now that what was coming was inevitable. Had lain awake nights just imagining the details, waking with a guilty flush on her cheeks. Normally she avoided eating anything starchy, but today would be an exception, though she'd not admit that to him. She'd make up for it with a salad tomorrow or even skip lunch altogether. She was far too nervous to eat, as it was, and only picked at her Veneziana. Gareth ordered wine. She had quite lost the thread of what he was saying, but that hardly mattered, he was confidently self-absorbed. He leaned closer to her with a look of intensity and, as though by pure accident, his fingers brushed hers. Edwina felt lightning course through her veins. It had been so long – too long. The words of the Streisand song burst into her brain and it was all she could do to keep herself from humming it. Moving off shop talk, he started describing an innovative new play he had seen just the night before, all the time studying her reaction. A first from an interesting young director from Los Angeles, raunchy yet well-written, stretching many boundaries. And starring an ageing Hollywood legend, who took off her kit every night, which was certainly brave. He asked if she had seen it.

Edwina shook her head. They didn't get out much these days since they'd had the child, what with finding a babysitter and so forth, and William was always reluctant to leave Morwenna. It was, he kept reminding her, the most crucial stage in a child's development. Suppose they should happen not to be there when she made that gigantic leap forward, whatever it might be. And who wanted babysitters cluttering her mind with mental popcorn? Childhood lasted for so very few short years. There'd be time enough for themselves once she was grown. Edwina said it with real conviction but Gareth sensed that she wasn't entirely convinced. The light in her eye was challenging; he responded in his groin. If it weren't for her middle-class conscience he'd be tempted to call it a day right now and not return to the office at all. Ring in and simply tell them they weren't coming back. Whisk her off to his bachelor pad or even go mad and do something really bold. Head for the coast or take the Eurostar to Paris. He loved extravagant gestures and they were, after all, on the brink of making their fortunes. If now was not the time to go wild, he would like her to tell him when it would be.

'Children are a tie,' is what he actually said, still in the role of the sympathetic listener. He had no wish at all to have any of his own, had so far succeeded in avoiding that sort of commitment. But he also knew when he was on to a good thing and reckoned Edwina might be almost ripe for it. He pushed his advantage and refilled her glass. Today she was looking especially delectable. He liked the way she'd started doing her hair, feminine yet also making a statement. She had great boobs too which along with those legs . . .

'How are things at home these days?' he asked, ready for her outpouring. She had been on the brink of confiding in him before. It was only a question of timing. He privately thought she was wasted on William, considered the man to be a dolt. What sort of wuss stays at home with a child, allowing his wife to support him? Edwina looked back at him with uncertain eyes, wondering how far she dared go. But her pulses were racing and her palms were damp; she couldn't rid herself of that pervasive dream. It invaded even her waking hours and made her feel very uncomfortable. She could hardly think straight any more, not when Gareth was around.

'Dull,' she said treacherously, seeing where this was leading but no longer able to hold things back. 'But that's what marriage is like. You find the perfect person then have to learn to adapt.' Once the ring is on the finger, romance goes out of the window. That's what she really wanted to say, to tell him how frustrated she was these days. And oh, how she longed to be enfolded in Gareth's

138

arms, to give in with grace and fly with him to the moon. He needed only to press the right buttons and she wouldn't be able to vouch for her reaction.

The waiter arrived and Gareth paid the bill.

'Thanks,' said Edwina simply. 'My turn next.'

He ushered her out of the restaurant and impulsively hailed a cab. 'Where to?' he challenged her and she barely hesitated.

'Surprise me,' she said, getting in.

Morwenna had developed an irritating cough, so William dropped in at the surgery. He knew he could sometimes be a bit of a fusspot but wouldn't risk dicing with her health. It wouldn't hurt to let the doctor have a look and ought not to take more than a minute. The Holland Park surgery had recently been revamped and shone now with sunshine and clean paint. There was a spacious area in front of the reception desk, strewn with brightly coloured, much-played-with toys. A couple of other toddlers were already ensconced there with mothers who smiled at him in friendly recognition. William smiled back and went across to join them. This was another part of parenthood he enjoyed, the companionship of the mothers. They were a nice lot, the ones he had met in the neighbourhood, civilised and welcoming, making him feel included.

'All right?'

Laura had had chicken pox but now was declared non-contagious. Nathan, like Morwenna, had developed a troublesome cough. They settled down for a good old gab till the receptionist called out their names. There was usually something of a wait in here but William had all morning to finish his chores. With, as it happened, his afternoon clear as well. When the other children and their mothers had been called, he picked up a magazine and embarked on the crossword. Not one he was accustomed to but far easier than *The Times*. He had almost completed it by the time their names were called and was tempted to take it into the surgery with him, but resisted. Mustn't be viewed by the doctor as anything less than a fully committed parent. Being in charge of a toddler was serious stuff.

The doctor was Asian and quite ravishingly pretty with glossy black hair drawn severely off her face. She had a slight look of Edwina. They both had magnificent eyes and the same flirty grin but, of the two, he would guess that his wife was the tougher. This woman was a committed healer; he could see the dedication in her eyes. Morwenna gurgled with pleasure when she greeted her and held up her arms to be lifted. The doctor laughed and did readily as bid. Morwenna was a favourite in this practice.

'And how are you today, young lady?' she asked as she settled the child on the examination couch. Morwenna beamed and drummed her booted feet. The doctor fished out her stethoscope and listened intently to her chest.

'Sounds all right to me,' she reported. 'Nothing very serious there. I'll prescribe her some cough mixture.'

'And how is Dad?' she asked as she scribbled the prescription. 'Coping with all this constant running around?'

She cocked an enquiring eyebrow at him and he grinned like a guilty schoolboy.

'Loving it,' he said heartily, really meaning it. He ruffled his daughter's silky head. 'They are almost edible at this age. Wouldn't have missed a second of it for the world.'

Nice man, reflected the doctor. Clearly a caring father too. Some women didn't know when they had it made. She had met the wife just fleetingly and hadn't warmed to her at all. Obstinate, vain and self-obsessed, preoccupied with her career. If she wasn't careful, one of these days someone was going to snatch him from under her nose. Given other circumstances, the doctor might even have been tempted herself. Men like William Huxley, with proper old-fashioned values, these days were very rare indeed. Plus he was terribly nice.

'Tell me something,' asked William as an afterthought when she ushered them to the door. 'Do you know a lot about blood?' It was a daft question, as he instantly saw, but he wasn't quite sure how else to phrase it. The doctor looked up at him with interest.

'What exactly is it you need to know?' She stood there, politely waiting, despite there being so many patients on the other side of the door.

'That's the problem. As yet, I'm not quite sure. Not till I've done some more basic digging and worked out what it is I need to know. But once I've done that, do you mind if I come back? I promise I'll try not to waste too much of your time.'

She laughed. 'I am at your service. Try me any time. Though I hope it's nothing too serious.'

'Nothing to do with us,' he reassured her. 'Just an odd little conundrum I've been trying to figure out.' He stopped, embarrassed, feeling a bit of an ass. He would have to work out the right questions before taking her up on her kind offer. He liked the warmth and interest in her eyes, knew that she was unlikely to treat him with scorn. It was too early yet to involve other people, yet comforting to know he had an ally. If only he knew what the questions should be. That was always the hardest part.

14

There was something about Howard Pilkington that instantly repelled me. Unctuous, smug, inordinately self-satisfied, with greased-back hair that gave him the air of a spiv. Not a person you felt you would ever want to know. An archetypal bank manager, I'm afraid. Even the MCC tie only added to his phoneyness. It had taken me so many tedious years to track him down that I ought to have been relieved I had found him at last. But I was not. The terrible mistake of killing those innocent schoolboys stuck in my craw till I very nearly choked and made me wish myself dead. But the grim truth was that the list existed, the promise still remained. There was no wriggling out of it, not even had I wanted to. I was bound by a sacred vow to see it all through.

I had sworn on that sad little coffin that one day I'd have my revenge and, since that's a dish best served up cold, was not backing off from it now. I hardened my heart by recalling that scene when she faded away in my arms. Someone had snatched my darling from me. Now was not a time for second thoughts.

*   *   *

The bungalow was precisely what might be expected of a man of his age with pretensions. Whitewashed, pebble-dashed, with boldly striped window blinds, permanently at half-mast to shield the furniture from the sun. Conformity at its stifling worst; I would not have been surprised to see garden gnomes. I traced him via the Rotary Club, his obvious environment, and wrote on one of my phoney letterheads with a PO Box address for his reply. Since I first embarked on this killing game, I've become quite an expert at deception. In his case, carefully chosen, raising funds for dialysis machines for diabetic Romanian orphans. Or some other twaddle like that. Tailor-made, I rather felt, to hit the spot with his sort of charitable groupie. From all I'd managed to dig up about him, I doubted he'd be able to resist. Definitely his Achilles' heel now that his children had left home.

He responded almost immediately, as I'd rather thought he might, and I made an appointment to meet him. As by now you are aware, I prefer to get to know my victims first. It gives my life some feeling of purpose, something it has been lacking all these years. Simply snuffing them out is no longer enough. I need the reassurance that they will suffer. The boys might have been regrettable, but this was a worthy victim. All of my rage came flooding back; I could hardly wait to get my hands on him. I would, I explained, be in his area later that week, and suggested that we meet somewhere mutually handy. I would not have the time, alas, to visit him at his home since my diary was already so crammed with pressing dates. I proposed that we convene at the bandstand at eleven. I would know him from his picture in the papers.

* * *

Also the flower in his buttonhole. I might well have guessed at that. And he by no stretch of the imagination could possibly recognise me. He was sitting in a deckchair, wearing a blazer and the aforesaid cricket tie, plump knees crossed, dark glasses slipping down his nose, and the morning's unfurled newspaper on his lap. The band, in their scarlet uniforms, had just struck up with a waltz, and a drift of strollers, local residents at a guess, were clustering around like pigeons keen for a crust. I took a seat right across from him but decided to bide my time. I didn't betray, by a flicker of recognition, the secret of who I was. Let him wait and wonder; what else did he have to do? Should I decide to make myself known, it would be at my own pace. There need be no hurry. The morning was cloudless and warm, and the mellifluous band music was lulling me into a torpor.

As the next on my hit list, he came as a welcome change with no sentimental plucking of the heartstrings. I confess I got a kick out of knocking off Jane Fairchild, felt she was better off dead, along with her dog. But the savage slaughter of so many innocent children was starting to drive me insane. I realised, with a jolt, what I was in danger of becoming. A totally depraved monster without an iota of pity. Lately I had problems even looking myself in the eye. I avoided the bathroom mirror whenever I could.

But a former bank manager, surely, has it coming. I had thought of confronting him and chatting him up for a while, spinning some ludicrous tale while I sussed him out. Get inside his head a bit, find out what made him tick. All the better to kill you with, my dear. But after I'd studied him for a while, I

145

found myself losing interest. On a magical morning like this, it was not worth the effort. Sitting here comfortably observing him was enough. I would catch him off guard, in a moment of weakness, and he'd never even know that I had been there.

He glanced fairly irritably at his watch a number of times and I could see him fast becoming crotchety. Certainly not the type to tolerate lateness, not even on a balmy morning like this. Soon, I knew, he would give up waiting, which is exactly what he did. I shadowed him through town, keeping at his pace, and saw how he puffed as he walked. Not a fit man, unhealthily overweight. He ought not to take too much effort to finish off. And when eventually he turned along East Cliff and entered the Grosvenor Hotel, a plan became instantly obvious. Casual barwork, as I'd proved before, was usually pretty simple to obtain. Especially in a resort like this, right at the start of the season. I could do the deed swiftly then lose myself in the crowd, just another of many faceless itinerants.

For those first few glorious years together we were deliriously happy, content just to be alone in each other's company. Every waking moment was uniquely just for the two of us. All that had gone before had been eclipsed. I regret all the damage we did to others, the wrecking of innocent lives. In particular I'm sorry about the children, though they survived. At the time we lived precariously, just for the moment. We even contrived to work together; the company obligingly slotted us both in. And once it was all out in the open at last, there need be no more deception. Happy and proud, in the flush of our new love, in those days I certainly walked tall. It seemed we had it all then, each other, our love and our health. The only thing we lacked was a child of our own.

Marina would say I was selfish to want it all. But greed has always been my particular failing. She had got her own life well sorted and children she knew adored her. Now it was my turn for a bite of the cherry while there was still the time. We begged and cajoled her but all to no avail. She said her piece then turned her back on us, refusing any sort of compromise.

So we had to go ahead without her, thereby committing a mortal sin. I suppose, on reflection, it was bound not to last. Idylls like ours rarely do. All my childhood teaching came flooding back to reproach me. I knew I could never face my mother again. We were damned in the eyes of both God and man, with me the main sinner on account of being the catalyst. But disaster was out there, waiting to happen, and just when we least expected it, it struck. One tiny misjudgement, an innocent error, that led to the total destruction of all we had.

Patience has, of necessity, become one of my principal virtues, and working part-time at the Grosvenor proved excellent cover. Occasionally I did the evening shift though they liked to move me around and, due to my obliging attitude, I found that I fitted in well. And living right there, on the sea front, brought back poignant memories from my youth. When not on duty, I would walk for many miles, breathing in the past along with the ozone. Things might never go right for me again but at least I'd already had my taste of paradise. Despite what

147

happened at the bitter end, which irreversibly set my course on this bloodthirsty mission.

Simply by eavesdropping at the bar, I discovered that Pilkington's wife was due to go off on a toot. Which meant, since the old buffer presumably couldn't cook, we'd be seeing a little more of him at the weekend. I used some excuse to alter the duty roster, then added the final touches to my plan. Timing was essential; there could be no second-guessing him and Sunday is a particularly busy day. Risk is something I had lately learned to relish. Without the possibility of something going wrong, killing, like anything else, becomes quite banal.

It went off like clockwork and nobody guessed a thing. By the time they had even found him, I was long gone. Lost in the crowds on the teeming promenade, a cipher whom no one in the Grosvenor even remembered. The police did their usual cack-handed job so that probably no one remarked on me or my absence. Once again I slipped on my cloak of invisibility and read the screaming headlines with satisfaction. I packed my solitary bag at my lodgings round the corner and was on the train to Cambridge by half past six.

15

There was a distinctly frosty atmosphere that morning at breakfast. Edwina had come home late with no explanation. William, while recognising the stresses she must be under, was fast beginning to lose patience with his wife. After all, they were supposed to be a team. Lately she'd been taking too many uncalled-for advantages. He had tried having it out with her but found her unreceptive. There were problems with the launch, was all she'd say, and a certain wariness in her eyes warned him roundly to back off. There'd been a lot in the papers recently about the plunging fortunes of all these bright young things. Millionaires one day, with the world at their feet, they could wake in the morning to find that their share price had plummeted. People were even starting to get off on it. Such largesse, so effortlessly earned, appeared unfair, especially amongst these brash twenty- and thirty-somethings. It was the lottery mentality that had taken over the world. Mindless greed which could surely not be healthy. He looked at Morwenna, playing contentedly with her building blocks. He'd do all in his power to prevent her growing up so grasping.

Morwenna, fortunately, being not much like her mother, had an altogether far sunnier temperament. She was bright and questioning but infinitely more relaxed, with a warm, cheerful nature like his. Provided the maternal grandparents weren't allowed too much leverage, there was a strong chance she'd make it into adulthood without the trailing baggage of her mother. He was encouraging her to express her individuality while at the same time not pressuring her to perform. They looked at things together and carefully discussed them, and he read to her whenever he found the time. She was a lovely kid and developing fast. She surprised him each new day with her sharp eye and intelligent grasp. It wouldn't be long before Morwenna became aware of the gathering tension, which he was keen, at all costs, to avoid.

'What are you doing tonight?' he asked carefully, as Edwina crashed around the kitchen, searching for her keys.

'What?' Edwina, her attention not upon him, was flustered and not at all her usual self. She was managing to tune out William altogether, could no longer face even having to talk to him. Just lately, with all that was happening at work, he'd started to get on her nerves big time. Watching him just sit there, engrossed in the morning paper, idly stirring his second cup of tea, really got up her nose. Wearing, too, that ratty old sweater that should by rights have been thrown out long ago. Soon he would lose all his self-esteem and even give up bothering to shave. It was bad enough at weekends when he did that.

These days, no longer with the discipline of an office, the least he could do surely was learn to conform. He was a nice enough looking man when he bothered to take the trouble but she couldn't abide this new thoughtless scruffiness. She blamed a lot of it, unfairly, on Mrs P. They'd become far too cliquey for Edwina's liking and she had to acknowledge that the woman was blatantly common.

And would be in shortly. She ought to get a move on. The taxi had been waiting twenty minutes.

'I'm off,' she announced brusquely, as she headed towards the door without having answered his question. For all she cared, he could do what he bloody well liked, provided he continued to look after the child.

'Tonight?' said William patiently, fighting a sudden urge to slap her. 'When will you be home and should I cook?'

She looked at him astonished. Who else did he think was going to do it? If *he* didn't cook, what on earth would they eat? Unless she made other arrangements, which was possible. Her heart beat uncomfortably at the treacherous thought. She hoped he couldn't see it in her face.

'I don't know,' she told him after a short pause. 'I'll try and call you later from the office.'

This new state of agitation really suited her. She looked even more beautiful than usual. Whatever it was distracting her was certainly having an effect. A twinge of wistfulness swept through William, though he didn't say any more as he watched her go.

Morwenna pointlessly waved at the retreating back. There had been a time when the child would try to stop

151

her, but those days of female bonding were long over. Now Morwenna looked on placidly as the tornado that was her mother whirled through. She was far more excited by the arrival of Mrs P, who regularly gave her the spoiling she deserved.

'Bye bye, Mummy,' she cooed dreamily to herself, then turned away, back to her toys.

After the first blast of shocked outrage, there was surprisingly little about Pilkington in the papers. This new case lacked the emotional impact of the little boys or the still-reverberating Marsh murders. Somehow the police appeared not to have hooked up, though William was still working doggedly on his theory. Either that or they were operating undercover. Even Susie Lamplugh's lot had finally, after fourteen years, got a lead. But so far no one official had spoken up, not in connection with these cases. Most extraordinary, as Mrs P agreed. She had started off sceptical but had been swayed by William's eloquence. It seemed there could well be a new serial killer whom nobody in authority was aware of. Or so it would appear from the lack of official statements. If only he could establish that one crucial link. Somehow he felt it might be staring him in the face. Which is why he couldn't let it go.

The card had been lying there on his desk all these weeks, submerged beneath a welter of tracings and roadmaps. It was only when William, frustrated out of his mind, began putting things in order that he found it. The annual meeting of the International Cartographic Association, to be held at the Royal Geographical Society. The following evening. He hadn't seen any of his former colleagues since his banishment into full-time fatherhood. It was time he got out there, back into reality, if only for a few stolen hours. He checked the date. Nothing in the diary that night, not for either of them. Edwina could damn well come home on time for a change and do a spot of hands-on mothering. It would be no bad thing, help to reacquaint her with her daughter. While he was out with the lads.

'It isn't convenient,' she snapped when he told her, but William, for once, remained resolute. He needed the break, to exercise his brain, to re-enter the solid male company of cartographers. So he left her grumpily tidying the living room, changed out of his customary jogging pants and sweater and into a halfway decent suit, and was off. The rain had stopped and the evening smelt fresh as he trotted over the hill to Kensington High Street. Twenty minutes' brisk walking at the most before he reached the dignified sanctum that still felt beguilingly like home. He hadn't fully realised till now how deprived he had been of the aura of academia.

He instantly spotted a few familiar faces and crossed the handsome panelled room to join them. After a brief reception and a number of hearty greetings, the president entered and the meeting kicked off to a healthy murmur of interest and affirmation. This year's president was William's former tutor, recently retired from Oxford Brookes. He was a distinguished-looking man, with a head of iron-grey hair and the weatherbeaten face of the much-travelled. William's heart started to buzz with anticipation. He was back in his proper environment. It felt good.

The address was inspiring and the following debate pretty lively, with William adding his bit along with the rest. All of them were united in a mistrust of computers and the geographical information service that was playing havoc with many of their lives. Things just weren't the same any more. Even Ordnance Survey no longer employed cartographers, with the result that the job had ceased to be aesthetically pleasing. His tutor, Martin Staveley, lingered for a word with him, then invited William to join him at The Goat. It was their customary stamping-ground from many years back and brought back pleasant memories. Despite the hour (it was almost ten) he felt no compunction at not hurrying straight home. Edwina would understand. She had done it herself often enough.

'There's something I'd quite like to talk to you about,' said William once they were settled. Staveley nodded and led him further from the jukebox. This pub was always busy, night and day. William wasn't quite certain how to begin, suddenly feeling a bit of a prat. His theory was so insubstantial as yet, but he'd started so he'd have to go on. The older man waited calmly as William assembled his thoughts. This was one of his brightest students ever. He was sorry things hadn't worked out better for him.

Slowly, aided by the back of an old envelope, William began to sketch out his spurious theory. Without going into specifics at all, he indicated the different murder sites, then linked them with his own connecting arrows. Staveley listened, instantly alert, totally understanding what he was driving at.

'These different places, for whatever reason, are, you think, linked by their topography?' His experienced eye didn't need an Ordnance Survey map. He was able to envisage the hilly terrain in his head. Take away the main motorways and their closeness was much clearer to the initiated. Cartographer's reality once again. Better than anything dreamed up by a computer.

'So you don't think I'm totally off my rocker?' asked William, once he'd filled him in. Staveley thought silently then slowly shook his head. William always had been amazingly quick off the mark. It was quite a different matter, of course, to try explaining it to an amateur. But as long as he could feel confident that he was roughly on the right trail he'd be happier following his theory through to its conclusion.

'Ever thought of teaching?' asked Staveley as he rose to go. William was exactly the sort of recruit they needed to keep the profession alive, full of enthusiasm and flair. Plus an almost uncanny eye for seeing things as they really were, and not being fooled by what seemed obvious. 'Give me a ring if you ever want to discuss it. In any case, do please now keep in touch.'

*   *   *

Working alongside Gareth grew more dangerous by the minute. Edwina had only to raise her eyes to find his fixed on her. Which was profoundly distracting, especially now. The German finance had not, in the end, been forthcoming. There'd been a last-minute hitch and they'd taken their money elsewhere. So now she was back to networking frantically, hoping to turn up another possible source. It was hugely frustrating, since everything else was in place. Nine thousand outlets and a rapidly rising share price. All they needed, and badly, was the seed money to keep them afloat.

The session in Gareth's flat had thrilled but also scared her. Fantasy was one thing and kept her senses buzzing, but actually doing it had never been part of her plan. Adultery was not a pretty word; she feared to think how her father would view such behaviour. Now, however, she could think of little else, at a time when she really needed her wits about her. She peeked again; he was still there, openly studying her, relaxed and nonchalant, hands clasped behind his head. He smiled as he caught her eye and blew her a mocking kiss. If he wasn't careful, the others would catch on and then she really would be in serious trouble.

It had to have been that extra glass of wine. She tried not to drink in the middle of the day. She liked to keep her head clear, especially now, but her nervousness caused by Gareth's close proximity had rapidly led her astray. He had tempted and she'd recklessly followed, too stirred by his sexy appeal to stop and think.

'Clerkenwell,' he had instructed the driver, giving the address of his loft. He had never invited her there before but she followed him docilely up the stairs, her pulses racing, her heart in her mouth, spurred on by a frenzy of desire. Once through the door, they fell into each other's arms and landed very neatly on the wide and serviceable bed.

'Shouldn't we call the office?' she whispered nervously.

'Later,' he said, beginning to tear off his clothes.

Total madness. She knew it immediately, shocked by her loss of control. But his hands were all over her, his lips at her throat, and she wanted him so badly she could no longer hold back. She had dreamed of this moment so many times and he certainly didn't let her down. His prowess as a lover was extraordinary and brought to mind all those pathetic other women who seemed not to be able to leave him alone. Edwina now discovered the man's secret power and found herself as helplessly ensnared. At five they surfaced briefly and he made the necessary phonecall. Stuck in a meeting, he blithely informed the office, unlikely to get back before they all went home. Everything was running smoothly, he reported as he crawled back into bed, bringing an opened bottle of champagne and two crystal glasses, thoughtfully chilled.

He grabbed two handfuls of her tangled hair, murmuring endearments that she had never imagined she'd hear. She knew she shouldn't trust him, remembered his chequered past, but was utterly unable to resist him now. William, in bed, was warm and cosy, but this man was a veritable tiger. She feared that his passionate embraces might physically leave their mark, but was unable as well as unwilling to put up a fight. She would take the consequences, work something out, say she had taken a tumble in the gym. Right now she was living entirely for the moment. And wanted it never to stop.

But that was two days ago, and now they both sat on either side of an open-plan room with a bunch of young technicians in between them. And she ought to be thinking about getting off home and resisting his raunchy animal magnetism.

'Drink?' he asked as he passed by her desk, pausing to finger her hair. She shook him off.

'Not tonight,' she said abruptly. William had been positively frosty when she got home, the dinner spoiled, the baby asleep, having called the office and found the answerphone on. A meeting in the City, she'd told him, trying to avoid his eyes yet hating herself for lying. Even last night's dutiful racing home had been insufficient penance. If she wasn't careful, she was going to lose him. She wasn't quite ready for that yet.

'When then?' Gareth's mouth was brushing her ear, his hot breath making her blush. She nudged him away. Nobody yet had a clue, she was certain, but it must only be a matter of time. And once they started to gossip here, who knew where it could lead? To public shaming and the end of her marriage, even – heaven forbid – the forfeiture of her child.

'Must go,' she said, starting to gather up her things. She dared not be late or William would start to suspect.

William, as it happened, was deep in the crossword, with Morwenna perched on the sofa beside him, engrossed in the end of *Pet Rescue*. What was it, he was thinking, as he wrestled with a quotation, that all those worthy citizens had had in common? Clean-living, hard-working, decent everyday folk. Like the cast of *The Archers*, totally sanitised. It drummed in his brain like the dripping of a tap – the tap he still hadn't managed to get fixed. Something uniting them, even though they were strangers. And had nothing else to connect them that he could fathom. Decent folk with a conscience, that was it. It hit him like forked lightning and he tossed the puzzle aside.

'Eureka!' he shouted out loud as he reached for his notes.

16

Six hardy stalwarts had turned out this dismal morning. Jasmine could hear them laughing together as she padlocked her bike outside the village hall. Mandy and Pam and Sarah and Maureen, all regulars. Oona and Jackie were making herbal tea. Usually there was also a handful of strays but not today. And who, in weather like this, could possibly blame them? The track was almost impassable, the village sheeted in rain.

"Morning, ladies,' she said as she entered, noticing that no one had bothered to switch on the heating. So she'd put them through their paces extra briskly to stop their joints aching or seizing up. She sneezed.

'Getting a cold?' asked Maureen with concern. 'I thought you were far too healthy a creature for that.'

Jasmine laughed as she stepped out of her tracksuit, revealing the aquamarine Spandex she wore beneath. 'Just a sniffle,' she said. 'I hope it won't develop.' There was nothing more dreary than having to take a class when feeling a little bit under the weather yourself. Mind over matter was what she preached, plus a mug of this excellent green tea they were making, to which, due to her, they had all become mildly addicted.

'Radish juice, that's the thing,' she said as she jogged up and down on the spot to shake out her legs. 'Whirr it up with your carrot juice in the morning. You'll find it does all kinds of wonderful things. Including slowing down a cold.'

'I know it's supposedly good for the bladder,' said Pam, cautiously unzipping her sweatshirt to test the temperature in the hall. Chilly now, but wait till they really got going. Already Jasmine was inserting one of her bouncy disco CDs. She didn't hold with wasting valuable time. Always on the go, she was, off to the next appointment. And right after this she had a very special client and particularly didn't want to be running late.

'Good for a lot of mild ailments,' she said. 'There's nothing to beat raw juice for keeping you fit and detoxed.'

They laughed. To the rest of them, mainly middle-aged and defeated, Jasmine, with her sparkling eyes and glowing complexion, was a picture of rude health. Straight off a poster for a spa, she looked. An excellent advertisement for what she peddled: fitness and exercise for the weary and overweight. Plus those with not enough to fill their day. The beat was starting so she turned up the volume and the class fell obediently into line, high-stepping vigorously to her lead.

'*One* and two, and *one* and two . . .' She certainly worked them hard, but this lot were loyal and had stuck with her for the six months she had been there. She

161

enjoyed the camaraderie of her general classes, though, if she were honest, got more satisfaction from the private one-to-one sessions she also gave. Like the one later this morning, to which she was looking forward. Individual yoga lessons for those who could afford them. Her reputation was growing steadily, her diary increasingly full. She had even attracted a couple of mild celebrities: a silver-haired actor famed for his sixties' stardom and an ageing footballer trying hard to get back to his form. She enjoyed the women but worked better with men, felt she had more to contribute.

It hadn't always been like this, oh no. As she mounted her bike after the gruelling session and pedalled back carefully along the sodden track, she wondered what they would feel if they'd known how she'd been in the old days, before she had sorted herself out. Too much drinking and too much sex. Too much everything, if the truth be told. Her memories of that period were hazy; like Mick Jagger, she admitted to huge gaps. She had not been rebelling against anything in particular, it was just her age and the times in which she'd grown up. Too much freedom, her father always said. Whatever it was, she'd made a right botch of things and had been rapidly deteriorating into a brain-damaged fool. Until she'd met Marco and he'd more or less saved her life by leading her off on a pilgrimage and thence to her ultimate salvation.

She would always be grateful to Marco, even though he had dumped her along the way. He had taught her to have more belief in herself and not trade her body for sex. To recognise her true potential and learn to stand up for herself. She had come off the booze, switched to a strictly vegan diet and gradually started to build up some self-respect. And as her spiritual consciousness grew and her physical strength increased, she slowly discovered an exciting new wholeness in the universe, a pattern she hadn't discerned before. She was part of a far greater entity, she knew that now. Whatever was up there would keep her from harm and give her the spiritual guidance she required. She remained on her own in an Indian ashram for a period of several years and there had discovered the benefits of yoga and deep meditation. Jasmine Brookes had returned to England a wiser and happier person, able at last to look forward to a proper future. Fuelled by her own determination, financed by the money she earned. Knowing that, at last, she was going to be all right and could face up to whatever lay ahead.

The cottage she rented in the village was small but sufficient. Room for herself, her bicycle and her cat, with a handy extra space that had once been a laundry room, which she'd converted into a studio for private lessons. Right on the main street, too, which she liked. People could literally stick their noses through her window. She got quickly sucked into village life. After the years of prayer and seclusion, she hugely enjoyed this new involvement. People, on the whole, were welcoming and kind; she had never really been aware of that before. And it felt good, she had to admit it. She was tired of always doing everything on her own. Being part of a community reminded her of the ashram. Only here she suddenly felt she was pulling her weight.

Her next class was at noon, with the fading actor, after which she would be free for a couple of hours. She might nip into Cambridge for tea and a film or see what the shops had to offer. Jasmine lived frugally, was more or less self-sufficient, but enjoyed the unaccustomed wealth of Western civilisation. It was still a bit of a novelty just to wander and window-gaze, though mostly she returned home empty-handed. Her needs these days were basically very frugal. She'd long grown out of the profligacy of her youth.

Gerry was waiting in his tracksuit on her step, having jogged the two miles from his mansion. He grinned as she dismounted, genuinely welcoming.

'No hurry, darlin', I'm early. Just felt like a breath of fresh air.' His famous night-black hair was streaked with silver; the pouches beneath his eyes gave away his age, though he was still in excellent shape for sixty-two, credit in some part to her. Their thrice-weekly sessions kept them both on their toes. For her it was a proper workout just keeping up with his constant amazing energy.

There had recently been a rumour in the papers that he was tipped for a comeback starring role. She hesitated to bring it up but knew she could count on his garrulity. Blowing his own trumpet came naturally to the man. These days, since he'd slid from the ratings, he had very little else to do but potter. Or pursue women, so the gossip columns would have it, though with her he had always remained a gentleman.

'Before you mention it,' he told her now with a chuckle, 'those rumours are not without foundation.' He listed those involved as she led him into her home. A Hollywood director, an impresario of note, and funding from a very reputable source. Couldn't fail.

'And get this, darlin', it's a musical this time! Can't you just see me up there struttin' me stuff?' He struck a pose and walked duck-like into the studio, then threw back his head and laughed heartily. Jasmine laughed too. She liked this rogue, even found him still quite sexy. If he did make a pass, she probably wouldn't object. The wife, his third, was rarely around these days. Spent most of her time in Portugal soaking up sun. And Jasmine deserved a break, it had been so long. Her sex life could do with a spot of geeing up.

'So we need to get you into tiptop condition.' She didn't use music for these private yoga sessions, but helped him to breathe properly and relax. She rolled out the mats on the sanded wooden boards and switched on a couple of strategically placed lamps. If she ever had real money she'd invest in a place of her own. Meanwhile, this cottage was adequate for her needs. This time, if she played it right, she might get to be part of his team. Official trainer to the major star, even with a credit of her own. That, most certainly, could do her career no harm. She was starting to covet some of the limelight for herself.

Which was how it always had been in the good old days when she'd still been the fashionable It Girl of her set.

The weather was still lousy when she got to her evening session – an aerobics class for the under-fifties, held in a school gymnasium in the next village. As she took off her tracksuit in the changing rooms, it steamed. There was a depressing smell of damp wool and old gymshoes, which reminded her all too vividly of school. Jasmine sighed as she did a few quick warm-ups. She was tired and unenthusiastic, aching to get back home. These were the sessions she liked the least, a spectrum of amateurs, few with their hearts really in it. After the inspiration of an hour with Gerry Handscombe, the prospect of these bumblers filled her with gloom. A hotchpotch of stragglers, many of them new, who could stray in off the street at whim provided they forked out the fee.

The lighting in the gym was harsh, and rain still rattled the windows. They stood around like disconsolate cattle, awaiting her signal to begin.

'Hi!' said Jasmine with an over-bright smile, belying the sinking dismay in her heart. She cranked up the volume of the worn-out music machine and tried to get them all performing in sync.

Forty, she counted, as they did their first swoops, most of them women, just a sprinkling of men. Many seriously out of shape who would not last till the end. Poor souls, she wondered why they let themselves get that way, with all that extra poundage to weigh them down. She would never get out of trim, even if she progressed to better things. At thirty-six, she still had firm thighs and a stomach that was the envy of her pupils. But how she had to work at it. She was, after all, only human, and occasionally liked to binge when she was unhappy. Staying fit meant punishingly hard work and never letting up, no matter what. She looked again at this bunch of pathetic no-hopers and privately despised the lot of them. She had dropped out of the social scene for reasons of her own, but at least had had some life before she did so.

There were a couple of newcomers tonight she didn't remember ever seeing before. A slim, dark woman with immaculate hair, who stood out because she was so supple. And a smoky-eyed youth with the grace of a dancer, a peacock among a flock of fattened-up geese. She watched them both curiously as they separately worked away, wondering why they needed to come here at all. Both had class and definite potential, though they seemed not to be together, an odd coincidence. This part of the country was primarily residential, most of the men commuting to the City. So who was this graceful mysterious man with the haunting, aesthetic beauty? Perhaps a professional, here from the town, using her class just to limber up. Even, perhaps, an acquaintance of Gerry Handscombe. The woman was undoubtedly just another bored housewife, whiling away some time till her husband returned. Jasmine made a mental note to seek them both out after class. She could do with making a few more friends; it wasn't just a lover that she needed. Being a teacher she found quite restrictive and was cautious of growing too intimate with her pupils. But, what the hell, she was new to these parts. And occasionally needed a little cheering up.

Gerry, of course, could well prove the exception. She had sensed a definite warming in him today, plus a spark in his eye that could well spell danger. She wasn't entirely clear about the ethics of it all, but it couldn't be as unprofessional as a doctor. And even though he was that much older, at least he still had fire in his loins. Jasmine instinctively tightened her pelvic muscles and doubled the speed of their dance routine.

By the time she had chatted and answered their various queries, collected their money and switched off the music machine, there were very few stragglers still left behind in the gym. Both the intriguing strangers appeared to have gone. Well, it wasn't the end of the world, thought Jasmine. Maybe they'd both come again. And, even if they didn't, she was hardly missing out. She didn't intend to remain here long and could always pop into Cambridge if she wanted new friends. Or back to London to do a bit of clubbing, perhaps look up some faces from the past. She'd been teetering on the brink of that, yet was scared of disturbing old ghosts. Life then had been so different from life now. She wasn't entirely sure she had the courage. Or the stamina to resist the inevitable temptation.

She pedalled home through relentlessly heavy rain, soaked right through to her innermost layers, her hair plastered wetly to her face. She could feel a drip forming at the end of her nose but her hands were too frozen to brush it off. There were times, such as this, when she wearied of this life, though she liked the money and freedom that it brought. Never again would she do a regular job; she needed the space and freedom to spread her wings. Though she could also use some company at times. Only the cat would be waiting for her at home.

She had left a window open right on to the street. She noticed that immediately as she dismounted. That was pretty stupid, considering the foulness of the weather. She hoped her curtains weren't ruined, that nothing in the room had been disturbed. She pushed her bicycle into the woodshed and wiped it down with a cloth. Then closed the door without bothering to lock it. People round here, on the whole, were very honest. She kept the heavy main doorkey on a string just inside the letterbox. It was far too cumbersome to lug around. Many of her neighbours didn't bother to lock up at all. Everyone here knew everyone else; it was supposedly very safe. One of the pluses of a small community after the adventurous life she had been leading.

The cat was usually waiting but this evening there was no sign of him. She took off her anorak and shook it outside, then hung it on a hook in the passage to dry.

'Orpheus,' she called as she went through to the

kitchen, switching on lamps to lighten the gloom and make the place feel more like home. His bowl was empty but of him there was no sign. She turned on the two-bar electric fire and longed for a wood-burning stove. Baked beans it would have to be again tonight, she was far too de-energised to cook. But first she must feed her hungry beast, unless he was out on the tiles.

'Orpheus,' she called again as she opened his tin, then went into the studio on an impulse.

When she saw what had been done to the cat, she very nearly threw up. He was pinned to the noticeboard with a skewer through his throat, his eyes popping out and scarlet with blood, his usually glossy black coat matted and repulsive. The poor creature's mouth was fixed open in a terrible silent rictus; whatever it was that had happened to him had caught him unawares. When, at last, she willed herself to touch his slimy fur, she found he was still warm. He could only have been dead for a matter of minutes. Whoever had done it might well be still around. Jasmine glanced nervously back at the front door, suddenly wondering if she'd remembered to lock it. And then she recalled the window and realised immediately what had happened. She hadn't left it open at all; some intruder had forced his way in. She moved instinctively to close it now.

Too late, she heard the movement just behind her.

17

*M*arina always used to say, in the days when we were still speaking, that the very best thing you could be given in life was good health. Children, she said, could turn out a disappointment, and love in the end always faded. Sexual attraction, the scientists had decided, lasted only a maximum of four years. After which you were stuck in a decaying relationship designed to drive you barmy in the end. I, the idealist, obviously didn't agree, but how much did I know then about real life? My own close-knit family had always got on well, a bunch of boisterous kids with tolerant parents. We'd been fortunate and I think it showed in our confidence and ease of manner. Based on that mercurial quality known as charm. Also, I suppose, our innate unquestioning selfishness. We accepted good luck as our natural due, expected people to let us into their lives. Helped ourselves to whatever we fancied, then thoughtlessly went on our way like a careless band of cuckoos.

But I never ever argued with Marina. She had a calm, madonna-like approach to life and, no matter what platitudes she occasionally came out with, put husband and, later, children resolutely first. She was a good woman, Marina; I am privileged to have known her and still feel pangs about what eventually happened. If I had it all to do again, I believe I would almost certainly desist. Too much anger and definitely too much pain. For what she thought about marriage turned out to be true. We are now both left to get on with our lives alone, when each, I suspect, could well use some propping up. It is lonely out here for us sinners. Once the passion is past, all that's left is the routine and the long dark suffering nights of endless regret.

She was there at the hospital right after the crash, but I was in far too much turmoil even to see her. She hung around but I slunk away and nursed my anguished emotions in anonymity. I ought to have been there for her – I see that now – but hadn't the guts, when it came to it, to stand up and continue with the fight. We had both loved colossally and both of us had lost. Or so it would appear at that bleak time. I tried writing her letters but always tore them up, unable to get my feelings down on paper. It was my fault entirely, of that there could be no doubt, so how could such a woman even start to forgive me? I badly needed to talk to a priest, but couldn't raise the courage to enter the church. When I needed Him most, He had apparently forsaken me. I was out there in the wilderness on my own.

God knows what Marina was thinking, I dared not imagine, but her agony must have been quite as profound as my own. I had staked my all on this one insane transgression, only to watch it disintegrate into ashes. I had wronged her right from the start, there was no getting round it. But nothing I could say or do could possibly make amends. At least she still had family to comfort her while I was now entirely on my own. One by one, she would turn them all against me, just as surely as I had alienated her. They would hate me forever, which I knew was only fair. It's just that, after everything else, it hurt so much.

Often at night when I cannot sleep, I stare at the ceiling and reflect. Is Marina's hatred as intense as my own and might she ever be fired to hunt me down? In a way, it would almost come as a relief to find I had my own personal nemesis stalking me. For the thrill has gone out of this creeping up behind. I would welcome a bit of combat face to face. Yet what would be achieved by that? You cannot restore the past. I'd do anything in my power to atone, but by now it is far too late. And even Marina must surely have moved on. I cannot begrudge her that, for she was blameless.

Not so Jasmine Brookes, however. A different story entirely. And I blamed her more than I did any of the others for the ultimate destruction of my happiness. I can't imagine what she expected, foolish woman, after the irresponsible way she had carried on. No matter how much, latterly, she might try to clean up her act, at no time had her life been a model of decorum. She was always a bit of a swinger, right from the start. I had learned that much from my years of detailed research. Indiscriminate in her choice of sexual partners, no telling what nasty diseases she might have picked up. For when she was growing up, in the early eighties, the London club scene was at its most frenetic. And Jasmine, fresh from suburban Ilford, was wide-eyed and easily led. I can well imagine what she

173

must have been like at that age – naïve and excitable, prepared to take dangerous risks. Always living life to the full, mindless of the damage she might be doing. A clone, in short, of my own capricious set, who hung around in a pack, ever on the pull. I'd not be surprised if our paths had actually crossed then. Who knows what we might have got up to when we were zapped. We were young, we were silly, in search of instant gratification. A bunch of thoughtless sybarites in need of a bloody good kicking.

I had to kill her and it made me feel better to do so. I studied her eyes as I watched her die and the baffled incomprehension gradually faded. I hadn't explained – there had not been time – and now I regretted my haste. Whatever relish I got from each new murder was somehow inevitably spoiled. Perhaps that is just how things are in life. Nothing is ever quite perfect until nirvana. Which is where, I'd discovered, lately Jasmine had been heading. I hope my action hurried her on her way. She deserved to die. As unpleasantly as possible. I struck her name from my list with vicious pleasure.

And yet, and yet. As I roamed those barren streets, contemplating the senselessness of it all, my grieving heart should have been enough to remind me that too much unnecessary dying is merely wasteful. I had lost everything in life that I cared about most while Marina, at least, still had the children. And would almost certainly make a new life for herself, of that I felt pretty confident. She'd always had her share of admirers, was not by any means remotely past it. Plus she had money of her own. And her generally prosaic attitude towards destiny would not preclude her finding another great love. Even though I had contributed to the shake-up of her life, I had done more than enough penance now, I felt.

I, on the other hand, was not in tremendous shape. I had tried to cure the insomnia with too much whisky, which had proved to be one of my less good ideas, for it seemed I'd developed an intolerance. After the night that I crashed the bike, I found myself in hospital, heavily sedated. To be released only into a private clinic where I stayed for almost a year, which I barely remember, sweating out the excesses that had landed me there and trying to come to terms with my terrible grief.

They used to bring me violets on my breakfast tray and hold back the newspapers in case they proved too disturbing. I lay there in a perpetual daze, thinking about nothing much at all, listening only to classical music on my headphones. Life had halted completely as far as I was concerned. I had no reason whatsoever to try to get better.

Until, quite by chance, I caught that brief item on the radio. And was hurtled back into reality, doubtless too soon.

18

William spotted it first as a single brief item of news, sandwiched at the back of the evening paper. It was so understated that he almost overlooked it, then flicked back as an afterthought to read it a second time. Some yoga teacher had been stabbed to death at home in a village outside Cambridge. Far from the scenes of the other crimes, but her cat had been brutalised too. Which was what initially caught his eye, triggering an instant twitching of the antennae. He tuned in hopefully to the lunchtime regional news, but that area was not included in the South East. For some unexplained reason, the plight of this unfortunate seemed not to have attracted general media attention. William, for the life of him, could not understand why this should be. Murder, after all, was murder and this a quite horrendous-sounding crime.

And then, in early evening, he happened to catch the fading sixties' filmstar, Gerald Handscombe, speaking live on air of his profound shock.

'A smashing girl, Jasmine,' he was telling the interviewer. 'One of the absolute best. We've worked closely together for the past few months. I'd grown to look upon her as a genuine friend. Shocking business, I'll certainly miss her.' And yes, I will soon be opening in the West End.

They had picked up on Handscombe because of his rumoured new starring role and were able to make a neat item of it on the pretext of plugging the show. Otherwise, so William thought, she might have been little more than a traffic statistic, for all the murder squad appeared to be doing about it.

Even Mrs P had completely overlooked it when she bustled in next morning, bursting with news. One of her many daughters was getting hitched, to a boy she'd known only a couple of months. For once she had no ears for William. All she could talk of, as she warmed the pot, were bridesmaids' dresses and satin shoes and the shocking expense of it all.

'Wait till it's your turn,' she said as she petted Morwenna. 'The years go by so fleetingly. It seems like only yesterday that our Sharon was still just a babe.'

William laughed cynically. Over his dead body. They would have to scale the fortress walls to get anywhere near his daughter. Slay a few dragons too. But that was not a priority right now, he was starting to become preoccupied with the fate of Jasmine Brookes. At last he did get Mrs P's attention when she temporarily ran out of steam.

'Another murder, you say? And with a sickle? Gracious, how grotesque can a person be? Do tell.'

'She was pretty near decapitated is all I've managed to glean. Head hacked half off, left bleeding on the floor. No one, for some odd reason, seems very concerned.'

'Too much in the papers right now about the American election. And all this miserable flooding everywhere.'

She was right. Lately the volume of sensation in the news was enough to pale the public's interest in a minor anonymous killing. Villains had even stormed the Dome in the biggest failed heist of all time. Whatever next? They both had a chuckle at the incompetence of the thieves and the way they had all been neatly nabbed by police-men disguised as cleaners. They had even had a speed-boat standing by for a clean fast getaway on the Thames.

'The diamonds weren't even real!' laughed Mrs P. 'De Beers swapped them for fakes just the night before.' One thing that could be said for the Brits, when it came to farce, they certainly topped the league. Straight out of an Ealing comedy, in fact. Pity flicks like that had now gone out of fashion.

But the murder, persisted William. The plight of this Jasmine Brookes was nagging away, he wanted to run it again past Mrs P. Though there wasn't a lot more to add, as far as it went. The item had been picked up by a local reporter, who just happened to have been the first one on the scene. He'd been riding his bike on a shortcut home and had noticed her open front door. Some pruri-ent curiosity, inspired by he didn't say what, had caused him to stop and investigate, and thus stumble across the bloodied corpse. If it weren't for this old actor chappie who'd managed to get involved and was bolstering his ego at the dead woman's expense, it was doubtful it would have appeared at all, not at national level. Shocking, really, when you considered the details. Not to mention the fate of the poor cat.

'You're not suggesting they're linked in some way?' Mrs P was instantly back on the ball. She had grown to understand the workings of William's mind as well as his many and weird obsessions. Was touched and intrigued by the interest he took, while privately believing he was probably wasting his time. Ought to be out there in the real world, silly fellow, finding himself a proper job, helping to bring in some cash. It wasn't quite healthy to be stuck home all day with Morwenna. No wonder he went off on these flights of fancy.

'I really don't know,' admitted William. 'I agree it is starting to sound a bit far-fetched. But there seems to have been a spate of motiveless murders, each of them gruesome in the extreme. And yet apparently unconnected. Doesn't that strike you as odd?' Which, put that way, it did.

'So how come the coppers aren't making a similar assumption?' Mrs P had little time for the police, her family had been in too many scrapes for her to view them as anything but inept. Talk about Ealing comedies; this beat the lot. Rather than harassing high-spirited kids, they ought to get their act together and do some proper detecting for a change. Protecting the community was supposed to be their main function. But they turned too many blind eyes to too many crimes. And it didn't help either if your skin was the wrong colour. She could continue in this vein for hours so William tactfully stepped in. He tried to explain his thinking so far. Without going into too much technical detail, he showed her on his map how the murder sites roughly connected, despite the fact they were all so widely spread out. Though, now he had another look, at fairly consistent distances. If only he could pinpoint the hub of this rough circle, he might get that much closer to the killer.

Mrs P stared at the map and tried to comprehend what he was saying. She didn't understand a word but the diagram spoke for itself, in a sort of way.

'Like a web,' she said slowly.

'With a spider in the centre.'

'And that spider is our murderer?' William nodded.

'So now you can see what they're up against.' Each of the murders had been in a different catchment area, with a separate local police force taking control. None of them particularly senior since the crime-scenes had all been fairly rural. A lot of these stations were increasingly under-manned.

'So why don't you go and tell them?' she said.

He laughed and shrugged and gave her a rapid hug. She was nobody's fool when she put her mind to it. He would rather rely on the cleaner than almost anyone.

'I've tried,' he confessed. 'They wouldn't listen. Which is why I'm thinking of going it on my own.' Edwina might think he was barmy but this woman didn't. 'I just happen to think I'm right,' he persisted.

'So do something about it,' she said.

'You don't think, then, that I'm totally barking?'

'Not if you say not.' She had a healthy admiration for William's intelligence. Pity that uppity wife didn't share her view. Hard as nails, was Mrs P's private opinion. Also totally devoid of charm. In a fair world, she'd come unstuck in the end. And Mrs P would definitely be there, cheering.

Edwina, predictably, showed her usual lack of interest when William tentatively outlined his master plan. It was as he'd expected – she was so immersed in her own small world, she found domestic trivia trite and boring. He didn't, for once, plan to involve Morwenna, but would leave her for the day with Polly's nanny. He was owed a good few favours by some of the local mothers, which he knew he could always call in if he needed to. Moral support when he felt he could use it, though now was not yet quite the time. He needed to do more investigation, to seek out any more details missed by the media. To get his facts in order before taking things any higher, or else they would think he was seriously out of his tree.

He overcame Edwina's immediate disapproval simply by telling a whopping lie, not his usual style. The less she knew, the better, at least for now. She would only scold him for wasting time and give him a list of household chores still waiting to be done. If only he'd put that sort of energy into finding a proper job. Nag, nag, nag; he was used to her acid tongue. It was easier not to tell her what he was doing.

'Cambridge?' she'd said, with only marginal interest. 'Who there can possibly be offering you employment?'

'The Fitzwilliam,' he lied promptly, without so much as a flicker. 'They want to extend their map division and I have the necessary knowhow.'

'Well, I hope it won't mean us having to uproot.' As usual, she put her own convenience first. She had no need to worry; he would tell her they'd turned him down. Nothing very new in that; it had happened so often before.

'Well, don't be back too late,' was all she said. She wanted that child safely fed and filed away before she got home from work.

The *Argus* offices were hidden up a narrow side-street, close to the town centre. William arrived there late morning and trudged up three flights to a shabby door with a peeling notice inviting him to enter. *The Evening News* was the dominant local paper, this just the also-ran. There was only one person in the large and cluttered office, a harassed-looking youth with specs and a crop of acne, studiously working on an ancient PC, surrounded by heaps of old clippings. Taking him for the office boy, William looked round hopefully for an adult.

'Yes?' said the lad as he bashed away. 'Anything I can help you with?'

William explained that he was looking for the reporter who had stumbled across the body of Jasmine Brookes.

The youth instantaneously brightened and pushed back his keyboard, glad of any distraction from a tedious job.

'That's me,' he said, extending one bony hand. 'Tim Hardy. Crime reporter. At your service.'

'Crime reporter?'

'Plus general dogsbody.' He grinned. 'A little bit of everything, in fact.'

Since it was very nearly lunchtime and the phones were hardly ringing, Tim was content just to shut up shop and lead William round the corner to the pub. Something about this visitor vaguely intrigued him, the familiar manic gleam of a driven man. This menial job was mainly solid drudgery with the occasional high spot in between. He grabbed his notebook and cheerfully accompanied his visitor down the stairs.

Tim turned out to be older than he looked, as well as considerably more clued up. They carried their beers to an out-of-the-way table where William sketched out his main thesis. Cautiously at first till he saw the reciprocal light in the younger man's eye. To describe himself as a crime reporter was stretching the truth quite a bit. Tim's actual job was a hotchpotch of minutiae as he learned the newspaper business from the bottom. But crime reporting was what he'd set his heart on, with Wapping, or something similar, his ultimate goal. He dreamed of one day having his own byline in one of the national dailies. If only he could chance upon that first elusive break. He was keen, committed and definitely up for it. William's sort of chap.

Without weighing him down with too much detail, William briefly outlined his thinking thus far. He had little more than a gut feeling, he was bound to admit, that the murders might, in some so far unspecified way, be linked. That, substantiated by his professional observations of the lie of the land on the Ordnance Survey map. The knowledge he'd gained from years of studying maps had given him an experienced eye for detail. He would sketch in more if Tim would let him, though it still remained very much a long shot. Tim listened alertly, scribbling the odd note, enthusiasm bubbling up as William talked.

'You're saying you think they could all be the work of one killer? Like the Yorkshire Ripper or his predecessor perhaps?' The crimes were certainly grotesque enough and might well have a similar MO. Only, instead of street trash and ladies of the night, aimed at the opposite end of the spectrum, the principled and clean-living. Tim had witnessed first-hand what had happened to Jasmine. It wasn't exactly how William would have worded it, but the younger man had obviously got the gist. He nodded. He was encouraged to have encountered a kindred spirit; these days such devotion to detail was all too thin on the ground.

'So what next?' Tim asked him, with rising excitement. 'Oughtn't you now be taking it to the police?'

William shook his head. 'Not yet.' He was adamant. He explained about the doltish bobby who had so witheringly dismissed him in Alton Coombe. And his later conversation with the Northampton police. He was not

184

going to risk another snub, not till he had more substance to back him up. It would only be counter-productive. If it worked at all.

'Tell me all you know about Jasmine Brookes.' Now it was William's turn to take notes.

'There's not a lot more I can add,' said Tim honestly. 'It looked, at first, like nothing much more than just a casual break-in. Not even that, to be strictly accurate, because the door wasn't even locked. Whoever it was must have been there waiting, since the cat had also been clobbered. Some sort of *crime passionnel,* I would guess. Even a revenge killing. Or a stalker.'

'Someone she knew, is that what you're suggesting? One of her pupils maybe?'

'Well, hardly.' Tim laughed and scratched his spiky hair. 'Yoga fanatics aren't usually quite that short-fused. Doesn't exactly go with the job description.' Not in a village this close to Cambridge. It was all far too civilised round here.

'Family or any significant others?'

'Not that we know of so far. It seems she'd always been something of a gypsy. Only back in this country a matter of months. There was one thing further,' he remembered after a pause. 'As I entered the cottage to check things out, I distinctly heard a powerful engine revving up in the background. A motorbike, I would say, with a hyped-up engine. Close to the cottage and going off hell for leather. I forgot all about it when I found her.' The trauma of the discovery had driven it out of his mind.

'Tell you what,' he added when William had replenished

their pints. 'What you've just told me might make an interesting filler. Mind if I write it up for the paper? All that stuff about cartography and studying the lie of the land? And your theory of linking the crimes together topographically. You never know what it might uncover.' Already he could see that dreamed-of byline looming.

William gave it serious consideration. Just so long as it didn't in any way implicate him. He dared not risk a ruthless killer getting wind of the fact he was possibly on his trail. That would be irresponsible because of the family. Yet it might provoke interest in the appropriate quarter, in which case he'd be doing a public service.

'Okay,' he said eventually. 'Provided you keep my name out of it.' Tim, as eager as a greyhound in the slips, nodded before he'd even had time to think.

'No problem,' he said, flicking to a fresh page. 'Now, mind if we run those details through one more time?'

William's heart softened. He was being overly cautious. It was good to encounter enthusiasm that matched his own. If the police wouldn't listen to a private citizen, a newspaper piece would carry much more of a punch. It wasn't a national, true, but a beginning. The *Argus* had a steady readership. One look at Tim's flushed face and bright eyes and he hadn't the heart to say no.

'Go on,' he said. 'And do your damnedest. The very least it can do is stir things up.'

19

More, as it happened, than William could have guessed. A hornet's nest of quite alarming proportions. For a day or two after his meeting with Tim he put it all out of his mind. Firework night had already been and gone, and the weather grew progressively wetter. A nasty draught blew in under the kitchen door and William promised faithfully that he would see to it at the weekend, when he had time to pop over to B & Q for the necessary bits and bobs.

'Don't forget,' said Edwina sternly, aware of the still-dripping tap. For the life of her, she couldn't see why he didn't go right away, but William had plans of his own for that morning which he didn't intend to discuss.

Edwina was fretting about Christmas already, refusing to pipe down till it was sorted. Normally they went to her parents in Highgate, to the grim rambling house at the top of the hill, with its book-lined rooms that were inadequately heated, where a child could lose herself for hours and not be missed. Her mother, harking back to her European heritage, inevitably cooked a goose, while the professor made a pompous flourish of carving, at the same time expounding on some weighty subject which sucked all merriment from the spirit of the day. William was always relieved to get away. At least, since the Fairchilds possessed no television, there was nothing to prevent them returning home as soon as the meal had been cleared. No waiting around for the Queen; no crackers or board games nor charades. Not even a reading from *A Child's Christmas in Wales*, something he always regretted. It had thrilled him to the core when he had listened to it in his youth, but the Fairchilds considered even Dylan Thomas trivial. Usually they were back in time for tea and the Bond movie in front of a roasting fire. Hillgate Village couldn't match the grandeur of Edwina's parental pile but at least it was friendly, brightly painted and warm, if cluttered with toys and general mess. A living environment for an active child. A home.

This year, for a change, Edwina was set on showing off. For the first time since their marriage she had decided to host the lunch herself and dazzle her critical parents with her newly found housekeeping skills. If William could handle it on a daily basis, it surely couldn't be that hard, and there were loads of trendy new books around on the subject of Christmas lunch. With a growing child, it was time to play domestic, and once and for all prove to her mother that she was finally a fully fledged adult. They would get a tree, a turkey and all the trimmings and, for a change, push out the culinary boat. William could take care of all the draggy details – the shopping, the tidying, the table setting – while Edwina worked her magic in the kitchen.

All her life she had craved centre stage but was far less hot on the chores. William didn't mind. Christmas to him, with a hyped-up infant in tow, was a season of genuine delight. He, in his role of protective parent, had the joy of seeing it all through her bedazzled eyes, while Edwina was seriously missing out. He preferred to keep quiet about the special treats. Hence this morning's furtive expedition to Harrods.

Mrs P was hoovering when they returned at half past twelve. She poked her nose round the living-room door and told him he'd had a phonecall.

'Someone called James Brown,' she said. 'Didn't leave a message or say what he wanted. I told him you'd certainly be back by lunchtime.'

William shrugged. The name rang no bells. Presumably, if it was important, he'd call again. He peeled off Morwenna's outer layers and switched on the television in the play-room. With a bit of luck, he'd have a relaxing half-hour before he needed to think about anything else. The door-bell rang.

'I'll get it,' he called to Mrs P, who was virtually out of earshot because of the hoover.

He opened the door and was halted in his tracks. A camera boom was looming in his face.

'James Brown from Anglia Television,' said a smooth young man. 'About your murder theories in the *Argus*.'

William, stunned, for a moment was lost for words. Then: 'What the hell are you talking about?' he said.

189

'The piece in yesterday's paper. About a serial killer. Is it true you believe that a new one is on the rampage? Mind if we come in and talk? I know all our viewers will be fascinated.'

James Brown himself was a mild man in a blazer; it was the cameraman who William wanted to hit. A sound engineer stuck his mike in William's face, causing him instinctively to step back. The very thing he had wanted to avoid, and now they were getting footage of his house. After a frenzied few seconds, he pulled himself together and managed to get back inside and slam the door.

'No comment!' he roared through the letterbox. Wait till he got his hands on that traitor, Tim Hardy. He'd have more on his face than acne to worry about.

'What do you think you were doing?' he asked when he finally got through to Tim. 'I expressly asked to be kept right out of it.' Now the whole world knew what he looked like and where he lived. Luckily he'd had the presence of mind to stay shtoom. Up to a point. His head began to ache when he thought about all he'd told Tim.

'Sorry,' mumbled Tim, though actually he was elated. When Anglia Television had called, he hadn't hesitated. Slip them a few good stories like that and who knew where it all might lead. He rather fancied a stint himself in front of the cameras. It was only a matter of time. And William was making too much of a fuss. He ought to be grateful for the coverage. Slightly mollified – he never stayed cross for long – William was forced to agree it had been nifty footwork. And he hadn't said a word on camera so, with luck, it could do him no real harm. Just never trust a journalist, he thought. Tim Hardy had his uses but must be watched.

It was extraordinary, really, how few people seemed to have caught William's fleeting moment of fame. Of course they ran the item, with James Brown outside William's closed front door, with the name of the street and number clearly visible. It simply went to illustrate how blinkered the public could be. He quietly heaved a grateful sigh of relief. He had to put up with a bit of flak from Edwina, whose colleagues had pounced on it and now wouldn't leave it alone. Kept ribbing her about amateur sleuths, which showed they knew her husband wasn't working. He might not care but she most certainly did. Especially when they had an irate call from the head of the Cambridgeshire police, ordering William to cease his meddling or else risk facing prosecution. If only he'd put his mind to getting a regular job, none of this sort of thing would happen.

'Why didn't you talk to me first?' she scolded. William simply shrugged as he dished up the meatballs. The truth was he'd known she would not be remotely interested and had wanted to avoid another domestic ding-dong. He had done his bit for the public good and was in no way fazed by the police reaction. Now that he'd even calmed down over Tim, he was curious to see what happened next.

* * *

'So you're actually doing the cooking this year?' Meryl and Sue were impressed. Edwina's blatant lack of domesticity had long been a bit of a joke, and the pair never tired of making fun of the house husband, eternally chained to the stove. Sue, as efficient as a field marshal herself, always had everything in order, but Meryl, the loner, only ever ate out and was secretly more than a little envious. Christmas to her loomed large and alarming; she was angling for an invitation to join them. Otherwise it would have to be the Maldives again, but she had no one she liked enough to go with. Again, the tragedy of the single life. She could not understand Edwina's discontent.

'How *is* Poirot?' asked Sue with a grin. She had caught the newsflash, been impressed by his air of authority. Especially the moment he had slammed the door. That had been perhaps his finest hour. There was clearly more to William than she'd ever imagined. He had even, in that one split second, looked rather dashing.

Edwina sighed and theatrically rolled her eyes. She was sick of the inevitable chaffing.

'I only wish he'd find himself a proper grown-up job.' The same old heartfelt cry, sincerely meant. She was worried about this new fascination with all these gruesome crimes. It wasn't quite healthy; she blamed Mrs P. And feared for what it might be doing to Morwenna. Too much morbid gossip in her presence. No telling the effect on her delicate psyche. She might end up an axe murderer or a doped-out anorexic. These days almost anything was possible.

'But he adores Morwenna,' said Sue with approval. She found the pair of them together very dear. If only her own husband could spare the kids more of his time, but Nick was increasingly out of the country and, when he came home, was whacked. Luckily they had the wherewithal to afford round-the-clock childminding, but from all she'd heard about Edwina's new e-company, she would shortly be in a similar position. More so, in fact, from the recent rave in the papers. Edwina and Gareth were set to make a killing.

Which brought them neatly to their regular topic, Edwina's budding affair.

'So how's it going?' Meryl, though openly covetous, was seriously eager to know. Some women, it seemed, had all the luck. It was positively piggy of Edwina to want Gareth when she already had the dishy William at home. Talk about dog in the manger.

Despite her natural caution, Edwina instantly lit up. It was currently her favourite subject and she loved to speak his name, though still feeling slightly awkward that they knew. Sometimes she saw what a fool she was being, couldn't believe he wouldn't dump her very soon. But she needed to discuss it, to run it through one more time, and these were her two closest intimates in the world. Especially now she seemed to be drifting away from William. Of course it was not something she could ever share with him, but she often yearned for his counsel, even on this. They had always been such buddies, before things had started to come unstuck. William was so calm and level-headed, he'd be the one to tell her what she should do. She bet that awful Polly Graham shared secrets of this intensity with him, occasionally wished he weren't so annoyingly discreet. She wasn't sure she trusted that woman at all.

'He wants me to go to Rome with him. Has a financial meeting there next week.' He'd even suggested that they do it quite openly; they were, after all, business partners. In the run-up to Christmas there would be loads of festivities. She could do her present shopping there as well. But Edwina knew she'd never handle the guilt. How could she look her husband in the eye and tell him such a major untruth? He'd see straight through her, was bound to do so. She would blush and stumble and give it all away. And then the shit would seriously hit the fan and, before she knew it, she would lose him. She had rehearsed this scenario over and over again and needed her two friends' wisdom and support.

They looked at each other, Sue with one eyebrow raised. She devoutly believed in preserving the bird in hand.

'Is it really worth it?' she said sensibly, guessing the inevitable outcome. From all Edwina had told them, the man was a louse. The flush on Edwina's cheek and the manic light in her eye told them all that they needed to know. Meryl, on her third consecutive cigarette, wanted more details of what he was like.

Edwina giggled like a lovelorn teen and buried her burning face in both her hands. 'I can't begin to describe it,' she said. 'Better than anyone else I have ever been with.'

'So tell us,' demanded Meryl. 'Chapter and verse. Remember some of us live through you vicariously.' It was a hard admission but accurate. She hadn't been sexually active for a while. There were times she could strangle Edwina, who had it all, and was vain and showy and heartless as she bragged. But Meryl loved a bit of lascivious chat; the dirt was far too tempting to ignore. Also, she still had an eye on Gareth for herself, was prepared to hang in there long-term.

'Well,' said Edwina, inhaling deeply. 'For starters, he has the most versatile tongue I've ever known.' And was off, amid gusts of infectious laughter, while Sue and Meryl couldn't help themselves, swept along by the sheer vulgarity of it all.

'It will all end in tears,' prophesied Sue as they filtered outside. Edwina had already left them in a rush, anxious to get home before she was missed. She was balanced precariously on such a sharp knife's edge, one slip and she knew she would be finished. And it wasn't just William she would ultimately lose, but possibly her beloved daughter as well. And what would her parents have to say about *that*? It was more than her fevered brain could possibly encompass.

'But she's having such a ball,' said Meryl wistfully. If only such a thing would happen to her. She was always on her own, eternally on the hunt. And he did sound total dynamite in the sack.

'And,' she added, climbing into a cab, 'she never did tell us whether or not she's going.'

* * *

They took a brisk walk when the rain finally ceased, though the storm clouds still lingered overhead. By half past three it would be almost completely dark so they couldn't stay out for very long. There weren't many people about in this weather and William thought himself crazy as they progressed. Just one fast circuit of the Round Pond, he told Morwenna, and then they would head for the Muffin Man and tea. She liked the shops, especially now at Christmas, straight out of the picture books they loved. All the Kensington lampstands were adorned with lighted fir trees, and Morwenna would clap her hands with delight and coo. He smiled at her predictability, then caught a glimpse of a figure he thought he knew.

Close to the palace, where the rollerbladers practised, a man in a shabby duffel coat stood forlornly watching the swans. A sharp breeze ruffled his thinning hair; he looked the essence of misery. For a second William was touched with compassion, then all his earlier misgivings flooded back. The man was nothing but a layabout and certainly up to no good. For what other reason would he be always hanging round children? They quickened their pace to hurry straight past him but the man had already turned and shuffled away.

She was a right little cherub once he'd got her into the bath, bright red cheeks and a rosy nose, with dancing raisin-black eyes. Her silky hair fell in a thick fringe like his own and soon would need to be cut. But now, freshly clean and wrapped cosily in a bath towel, she looked so scrumptious he could eat her.

'Grrrrr,' he said fiercely, pretending to nibble her toes, and she squealed with spontaneous delight. How could anyone hurt them? thought William as he carried her gently up to her bed. Predictably, Edwina was still not back from work. He was becoming seriously irritated by these over-extended absences. Even if she had stopped loving him, she ought to be here with her daughter. Two years old was a precious time and a small baby girl needs a mother. It was all to do with this damned dotcom rubbish. He wished she had never got caught up in it. She worked far too hard and was turning into a shrew. He couldn't hold her attention any more.

He was closing the book when the front door slammed.

'Hi!' called Edwina breezily up the stairs.

'Shush!' said William fiercely, going out on to the landing. Morwenna had just dropped off to sleep; it would be criminal to wake her now. Edwina shrugged and slipped out of her coat, then went to the fridge for a glass of wine. She looked entirely ravishing, with her mass of luxuriant hair and a heightened glow to her cheeks, he presumed from the cold. She was wearing a suede skirt he couldn't remember seeing before, and her hair had sprouted subtle aubergine tints. If he didn't love her so much, it would be that much easier, but it still gave William a pang to see her this way. They met at the foot of the stairs and she gave him a hug. She smelled deliciously of some expensive soap, and he led the way back into the kitchen.

Supper was almost ready; he poured himself a scotch. He only needed to microwave the veg and then they could sit down.

'Oh, by the way,' said Edwina later, after they had made a makeshift sort of peace. It was Friday night, with the whole weekend ahead, and he'd privately vowed he would try to woo her back. It was not her fault, the way she had been raised, driven to excel in everything. If only those monsters in Highgate had given it any thought, they'd have allowed her a proper childhood. She was, after all, Morwenna's mother, and at times he saw flashes of it in her smile. Like now. He reached across to stroke her peach-like skin. Perhaps tonight, if he offered to rub her feet . . .

'I have to go to Birmingham on Wednesday,' said Edwina. 'For a two-day convention, an electronics fair. I may stay on through the weekend, too. We all of us at the office agree it's important.'

The slight edge in her voice challenged him, as though she expected some opposition yet was ready to fight her corner if she had to. It was she, after all, who currently paid all the bills.

William had heard it all before and no longer particularly cared. He returned her challenging stare without comment; it simply wasn't worth it. Just when he was beginning to warm to her again, he saw her as a shallow conniving bitch whom he didn't much like any more. He was well accustomed to being shoved around. She would doubtless just assume that he would cope.

20

*I*t was purely by fluke that I happened to catch that news-flash. I had lost the habit of watching television when I embarked upon all this cloak and dagger stuff. Even a small portable would be cumbersome to lug about and was likely to slow me down if I needed to run. Mostly I spend my evenings nose in a book, though I also read the papers pretty thoroughly. Somehow I'd managed to miss the Argus piece or, believe me, I'd have been out of there faster than light. As it was, the shock was enough to have given me a coronary. I swear my heart stopped in my chest for a solid second.

I had been pondering who on my hit list should be the next: the social worker, the politician, even the unfortunate bank-rupt. Though he, poor fellow, had taken so many low blows and even I am not entirely without heart. Except that his current sad state didn't excuse him or alter the past. He had not been quite so community-spirited in the days before his fortunes took a tumble. Of the three remaining, he'd be the hardest to pinpoint, though already I had an approximate lead as to where he might be found. It would mean another massive upheaval, but by now I am more than used to that. I never stay anywhere longer than I need, except, of course, for the covering of my tracks.

It was largely a geographical choice as I worked my way around my web. The politician would, of course, be the hardest of all to finger, but I rather relished the danger of it all. My victims so far had all been relatively ordinary. This man was known to be wily and corrupt as well as constantly surrounded by heavy security. It was the challenge that most attracted me here; I saw him as the acme of my desires. Meanwhile I'd be patient and sharpen my teeth on the rest of the list. At least he was unlikely to slip out of sight, with the eyes of the world's media upon him. Also there was a general election brewing. The ideal time to strike for mega publicity.

I came home early with the start of a shivery cold, to be waylaid by my landlady the moment I opened the door. She was hovering in the hallway, as she very often did, anxious for some company, poor soul. She invited me into her chintzy parlour for a glass of sherry while she watched the evening news. Sherry would not normally be my preferred choice, but my head was pounding, my nose bunged up and I found the cosiness of the room enticing. Upstairs my own quarters were depressingly sparse and chilly. A few moments lingering down here could do me no harm.

'Dreadful business about the murder,' she said cheerfully, passing me the macadamia nuts. And there he was on the screen right behind her, some keen young news reporter in a blazer, standing outside a closed front door in a street that looked up-market, even for Cambridge. 'Hillgate Street,' the sign said clearly, plus 'Royal Borough of Kensington and Chelsea'. London, then; I looked that much more intently. What in the world had this to do with them?

'Pull your chair a little closer to the fire.'

I wanted to tell her sharply to shut up. He spoke with solemn authority about this latest murder and seemed to have a theory he was aching to share. Something to do with an article in the Argus. And a possible serial killer striking again.

'It's parky out there tonight,' she chirped, unaware of my palpitations. 'You don't want to go taking too many risks with your health.' If she only knew the half of it. She must have noticed my pallor. 'Some yoga teacher,' she explained, once more drowning him out. It turned out she'd seen it all before, at lunchtime.

'Murdered in her own cottage. No more than a half-mile from here.' She shuddered with positive relish as she topped up my glass. Twelve years a widow with her children flown the nest. It was clear that she was lonely and looking for friends. But what was it he was saying now? I did my best to shush her. No disrespect, but I desperately needed to know. My safety could well depend upon it, perhaps, indeed, my life. I couldn't believe I had possibly been so careless. It turned out this was one James Brown, a rising Anglia star, following up a story from yesterday's paper. Based on the ingenious reckoning of some unknown backroom boffin, who had talked, it appeared, quite expansively to the Argus. I leaned a little closer, straining my ears, and finally, thank goodness, she got the message. Together we sat in silence and listened to the rest.

'This is where Mr Huxley lives. A cartographer by profession.'

It wasn't exactly Number Ten but looked very nice all the same. He strode up purposefully and rang the doorbell, and then came the humorous part. After a short pause, the door was flung open by a man with shaggy dark hair and an engaging grin. Until he heard what Mr Brown had to say, when he acted like a badly scalded cat. Backing off with one arm protectively raised, he virtually told the crew where to stick their sound boom. Before brusquely slamming the door in their foolish faces. I have to say, I warmed to him for that. And also to them for the fact that it hadn't been cut. They were either inept or else had airspace to fill. But now I knew what he looked like, this William Huxley, as well as, even more handily, where he lived. Obviously Mr James Brown hadn't thought about that.

The programme cut to a newspaper office, where the youth responsible for the original article was eager to expand on the little he knew – or thought he knew; it was clear he hadn't totally grasped it. A lot of cheap blah about maps and things; I almost expected the phases of the moon. I would have been smirking along with the rest, if only I hadn't been so scared. For this total stranger, this amiable Mr Huxley, seemed unnervingly right on my wavelength. Something I'd never encountered before, other than that one occasion, long ago. And look at all the damage that had led to.

It is seven long years since I embarked on this crusade, the first months simply spent in detailed research. After I discharged myself, when the crying finally ceased, I wandered alone in a hostile world, not knowing what to do with the rest of my life.

Steeped in self-pity, half crippled with grief, I must have cut a very sorry figure. When I'd held that frail dying body in my arms, I had cursed the God who'd forsaken me and vowed that somehow some day I would have my revenge. For whatever my sin, it did not deserve a punishment this harsh. All I did, after all, was fall in love. No wonder, in the end, they locked me up.

Often I have wondered about Marina and whether she'd have the guts to try tracking me down, when all the while, unsuspected by me, this amateur sleuth had been stealthily closing in. My entire campaign appeared suddenly under threat; I hadn't felt quite this crazed since I left the clinic. My heart was hammering in my chest; my forehead dripped with sweat; I found myself starting to hyperventilate. What I needed more than anything was a drink – a real drink, not this pathetic old-lady sherry. But I knew that she kept no whisky in the house. I longed to be able to crawl into bed but my time, it now appeared, was running out.

I emptied my glass then tottered upstairs to pack. Whatever I did, I must not risk arousing her suspicions. She followed me into the hall and patted my arm. Said she hoped I realised how welcome I was and that she'd like to get to know me better. I felt almost sad for her in her solitary cocoon until I recalled the imminent danger and dragged myself upstairs to think of a plan. Talk about the biter bit, I could hardly credit I could have been so blinkered. For in all this time it had never once occurred that I ought to be keeping watch over my own shoulder.

*   *   *

After a sleepless night, I managed at last to get a grip and hastily threw my few possessions together. Whoever this man Huxley might be, he had to be stopped immediately before his meddling attracted any more attention. Of one thing, though, I did remain smugly confident. Smart though he might be, he was not as smart as me.

I told my landlady that I'd had bad news and regretfully had to be leaving right away. She seemed to be genuinely sorry. I rather think she liked me quite a lot. One good thing, she was well in pocket since I had paid my rent a month in advance. So we parted friends and I promised to keep in touch as she stood on the doorstep, tearfully waving me off. I have to say, I found that incredibly touching.

'Where to?' asked the driver.

I thought fast. 'The station. As quick as you can.'

For I had a pressing assignation in London that couldn't any longer be delayed. And was adding another name to the original hit list.

Part Three

21

Edwina held a deeply rooted conviction, relic of her own over-protected childhood, that her daughter's life could well be endangered should she fail to receive her regular jabs. William didn't agree with such faddishness. His own haphazard childhood had been virtually illness-free without the intervention of any induced antibodies. A good healthy diet of dirt and germs was guaranteed to inoculate you naturally against the minor hazards of growing up. He believed in allowing nature to take its course, was wary of unnecessary meddling. But anything for a quiet life. Edwina, of late, had been acting like the proverbial bear. Or, perhaps more aptly, a cat on a hot tin roof.

He had held off fixing a date with the surgery until they'd got safely clear of Christmas. There was too much action on the party front right now for him to want to risk Morwenna being out of sorts. Which these jabs, he knew from past experience, were more than likely to make her, poor little mite. So much for modern medicine and all the phoney jargon they spouted now. Once, however, the twelve days were past and the tree and all the litter

207

cleared away, he did give into Edwina's viperous tongue and arranged the necessary appointment. Reluctantly, though it could have a silver lining. There was, after all, always the possibility that he might encounter the delectable Asian doctor again. And thus have a chance to continue their conversation. He was far too bashful to seek her out directly.

The waiting room was packed – he had never known it this busy – with miserable adults, most surely skiving, though with runny noses and convincingly hacking coughs. William's immediate instinct was to turn right round and leave. Morwenna stood a far more likely chance of picking up infection here than from roaming the streets with him, safe in her stroller, in the bracing freshness of the outdoor air. But, with the receptionist's gimlet eye already upon him, it was now too late to run away. He meekly gave her their names, then found himself a vacant seat and picked up an ancient magazine.

He was pissed off with Edwina and glad of some space in which to brood. She had behaved throughout Christmas like the prima donna she was, and the presence of her parents hadn't helped. Whatever she did now was glorious in their eyes. The endless nagging criticism of her somewhat oppressed childhood had changed to near beatification. Her father, especially, was thrilled with her recent achievements and crunched numbers over lunch until William wanted to scream. This was supposed to be a joyous family occasion. Primarily for the child. It was the height of bad manners to talk business at table. If anyone should be the focal point, it was Morwenna, not her mother. Her doting grandmother fawned upon her but Arnold, as always, ignored her. No wonder Edwina had grown up the way she had. Invisible to her father, too, until she had gained her post-pubescent looks. And now he behaved like an ardent suitor. With her heightened beauty and sparkling eyes, William could well see why, though he didn't approve.

Something in Edwina had subtly altered, more than just the promise of huge success. She flirted with her father as he praised her hit-and-miss cooking, while acting as though William were barely there. He was allowed to serve and carve and clear away, but the accolades were exclusively for her. Doing it here had turned out to be a mistake. At least in Highgate they could gobble their food and run without being bored to death by the pompous old fart.

'Next, please.'

A tottering elderly woman, bent double with age or arthritis, followed the doctor meekly into her surgery. William glanced around. Three receptionists were at it full tilt while a drably dressed minion lurked silently at the back, mindlessly filing papers from a trolley. The phones never ceased. Was it always this bad, or was the post-holiday pestilence really a fact? He looked around for his daughter and saw her happily occupied on the floor. She sat alone amid a sea of discarded toys, triumphantly queen of her own domain, unchallenged. No Nathan nor Laura to bicker or interfere. She was having the time of her life. William returned to his morose train of thought, comfortable in the knowledge that she was safe.

It was the four days in Birmingham that had done it, he was positive. Before that Edwina had been jumpy and overstrung, but William had always understood because of the dotcom launch. They were calling the company fast.bucks.com, which seemed to sum it all up: gambling with other people's earnings. Privately, William wasn't sure he approved. He had long suspected that things weren't quite as rosy as she painted them but had learned, since their marriage, when not to interfere. When she needed him, she would let him know. He was prepared just to sit and wait. She hated anything that smacked of advice and was liable to accuse him of being patronising. Which was all well and good. His own talents lay more in the artistic field; he had never laid claim to much of a business brain. But he was good at logic and could usually see things clearly. And certainly didn't share her erratic temperament. Birmingham appeared to have been some kind of watershed. His wife had returned an entirely different person – spiky and unravelled, inclined to shouting fits. And William still hadn't worked out why.

They had been there already close on fifty minutes and Morwenna was growing bored. She started to miss the company of her peers and let out a loud and imperious wail. William resignedly closed his *Country Life*, of which he had read not a single word, and prepared to go to her aid, the attentive father. But when he looked up, he saw someone had got there first. The drably clothed woman from the filing area was squatting on the floor beside the child.

'Sorry about that,' said William apologetically, swinging Morwenna up into his arms, thus detaching her from her chosen toy. Tears of frustrated anger ran down her flushed little face and she kicked him sharply with her sturdy boots, causing him to wince and almost drop her. The woman instinctively held out her arms and Morwenna went into them uncomplainingly.

'What is it, babe?' asked William, stroking her face. She was obviously on the brink of working herself up into a tantrum. 'It won't be long now.' He smiled and grimaced slightly at the woman. She quickly returned Morwenna to him, then hurriedly backed away to her laden trolley. She was slight and dark, some kind of foreigner he thought. He couldn't even be sure that she understood.

'Not long now, sir,' said the receptionist, who had been watching. 'You are high on the list to see the nurse. I am sorry you've had to wait so long.'

'No problem.' William, with his customary good manners, smiled and nodded and soothed Morwenna until her frustration gradually ebbed.

'Good girl.' He kissed her on the forehead, then joined her on the floor to play with the Lego. Little hope now of seeing the Asian beauty. There had been so many comings and goings but still not a glimpse of her. He was out of luck.

*   *   *

Edwina, poor darling, was frantically busting a gut in a frenzy of anguish at what she had done. Which was go far too far. This was not what she'd intended, not at the very start. She was paralysed with terror now that William would find out. She loved him, yes she loved him still despite their drifting apart. It was just that their daily routine had become pretty jaded.

'That's what starting a family does,' Sue had explained to her sensibly last night. And even Meryl had nodded her head. It was part of her wildest dream.

'Sameness,' Sue echoed. 'It's as well to get away from it.' But how? Edwina wanted to cry, when one of you's out of work? At least Sue's Nick spent much of his time abroad. William was constantly there underfoot, waiting for her to return, with a meal cooked and ready. Saintly and uncomplaining, hard to take.

'You should be so lucky,' said Sue. 'Most women would kill for what you guys have got.'

'Enough of all this,' said Meryl with hopeful relish. 'Cut to the chase. Tell us about Rome.'

It had been beyond all her wildest expectations and now she was horribly scared that she might be in love.

The Via Veneto two weeks before Christmas. Where better for the start of an affair? The sky was cloudless and a deep vibrant blue, and the air as soft and balmy as early spring. Edwina, dressed for her Birmingham subterfuge, discarded her boots and topcoat on the spot. She had had the intelligence to pack a lightweight pantsuit and soon was even strolling in her shirt-sleeves. Gareth steered her in and out of the smart boutiques and wanted to buy her something as a memento. Edwina refused. What they were doing was already quite sinful enough without him compounding it with gifts. And how in the world could she ever explain them to William? He wasn't particularly observant, not about fripperies like clothes, but still she knew she'd be crazy to take such a risk.

He had booked them into a chic hotel, more opulent than Edwina would have chosen, where champagne on ice was awaiting them in the suite. They were, he reminded her, on the brink of mega riches. If they didn't start sampling it now they were out of their minds. And look what could happen when the sluice-gates finally burst. They might be too swamped with work to have time to spend.

'Here's to you, my darling,' he said, kissing her softly, then hung up the 'Do Not Disturb' sign on the door. The meeting, of course, was a fake; he had made it up. It was simply a devious excuse for a spot of dalliance away from the prying eyes of their business associates. About the husband he really didn't care. He was far too wet to be likely to cotton on. And what the hell if he did? It wasn't Gareth's marriage that was at risk.

For three solid days they hardly left that room, except for occasional forays into the street. At the cocktail hour, when the locals began their stately evening promenade, they would throw on some clothes and go out to observe them, clutching each other with poorly concealed lust, anxious only to knock down their drinks and scuttle back up to their suite. It was magic. She had never known sex as raunchy or as thrilling. She surrendered herself to him completely.

'So you didn't get to see much of the sights?' grinned Meryl. Edwina shook her head. They had taken a coach tour on that first afternoon, but from then on their pursuits had been more libidinous. She was sated, she was ecstatic, still high on an adrenalin rush. Her mind was entirely preoccupied with Gareth; she wasn't thinking straight any more.

'So what happens next?' asked Sue, the hardened prag-matist. She hated to see Edwina in such a state. She had so much to be grateful for with that really decent marriage. Surely she wasn't going to risk it all on a whim. And from what they'd heard, Mr Prendergast wasn't to be trusted. It very much looked like a disaster in the making.

'All I know,' said Edwina defiantly, 'is that I love him. He is far more exciting than William ever was. Has shown me things I never even imagined.'

Sue and Meryl exchanged a sly glance. Meryl was dying to hear the sordid details but spoilsport Edwina announced that she had to go. She needed to come down to earth for a while until she could talk things through properly with her lover. Christmas away from him had been purgatory. She just couldn't wait to reconnect.

They walked home briskly through the biting cold, William singing rousing choruses of 'Incy, Wincy Spider' in order to sustain Morwenna's flagging spirits. Her nose was running and he stopped to dab it dry. He knew he shouldn't have taken her into that polluted atmosphere. If she'd caught a cold he'd be very angry indeed and blame it all on the hapless Edwina, who was currently well out of favour.

Right on the corner of the turn-off up the hill was a tiny French patisserie and, impulsively, he pushed the stroller through the door, into the delicious warmth of the sugar-sweet atmosphere, and allowed Morwenna to choose whatever she wanted to go with her juice. Doctor's appointments always included some extra pampering. It was part of the unwritten law of being a parent. Morwenna brightened instantly and chose a cheery meringue snowman with a cherry nose. The girl was about to pop it in a bag but Morwenna insisted on eating it there on the spot. When she put down her foot that was it; she was very much her mother's daughter. William smiled apologetically and ordered a cappuccino. Come to think of it, he could do with a treat himself and he liked the vanilla-scented snugness of the place. There were four small wrought-iron tables ranged along one wall, so he unbuckled Morwenna from the stroller and plonked her on one of the chairs, while he went to examine the pastries.

When he returned, someone else had come in and was seated at the table by the window. A man in an overcoat, absorbed in his newspaper, facing away from Morwenna towards the door. Morwenna, with icing sugar all over her chin, beamed her little angel's smile and kicked her feet in delight. She was very easily mollified, this child. That was his own sunny nature shining through. William smiled down at her and ruffled the glossy dark hair.

'All right, pet? Would you like some juice? I'm quite sure that, if you are very, very good, they can rustle you up some orange.'

The waitress obligingly brought their drinks over and lingered awhile for a chat. William, a regular, was in no hurry. They had half the morning still ahead as well as the afternoon.

'Nasty weather.'

'Freezing.'

'Wouldn't be surprised if it snows.' She had lumpy thighs and a too-short skirt but her smile was positively seraphic. She tickled Morwenna under the chin then generously topped up her orange. She admired this man who was such a great dad, dreamed of knowing him better. The man at the next table coughed politely as he waited for his bill. The waitress scribbled it and he paid in loose change. William, glancing up, recognised him immediately from his bony wrists and chewed nails. The man from the playground, still evading his gaze. Making a quick retreat now he'd been spotted.

'Morning,' said William but received no response. Either the man was pathologically shy or maybe something worse. He was certainly reluctant to engage in conversation. He muttered something bland and was out of the door while the waitress watched his exit with a chuckle.

'Funny bloke that. Comes in here quite a bit. Never seems to have anything much to do.'

William watched the retreating back, narrow shoulders slightly hunched, the threadbare overcoat flapping, his hair blowing wispily in the breeze.

'Do you happen to know who he is?' he asked, but she shrugged.

'Some poor blighter whose wife has chucked him out. Lives somewhere near here, I think.'

Paddington, thought William silently, which was a fair step away in this weather. He wondered where he was headed now, but kept his thoughts to himself. None of his business and he'd do well to remember that, though he still viewed the fellow with distaste.

'Time we were moving on too,' he said reluctantly. Mrs P would be almost through and he ought to be back there, sorting out the laundry. He zipped Morwenna into her bulky snowsuit and buckled her into the stroller. Life for them both was one long extended jolly, or so Edwina would imagine. They waved their goodbyes and set off to brave the elements, father and daughter with their ingenuous matching smiles.

From somewhere across the busy main road a powerful engine fired suddenly into life and a motorbike wove its way swiftly into the traffic, its rider's face obscured by the black smoked visor.

22

'Get the fuck out of my way,' snarled Edwina, rudely shoving William aside. William, still at the cooker making breakfast, merely raised an eyebrow. She had been like this for a week or so, almost as though she couldn't bear him. He hated the language she used in front of the child but was reluctant to chide her now. One of these evenings, when she wasn't so het up, they needed to have a calm and considered talk. Something was clearly badly wrong in her life. He just wished she'd tell him what it was. Before it was too late and the cracks grew any wider. Before they ended up having a major fight. He was making French toast, and Morwenna was patiently waiting, crooning quietly to herself as she spooned up her melon balls. What a joy she was, his little ray of sunshine, who made this domestic disharmony almost bearable.

William had been studying Edwina's stock price in the paper and knew things were more precarious than she let on. So many of these fly-by-night dotcom companies had burned out immediately after take-off. Although Gareth and Edwina had found additional backing, things were

218

significantly rockier than they had been. The financial forecasts were glum in the extreme. The new year had got off to a wobbly start. He would talk to Arnold Fairchild if he liked him a little better but could not face up to the man's pontification and smug superiority. Besides, it would be disloyal to Edwina. In her father's eyes, at least, she could do no wrong. He would not go telling tales out of school.

Edwina returned wearing a new cherry red coat which did wonderful things for her complexion. She had taken to leaving her long hair loose instead of severely scraped back. She was even more striking now than when they first got married, her skin a luminous creamy peach, her figure as good as they get. If it weren't for the now habitual scowl, she would be sensational.

'Got your homework?' His attempt at levity failed. She simply looked up from stuffing her briefcase with a truly malevolent stare.

'Don't wait supper for me tonight,' she said. 'I'll be late.'

So what else was new? William made no reply, just slid the perfect French toast on to Morwenna's plate.

'Eat it now, darling, while it's still crisp.' He stooped and kissed her head. She smelled so wholesome, with the fresh innocence of youth. How long before she went downhill like her mother?

'Look . . .' he started, aware that the timing was wrong. 'I know you're going through a crisis period. Couldn't we just sit down some time and talk?'

She didn't even honour him with a reply. Just snatched

up her things and stormed off up the steps. He heard the taxi door slam.

Right, he thought as he swabbed down the stove, subversive action was called for. He glanced at the clock. As soon as it was a remotely decent hour, he would call up Polly Graham and postpone. No more sitting around in cosy kitchens. He could feel himself softening as the weeks went by, and all that girlie chatter was starting to emasculate him. Today, now the weather had brightened, called for a radical change of plan. They would go on another of their enchanted excursions and put aside the misery of this morning.

'Come along, Morwenna,' he called. 'Chop, chop! Get your shoes on. We're going on an adventure.'

Right from his earliest childhood William had loved the zoo. To him it spelt excitement and a sense of mystery, all those exotic animals seen up close. Although it had been developed over the years, the timeless essence remained the same, and once they were through the turnstiles and facing the signposts, he felt the old magic returning. 'Where to first?' he wanted to know, and, when Morwenna hesitated, struck out towards the elephants. Start with the big mammals and gradually work down. She was still too young for the insect house, and they had already been to an aquarium. They settled on a bench by the outdoor enclosure and watched a couple of African giants doing their stuff for the visitors. Squirting water and picking up things with their deftly manipulative

220

trunks. They used to have one that played the mouth organ but that must have been decades ago. Probably dead by now. Even though they lived extraordinarily long.

Morwenna loved it until one came a little too close and stuck out an enquiring trunk to see what he could scrounge. She screamed and shrank into her father's arms and he patted her head and reassured her.

'He won't hurt you, pet. He is only being friendly.' He had been going to suggest a ride but could see that the prospect appalled her. With one hand holding hers, the other pushing the stroller, he led her away to the big apes' house, which he reckoned she'd find more fun. Start her off slowly and let her make her own decisions. There was just no telling what turned kids on, all part of the fun of these expeditions. Ham sandwiches spiked with Colmans mustard. The memories came rolling back. They would eat them under the trees by the polar bears or sometimes on the bank of the canal and watch the barges glide by. He wished now he'd thought to bring a picnic, but the weather was still dicey and probably too chilly. They'd come back properly in the summer as a family, provided the Huxley unit was still intact. Not a thought that he liked to dwell on, but something that clouded his mind.

Again he wondered what could have happened to Edwina. He couldn't bear the way she seemed to have changed. One moment she had still been his lovely, spirited wife; the next she'd turned into a sour old crone with scarcely a civil word for him or Morwenna. The pressures of the business launch were clearly weighing upon her, but there had been a time when she'd have shared it all with him, not left him out in the cold to worry and wonder. He had a guilty feeling it was because he wasn't working, that she'd begun to lose her respect for him the day he had quit his job. They really needed to talk about it, though the thought of a showdown made him extremely uneasy. If they really had grown so far apart, his intrusion could bring down the whole edifice. And then where would they be? He dared not think.

The monkey house was practically deserted, it being a weekday morning. It was too early in the season for the usual busloads of schoolkids, and even the tourists were thin on the ground, despite the milder weather. A goofy-looking orang-utan swung lazily back and forth in his motor tyre, while a couple of chimpanzees did stylised acrobatics and brought the smile instantly back to Morwenna's face. This was more like it; she broke away and went to stand close to the rail. William watched her enjoying herself and was suddenly hugely glad he had brought her here. Although intellectually he disapproved of zoos, it was marvellously educational for the kids. These days too much of their lives was virtual reality. Computers were it, they controlled the world, now even on a domestic level. Nothing could compare to the hands-on experience of seeing real animals up close. The smell might be pungent but that was all part of the experience. Nostalgia came flooding back and William was a schoolboy once again.

Next they went to look at the polar bears and then on to the penguin enclosure. Morwenna loved these quaint-looking creatures, like miniature waiters in their sleek black coats, diving and swimming and having the time of their lives, jostling each other as they lined up for the chute, enjoying a thoroughly good natter. A couple of other children were there, each with a single man. Weekend fathers, William supposed, though he wondered why they would be there on a Tuesday. The whole bleak prospect of single parenthood brought down his spirits once again. He must make his peace with Edwina, and soon. The alternative was too frightful to consider.

Seeing the penguins flopping into the water reminded Morwenna of her favourites. 'Swans,' she said brightly, with rising hope on her face, and pulled him by the hand towards the gate. William laughed and allowed her to lead him. They had been there two hours already. They would come back again on a regular basis and work their way through the different sectors. But if swans she wanted, then swans she should certainly have. He had done quite enough today for her education.

Office morale had reached an all-time low. What had started off with so much energy and enthusiasm was wobbling now on the edge of catastrophe as the workers watched their golden goose sicken and die. The boom was over, reality raising its head. They hadn't thought their strategy through sufficiently and the fast.bucks stock had plummeted overnight. They were in big trouble, not least with their City backers. Edwina was seriously concerned.

Gareth, as usual, had not yet made an appearance.

Always a tardy riser, he had been slacking off more and more. She grabbed his diary and scrutinised his day. He had a table booked at Vertigo for one; apart from that, nothing else.

'Where is he?' she asked his snooty PA, who just shrugged and turned back to her screen. One of Gareth's more irritating affectations was to hire them for looks rather than ability. This one, with her coltish legs and twenty-four-inch waist, resembled a polo player's moll. Her clothes were all designer, her hair expensively mussed. Her highly glossed nails were far too long to cope efficiently with a keyboard. Her attitude was of cool indifference, which made Edwina long to fire her on the spot. Though she hesitated from doing so because of what Gareth might say. Pathetic. She hated herself for her weakness, not at all her usual style.

'Well, tell him I need to talk to him,' she snapped, horribly afraid she was making a fool of herself. She was jealous, it was as simple as that, and no longer knew how to conceal it. She sensed the sneer on the younger woman's face and stomped back to her work station in a rage. She regretted ever getting into this mess but was powerless to help herself now. Gareth had become an almighty obsession. She feared where it might be leading.

Almost an hour later, without being aware of his presence, his lascivious e-mail flashed up on her screen.

i'd like to ravish you on the spot and tear off that black satin thong . . .

Edwina looked guiltily over her shoulder and he raised one hand in casual salute. He was wearing his trademark designer suit over a white silk polo. He looked so gorgeous, she felt her knees weaken and longed more than anything for his touch. He had made her his sex slave, she had now become insatiable. Small wonder their business was in such a mess. She ignored his e-mail but he didn't desist, his messages growing progressively more lewd. Aware that others could hack into the system, she wanted to warn him not to be so reckless. But she hesitated to talk to him with that icy bitch looking on. She no longer had total control of her turbulent feelings. A few minutes later he leaned across her desk, a look of mocking amusement on his face.

'Lunch?' he said, with a question mark.

'You already have a date.'

'Lord, checking up on my movements now, are you? Just like a jealous wife.'

Edwina was furious and badly wanted to hit him, but restrained herself because they were not alone.

'We need to talk,' she said through gritted teeth. Their whole world was balanced on the edge of an abyss and all he wanted to do was fool around.

'So, lunch?'

'You already have a table booked.'

'For us.' His cool grey gaze put strictures on her heart; she knew she was weak as a kitten in his hands. Though she still had claws, let him not forget that. All her resolve went flying out of the window as he traced her eyebrow lightly with his finger. What a wimp she was becoming, a lovesick fool. Yet, try as she might, she knew she could not resist him.

'I'll meet you by the lift,' she said. 'In twenty minutes.'

'That's my girl,' said Gareth smoothly. He knew when he was winning and it showed.

They had milkshakes and burgers in Regent's Park, then drove back to Kensington for the swans. That was how Morwenna preferred it. In some things she was quaintly settled in her ways. The sun still shone, it was a beautiful afternoon, a boon after so many months of inclement weather. He helped her out of her little quilted jacket, revealing the black and red tartan dress her granny had made her for Christmas. *His* mother, needless to say, the granny in Devon. The other side had bought her an expensive educational toy, which they'd made her play with for half an hour before she was allowed to open any of the others. Her glossy dark hair was freshly washed. She wore little red sandals to match the dress, too good for a mucky outing to the zoo. But the swans would approve. Her face was wreathed in smiles as they reached the Round Pond and saw the whole flock of them there. He hadn't brought any bread, which was no bad thing. He'd not expected to come there that afternoon and was anyway cautious of letting them get too close. A swan aroused could kill a small child with one stroke of its powerful wing. Morwenna was in heaven and he laughed to see her delight. Why bother with thinking out new and exciting jaunts when a bunch of white birds in a local park gave her so much joy?

They found an empty bench full in the sunshine and settled there for a while. The sun made him drowsy and he dropped off for what seemed like only a matter of seconds. Until he heard voices loud and clear and was awake abruptly, to see who she'd picked up now. It was pointless, William had long ago discovered, to try to teach this child to be wary of strangers. She was cute and appealing, with no real concept of fear. It would be a shame to make her over-cautious but he tried to keep his eye on her all the time. For these days you just couldn't tell. Worse and worse things were happening in the world. The crime rate was rapidly rising. An image of the ratty man flashed like a warning across his inner screen, but when he shaded his eyes and focused properly, he saw Morwenna in conversation with a woman. A slight, dark stranger whom he didn't think he knew was listening to her gabble most politely. He lurched to his feet.

'Daddy, Daddy!' called Morwenna in excitement, beaming broadly as she held the woman's hand. They were standing by the neighbouring bench where the woman had been sitting on her own. She looked a bit abashed when William approached and tried to disentangle her hand from Morwenna's.

'Hello!' said William heartily, suddenly knowing precisely who she was. The air of slight self-effacement gave her away. The woman from the surgery they'd met on their recent visit. Her thin, pale face was flustered now and she tried not to meet his eye. William was quick to apologise.

'I do hope she's not being a pest. We're here to see the swans.'

The woman smiled faintly and shook her head, indicating sandwiches and a Thermos on the bench. 'I'm having my lunch,' she explained in correct but accented English. He'd been right. She was a foreigner, though appeared to understand, unless she was just terribly polite.

'Isn't it rather late for lunch?' He glanced at his watch in surprise.

'I have to fit in with the surgery's hours. We work on a strict rota basis.'

'Well, we'll be off then and leave you in peace.' William attempted to prise away Morwenna, still clinging like a limpet to the hand. She was eyeing the sandwiches hopefully, her mind fixed firmly on the swans.

'Would you like to feed them?' asked the woman, getting the message.

'Daddy, Daddy. Let me! Let me!' And she drummed both tiny feet in their smart little sandals.

'Please,' added William automatically. 'I'm sorry,' he said apologetically. 'She's not normally quite this pushy.'

'I know how it is with the young,' said the woman, handing over a piece of buttered bread. She looked up at William with a tentative smile which immediately softened her face.

Nice, he thought. *Gentle and possibly scared*. She brought out in him a strongly protective feeling. Which he had to admit felt good.

228

23

Tim Hardy rang out of the blue. He had to pop up to town unexpectedly and wondered if William would care to meet up. William barely hesitated. He would welcome the chance of some adult male company, all too lacking in his life these days. Also there were things he wanted to run past Tim. The visit could hardly have been more timely. Polly's nanny said she would be only too pleased, so William called Tim straight back. They arranged to meet in a pub in the Gray's Inn Road, not a stone's throw from King's Cross Station. They could fit in a few quick beers and perhaps a spot of lunch before Tim went on to his journalistic assignment, an interview at the House of Commons with a rather uninspiring back-bencher. Hardly exciting, he explained with a sigh, yet another weary step up his career ladder. Wapping remained still a distant dream unless something unexpected fell into his lap. Which is why he secretly pinned his hopes on this meeting.

'Any more news on the yoga teacher front?' asked William as soon as they were settled. To suit the occasion,

Tim was wearing dashing yellow aviator specs, which gave him a slightly sinister air though did little to disguise his obvious youth. He looked about seventeen and somewhat pimply, like a schoolboy out on an illicit razzle, despite the pale designer stubble he was now self-consciously affecting. With his colourless hair centre-parted and plastered down like an Edwardian dandy's. William greeted him with unfeigned affection. Tim might be slightly odd, but he respected the younger man's pioneering spirit. He warmed to his enthusiasm and determination to forward his career. Made him feel lazy and insufficiently ambitious, not that he really cared much any more.

'Somewhat surprisingly, no,' said Tim, sliding the shades into his pocket. 'It would appear they've come up against yet another brick wall. Not that they seem to be trying all that hard.' The truth was that, despite his terrier-like tenacity, the Cambridge police were refusing to be drawn. He might be the one who had stumbled across the crime scene, but that was about as involved as they'd let him be. The press corps did, on occasion, have its uses, like when they needed publicity to help flush out a suspect, but at this crucial stage in almost any inquiry, they played their cards close to their chests. Which did make sense. Hugely frustrating for Tim, but still. Until they were ready to make an arrest, they were unlikely to spill any beans. Not to a tyro reporter who looked like a child. William sympathised but could offer little solace. Certainly not the lead for which Tim was hoping.

He ran through the list of victims again, starting with

Edwina's Aunt Jane – the point at which he had first got involved himself, though not necessarily the earliest of the murders. For all he knew, there might have been others before that, though somehow he didn't believe so. It was hard to be retrospective at this stage. The second crime to have caught his attention was the truly horrendous butchering of the Marshes. Killing those little girls had been gruesomely over the top, hugely more disgusting than the impalement of Jane's little dog. And now the yoga teacher's cat. A macabre pattern of sorts was emerging. Tim grew quite excited as William explained, pulled out a notebook and started to jot things down.

'Who next?'

William thought a bit. 'That schoolmaster with his vanload of kids. More innocent lives lightly squandered, almost as if just for the hell of it. The man's throat had been savagely cut so he was presumably the designated target. The boys were simply unlucky, I would guess. In the wrong place at the wrong time.'

'You think?'

William nodded. 'Whoever is doing it must have some sort of game plan from the little I know of the criminal mind. Another thing they each have in common is the violence, which ought to tell us something. A very angry man indeed with a personal grudge to settle. Or else a loony fanatic with some sort of message.'

Tim was duly impressed. There was clearly more to William than he'd first thought. 'What exactly?'

William shrugged. 'Who knows? That's for us to surmise

and then work out. Think of the Unibomber and those chaps who walk into McDonald's and open fire. They all have enormous chips on their shoulders, even if their thinking is screwed up.'

'So what did they all have in common?' asked Tim. 'Apart from the sheer brutality of their deaths.'

'That,' said William slowly, 'is the crucial question. Answer it and, with luck, the rest will slot into place.'

'Where, for example, does the bank manager fit in? According to your theory. No pets, no kiddies, no other vulnerable dependants. And, when it happened, all on his ownsome. In the supposed safety of a plush hotel where he was pretty well known by the staff.'

'With his main artery punctured by a common or garden icepick. Not a pretty way to die, gagging to death on his own blood.' There it was again, the blood theme, nagging away at the periphery of his mind.

Tim's sallow face turned another shade of pale, sickened by the horribly graphic imagery. He would need a stronger stomach for crime reportage. He was going to have to learn to toughen up.

'And now this yoga teacher. And her cat. Another unlikely scenario. I thought her sort were supposed to be clean-living. Vegetarian, that sort of thing.'

'You never can tell. She had kicked around quite a bit. A fairly recent newcomer to the district, no longer in the first flush of youth.' Tim had certainly done his homework. It was William's turn to be impressed. The lad had promise and should go far, if only he could get that longed-for break.

'Including some years in an ashram in India,' Tim continued. 'Which isn't exactly my idea of decadent. A bit of a flower child, from all accounts. Devoting her life to spiritual matters.'

Like Aunt Jane, arranging the flowers in church. And Robert Marsh, another stalwart of the community. And Pilkington, with his strong Rotarian connections, steeping himself in fund-raising and charitable works. And then the schoolmaster, revered by both pupils and staff. William stared at Tim as something clicked. *That's* what it was. The connection. It was obvious.

'Blameless reputations,' he said slowly. 'Each and every one of them.'

'All condemned to particularly bloodthirsty deaths.'

'As if someone were targeting the saintly and the good.'

'Precisely. But why?'

'There,' William said, 'you have me. But it's a start. The pets and kids are all thrown in to make some sort of a point. Someone is methodically hunting them down and seems to want the world to be aware. His MO is not exactly subtle with all that battery and violence.'

'Revenge killings, do you suppose? Planned executions?'

'Possibly. Though it's hard to imagine what people like that might have done. All those godly folk, to deserve such a fate. It fairly boggles the mind.'

Tim said reluctantly that he'd have to be heading off. Though he'd far prefer to stay here with William than talk to some fusty old country squire about the joys of hunting. Criminals were much more enticing than foxes. He

233

felt that at last they were getting somewhere.

'Any chance of our getting together again?' he asked. William hesitated, his enthusiasm suddenly dampened. He had got so caught up in it all, part of him wanted to continue, yet prudence, at the same time, warned him off. Since the fiasco of the television exposure, he knew he was pretty much a marked man. Who shouldn't be risking his family's well-being, not with a frenzied killer still at large.

'I'm not sure,' he said slowly, 'that I want to get any more involved.'

Tim's face fell. 'You can't quit now!'

'It's your own bloody fault. I told you I didn't want to be identified. If you hadn't tipped off Anglia, I'd be safe.'

'They came after me,' said Tim, still pleased to have attracted their attention. 'And I can't drop out of it now. My readers are waiting.'

'Nothing to stop you going it alone. You're the news reporter, after all.'

'But you're the one with professional expertise.' Also the intuition.

William sighed. He hated giving up on anything and also didn't want to let Tim down.

'All right,' he said finally as they parted on the pavement. 'Give me a ring in a couple of days and we'll see. But no more risks, mind. Unlike you, I am no longer fancy free.'

Charity workers, do-gooders, genuine altruists. People who put something back into the community. It nagged away in William's brain as he hurried to the tube. Aunt

234

Jane might have been a bit of a handful but she certainly hadn't deserved to end up dead. Not in such a particularly nasty way. Whoever was out there committing all these murders certainly had to be stopped. This was far more engrossing than any crossword puzzle. William felt sneakily elated by it all.

The headline on the billboard stopped him in his tracks and he fumbled in his pocket for some change. *Big Issue Seller Hacked to Death*, it said. *Read all about it in the Standard*.

It had happened close to where William was standing now, in a badly lit side-street off the Caledonian Road. In the early hours of the morning, they thought, when only the winos and prostitutes were about. His name was Jed Hunter; he was fifty-five years old. And had been inching himself back from recent bankruptcy. The police tracked him down to a shelter for the homeless where the warden spoke of him with genuine warmth. Once she'd recovered from the shock.

'What a terrible thing!' she said. 'He was always so mild-mannered. A genuinely decent man with gentle ways who'd just happened to fall on hard times. Why would anyone want to do something like that?'

The policeman neither knew nor particularly cared. It bore all the signs of a drink-related brawl, only too familiar in this area. It was, at the best of times, a pretty unsavoury neighbourhood. And he a hopeless down-and-outer who had once known better days. Obvious, it was implied by his lack of real comment. Scum of the earth like that. But the woman refused to agree.

No, Jed was one of the brighter ones. Had never lost his dignity despite all he had been through. Business partners who cheated him, a wife who ran away and took the kids. Yes, he had hit the bottle for a while, but certainly with ample provocation. And lately he'd been on the wagon. She could vouch for that. His body had been found with his throat slashed wide open and one of his hands cut off. But the odd thing was, they hadn't touched his stash. He had been working long shifts, selling the magazine, and had on him fifty-five pounds in coins, which in itself was pretty remarkable.

'He was a nice man,' she said, 'with a great sense of humour. Made friends easily, was getting back on his feet.'

'Where did he actually hail from?' asked the policeman with little interest.

'Originally the West Country, I believe. He had a bit of a burr to his voice, Bristol, I'd guess, or somewhere like that.'

The policeman shut his notebook. He would not be exerting himself. Not for a homeless vagabond living rough.

It was mentioned briefly on the evening news, but after that there wasn't another word. The same sort of lethargy appeared to be recurring. Another wasted life and nobody cared.

'Do you really think it's connected?' asked Tim when he rang.

'Yes,' said William confidently. 'I do.' The infliction of the injuries, the callous brutality. It had all the marks of the same quite conscienceless killer. Still very much at large and apparently now in London. A tiny frisson of fear ran down William's spine. A Jack the Ripper of modern times, though his victims came from entirely the opposite pole.

'So where exactly is the match? This homeless person with the others?'

'Selling *The Big Issue*. Pulling himself up from the gutter. Yes, it fits. It has all the same hallmarks. A man with no criminal past who has known better times.'

'But the locality,' objected Tim. 'London.'

'He was only recently arrived, they think. Probably from the West Country.'

Both men fell silent, then made a date to meet. There was absolutely no question now of William pulling out. Even the danger element began to fire his excitement; he would just have to be extra vigilant where Morwenna was concerned. It was heady stuff, this detective work. He hadn't felt quite this empowered since losing his job.

'Come along, cherub,' he said, after hanging up. Time to get a move on. Edwina would soon be home. He felt a touch guilty at having neglected Morwenna, who was placidly watching television on her own. He gave her a quick cuddle and she snuggled up against him, thumb in mouth, her eyelids starting to droop. The world out there was a harsh and dangerous place. He would always do his utmost to protect her. Tonight, for a special treat, they were having fish and chips. He had bought them from the pub at the top of the hill. Edwina, with her faddy ways, would simply have to lump it. She could make herself a salad if she was hungry.

Edwina, however, failed to come home at all. She called at nearly nine to say she was eating with Sue and, since there was so much still to catch up on, would stay overnight at her house. William was surprised. This had never ever happened before. Sue, who lived south of the river, in Clapham, certainly had plenty of space, but Edwina's rightful place was here, with her family. Once more she was shirking her duties and it just wouldn't do. The ice in his tone was unmistakable and Edwina lowered her voice. Problems, she hinted, with her hand muffling the mouthpiece. Something to do with the state of the marriage. Not good. William sighed resignedly and said that was all right then. If Edwina detected his irony, she didn't let on. He was surprised if the brisk and well-organised Sue was having emotional problems. She was one of the most capable women he knew. He wondered if the husband had been straying. It was happening more and more these days, in even the happiest of ménages. And Nick spent much of his time in Brussels where fleshly temptations were supposedly rife.

He tucked in Morwenna and switched off her light, leaving the door ajar. He would hear her if she woke in the night, though normally she slept straight through. He collected her scattered clothes from the floor and dropped them into the basket for Mrs P.

William, alone in his study, at last relaxed. In a way, not having Edwina around with her spiky, sullen presence, was a relief. He had carried upstairs a glass of Glenmorangie and sat there slowly sipping it while he gazed again at his maps. The window was open and the cool night air filtered in, lavishly laced with the scent of the wisteria. Perfect. He idly ran through his mind again that day's conversation with Tim. Then put down his glass and ran downstairs for his chequebook.

He studied the diagram he had made for Tim and his mind began to clear. He listed the murder sites then laughed aloud. He'd been studying entirely the wrong map. For what these places had in common was suddenly stunningly obvious. So obvious, in fact, he'd have got to it sooner, if only he hadn't been chasing so many hares.

Alton Coombe, Northampton. Dorset, Bournemouth and Bristol. Even Cambridgeshire fitted, for they all had one major thing in common. William Smith, the 'father of British geology'. One of his old framed maps was hanging here on the wall. William crossed to look at it now and could scarcely prevent himself laughing aloud. Sedimentary rocks, all fossil-bearing, Jurassic or else Cretaceous. Ha! He took a step backwards to get better focus. There they all were, the murder sites, in one bold geological circle.

24

They were in the farmer's market when they encountered her again, a slight, sallow-skinned figure in a serviceable navy coat, a silk scarf knotted elegantly at her throat. She was carefully selecting apples and dropping them into a bag, frowning with concentration as she chose them. It was Saturday morning and the place was packed. Morwenna spotted her first so William hailed her.

'Hello again,' he said, and touched her arm. He was startled by quite how nervously she reacted. This was one jumpy lady, he would need to tread with care. But Morwenna was starting to clamour and he knew he would now get no peace.

'Oh,' said the woman, instinctively backing away. 'It's you.' She looked at Morwenna, riding high on William's shoulders, and gave them both a fleeting, tentative smile. William lowered the child to the ground, glad of the chance for a breather. She was a sturdy little madam these days and growing fast. Soon she would have to learn to walk without the constant complaints. They were, after all, no more than a block from home.

'Lovely morning,' said William breezily. 'Nice to see some sunshine for a change.' The weather had been horrendous but the rain had finally stopped. And the mornings were visibly brightening by the day. Edwina was off on some jaunt of her own while taking the car to be serviced. William was buying the Sunday lunch, a nice leg of lamb to be seasonal. With peas and broccoli and Jersey new potatoes, which were all piled up in the stroller. So now the infant had no choice but to walk since he seemed to have run out of hands.

'Do you live around here?' he asked chattily.

'Not far away. It's convenient for the surgery.'

Property in this part of the world was all high rent. He wondered how she could possibly afford it. But perhaps there was a husband in the background. He glanced around the crowded carpark but no one stepped forward to claim her.

'We're just up the hill,' he said, nodding in that direction. Something about her he found inexplicably appealing. She had soulful dark eyes and a low, husky voice. He couldn't quite identify her accent.

'Well, better be getting on,' he said when she seemed to have run out of words. Not one of life's natural chatterers, that was clear, but it gave her an air of contained tranquillity. Apart from the obvious shyness when confronted by a stranger. Well, that was no bad thing at all, only made him respect her the more. Wherever it was she hailed from originally possibly had different manners. He'd do well to bear that in mind if he ever ran into her

241

again. He found himself thinking that he rather hoped he would, though wasn't entirely sure why. Loneliness, probably, he told himself sternly; moving in too restricted a circle.

Morwenna set up a bit of a squawk but they said their goodbyes and moved on. They still had more shopping to worry about and only an hour until lunch. There were times when William marvelled at this endless round of meals, the planning, the shopping, the cooking, the clearing away. Not to mention the actual brief moment of eating. No wonder so many married women cut and ran.

Edwina, in her weekend tracksuit, was driving fast towards Clerkenwell, frantic for even a glimpse of Gareth, appalled by her loss of control. Never before in her life had she sunk this low. Marriage to William had proved to be a stabiliser; she hadn't acted so erratically since her youth. They had parted the night before last as the dawn was beginning to break, and she'd gone on direct to the office after a shower. William had to be rung and appeased, the fib about Sue fleshed out. The baby chortled at and reassured, the usual false promises made. Gareth, of course, had remained in bed, unwilling to alter his habits just for her. And they dared not be seen together, not first thing in the morning. A single whiff of scandal would totally blow it. He had followed her in, infuriatingly late, but this time hadn't mentioned lunch. She had a nasty gut feeling he was seeing someone else. Had noted the snooty assistant was missing too.

It filled her with such agony, she was no longer thinking straight. She had muttered an excuse to William about the car and driven off furtively across town. She had to see him, had to make absolutely sure. Was almost on the edge of phoning just to hear his voice.

'Get a grip!' she hissed at herself as she wove through the Saturday traffic. Luckily William was so obtuse he would scarcely be aware of her absence. She would drive past the converted warehouse and check if his blinds were still down. Failing that, she'd try him on the mobile and hope he'd not be able to trace the call. Not that he'd care either way, she was sure. He was laid back to the point of indifference. The reason she was in such a sorry state.

For despite the intensity of their now regular sex sessions, he'd still spoken very little to her of love. Yes, he paid her the occasional compliment, fired by momentary passion, but rarely got into serious mode while continuing to mock her with his eyes. Which served only to intensify this craziness and fuel her insatiable desire. She had never felt this way before for any other man. Was scared to death of where it might be heading.

She was also terrified about the current state of their business, afraid that the bubble might soon be about to burst. She could never get Gareth to talk about it seriously, he appeared to have his head firmly in the sand. And yet the share price continued to wobble while all around them companies were going bust. Pride had prevented her from consulting her father. She couldn't bear the indignity of losing face in his eyes.

Which left her with only William, and that was a joke. He knew nothing at all about city trading or the intricacies of the internet. Had no particular interest in money; was content to allow her to support the family without ever asking real questions. Part of her despised him for being so compliant, though she did appreciate all he had done to keep the marriage intact. She knew she couldn't be easy to live with, was aware she was turning into a shrew. She suspected she might respect him more if only occasionally he would tell her to shut up. Or even, in extremes, belt her one. She had a nasty suspicion she might even find that sexy. Much-needed evidence, at least, that he still cared.

Edwina was grumpy at lunch and monosyllabic. She had turned up late and in a bit of a state, her long hair tangled, an unhealthy flush on her cheeks. Perhaps she was sickening for something. He touched her forehead, but she brushed him away with her usual sneering contempt. William toughened inside. If that was the way she preferred it, two could play at that game. Morwenna had nodded asleep at the table so he carried her up to her cot for a nap then continued on to his study without a word. Edwina, for once, could deal with the dishes and not before it was due. Lately she'd been treating this house like a hotel. He heard himself echoing his mother in one of her self-righteous moods as he shut himself away for the rest of the afternoon.

As he sat at his desk, absorbed once again in his maps,

William felt his blood pressure gradually readjusting. He was totally convinced now that his geological theory held water and that somewhere within the circle he had drawn lay the elusive solution to the puzzle. He knew he ought not to be endangering Edwina but she was hardly doing her utmost to make amends. He picked up one of his boyhood fossils and traced the intricate pattern with his finger. He needed to put in a great deal more hard work. It was not in the Huxley genes to face defeat.

Downstairs Edwina banged the dishes into the washer, rolled up the tablecloth, ignoring the stains, and thrust it back into the drawer, along with the mats. It would last for at least another meal and William could take care of it then. She ran frantic fingers through her tangle of hair and glared at herself in the mirror. The light in her eyes verged on the manic and she felt herself starting to shake. She had got to find a way of calming down. If William realised the state she was in, the balloon would go up well and truly. With his customary tact, he had removed himself from the scene, apparently anxious as always to avoid a spat. Though how much longer his patience would hold out, she had no idea. She was beginning to think she hardly knew him at all, that they were starting to go their separate ways.

She stared at the telephone, willing it to ring, while all the time knowing it was unlikely to. Gareth had a life of his own and appeared quite unmoved by the obstacles in their way. All she wanted to do these days was be with him, touch him, make love to him. His words ran endlessly through her head as she looked in vain for hidden meanings. He might not actually have spoken to her of love but surely his actions belied that. He was, at times she was certain, a man who was equally smitten. For what other reason would he be taking such risks? And then her confidence failed her again and she saw what a miserable fool she was becoming. Gareth Prendergast was an accomplished seducer. She had known that all the years since they'd first met. She remembered how she had sneered at those foolish needy women, plaguing him with phonecalls, provoking his biting scorn. She, Edwina Huxley, had maintained the moral ground. Yet now was starting to act no better than them.

It was half past three, with the afternoon stretching ahead and nothing she wanted to do in this state of mind. She paced the spacious kitchen and picked up a couple of toys, then went to the door and listened hard in case there was movement above. Nothing stirred. Morwenna was clearly more exhausted than she'd looked, while William had simply blanked Edwina out. He would stay up there till he sensed the storm was past, and then come down with a smile and even a hug to rustle up something for their supper. He truly was a saint – her friends were right – and she knew in her heart that she really didn't deserve him. If only he didn't irritate her quite so much.

Her thoughts flew back to Gareth and she wondered what he was up to. There had been no sign of him when she circled his block and the telltale blinds were still down.

Now she wished she had dared ring the bell with some off-the-cuff excuse. Surely, with all they now meant to each other, she had every right to intrude. They were lovers as well as partners and mad for each other. Every single moment apart was a strain. She considered phoning him now but feared William might pick up the extension in the study. So she dug out her mobile and went out on to the patio to have another shot at self-degradation.

The improvement in the weather meant they could return to the playground and that's where William chanced to see her again. He was pushing Morwenna on the swings when a soft voice beside him said hello and there was his bashful lady from the surgery. Not the glamorous Asian doctor, the shy one. Smiling a shade more warmly than before but looking slightly uneasy all the same. William was delighted and slowed Morwenna down despite her indignant protests and kicking feet.

'More, Daddy, more,' screamed his imperious little princess, but William, for once, paid no attention. He was far more concerned with not letting the woman get away. She was wearing the same navy coat and silk scarf, with neat low-heeled shoes and leather gloves. Her straight dark hair was sleek and immaculate; large sunglasses hid her eyes. She was, she explained, on her way to work but still had a little time in hand. He led her to a nearby bench, leaving Morwenna to her own devices. Something about this stranger charmed and intrigued him. He suddenly wanted to get to know her better.

'Do you come here often?' he asked, unwittingly using the tired old pick-up line.

She nodded and smiled and admitted that she did. 'I like to watch the children,' she shyly explained.

William warmed to her instantly. There was something exquisitely poignant about her, he felt. He longed to ask more questions but was reluctant to scare her off. A single misplaced word and he sensed she might run. He could tell from the tense way she sat that she wasn't entirely easy in his presence. He wished she would take the glasses off so he could gauge more precisely her thoughts. Morwenna came toddling up which instantly broke the ice. She placed her small hands on the woman's knees and bounced up and down with delight. Both adults laughed. She was just so cute.

'Come here!' said the woman, overwhelmed with affection, and snatched the child on to her lap.

Her name, she told him, was Luisa Salvoni and she came originally from Sicily. It was a long, not particularly interesting, story but she'd been here now for quite a while. No, she had no children of her own. That was one of her many regrets. She had taken off the dark glasses while she talked and he saw that her warm, dark eyes were verging on moist. He placed one hand daringly over hers then rapidly changed the subject. He thought of Edwina, with her callous disregard, as his heart went out to this stranger. There was a strong streak of heroism in William Huxley. He wanted to be her protector.

But time was passing and she had to get going. She

would be a little late as it was. She handed Morwenna back to him, then solemnly offered her hand.

'Thank you,' she said simply, replacing the sunspecs. 'It has been a real pleasure to meet you both.'

'Hang on,' said William, in alarm, before she could turn away. 'Will we be seeing you here again? I really would like to go on chatting.'

The same faint smile and the slightest of shrugs. She didn't apparently believe he could be serious.

'Who knows,' she said vaguely. 'I often come this way. It helps break the monotony of the day.'

He watched her as she walked away, a small determined figure with a purpose. Morwenna pulled a tragic face as though about to cry so William swiftly diverted her by taking her back to the swings. For the first time he could remember in years, he understood precisely how she felt. Like a child deprived of a shiny new toy before she had even got the wrappings off. Yet that was absurd. There was nothing particularly special about the woman. She was certainly no beauty and older than him, he would guess. Yet something about her, her loneliness perhaps, had touched him in a very sensitive spot. He wished he'd been bold enough to ask to see her again, yet knew that, as a married man, he really hadn't the right. Though at least he knew where she worked. Which was a start.

William was still brooding and languidly pushing the swing when his attention was caught by a minor commotion on the opposite side of the playground. A lone man

249

had entered and was talking to two small boys while a woman was hysterically complaining. William sensed the urgency of it immediately.

'Stay here, sweetie. I'll be back in a jiffy.' He was over there like a shot. For the man was all too recognisable in his flapping, threadbare coat. And clearly, from the state of the woman, up to nothing good. The man backed away as William approached but the woman continued shouting, out of control.

'You dirty devil! Clear off!' she shouted, ineffectually waving her fist. The small boys cowered and she shielded them both with her arms as William, slightly breathless, came pounding up.

'Everything all right?' he asked, though that clearly wasn't the case, and the man, defeated, turned away, and beat a hasty retreat, The boys stood mutely staring at William, unexpected figure of authority, while the woman continued to flutter around like a chicken. Her face was beet red; she was snorting hard. For one alarmed moment William feared she might be on the brink of some sort of attack. Eventually, once she'd calmed down, she tried to explain.

'I'm the next-door neighbour,' she said. 'Their mother works long hours. So I pick them up occasionally from school. Sometimes, because of my own erratic timetable, I can't always get there on time. So I meet them here in the playground instead where I know that they'll be safe.' She sniffed. 'At least, that's how it's always been up till now. Till he started sniffing around.'

William soothed and calmed all three and checked that the boys weren't too shaken. They looked at him politely out of innocent glass-clear eyes and nodded in affirmation of everything he asked. Yes, they knew him, they said politely, and no, there wasn't a problem. Having ascertained that the woman was who she said she was, William left them and returned to Morwenna, still seated happily on her swing. The man was most likely deranged, he thought, but at least no lasting damage had been done. Though you couldn't be too careful and he was glad he'd intervened. And it was certainly time that Morwenna had her tea. He sang to her briskly the entire way home and renewed his resolution that, no matter what, he would always be around to keep her from harm.

25

Mrs P rang in to say that she was poorly so William told her not to come back until she was feeling better. The poor woman worked hard enough as it was and he didn't want to risk germs around Morwenna. Deprived of his partner in crime for once, he found himself at a bit of a loose end. He enjoyed their regular morning sessions; the house seemed so empty without her cheerful chatter and the pervasive aroma of cigarette smoke. He emptied the dishwasher and restacked it with last night's dishes, then wiped down the surfaces in a desultory way before turning his attention to the rest. Four floors and a basement was a lot for one person to tackle. If he let things go, they would rapidly get out of hand and he didn't want Edwina any grumpier. He decided to start at the top and work down, doing just the essentials for today. If she stayed off any longer he would have to rethink but a basic lick and a promise would do for now.

Morwenna's favourite *Cobbleywobs* was on so she was glued to the set. He left the door to the playroom ajar so he could hear her if she needed him, then trudged on up to the attic floor with the hoover tucked under his arm. He would kick off there then move methodically down. The bedrooms always took up most of the time. He calculated rapidly and decided to change the sheets. Nothing nicer than the scent of fresh linen; he was becoming rather expert at hospital corners. He was in the airing cupboard selecting sheets when the doorbell unexpectedly rang. He was surprised. It was still not quite nine and he wasn't expecting anyone. Unless Mrs P had changed her mind, which did seem unlikely so soon. Besides, she had her own key.

He answered the bell from the bedroom floor and a male voice shouted out, 'Gas board!' So he pressed the upstairs buzzer to admit the man and said he would meet him in the hall. It was ages since they'd had the meter read. He'd been paying recent bills just on their estimates. With a bit of luck, he might be in for a refund, though when he remembered the awful weather and amount of heating they'd been using, he changed his mind. This rain had lasted for almost a year; even now, at the beginning of spring, he'd be paying through the nose. Luckily Edwina earned a fair whack and her prospects had never been rosier. Once her ship came in, he would start by clearing the overdraft and hope, at the same time, perhaps to pay off the mortgage. Edwina might be the earner but William, along with all his other chores, always took care of the bills.

The hall, when he got there, was deserted. No sign of the man from the gas board anywhere. William glanced around but all was still except for distant voices from the playroom. He headed that way then stopped in his tracks at the sight of a stranger wandering around the living room.

'Nice place you've got here,' said the man with an amiable smile, his eyes on the valuable eighteenth-century clock. William looked at him with sudden suspicion. He didn't look much like a meter man at all; he was middle-aged and dressed in country casuals with expensive shoes, one detail that William always noticed. He had rimless spectacles that gave him a studious air, and the only indication of any official capacity was the plastic-coated label hung round his neck. Surely they normally wore uniforms and carried torches. This one looked more like a college lecturer with a highly defined interest in snooping. William stood disapprovingly in the doorway while the man continued to scrutinise the room. He even had the affrontery to cross to the fireplace and study some etchings inherited from Aunt Jane, which Edwina particularly liked. Jane Fairchild might have been a disagreeable old bat but couldn't be faulted in her taste.

'Turner,' said the man, with an approving nod, smiling at William good-humouredly. 'Have you seen the water-colours at the Royal Academy? Very collectable they are. Especially the ones of Swiss scenes.'

'The meter's downstairs,' said William stiffly, leading the way to the basement. He hated himself for being so uptight but didn't trust this stranger one bit. For all he knew, the badge might well be fake. He had made no particular

254

effort to draw attention to it. And William didn't like inter-lopers snooping around his house without so much as a word to ask permission. He opened the door of the cupboard under the stairs and the man at last did produce a flashlight from one of his voluminous jacket pockets. He scrawled down the figures on his clipboard, then stepped uninvited into the kitchen. The dishwasher was chugging away and the table had luckily been cleared. Not that it mattered what this gasman thought. He was already way out of line.

Just then Morwenna called out from the playroom and William, torn, had to go to her.

'You can use the kitchen door,' he said, meaning the tradesmen's entrance. This meter reader had one colossal nerve. Soon, if not stopped, he'd be also invading the playroom, and William was determined that he should not set eyes on Morwenna.

'Mind if I use your toilet?' asked the man super-casually, to which William reluctantly had to agree. He directed him to the one by the basement door, didn't want him intruding any further.

Morwenna was all right, just curious to know who was there, but William didn't encourage her to join them. Something about this man's overt curiosity made him feel positively prickly with distrust. He wanted to get rid of him as fast as he possibly could and hoped he wouldn't be troubling them again. Though he couldn't have explained why he felt this way. Just some instinct that wouldn't be shaken off. Must be getting jumpy in his old age; certainly all this murder stuff didn't make him breathe any easier.

'Stay here, sweetie,' he instructed Morwenna, 'and I'll bring you a glass of milk and a biscuit.' It was early for that but he didn't want her emerging. Not till this dubious stranger was out of the way.

The man was back in the kitchen by now, taking a snoop at the patio.

'This place must be worth a bomb,' he said. 'Lived here long?'

'Four years,' said William, slightly mollified. He liked it when people admired his house. He and Edwina had worked their butts off to get it into this shape and the value had virtually quadrupled in as many years. But the man was behaving like a friendly neighbour instead of a gas official, which didn't quite fit.

'Well,' he said reluctantly at last. 'Guess I had better be moving.'

'Have you got the rest of the street to do?' asked William, remembering the television clip and therefore back on his guard. He would watch him and see if he went next door; somehow he guessed that he wouldn't.

'Just the few we missed last time. When people either aren't home or don't answer their doors. You'd be surprised how many people just can't be bothered.'

William watched him saunter up the steps as casually as if he had all day. For a second, he thought of checking him out with the gas board, then decided he was over-reacting. In all probability, just another poor sucker,

256

temporarily down on his luck. William, himself unemployed all this time, was scarcely in any position to be so distrustful. But the man continued to linger in his mind for much of the rest of the morning. You couldn't be too careful when you let strangers into your home. He might be back with a removal van to collect all the things he had admired. You heard it all the time these days, homeowners being ripped off. And the man had possessed that sort of easy charm which often denoted a fraudster.

Not enough to occupy his mind, thought William impatiently as he started stripping off the sheets. He was turning into a regular old woman, looking for bogeymen under the bed. Time he was thinking about getting himself a job. He spent far too much of his time on his own, and it couldn't be healthy.

Edwina came home in another of her foul moods, with barely a civil word for either of them. She even made Morwenna cry by scrubbing her face too hard, so that William protectively took her up to bed and read her an extra chapter for a treat.

'Mummy didn't mean to hurt you,' he said. 'She's just got a lot on her mind.' And not enough time for her own precious child, who occasionally she treated like a nuisance. Don't take it out on Morwenna, he wanted to yell. Whatever it is that is turning you into a shrew. But the last thing he needed was another ugly row so he made a big effort to button his lip. They would have to have it out some time soon before the structure of the marriage fell apart. He could tell that Edwina was deeply unhappy but still hadn't figured out why. The way things were going according to her, she ought to be over the moon. Instead of which she grew more listless by the day and even appeared to be quietly losing weight, something she would usually be proud of.

Despite his best intentions, his thoughts kept straying back to the slight Sicilian stranger with the hauntingly beautiful eyes. There was a contrast, if ever he saw one: the strident, abrasive Edwina and this woman with genuine class. He regretted he hadn't arranged another meeting. There couldn't be anything very much wrong with an innocent stroll in the park. He found himself watching out for her, pushing the stroller to places he'd seen her before. The farmers' market on Saturday morning, the Princess Diana playground. Most of all, back to the Round Pond and the swans, praying she might materialise there.

Since he'd first met Edwina, William had been ensnared, but lately it was obvious that the magic was wearing thin. She still looked great, when she bothered to make the effort, yet was growing increasingly slatternly at home. She went whole weekends without putting on make-up and usually only dolled herself up for the office. Which was, William felt, the clearest of indications that she didn't really care for him any more. She rarely listened to what he was saying, had developed a nasty habit of cutting across him. And she snapped at Morwenna, making her miserable too. Their home was no longer the haven it always had been.

This particular Saturday morning he chanced the Portobello Road. Though packed all year round and thronging with tourists, it usually gave him a buzz. And he thought Morwenna might find it fun. They could come away quickly if she didn't.

'Hold very tightly to Daddy's hand,' he warned her. 'We don't want to risk you getting lost.'

He carried her through the densest part, having deliberately left the stroller at home. The crowds were streaming past The Sun in Splendour and he battled to get through to where it eased off. And then he put her down and took her hand. She was growing fast into a real little girl whose bright inquisitive eyes missed very little. They stopped and browsed at the bric-à-brac stalls and laughed at the long-haired man with the didgeridoo. Morwenna pleaded to be allowed to have a go but hadn't the breath to coax out any sound.

'Never mind, pet,' said the friendly Australian. 'Come back when you have bigger lungs.'

There were Rastafarians dancing in the street and plenty of ethnic food they were tempted to sample. The sun came out and it almost felt like spring. Morwenna was really having the time of her life. And then he spotted her, just one stall ahead, and his heart did a sudden backflip in his chest. Elegant as always, in jeans and a cashmere sweater, her large dark glasses pushed up into her hair as she studied the intricate workmanship of a brooch. It was clear she hadn't seen them yet, and she gave a perceptible jump when William stopped beside her and spoke her name.

'Luisa, great to see you,' he said while Morwenna clapped her hands in real delight. For one second Luisa appeared confused, then a smile slowly softened her face and she swung up Morwenna in an impulsive embrace before placing her back on her feet.

'How are you?' she said.

'We were just thinking of getting a spot of lunch.' Which wasn't quite true. 'How would you like to join us?' he asked impulsively.

Luisa looked uncertain and he was sure she was going to decline, but the look of joy on Morwenna's face would have melted the heart of a gorgon. She glanced at her watch.

'I can't stay out long. I have things to do at home. But, yes,' she said simply, 'I would like that.'

'Pizza Express all right with you?' There was no point in staying in these crowds.

'Perfect,' said Luisa politely, grabbing hold of Morwenna's other hand, and the three of them pushed their way back to Notting Hill like any Saturday family on an outing. Morwenna started gabbling and telling her about the *Cobbleywobs* and Luisa laughed then listened very solemnly to every word she said. Nice person, reflected William again, very much liking the way she was with his child. Politely attentive yet without condescension, treating her exactly like an equal.

The Pizza Express was packed with kids, as it usually was on a Saturday. Morwenna, out with two of her favourite people, was entirely in her element. She sat and chattered with a radiant smile as William chopped her pizza into manageable slices. Luisa, who ordered only a salad, focused on her completely.

'They are so lovely at this age,' she said dreamily, smoothing Morwenna's shiny hair and helping to tuck in her bib.

Edwina, conveniently, had taken herself off to Highgate for a rare visit to her mother, who wasn't well. Something inconsequential and gynae, she'd mentioned over the phone, but Edwina, interpreting the sub-text correctly, responded with alacrity to the summons. It wasn't like her mother to make any sort of fuss. She had better check her out, just to be on the safe side.

'I'll be back in time for supper,' she'd said vaguely, meaning she assumed that William would cope.

Right now, though, he'd forgotten all about Edwina, enthralled as he was by his unexpected guest. This was turning out to be more of a treat than he'd expected. With the result that he felt quite giddy and skittish.

'Where exactly is it you live?' he asked, seeking for something inoffensive to say. He sensed she was wary of telling him too much and reminded himself she hardly knew him. It was a very long time since he'd chatted anyone up. He was anxious not to make a fool of himself. Besides, he was married, but he shoved that thought from his mind. He hadn't made a secret of it; Morwenna was there as the proof.

'Close to the Portobello Road,' she said, 'which is where

261

I usually do my weekend shopping.' There and in the farmers' market; she obviously cared about quality and if this was all she ate for lunch, small wonder she stayed so slim. William had a crazy impulse to stretch out and touch her hand. He managed to restrain himself; he was afraid of driving her away. Her soulful dark eyes were still fixed on the child as she listlessly picked at her salad. Morwenna, by contrast, was tucking in heartily, her face now heavily streaked with tomato sauce. William damped a tissue and carefully cleaned her up. Table manners were not yet one of her strengths.

'Tell me more about yourself,' he risked and Luisa gave it careful thought.

'There isn't a lot to say,' she said, 'apart from what you already know. I came to this country, things didn't work out and now I seem to be stuck here.' She looked him suddenly straight in the eye and he felt again that sharp spasm of excitement. She wasn't quite a beauty, but haunting, nonetheless, with a tantalising hint of passion beneath the calm exterior. He wondered idly how old she was but knew he couldn't possibly ask. Not that it made any difference, not at this stage.

'And do you like your work?' he asked, embarrassed at his banality.

'It's a job,' she said simply, 'and helps pay the rent. And now I'm sorry but I really have to go.'

William silently cursed himself for so clumsily driving her away. He rose to his feet and helped her from her chair. 'Look,' he said awkwardly, 'I know it's a bit of a nerve, but I'd awfully like to meet up with you again.'

She looked at him long and thoughtfully then flashed him a radiant smile.

'All right,' she said, surprising him, 'I think I'd like that too. Perhaps one morning for a quick cup of coffee before I begin my shift.'

He whistled cheerfully all the way home and treated Morwenna to a piggyback. He didn't have a number for her but at least they'd arranged to meet, which was a start.

26

'Have I got a treat for you,' said Gareth, eyes gleaming wickedly as he tossed an opened envelope on to her desk. Edwina looked up at him sharply. He hadn't appeared at all the previous day. She was still awaiting some sort of an explanation. But could hardly ask him now, with the rest of the team looking on, including Portia, the snooty PA with the cold and insolent stare.

'What?' she asked ungraciously, with a poor pretence at cool.

'Suck it and see,' he said and walked away.

She carefully completed her network search before succumbing to the bait. Mustn't be seen as too eager, but what had got into him now? Two tickets fell out of the envelope, for a trade fair next month in Vancouver. What did he think he was playing at? Had he finally lost his mind?

'What's this?' she demanded sharply, flinging the envelope back at him. Gareth looked up with innocent eyes.

'I thought we should go to it,' he said. 'Together.'

Yeah, and leave the child and the house and now her

ailing mother, not to mention the potential crisis the company was breasting right now. She knew that William was bound to put his foot down, would finally throw her out and who would blame him?

'You're mad,' she said but she liked the thought. Three days alone with him, six thousand miles from home. Away from people with snoopy, gossipy eyes where they might find a little privacy for a change.

'Think about it. It's a very big deal and I feel we should have a corporate presence there. To show the world that we're finally up and running, a company to be reckoned with. Call it PR, if you like, and cheap at the price.'

'Have you ever been to the West Coast?' he asked later, over lunch. Edwina shook her head.

'Vancouver is glorious, one of the world's greatest cities. I'd love to be able to show it to you first-hand.'

When he was not being caustic or suave, Gareth had incredible charm. His clear grey eyes simply swam with sincerity; he could tell how much she was longing to give in.

'Take someone else,' she said, immediately regretting it. Gareth shook his head.

'Has to be us together,' he said. 'Giving it all we've got.' The two fast.bucks.com musketeers confronting a possibly resistant world. He could see her resolution rapidly wavering.

It was a temptation, she granted him that and took time to study the brochure. They'd expended so much effort just raising the cash, she knew a little more would not be wasted. Her father would approve, with his grasp of global finance. It was pointless to risk a fall at the final fence. A thing's only worth doing if you do it properly. And all that stuff she'd been raised on since a child.

'All right,' she said finally, after a long, considered pause. But how was she ever going to explain it to William?

William, unknown to her, had other things on his mind. Eyes the colour of liquid coal had etched themselves into his soul. No matter how hard he might try – which wasn't very much – he could not shake Luisa from his inner-most thoughts; she haunted him night and day. And all based on what? A few casual meetings and a feeling they might be soulmates under the skin. William, after years of single-mindedness, found himself, out of the blue, suddenly smitten. Which was disconcerting, to say the least, yet hugely uplifting to his spirits. He had become accustomed, since losing his job, to being considered a bit of a useless berk, certainly by Edwina and her friends. Now all of a sudden he had found this attractive stranger who not only listened intently to what he said, but also appeared fairly besotted with his child. He could scarcely believe it was happening to him, kept on expecting to wake up. Could barely wait to see her again, maybe even take things further.

Edwina regarded him suspiciously when he greeted her with unusual bonhomie. He even tried kissing her though she pushed him away and went to check her messages on the machine. William shrugged; he no longer particularly cared. His heart was quietly singing as if it were spring. Which indeed it was; the clocks had just gone forward and the mornings were getting lighter every day. Best of all, tomorrow was magical Thursday. The day of his next planned meeting with Luisa.

He left Morwenna with Polly, explaining he had a check-up with the dentist. He hated to lie, but a small one wouldn't hurt and he didn't want Morwenna blowing his gaff. Not to her mother nor even to Polly; he wanted to keep this thing private as long as he could. Also, no matter how adorable she might be, she always wanted to hog centre stage.

'Won't be long, ought to be back by noon.' He waved to them cheerily as they watched him from the porch, then headed to Notting Hill and his assignation. He had spent an unusual amount of time deciding on what he should wear. Nothing too smart – no need to overdo it – but he wanted to look his best for her nonetheless. He chose a denim shirt that was almost clean and teamed it with his dark blue Guernsey that went so well with his jeans. He could do with a haircut but had left it too late so used Edwina's expensive shampoo instead. He also polished his shoes, a rare event. He surveyed himself in the bedroom mirror and was more or less pleased with what he saw. He had added some pounds since he'd given up his freedom but was still in fairly good nick for a man of his age.

She was there already, seated quietly in the corner, reading a paperback novel by Isabel Allende. She raised her head gracefully as he blundered through the door, full of apologies for being minutely late.

'Don't worry.' She smiled. 'I was happy with my book.' She inserted a leather bookmark and returned it to her bag. They both ordered coffee, his a cappuccino, hers a filter, then found themselves faced with sudden silence. They had come this far, acknowledged some sort of attraction, yet what in the world was there left for them to say? He had asked her various basic things yet still knew little about her. Not even if she lived alone or had some sort of partner in the background. She wore no rings, but these days that meant very little and he'd learned already not to ask too many direct questions. William ponderously scratched his head then was struck by inspiration. For the next half-hour he proceeded to regale her with the aesthetic delights of cartography.

After the lunch, despite her protests, he rushed her back to his loft for a rapid screw. This was the aspect of Gareth that really thrilled her, the ruthless, powerful maleness of the man. He started ripping her clothes off as they climbed the concrete stairs and fell upon her hungrily the moment he opened the door. His bed was still in darkness and unmade. The sheets smelled fusty and the room needed airing but that was all part of the feral allure of the man. After they'd finished and she'd started to dress he brought in a bottle of ice-cold Krug, which had become a key part of the ritual.

'Gareth, no!' said Edwina, laughing. At the rate he was corrupting her, her liver was in as much peril as her conscience.

'Be a good girl and drink it up. It'll do you good.'

'It's such a waste to have to glug it down.'

'Then we'll stay here until it is finished.' He was wearing only a not-too-large towel which he tossed across the room. Edwina laughed again, this time unsteadily, drawn by the sight of his obvious re-arousal. There seemed to be no stopping the man; she sighed and graciously gave in. She knew it was wrong but shut her mind to the terrible sin she was committing. She was relieved he appeared to want her still, that his ardour was undiminished. Of course there were moments when her confidence failed, but what woman has not sometimes felt like that? She needed to believe that he genuinely loved her and closed her mind to all doubts, at least for the moment.

She felt guilty when he phoned in and lied, told the office one more time that they'd both been caught up in traffic. She stretched across the crumpled sheets and studied his long, lean back. Compared with William, who was getting a little pudgy, Gareth had kept the fit silhouette of his youth. She ran her hands over his shoulder-blades then down to his small, taut bum. He had long athletic legs that would do credit to a girl and a hard, flat stomach that made her green with envy. She must step up the aerobics classes if she wanted to keep up to speed. Although lately she was barely eating, she could still only just fit into a size twelve, which wasn't nearly thin enough, certainly not without her clothes. Not for a man like this, a true connoisseur.

She finally dragged him away at a quarter past four and into a cab for a breakneck drive back to the office. There was an eerie silence as they slid through the door, though the computer screens were all functioning. A small knot of their colleagues were gathered together round one work station and they hardly raised their eyes to the guilty pair.

'Everything all right?' asked Gareth smoothly, the consummate master of bluff.

'No,' said Barry, the resident bean counter. 'It's not.'

They were into the Dow Jones and watching with horror the rapid descent of the stock market. Before their eyes, the figures were plummeting. There wasn't a lot further they could go.

'It rather looks,' said Barry grimly, 'as if we're well and truly fucked.'

They had dropped ten points in a matter of hours and the spiral had hardly begun. Gareth embarked on a light-hearted quip but Edwina told him fiercely to shut up. This was worse even than anything she had imagined. She should never, not for a second, have taken her eye off the ball.

'I'm going out,' she said, without explanation, grabbed her bag and stalked straight out of the door. When the chips were down and she needed advice there was only one man in the world she could really turn to. The one she trusted, whose strength she could always rely on, who would never let her down, no matter what.

'Highgate,' she told the driver curtly, and hurried on home to her daddy.

Rather to William's surprise, Luisa appeared quite absorbed by what he was saying. She focused her beautiful lambent eyes on his and never, for even a second, glanced away. William, into his favourite topic, rattled on without ever drawing breath. When it came to maps, he could bore for Britain. The wonder was, she didn't appear to mind.

'I'm sorry, am I talking too much?' He stopped himself abruptly in mid-flow.

Luisa smiled and shook her head. 'It's fascinating,' she said. 'And I really mean that. Please go on.' She seemed sincere so he took her at her word, then realised that his coffee had grown cold.

'I feel such a fool,' he said in sudden embarrassment. 'I wanted so badly to get to know you better and here I am hogging the conversation.'

'It really doesn't matter.' She gently touched his hand. 'I hadn't realised that maps could be so addictive.'

He wondered if she was laughing at him then decided she was not. She wasn't like Edwina, with her treacherous, spiteful tongue. This woman was gentle and intellectually alert; she obviously cared for the finer things in life.

'Unfortunately,' she said, 'I now have to go. But I'd love to hear more perhaps another time.'

She meant it; she was smiling now as she picked up her bag and sweater.

'When?' asked William, eagerly, entirely forgetting, in the rush of blood to his head, to try to seem nonchalant and calm. She liked him, had virtually said so, and wanted to see him again. This fragile creature with the searching dark eyes apparently didn't regard him as a joke.

'How about here next Thursday?' she said and allowed him to pay for the coffee.

Had he been as young as he suddenly felt, he'd have tossed his cap in the air. William whooped like an exuberant child and ran nearly all of the way home.

Her father had been quite adamant on the subject. Now all she had to do was try to convince William. There were moments, he'd said, when it paid to take risks like throwing more good money after the bad. The trip to Vancouver was worth the expenditure, provided they made it work to their maximum advantage.

'Remember it's not just a junket,' he warned. 'But an occasion for really solid graft.'

Do their homework, establish the right connections. Put themselves about by working the fair. A few expensive new clothes would not come amiss and he also suggested that they travel business class. Let the world see that they were confident and unruffled; never, for even a second, reveal their fear.

'These people who are investing in you need constant reassurance that their money will be safe. The current state of the markets, with luck, will be merely a temporary glitch. You'll not achieve anything by chickening out now. For real success in business, it pays to be bold.' She was truly his daughter, he was mightily proud of her. She had developed into such a fine young woman. He hugged her benignly as she climbed back into the cab and waved until she was finally out of sight.

William appeared to be in unusually high spirits. Edwina couldn't remember when she'd last seen him like that. She felt a guilty stirring when she thought what a bitch she had been. He worked so hard and for such little praise. The least she could do was make some attempt to be nice. Also, of course, she had a guilty conscience.

'Why don't I treat you to supper out?' she wheedled. For once in her life she had come home early, before he had even thought of preparing supper. He looked at her in vague surprise, as though it wasn't really sinking in.

'Our daughter,' he said finally. 'Or had you forgotten we've got one? Were you thinking of leaving her all alone at home?'

Edwina bit back her sharp retort; confessed she hadn't properly thought it through. They could ask the neighbours but he wouldn't even hear of it. And they couldn't take her with them, not at this age.

'Takeaway, then!' said Edwina, rallying. 'Thai? Or Chinese? Even Indian? My shout.' She had some uphill work before her and would bribe him with as much as it took.

William paused and considered very carefully. It would certainly make a change from him having to cook. He was slightly suspicious of her subtly softened mood but couldn't really be bothered to think about it now. He was still engulfed in a shiver of silent ecstasy at the memory of his Luisa and their talk. Like a passionate adolescent or a child of Morwenna's age, he was fervently counting the minutes until their next meeting.

'Whatever,' he said finally to a thunderstruck Edwina. Then left her alone in the kitchen and went upstairs.

27

The powerful roar of a motorbike engine woke Minna. She'd had a constantly interrupted night. She opened her eyes reluctantly to another uninspiring morning. Sleeting rain behind grimy curtains and a sharp nagging pain inside her head. She reached across to the alarm clock – five to eight. She groaned and wanted to roll straight back into soothing sleep but the violent revving had shattered her concentration. Besides, there was work to be done. The room was about as depressing as it could be but the best she could afford on the money she earned. She crawled out of bed and into her battered slippers, then shuffled across to the poky kitchenette to put on the kettle for her tea. The radio did nothing to raise her lagging spirits; the foot and mouth plague, currently dominating the news, seemed to grow more threatening by the day. They were even talking now of postponing the general election, which Minna had to agree was probably right. She was starting to suspect this prime minister couldn't hack it, though she'd been a Labour supporter all her life.

She looked at herself in the mirror after she'd dressed, the round pale face corroded by worry lines. Her listless hair grew thick and unkempt but she hadn't the heart, nor the money, to put it right. There had been a time when she'd cared about her appearance but all traces of vanity had left her long ago. Along with Roger . . . but she firmly stamped on that thought. Life was depressing enough as it was without dredging up bleak memories from the past. And, anyhow, she really had to go.

The street was noisy and littered with rubbish, with a bunch of black kids on the corner engaged in a fight. Minna, always a timid person, crossed quickly in an effort to avoid them. If she didn't make eye contact, she would probably be all right. She hated this area as well as the job but it was handy to be close to her casework. She had two school-age mothers to look in on today and make sure they were keeping up with their basic studies. Teaching had been bad enough; she had quit because she found she couldn't cope. But the hopelessness and squalor she encountered every day had driven her to the edge of another breakdown. If only this dire weather would brighten up a bit she might stand a chance of ridding herself of her chilblains.

Minna's childhood dream had been to be a dancer and she'd made it into the ballet school at eight. Her parents had always been inordinately proud and fantasised about her becoming a second Fonteyn. As an only child, they lavished everything upon her, but could do nothing about the way she had failed to grow. Short and stocky without the requisite long legs, she had also lacked the distinction of being pretty. At fifteen she'd been faced with the crushing truth. Her face was just too round for the *corps de ballet*. She'd had to transfer to the local comprehensive and after that her life had been all downhill.

Or so it appeared to her now, battling with rush-hour traffic, miserably wet and already shivering with cold. She hadn't the heart or the talent for teaching ballet so had opted instead for an undistinguished Dip.Ed., which had landed her with a bunch of unruly kids in an area of London she feared to go. The wilder reaches of Hackney in those days were like a jungle, and violent assaults upon teachers increasingly common. It had brought on eczema and anxiety attacks till the school, and the doctor, had suggested a radical change. She wasn't cut out for teaching, they said, it was taking too much of a toll upon her health. And when she started to vomit, they let her go.

She had had a shot at a number of different jobs: working in a shoeshop, helping in a home. The customers in the first she had found unacceptably fatuous; the residents of the second merely depressing. She longed to do something worthwhile with her life yet lacked the basic stamina for the caring professions. Nursing was out, she hadn't the requisite O Levels, and in any case doubted her health would stand up to the strain. She had muddled around for a while, with not much help from her parents, who seemed to have given up on her when she shattered their cherished dream. She also showed no sign at all of finding herself a boyfriend, thus depriving them also of grandparenthood. A washout.

The course in Swindon had beckoned her out of the blue. She read about it in the *TES* and grasped it with both hands. Social Studies sounded challenging and respectable as well as fulfilling her long-held desire to do good. If she couldn't handle a whole class of brawling kids, at least she could help sort out their troubled lives. She was just in time to enrol for the following autumn so turned her back on the family home in Enfield and went eagerly to Swindon to embark on a whole new life. That had been thirteen years ago and now she was pushing forty. It hadn't exactly fulfilled a dream but it helped.

Swindon was hardly the mecca of the universe but to Minna, after all she'd been through, it glowed. She liked the course and the other students and even succeeded in making a couple of friends. They shared a house in a dowdy suburb and got involved in Greenpeace and nuclear disarmament. Occasionally, at weekends, they went up to London for concerts at the Festival Hall or to queue at the National Theatre just in case. Men didn't feature much in their lives but they, modern thinkers as they were, weren't too bothered. They had their cosy domestic life, cooked for each other, shared all the bills, and turned their dingy surroundings into a home. Looking back now, after all this time, Minna reflected wistfully that those had been the happiest years of her life. Until she met Roger, who had swept her off her feet, and she abandoned her trusted friends to move in with him.

Roger was also a social worker, a couple of years older than Minna. He was tall and intense with a ferocious beaky nose and firmly held opinions on most things. They met one weekend on an anti-nuclear rally and for some odd reason, which she never quite understood, he had focused on her throughout and then closed in. They fell into an unequal friendship which slowly developed into love. Love, at least, on Minna's side. She was never quite certain about him. But he must have had some real feelings, surely, to allow her to share his bed. Minna brightened up considerably and, for a while, became almost pretty. She cut her springy hair really short, which softened her puddingy face, and made new clothes, with the help of her friends, that gave her a more vulnerable look. Roger approved so she started using make-up, a daring touch of blusher, a timid hint of mascara, which enhanced the new natural sparkle in her eyes.

Her parents, when they met him, approved; another huge burden was lifted. They didn't like the fact, of course, that their daughter was living in sin, but at least it was a step in the right direction.

'Bring him home for Christmas, dear,' said her mother with meaningful emphasis. Minna was almost twenty-seven and had finally found herself a man. The sooner it could be consolidated, the better. Her mother was nobody's fool.

*   *   *

He couldn't come for Christmas that year. His parents in Shropshire were expecting him. Nor, a year later, could he manage it again, off on a long-fixed trip with old college friends. The parents glowered but Minna continued to trust him. What they had together was sacrosanct. He couldn't behave as he did if he didn't love her. And repeatedly told her that what they shared was better by far than any marriage. He was with her because he cared, it was that simple. With which, as a modern, free-thinking woman, she concurred. Equality was what counted and not the shackles of marriage. She was proud to be seen as the woman in his life. Beyond that, nothing else mattered. At least, not then.

The months slid by; it was Christmas again. This time he was off to Brazil. A project to do with street children, he said. He would take her too if only the funding would allow it. She spent a miserable time with her disillusioned parents and tried to convince them it was still just a question of time. Roger was on the up, she said, with important social issues to decide. The best she could do was stick around to support him, a comfort in his life as well as a rock.

By Easter even Minna was beginning to lose faith, especially when he was seen out with his new assistant. Angie, she was called, and was all of nineteen. They were working together on an undercover project he wasn't allowed yet to discuss. Four gruelling days with her over-anxious mother caused her to force his hand in a reckless way. Two and a half years in an uncertain relationship; she needed to know precisely where she stood. Roger was contrite and took her in his arms, blowing soft kisses into her receptive ear, asking her, please, to indulge him a little while longer.

'I care for you, doll, too much to short-change you. When we do it, I promise you, we'll do it in style. Let's not risk wrecking it now.'

Another Christmas, another disappointment, and Minna was willing to walk. Nothing he promised ever came to fruition and he seemed to be spending less and less time at home. On her thirtieth birthday she finally took the plunge and asked him outright what his intentions towards her were. The biological clock was ticking. She wanted security and a family of her own. He hummed and stuttered and generally prevaricated then told her there was something that she probably needed to know. Angie, he said, was carrying his child. And came from a family of Roman Catholics.

Remembering all this now on the tube on a miserable ride home, Minna found herself fighting back the tears. She had loved him so much, had believed they were going to make it. But once he had mentioned the baby, he was gone. Her friends said she was well out of it and her parents refused to discuss it. She had made her bed was the implicit message, and now would have to lie on it. Alone. She had moved back to London and found this ghastly job and a nasty little flat on the outskirts of Acton. Which was more or less all for the past uneventful ten years. She wished she could turn off the faucet and simply forget him.

The sole faint glimmer in her life right now was her new plan of enrolling with VSO. She had recently seen an ad on a cinema screen which had got her instantly hooked. The thought of escaping another dreadful winter was a temptation she couldn't resist. It would only pay peanuts but that's all she earned already and her lodgings and minor overheads would be met. And it might extend her social life; she couldn't sink lower than rock bottom. So she filled in the forms and bravely sent them off, dreaming of starting a brand new life in some emerging tropical country. She started browsing through travel books and even thought of brushing up her languages. The library carried cards for all kinds of new things she could learn. Just having a dream kept her going at night and sustained her through the miserable working day.

It was raining again by the time she reached her station and swirls of filthy water splashed over her feet. She stood and waited for the traffic lights to change and felt the icy damp seeping into her coat. Her throat was feeling prickly and she still had that pain in her head. She hoped she wasn't getting another cold. She would make herself a hot toddy but couldn't afford the whisky and all she had in the fridge at home was bread. She started to cross and was very nearly knocked down by a motorcycle coming at her at full belt. Its heavily helmeted rider was clad entirely in black leather and crouched like a steeplechase jockey over the handlebars. These deadly machines were a law unto themselves and thought nothing of cutting through traffic and jumping red lights. At least in her island paradise, she'd be safe from such city scourges. She imagined walking barefoot through rippling surf and never again needing to carry a mac or umbrella.

The flat smelled fetid and there was a widening stain on the ceiling. She had asked the landlord repeatedly to fix it, but he never even bothered to reply. It would have to be toast and Marmite again, but first she must warm herself up. Her chilblains were aching as she pulled off her sodden shoes and all of a sudden she started to shiver uncontrollably. She sneezed and sneezed and searched for a packet of tissues, but had to make do in the end with just a loo roll. She lived as impecuniously as even her hardest-up cases. Something would have to change or she wouldn't survive.

The water ran sluggishly into the rusty tub but when she cautiously tested it, it wasn't hot. Tepid as usual, so she couldn't have a bath but would boil the kettle and at least bring relief to her feet.

She was sitting huddled in her candlewick bedspread, waiting for the toast to pop, when the doorbell rang with shocking insistence, causing her to spill her mug of tea. It rang so rarely, it always gave her a start, and there was no one at all she could think it might be. Around this area there were very few random callers. It didn't pay to open your door on a whim. She sat in petrified stillness, hoping whoever it was would go away, wishing she had a peephole through which she could check. It rang a third time, more stridently. They clearly weren't about to take no for an answer.

'Who is it?' called Minna, in an unnaturally quavery voice, slipping on the doorchain just to be safe.

'Pizza,' called a muffled voice, and she instantly relaxed. The fact she hadn't ordered one didn't matter. She was so relieved, she thought she might even accept it, and glanced around for her purse before opening up. Then she remembered that she hadn't any cash. Only enough for her tube fare tomorrow morning.

'Not for me,' she said, her face now close to the door. 'I'm afraid you must have been sent to the wrong address.'

'Pizza,' repeated the voice impatiently and somebody thumped on the door. Perhaps he couldn't quite hear what she was saying. She couldn't bear to leave the poor fellow standing, and somebody's order was rapidly getting cold. It wouldn't hurt to open the door just a chink and repeat what she was saying to his face.

He appeared to be only a lad, dressed in leather from head to foot, the smoked visor of his helmet still down, which was odd.

'I'm sorry,' repeated Minna clearly, but a boot was jammed in the door and the knife went into her chest before she could scream.

28

'Talk about losers!' said Mrs P with relish, slamming down the paper on the table. William, looking suspiciously cleaner than usual, stared at her abstractedly as if uncertain who she might be. He had also shaved by this early hour and his hair had been properly cut. And his shirt looked suspiciously crisp for him on just another routine weekday morning. She clicked her fingers to bring him back to earth. It was hard to imagine how he'd cope without her chivvying.

'Hello! Anyone at home?' She had only been off for a few days yet light years might easily have passed. He seemed spaced out.

'The social worker?' she ventured at last, lighting another of her endless cigarettes. Still the blank expression, combined with a questioning look. A portrait of a woolgatherer caught on the hop.

'Lord,' said Mrs P with a knowing twinkle. 'If I didn't know you better I'd almost think . . .'

It was true, he was backsliding. He pulled himself together. Mustn't allow this dream of his to get in the way of real life. But he still didn't know what on earth she was blathering about. She placed one jewel-bright nail on the relevant item.

'Social worker,' she repeated. 'Stabbed in the heart through a barricaded front door. No sign of breaking or entering either. Or even unnecessary force being used. Another apparently motiveless murder, or so the local police are quoted as saying. Dangerous profession that, the social services. Mind you, though, it's a pretty unsavoury neighbourhood. Wouldn't catch *me* setting foot there after dark.' Then she sat back, puffing contentedly, and watched him grab the report and finally read it.

Minna Bassett, social worker, forty years old, unmarried and alone. That was the sub-text in the morning's *Mail*. The few sparse details of her dreary-sounding life certainly made depressing reading. Alarm bells clanged instantly in William's befogged brain and suddenly Mrs P had his full attention. If this was yet another in the series of savage murders, they seemed to be unnervingly closing in. He thought, with renewed embarrassment, of that ill-advised *Argus* piece and the television fiasco that had ensued. He should never have given in to Tim's skilful underhand wheedling. Had risked his own family's safety and all on a whim.

'So what's your opinion?' asked Mrs P, straining the last few lukewarm drops from the pot.

William sighed and thoughtfully scratched his head. 'I really don't know,' he admitted.

*   *   *

286

Tim, when William spoke to him, had spotted it too. 'I was just about to call you,' he said, with all the familiar ebullience. He was like a terrier or eager boy scout, straining at the leash, just raring to go.

'This has got to be part of the series,' he said. 'The killer's MO seems to fit it to a tee.'

'The one thing that's different,' William pointed out, 'in this particular instance, is location.' It didn't match his geological theory, a shame because he was now hooked on William Smith. Not part of his mythical magic circle, meticulously copied on to proper paper and carefully shaded in on his study wall. Amazing they'd sussed all this out in the eighteenth century – pale blue for limestone Jurassic rocks. The discovery had electrified him. An integral part of the endless fascination of maps, detective work made visual.

'What exactly do you mean?'

'No limestone.'

'Then the same must apply to the homeless man.' Butchered in cold blood outside King's Cross Station.

'Ah, but newly arrived from the West Country.' Perhaps the killer had stalked him on to the train. William recoiled at that particularly chilling thought and realised he was mad to have got so involved. Tim was a bad influence, he really ought to avoid him. Couldn't imagine what Edwina would say if she knew.

'I have to be going,' he said hurriedly. 'Will try to catch up with you later.' Right now he had something more urgent on his mind.

* * *

'Got a date?' asked Mrs P saucily when he reappeared in his jacket, hair neatly combed. Little escaped those needle-sharp eyes. It was as well she rarely encountered Edwina these days, though her loyalty was solidly with him. There could be no debate about that.

'Just dropping Morwenna off at Polly's,' he said casually. 'She's going to play with Miranda for the morning. And then I'll probably do a bit of shopping. It's a glorious day. I might take a walk in the park. You'll be all right on your own for a while?'

She laughed. 'I would certainly think so after all these years. Go on then, lovie, and enjoy yourself. You deserve a bit of fun.' She had never known him spruce up before, certainly not for just shopping.

'I shan't be long,' he said, ignoring her leer. 'You'll doubtless still be here when I get back.'

She was dressed a little more casually this time because of the milder weather. The whole of the Holland Park area was a mass of pink and white blossom, the royal borough at its resplendent best.

'It's a shame you have to work,' he said, 'or we might have taken a stroll in the park.' He imagined them wandering together under the trees, talking about all sorts of things, matters of the soul. He had certainly bent her ear enough with his own rather drivelling thoughts. He was surprised she'd agreed to meet him again. Still hadn't worked that one out.

288

The smile she gave him held genuine warmth and her lucid eyes glowed with sudden happiness. 'I'm fine just sitting here,' she said, clearly meaning it.

He fetched them each a coffee, with a sticky bun for himself. Edwina was always banging on about his weight but this morning he felt quite ravenously hungry.

'You are sure you won't?'

She shook her head. 'No thanks.' No wonder she managed to stay so ethereally slim. She looked as though she existed just on air and her skin was as clear and luminous as alabaster. The shirt she was wearing was pure white silk and she had tiny seed pearls in her ears. He admired her casual continental chic and the way she put herself together, with none of the opulent flashiness of Edwina. He couldn't remember when he'd last felt this light-headed. Had an overwhelming urge to touch her hand.

'How've you been?' she asked softly, her chin on her laced fingers, so he sketched out a few domestic nothings to amuse her.

'Why aren't you working at the moment?' she asked and he gave an expressive shrug.

'I guess you could say it was simply bad luck. I was made redundant. There's not a lot of scope these days for those of my chosen profession. Trust me to have picked one just on the verge of extinction. It seems to be the story of my life. Now they do most of the work by computer. Effective but hardly aesthetically challenging.' He would love to show her all his fine old maps. Perhaps

289

at some later stage when he knew her better.

'But it means you get to spend precious time with your daughter. I must say, I envy you that.'

'And I wouldn't exchange it for the world, I can tell you.'

When it was time to go he paid, then walked with her to the surgery. 'Speaking of which,' he said, 'how about yourself? I wouldn't imagine your job was particularly enlivening.' Not for a person with her fine intelligence, just shuffling papers and updating tedious files. Not even dealing with patients or anything rewarding like that.

It was her turn now to smile and shrug. 'I took what was available at the time. Recently my circumstances have altered fairly radically. I was lucky to find a job at all, especially one round here.'

And that was all she would tell him. William, hugely daring, pecked her awkwardly on the cheek, then asked if they might do it again. Luisa beamed.

'A week today? Same time, same place,' she said. And left him turning mental cartwheels of joy as he raced back to pick up Morwenna.

'How come the police aren't more concerned?' moaned William to Mrs P. He had risked a call to the one in Alton Coombe, who still refused to talk to him, let alone listen to his theory. And, from the little there'd been on the news, it appeared that those in Acton were similarly sluggish. William, suddenly defeatist, hadn't even bothered to approach them since his theory about terrain didn't seem to fit. In any case, what would be the use? She had been a mere social worker with no one in her corner to fight her cause. Small wonder the country was going to the dogs.

'I blame the government,' said Mrs P darkly. 'These champagne socialists are all fat cats, concerned only with private education and foreign holidays. Always strutting around with royalty, holding hands.' A dyed-in-the-wool Conservative herself, she could go on like this for hours if he let her, with her theories of how the country should be run. Not that she was wrong; she was very canny. Salt of the earth, as his grandmother used to say. But there wasn't time now for idle chitchat; William was still searching for a link. He remained convinced that the crimes were connected. If topography wasn't the answer, then what was?

He bounced it cautiously off Edwina, who still hadn't forgiven him for the television gaffe. Luckily she hadn't really tuned in to what he was saying, or else she'd have acted like a scalded cat and whisked Morwenna away. She seemed permanently distracted these days, though with an inner sparkle that she tried in vain to hide. Things at work must be going better than he'd thought, though, as usual, she appeared not to want to discuss it. Well, that was all right with William; he was long accustomed to doing things on his own. All he felt the need of was a clued-up co-conspirator now that he'd made the decision to steer clear of Tim.

For the remainder of the week he walked on clouds,

brimming with dizzy excitement about Luisa. Each nuance of their conversation ran through his brain in an endless loop and he heard new subtleties every time and tried to figure out how much she liked him. Which had to be a little, at least, or else she wouldn't have agreed to see him again. He had never been much of a ladies' man and solidly faithful to Edwina. Now he was acting like a school-boy with a crush and could scarcely sit still for anticipation. The days seemed to drag as he went about his chores, cramming each second with activity. Whenever he could, he returned to his maps, sticking red pins into relevant sites, trying, with a protractor, to figure out a possible epicentre. Which got him nowhere, he was forced at last to admit, since it landed him bang in the middle of Salisbury Plain. Unless he were to concoct a fanciful theory about Stonehenge, which might act as a useful red herring to ward off the indefatigable Tim.

At last it was Thursday again and William sat opposite Luisa, this time with Morwenna along since he didn't want to dump her all the time. Morwenna was thrilled and self-important as she sat between them, spooning up ice cream, chattering non-stop to an enchanted audience. Everyone in the café seemed to be listening in. Luisa gazed down at her fondly and wiped a splodge of vanilla off her chin.

'They are really lovely at this age,' she said. 'It's a pity they grow so fast.'

With her attention fixed on Morwenna, William was able to study Luisa sneakily. She was looking slightly peaky, he thought, as though she had not been sleeping. But her hair was as sleek and well-groomed as ever and the simple linen suit immaculately cut. She caught his gaze and her cheeks flushed slightly, causing him to shuffle around and nearly spill his coffee. He was such an idiot to be in this state but simply couldn't control it. If he wasn't careful he would blurt out something silly and then she'd be off in a flash. He was certain of that. Luckily there was Morwenna to distract them, still babbling on about *The Cobbleywobs*.

'Where had we got to?' asked Luisa at last, settling back and finally focusing on him. William, at a loss for words, found that his mind had gone blank. Just one straight look from those glorious eyes and he was putty.

'Your maps,' she reminded him with amusement. 'You can't have forgotten already.'

'Oh Lord, that time I bored you to death.'

'Not at all,' she said sincerely. 'It was fascinating.'

Which was when it occurred to him that he couldn't do much better than involve this intelligent woman in his quest. The worst that could happen was she'd find it far-fetched, but she wouldn't be rude and dismissive like Edwina. She was gentle and sweet and her manners were far too good. And it could be that she'd throw new light on it all. It was certainly worth a try. Two heads are better than one, and now he'd decided to jettison Tim, he'd be glad of a fresh point of view. So, picking up where he'd last left off, he embarked on an exposition of William Smith. And soon had her totally absorbed again, which gave him an inward thrill of satisfaction.

One thing led to another, of course, and soon he was telling her about the murders. Keeping off all but the sketchiest of details, because of the listening presence of Morwenna, but outlining the salient events and his unshakeable conviction that somehow they might all be linked.

Luisa listened with rapt attention. 'Where do the police come in?' she asked.

'I can't seem to get them interested. They refuse to take me seriously.' Not that he'd really tried very hard.

Luisa stirred her second cup and thoughtfully ran it all through.

'That's a lot of murders,' she said at last. 'Have you any idea who might be doing them?'

None, he told her, which was so frustrating, though he could see a rough connection via his maps. At which she laughed and patted his hand. She loved his boyish enthusiasm and let it show.

'Well, just be careful,' she told him sternly. 'You don't want a ruthless killer on your trail.'

At which he felt bound to confess to her the awful *faux pas* he'd already made.

'I trusted Tim,' he said with shame, 'and he very nearly landed us all in the soup.'

So now she was curious to hear about Tim. William filled her in. The thing about him, apart from his ingenuity, was his useful entrée into newspaper libraries. Because of his press card and persuasive charm, he could usually wheedle access and was reading his way through old files when he had the time.

'He's got bags of energy and a tireless questing nose. Dogged persistence, I suppose you'd call it. Can't do enough to help me, bless his heart, though he does go that bit too far a lot of the time. Is keen to crack it to embellish his own reputation, dreams of being on a national daily with a crime byline of his own.'

She asked what he thought the outcome might be and William told her proudly, 'All we really need is that single breakthrough. And then I truly believe we might well crack it.'

Luisa, spontaneously, leaned across and kissed him and then did the same to Morwenna. 'Well, just take care,' she repeated with mock severity. 'Think of your lovely daughter and please don't go taking unnecessary risks.'

29

When it came to the crunch, Edwina knew there was no way she could tell him that Gareth was accompanying her to Vancouver. Her father had strengthened her resolution and given her the necessary courage to fight on. Yet telling William would be going just one step too far. She felt so incorrigibly guilty as it was. Lately he had seemed a bit abstracted; the chances were he wouldn't suspect a thing. But she didn't want to risk stirring things up, was not yet prepared for a showdown.

'Vancouver?' was all he said mildly, surprising her. 'I hear it's a beautiful city.'

'You don't mind?' she found herself asking quite anxiously. 'I hate to lumber you at such a late stage but it really is important. And I'll only be gone for about four days. At the most.' Gareth was taking care of the travel arrangements, him and that snooty PA.

William astounded her by appearing not to care. He hummed as he set about laying out the breakfast and told her to stay away for as long as she liked. He was perfectly able to cope alone. Had done it often enough before.

'It's a pity to go all that way for such a short time. Why not give yourself a break and drive on down to Seattle? You've always been such a *Frasier* fan. Might be fun to actually visit all those locations. Or even San Francisco, while you're over there.'

Edwina blinked but said nothing. She hadn't expected him to be quite so co-operative and not even ask her any questions.

'So it's okay then?' she repeated.

'I've just said so. Now come along, blossom,' (to the child) 'and finish your juice. We've a lot of exciting things to fit in today.'

Maybe he was sickening for something, but she'd actually never seen him look healthier. He had bothered at last to get himself a proper haircut and was wearing his new, really well-fitting jeans, which made him look positively sexy. She watched him for a while as he went about his work then, recalling the time, pulled herself together and rocketed out of the door. Just as long as he didn't appear to mind, there was no point in upsetting this precarious apple-cart. Her friends were right when they called him a saint. Her guilt was weighing down on her more with every duplicitous minute. Not even her father had yet cottoned on; for him the sun still shone from her eyes. If he ever got a whiff of it, of how she was carrying on outside her marriage, the fall-out would be worse than World War Three.

But what mattered most to her at this precise moment was Gareth and saving fast.bucks.com. The two things went together, hand in hand. If one went wrong, she felt the other would too. She had made no advance on ascertaining his true feelings, but had hopes the Canadian trip might clarify things. If he hadn't wanted to be with her, he would surely not have suggested it at all. It felt like a last ditch action on both fronts.

Meryl was envious and Sue disapproving when she joined them for their usual Thursday drinks.

'What are you going to do when he finds out?' Sue, of course, on one of her moral crusades, tolerant and affectionate yet stern.

'He won't unless something should go drastically wrong. In which case, I'll simply have to bluff.'

'Is it really worth risking your whole marriage for a fling?' Philanderers like Gareth were dyed-in-the-wool bad guys while William was, by consensus, a genuine sweetie-pie. It privately occurred to Meryl that it might be worth sticking around to pick up the pieces. But Sue, a mother herself, was more far-seeing and shuddered at what the outcome could be for the child. But there was no convincing Edwina, who had clearly made up her mind, so all they could do was support her and drink to her trip.

'Lucky devil, I wish I was coming too.' The winter had been interminable and now, unbelievably, it was raining again with further storms on the way.

'It won't be all fun,' said Edwina defensively. 'Most of the time, remember, we'll be working.' And those long-haul flights could play havoc with the system: loss of sleep, monumental jet-lag, dehydration. Not to mention the fashionable scare about thrombosis. She remembered all too well the Australian trip. What it did to her skin and her sinuses. And her ankles.

'Yeah, yeah,' scoffed Meryl. 'Try pulling the other one.' Then they settled down for a serious discussion of what clothes she was planning to take.

William continued in a state of euphoria, unable to think of anything but Luisa. He loved the way she looked and dressed and talked. That soft lilting accent ran constantly through his dreams. There had been a time, which he now only dimly recalled, when he must have felt much the same about Edwina. But her recent harshness and changed attitude towards him had finally worked their trick and he no longer cared. If she was prepared to throw away all they had worked for in their marriage then he would take his loving elsewhere, to someone he felt might return it. He found himself acting like a total sap, haunting the places where he might see her. All the corny love songs of his youth came crashing back into his consciousness. He even found himself listening to Sinatra.

He had managed to keep away from Tim, had lately lost his zest for detective work. The social worker, it seemed to him now, might well have been a genuinely random killing. People in those professions took great risks, as Mrs P had already pointed out. The area where it happened was sleazy and oppressed. If it hadn't been for Mrs P he'd have missed the item altogether.

He embarked on sneaky press-ups in the bedroom, but only when Edwina was out of the way. How she would scoff if she ever caught him at it. She had lately given up nagging about his paunch. He even cut down on his beer consumption and started eating his burgers without the bun. Was now able to tighten his belt a couple of notches as he felt his chubby love handles melting away.

He ventured into the Portobello Road with the prepared excuse that he was hunting for antiques. There wasn't really anything new they needed for the house, but inspiration would doubtless strike should he chance to bump into his quarry. He felt his heart give an involuntary lurch at the sight of any slim woman with glossy dark hair. He followed one foolishly for a couple of blocks, only to discover, when she finally turned her head, that she was Asian. His appetite was waning, he could no longer sleep at night. Simply put, poor William was a mess.

In the office the team was on tenterhooks, watching the crazy fluctuation of the share price. At the start, they had enjoyed a dream flotation and even Arnold Fairchild had been impressed. On the first day of trading it had leapt by more than three thousand per cent, sending them spinning euphorically into the stratosphere. They hugged each other in disbelief and danced around the room, their eyes all glued to what was happening on Dow Jones.

'We've done it, girl!' said Gareth, giving Edwina a whopping kiss. 'My looks, your brains and we're millionaires overnight.' And most of them still in their middle twenties.

On paper they were, in an instant, phenomenally rich, with these two founding partners controlling the lion's share. The younger ones started planning a vast party, made lists of the undreamed-of luxuries they could soon afford. It had been an initial gamble but was paying them back in spades. Only the bean counter, Barry, retained his cool. He had seen it all happen so many times before and remained a cold-blooded cynic. A bubble that grew this fast could just as quickly burst. Indeed, the market began to correct itself and soon they all crashed back down to earth. It was almost too painful to perceive.

'What can we do to halt it?' whispered Edwina, watching their newly found fortune haemorrhaging away.

Barry turned his gaunt face to hers and gave an eloquent shrug. Easy come, easy go. Over the years he had developed nerves of steel.

'All you can do now,' he told her grimly, 'is say your prayers and wait. And go to that goddam convention and make like stars.'

'I'll run you to the airport,' said William, unaware she wasn't travelling alone.

'That's okay,' said Edwina off-handedly, deciding which luggage to take. 'It's just as easy on the Paddington Express and then you won't have all that snarled-up traffic to manoeuvre.'

He glanced up, surprised, but could see she really meant it. It was not like her at all to be so unselfish.

'No problem,' he said. 'We'll set out in good time.

Morwenna can come along too for the ride.' Another new experience to share with her; he would afterwards take her for a closer look at the planes. And then they'd come back by a circuitous route and he'd think of something else with which to beguile her. Not that, these days, he could think coherently at all since he'd fallen beneath the spell of the Sicilian temptress.

Edwina thought swiftly, trying hard not to panic. If she protested any more vehemently, he'd grow suspicious. And although, on the surface, she was up to nothing wrong, she doubted her husband would view things quite that way. He had been so generous in letting her go at all. If he found out Gareth was going too it was unlikely he'd remain so benign. And she certainly wasn't about to push her luck.

'All right, sweetie,' she said in a muted tone. 'Thanks.' It would save her a lot of hassle to part as friends. She would allow him to deliver her safely to the airport. And make sure that Gareth stayed discreetly out of sight until they were in the air.

He was dying to see her again though not at all sure how to accomplish that. He didn't want to come on too strongly, was in no position to woo her. Yet just the thought of her was driving him demented and he walked around all day with a foolish grin. He was heartily relieved that Edwina was going away. The timing could not have been more perfect. What he needed more than anything now was quality time with Luisa. Time to get to know her better and figure out how he really felt.

He still knew virtually nothing about her and that was particularly tantalising. He imagined all sorts of scenarios for her and couldn't believe she was single. A woman like that, with her understated beauty, could not possibly have got this far alone. On first impression, she was a mousy little thing. It was only on closer acquaintance that the light shone through. Something leapt in the pit of his stomach and he longed to pick up the phone and ask her out. But if he rang her at the surgery he knew she might be annoyed and he didn't want to risk losing the ground he had gained.

Yet he knew so little about her, that was their only contact point. If he haunted the surgery, he might well bump into her, but then surely she'd guess his reasons and fend him off. Courting Edwina had not been at all like this. She was bold and upfront and always slightly pushy. She was totally confident of her sexual power and treated most men with disdain. It had taken months before she started to take him seriously and even then only because she was bored. Edwina had been a real feather in his cap. He sensed that most of the world still saw it that way.

But Luisa was quite different. Diffident, cautious, eternally on her guard. He longed to be able to share his true feelings, yet was reluctant to scare her away. He had, he reminded himself, nothing at all to offer, for his loyalty to his marriage still remained.

Of all places, it was in Blockbuster on the High Street that he finally saw her again. The door creaked open and in she came, just as bold and friendly as could be.

'I just happened to see you,' she told him gaily, 'and thought I'd pop in to say hello.'

William, overwhelmed with surprise, felt his blood pressure sharply rise. He hoped he wasn't giving too much away as he stooped to give her an amateurish kiss. Morwenna, as always, simply crowed with delight and insisted that Luisa should join them for tea. And when Morwenna wanted anything, she invariably got it. Luisa laughed and cuddled her and said that she hoped he didn't mind.

'We're going to the Muffin Man, a favourite of ours. Nothing spectacular but cosy and nice.' A place for them to relax at last and try to get better acquainted. His luck was in. He paid for his videos and ushered them both outside, dizzy with the thrill of being with her.

He hesitated to mention that Edwina was going away. Somehow it sounded too bald and opportunistic. He knew he had to tread carefully and not come on too strong, yet chances like this of really talking to her were few and far between. He had to learn to seize opportunities and not just rely on chance encounters. Or else she'd lose interest and vanish from his life and he simply couldn't bear the thought of that. A more worldly man would try flirting outright but that had never been part of William's style. So instead he resorted to murder, a safer subject.

She'd been thinking about it a lot, she said, even making notes.

'You are absolutely convinced it's the same person doing them all?'

'Pretty much so. From the modus operandi.'

'And what do you consider might be the motivation?' She pulled out a leather-bound diary and prepared to take notes. It was almost like being with Tim again, only this audience was a hundred per cent more delectable. Flattered, William expanded upon his theory and as he grew enthused, he also relaxed. That, he was forced to acknowledge, was the stumbling block. He really hadn't a clue what they all had in common. Apart, of course, from the worthiness of their lives. A teacher, a social worker, even Aunt Jane with her dedication to doing good works.

'But why bump them off? It doesn't make sense,' she said.

'The scary thing is,' he confided, 'the murders appear to be creeping closer. First that guy at King's Cross station and now this woman in Acton. Most of the others were dotted around the West Country. The reason I suspected a possible link.' That and the sheer brutality of the crimes.

'Hmm,' she said and scribbled a couple of notes. Then tore out a page and doodled a cat for Morwenna.

'You and your maps,' she said, eyes now delightedly sparkling. 'You certainly have a most unusual brain.'

Which, he could see, she meant genuinely. He felt quite puffed up with pride.

'Just a way of looking at things. Derived from a childhood spent constantly doing puzzles.' His father had often scolded him for not getting on with his studies. Had hoped he might have made more of himself instead of ending up drawing maps. 'Think laterally,' William explained to her, 'and always ignore the obvious. Assume the murderer's as smart as you are and try to wrongfoot him with your brain.'

'Though not the police?' said Luisa with a smile.

'No way! They are all a bunch of morons. Who couldn't detect their way out of a paper bag. Not the wretched fellows I've encountered.'

It was time to go home, Morwenna was growing restless and Luisa still had shopping left to do. They parted on the corner and promised to meet again, then Luisa shyly rose on tiptoes and gave him a fleeting kiss.

'You're a very decent man,' she said. 'And I'm really proud to know you.'

William could barely contain himself as he pushed Morwenna's stroller up the hill.

30

'Don't bother coming in with me,' said Edwina as William pulled up outside Terminal 3. It was fairly early in the morning and, for once, surprisingly un-crowded. There were even parking spaces to be had, which was unusual.

'I'll just stick it over there,' said William placidly, 'and then help you with your bags.' He was ever the epitome of male chivalry, even when dealing with his lately trucu-lent wife.

'No need,' said Edwina hastily, leaping from the car and grabbing a vacant trolley. She was travelling comparatively light, for her a first. Morwenna, in her car seat, began to drum her heels. Her mother gave her a lingering kiss then started assembling her things.

'Why not get off?' she suggested anxiously. 'Before she gets too restless.' A trip to the visitors' gallery had been promised and then, perhaps, a stroll along the river.

'Are you absolutely sure?' William hesitated, but she seemed to have her mind made up. Edwina always loathed goodbyes, especially now when she already felt so guilty.

She was also nervous that Gareth might appear. Although she'd warned him off, he was never predictable.

'Okay, then,' said William, pecking her cheek. 'Bon voyage and have a good time. Don't work too hard and allow yourself some fun. And let me know when you're coming back and I'll meet you.' She had deliberately left her ticket open-ended.

Edwina waved to them both as they drove away, then pushed her trolley through the automatic doors. Business Class was virtually deserted and she was through, all checked in, in no more than a matter of minutes. She headed towards the departures gate. She'd arranged to meet Gareth in the VIP lounge and looked forward to a leisurely and intimate breakfast, away at last from the world's prying eyes, which was long overdue.

Alas, it was not to be. She found him waiting by Passport Control, accompanied, she was dismayed to see, by the supercilious Portia. Who was dangling his laptop from one limp-wristed hand while helping him adjust the strap of his travel bag.

'Ah, there you are,' said Gareth lightly. 'The lovely Portia's consented to join us for breakfast.'

Why? Edwina wanted to scream but couldn't. Instead she followed them to a restaurant nearby and ordered herself just orange juice and coffee while they both went for the full works. Even this early, Portia's make-up was flawless, her skin as soft and dewy as a teenager's, her tangled hair a marvel of artifice. Her skirt was brief and her legs a perfect bronze, her toenails painted a brilliant lustrous pink. She said very little, just tucked in manfully while Edwina glared at Gareth with barely suppressed fury. A fine way to start their illicit expedition. And how come, this early in the morning, Portia was already at his beck and call?

Gareth could see the questions in her eyes but simply smiled relaxedly and made small talk.

'Portia was good enough to drive me to the airport. I didn't want to risk leaving the car here for the interim.'

So what's wrong with a taxi like everyone else? Or even the tube or the airport bus? Or the super-efficient Paddington Express? But she didn't say it, just silently clenched her teeth and hoped this darkening mood would pass by the time they finally took off. Nine hours trapped in the air with him had seemed like a dream come true. But now this cow with the haughty stare was risking ruining it all. She glanced at the clock. They ought really to be going. The flight was on time and they still had to get through security.

'Better be off,' she said briskly, as pleasantly as she could muster. Then winced as Gareth kissed Portia warmly and gave her bottom a squeeze. What a bastard he was, always trying it on. She had known him all these years yet still hadn't learned. She couldn't determine if Portia was in accordance or simply just being polite. Certainly not so much as a flicker of response disturbed her exquisite *maquillage*.

'I'll call you when we get there,' he promised, giving her one of his extra special smiles. Then they both watched her walk away with her confident stride, tossing the messed-up mane with an air of supremacy.

The actual plan was to meet up with Luisa, then drive the three of them back to Hammersmith for lunch. The weather, at long last, was making a slow improvement. A stroll along the towpath should do them all good. He hadn't spelled out the details to Edwina, was pretty certain that, in any case, it would hardly be of interest to her now. Her concentration these days always seemed elsewhere. Whatever it was, to be cutting them out altogether. Morwenna sat happily at the back in her car seat, repeatedly chanting one of her daft little songs. She was a perfect child to travel with, sweet-tempered and benign. Content just to be with her daddy, no matter where.

William's emotions were still very much in turmoil. He could barely sit still with the prospect of seeing Luisa. That swift little kiss had given him sudden wild hope that this lunch today might lead on to more promising things. Preferably soon, while Edwina was still away, for William was quite unaccustomed to subterfuge. They would go to The Dove and eat lunch out on the terrace and watch the barges and rowing eights glide by. Provided it wasn't too chilly outside. Luisa appeared such a frail little thing, he would hate to be responsible for allowing her to catch cold. It was twenty to ten, Edwina would soon be off. They would not have been apart this long since they married.

* * *

Despite all her best resolutions, she just couldn't manage to button it.

'Are you sleeping with her?' she demanded, then bit her tongue.

Gareth turned pale and inscrutable eyes on Edwina then, without responding, wandered over to the free bar and helped himself to a gigantic Bloody Mary. At this hour in the morning, too. She shuddered.

'Want anything?' he called but she peevishly shook her head. He needn't think he could get round her quite that easily. He picked up a plateful of small and delicate sandwiches and brought them back to the table for them to nibble.

'I really don't know where you put it all,' she said. Despite his endless appetite, he seemed never to gain an ounce. Whereas she worked harder and harder in the gym yet it still felt like wading through mud.

'I work it off,' he said calmly, without a flicker. Then settled down with the paper to wait for their call.

Edwina silently cursed herself for being so unsophisticatedly uncool. She hated the way that he held her in sexual thrall. Despite these flashes of insecure rage, she still couldn't get quite enough of him. Had anticipated this brief Canadian break with all of her hormones raging. But the Portia incident had tarnished it already and brought back her rampant insecurity. Portia was rich as well as at least ten years younger. There simply wasn't a contest. Enough said.

* * *

The traffic congealed as they approached the Hammersmith flyover and William resigned himself to probably being late. He drummed his fingers impatiently on the steering-wheel and glanced in the mirror to check on his back seat passenger.

'All right, sweetie? Soon be there. Is there anything you need?' She didn't even bother to reply, just continued crooning to herself. He loved the way she was so self-sufficient, exactly like himself as a child, content in her own interior world. William smiled and allowed himself to relax. Soon, despite the traffic, he'd be with Luisa again and his mind drifted off into all sorts of improbable scenarios. If only, if only . . . They were infinite. He checked the time to see if Edwina was yet in the air. Twenty minutes to go and then at last he'd feel free, even if only temporarily. Without her on his conscience for a while, able to follow his instincts wherever they led.

As they reached the flyover, the speed of the traffic picked up and William, with relief, put his foot down. Not long now, he raked his fingers through his hair and glanced at himself in the mirror to see how he looked. He crested the flyover and that's when he saw it, a mammoth new billboard staring him in the face. A grainy black and white photograph of a man several times fullsize, with a shoutline that knocked the wind right out of his sails. ***This man is going to save a life today. Yesterday he gave blood.*** William was stunned. For a moment he wrestled not to lose his place in the queue. With a resounding clang, the penny finally dropped.

*   *   *

As simple as that and yet it had never occurred. He ran through the list of the victims in his mind. A schoolmaster, a yoga teacher, a prominent Rotarian. A welfare officer . . . it slowly began to add up. The conscientious sort with an active social awareness who certainly, now he thought of it, would be donors. Aunt Jane with that gold disc she always wore round her neck. He glanced again at his watch; seven minutes to go. Then rapidly dialled Edwina on her mobile. If only she hadn't yet switched it off, was still in the lounge awaiting take-off.

Edwina just couldn't leave it alone. It was one of her fatal flaws. She fretted away in belligerent silence while Gareth remained beside her, impassively reading. They would soon be boarding and she needed to have it out before they were in the confines of the plane. She didn't intend to wreck their whole journey by having a public scene on a nine-hour flight.

'Well, are you?' she repeated. 'I really need to know. She certainly looked like the cat that swallowed the cream.'

'So to speak.' Gareth smiled slowly as he folded the paper. 'It's always a cat when it's somebody else,' he remarked.

Edwina, stung, flushed angrily. He would never take her seriously and yet he had been the one to set this all up.

'I can't understand what you see in her,' she snapped. 'Lazy, incompetent, with a definite attitude problem. Barely even acknowledges me even though I am nominally her boss.'

'She's shy,' he said with a wolfish smile. 'Is it my fault if she finds me irresistible?'

She wanted to throw her coffee cup at him but managed to hold herself in check. One of her lenses was starting to give her trouble. She was terrified he might think she was actually crying. She groped for her compact and poked the lens around until the speck of mascara had floated away. Then blew her nose fiercely and powdered it before squaring up again to his questioning grin.

'You're a bastard,' she told him. 'And I hate you. You've never really cared for me at all.'

And now she was suddenly on the brink of genuine tears as a crashing wave of self-pity completely engulfed her.

'Now, now,' he said, leaning forward to grip her knee. 'Steady on, Edwina. Let's not have a scene.' He glanced around at the other bored passengers and flashed the listening few a complicitous smile. *Women,* was the implication. They all knew what they were like.

He's treating me like a child, she thought, and once again longed to thump him. Yet knew that the moment she touched him, all would be lost. For this was the aspect of Gareth that physically turned her on, the cavalier bachelor who gave not a shit, who would always be likely to fight to preserve his freedom.

'Tell me the truth,' she said, before she could change her mind. The ground staff were beginning to make meaningful moves. The authoritative one at the desk had the mike in her hand. Any second now they'd be asked to

314

proceed aboard. But this was a necessary showdown that couldn't wait. 'Have you ever really loved me or am I just another bit on the side?'

The question caught him unprepared, quite stopped him in his tracks. It wiped the insouciant smile right off his face. The other passengers were starting to move, in anticipation of the announcement.

'Well, have you?' She was imperious now as her dignity returned.

'Edwina . . .' he began, for once at a loss for words.

But right at that moment her mobile started to ring.

'Thank God I caught you,' said William breathlessly, still weaving his way through dense traffic. 'I was afraid you might have already boarded.'

'We're just about to.'

'There's something I need to know about Aunt Jane.'

Edwina mentally groaned. Not now, she wanted to yell at him. It was the last thing she needed to hear. 'I've got to go.' And was about to switch off when she took in the urgency in his voice. And waited.

'Hang on a sec! This could be really important.'

'Go on.'

'What was on that gold dog tag she always wore? It could be a crucial piece of evidence.'

Edwina was completely taken aback. What in the world was he on about now? She was heartily sick of this morbid preoccupation, wished he would give it a rest and get a real job. She had far more important things on her mind right now, questions of life and love. And destiny.

'Why, her blood group, of course. I'm surprised you didn't know that. She always made a thing of it because it was apparently so rare.' As if she were royalty, Edwina's father always laughed. Just another of her petty affectations.

Of course. It fitted. He should have thought of it himself. William's breathing slowly relaxed as comprehension dawned.

'What *was* her blood group? Have you any idea? This could be the major breakthrough we've been looking for.'

Now, at last, they really were calling the flight and everyone was surging towards the gate.

'I really haven't a clue,' said Edwina impatiently, watching Gareth starting to gather up their things. But then, as a sudden afterthought, she added, 'You can easily check that out for yourself. She left me all her jewellery, remember? It's in the box on the dressing-table.' Where it had been, unlooked at, all these years.

Something, he realised now with a twinge of guilt, that he really ought to have known and remembered before.

Part Four

Part Four

31

At first Luisa was reluctant to come inside. Felt uncomfortable entering another woman's home in her absence. But William explained it would be only for a minute. Besides, it was his house too. He had intended at first to leave them both in the car till Morwenna piped up that she needed to go to the lavatory. It was then that he realised it could surely do no harm. And he rather wanted to show it off to her. He left them in the kitchen, admiring his latest chalk masterpiece, while he shot upstairs to the bedroom to look in the box. There was a lot of clutter here that he didn't believe he'd seen but he quickly located the fine gold chain with the dog tag at one end.

'Got it!' he said triumphantly, swinging it from his hand. Luisa showed only the mildest curiosity. She still hadn't quite understood what it was he was after, only that he had said it couldn't wait. He dropped it into his jacket pocket to look at later at leisure. It was early for lunch but they had to get there and park. And the weather was brightening nicely.

'Your house is lovely,' said Luisa.

William beamed. 'You should have seen it when we first took it over.' A shambles just wasn't the word. It had been lived in before by an elderly lady who had done nothing at all to improve it in years. A virtual wreck but at a price they could just afford and they'd enjoyed the toil and sweat they had both put into it. Therapeutic, it had been, and had helped to cement the bond of their brand new marriage. None of this did William say but it gave him a twinge of conscience all the same. Only four years and look where they'd got to now. He took Morwenna very firmly by the hand and led them both back to the car.

It was just about warm enough, though Luisa kept her coat on as they sat with their lagers and salads outside on the terrace. The Thames was grey and lightly scuffed with ripples as they watched the rowing eights practising for the regatta. The sky was mackerel, with the promise of more rain to come. Still, it was the most spring-like they'd seen in ages. Morwenna sat poised triumphantly between them like a little princess, chortling and waving her fork.

'Eat up, lambkin,' said William tenderly, unable to resist dropping a kiss on her glossy head. His eyes met Luisa's and a glance passed between them. For one second he thought he might choke with sheer happiness. Now that they were sitting here, content and no longer in a hurry, all the things that had been worrying him faded away. He fished in his pocket and brought out Aunt Jane's gold chain. Laid it carefully on the table between them to study. Luisa remained politely mystified, uncertain what it was that was so much exciting him.

'It's her blood group,' he said, rubbing the tarnished gold with his finger. 'And, with luck, the vital link I've been searching for.'

Luisa quizzically cocked her head. 'How so?' She really was irresistible when she was solemn. He had an urge to take her in his arms but that would never do in front of the child.

'The connection between all these random murders. I remain convinced that there is one. And now this could be a real clue.'

Luisa, baffled, shook her head. 'I'm afraid I still don't understand.'

'You'll see,' he said mysteriously, slipping the chain back into his pocket. He had said enough on this grisly subject. The day was far too magical to continue it now.

The person he needed to talk to was really Aisha, the Asian doctor. He asked Luisa what she knew about blood but she told him very little. Hers was simply a clerical post; all she really did was collate and file. And occasionally stand in as receptionist. He should ring the surgery and make a proper appointment. Aisha was, indeed, a lovely person and if she had said she would help, then she certainly would. William glowed; two birds with one stone. He could use it as a transparent excuse for getting to see Luisa again. For he was smitten. He couldn't believe he could feel this way so quickly.

Morwenna started babbling about Mummy but he headed her off. He didn't want Edwina's intrusive presence spoiling this perfect day. A wary sun crept out from behind the clouds and Luisa unbuttoned her coat and slid the trademark dark glasses over her eyes. She looked a little like Jackie Onassis with her sleek dark hair and finely sculpted features. Of course, not quite as spectacular but pretty damn good, nonetheless. Today she seemed softer and younger than he'd thought, with many of the care lines wiped away. He longed to know more about her but didn't dare ask. Not without some opening from her.

Watching her smile at Morwenna's antics emboldened him to try a little fishing. All she could do was rebuff him, though he couldn't see why she would want to. Since those initial tentative conversations, he felt they were developing into genuine friends. Otherwise she'd hardly be sitting here with him now, being so openly affectionate to Morwenna.

'You say you have no children yourself,' he said.

She shook her head. Then, after a quite significant pause: 'I did have one once. A little girl. She died.'

William, shocked and embarrassed, was contrite.

'I am so sorry. How clumsy of me. I really had no idea.'

Luisa smiled sadly. 'How could you? I try not to talk about her much. It was all so painful.'

'What was her name?'

'Adriana.'

'How long ago?'

'Nine years.'

'How old was she? That's if you don't mind my asking?'

Luisa mutely shook her head and looked at him over the glasses. Her fine eyes were swimming and she dabbed at them. William could have cut out his tongue with remorse.

'Two,' she said simply with a huskiness in her throat. 'The exact age Morwenna is now.'

'What happened?' But she simply shook her head, too overcome with emotion to continue.

William grabbed her hand and squeezed it tight, wishing he could do considerably more. He couldn't bear to see her in so much pain. Began to comprehend her air of withdrawal. This was a person still deeply suffering and all he'd succeeded in doing was making things worse. But Luisa, sensing his deep discomfort, returned the hand squeeze and kissed him on the cheek.

'I'll tell you all about her some day, I promise. It's dear of you to ask.'

And so he had to leave it for a while. But was cheered at the prospect of a continuing relationship. If he played his cards carefully and did not move too fast, there was simply no telling where all of this might lead.

Edwina rang in to confirm her safe arrival. The flight had been fine, she said, yet sounded oddly subdued. Vancouver was indeed a wonderful city though, so far, she had hardly been out of the hotel, which was conveniently part of the conference centre. They were right down on the water's edge and she planned to take a walk to look at the cruise ships. She asked to speak to Morwenna, who had long been asleep.

'What time is it there?' she asked and William told her nine. She was getting confused about the different time zones.

'Did you find the tag?' He told her that he had, though noticed she didn't seem interested or particularly want to know more. He realised how preoccupied she had become and surprised himself by finding it less hurtful than usual. Their marriage appeared to be quietly disintegrating. He was shocked to discover how little he really cared.

Then someone at Edwina's end spoke to her fairly abruptly and, after a muffled conversation, she told William she really had to go.

'Don't work too hard,' he said cheerfully, hanging up without an iota of regret. He hugged himself as he wandered about the house, too restless and fired up to want to relax. He had thought about ringing Tim . . . and then given in. To hell with it! Whatever the danger, he couldn't not share this latest breakthrough with his buddy. It wouldn't be fair and he needed Tim's expert back-up. It hadn't felt right not to have him along. Frustratingly, for once Tim wasn't there so he would just have to leave it till morning.

Meanwhile, his head was still full of Luisa and the giddy effect she was having upon his life. Telling him about her child had seemed like a big leap forward. He longed to know the exact circumstances, including where the father was now. But he needed still to step very carefully or else she might cease to trust him and back away.

Aisha said she could fit him in before evening surgery, so he pushed Morwenna over to her just before five. The waiting room was less crowded than usual and he looked around hopefully for Luisa. Alas, today there was no sign of her. Obviously not her shift. Aisha came down to fetch him and ushered him up to her bright, airy room over-looking the blossom-filled garden. These wedding-cake houses in Holland Park were marvellously spacious and light. How the practice could still afford the rent was something he had long wondered. Perhaps they had a peppercorn rent or else a silent benefactor.

William reminded her of their previous conversation and, without going into details, produced the chain with its tiny gold lozenge. He explained what he wanted to know about the blood group and Aisha took it across to the window and squinted at the minuscule inscription.

'AB negative,' she told him after a while. 'Perhaps the rarest blood group of them all.'

So no wonder Aunt Jane was so proud of it, in her pathetically superior way. And perhaps that accounted for her charity work, raising funds for the Haemophilia Society. He knew he ought not to make fun of her; she had been, at heart, a good woman. But her continuous posturing had not been easy to take, one of the reasons they had visited her so rarely. Which, in retrospect, still made him feel guilty, especially since she had left Edwina the lot.

'What precisely does that mean, in layman's terms?' he asked. Aisha flashed him her radiant smile and explained.

'Everybody has a blood group in the ABO system. Forty-seven per cent of people are O. Forty-three per cent are A. Whereas only seven per cent are B and just three per cent AB.'

William whistled softly, impressed. 'So pretty rare then?'

'Rarer even than that since she's AB *negative* whereas eighty per cent of people are Rhesus positive.'

Aisha was clearly intrigued to know what William's interest could be.

'Is this person a relative of yours? And have you a special reason for wanting to know? Blood types aren't hereditary, you know.' She glanced at Morwenna. 'Not always.'

'My wife's aunt,' said William, 'and it's academic. The poor woman has been dead these past five years.'

Without explaining further, he thanked her and left, promising to tell her all when he felt he could. He didn't want to waste more of her time and feared she might think him foolish if he explained. It was still very much a long-shot, but he did feel he might be getting a little closer. Now he really needed to get hold of Tim and set the boy detective back on the case.

Tim was thrilled when William finally tracked him down and told him of this latest potential development. He appeared not to have taken in that William had been avoiding him. Was far too hot on the trail to imagine such things.

'What do we do now?' he asked, bursting with enthusiasm.

'Find out if there's a blood group match,' said William. Otherwise, they were off on another false trail which, after all this time, he couldn't bear.

'How do we do that?'

'I'm not entirely sure.' The police, so obstructive up till now, would hardly be likely to dish out such information. Not to a couple of amateurs. William ran through the murders in his head; according to his own chronological reckoning, next on the agenda would be the tragic Marshes. But Robert Marsh appeared to have gone to ground. A few selective calls from Tim established that.

Then William had another inspired thought.

'The school,' he said. They were bound to keep a record. And might be more compassionate to a discreet, unauthorised enquiry. Tim got back on the case and pulled a few favours with the Northampton *Chronicle & Echo*. It cost him a lunch but turned out to be well worth the effort. A sympathetic female reporter actually went round to the school and conned the head into letting her have the relevant information. The woman could see no harm in it; it might even do some good. Anything that might help convict the still uncaught murderer.

'Those poor little girls,' she said. 'Who could have done such a vile thing as that?' Privately, she had long suspected

327

the father, though he seemed such a decent fellow. At least, on the surface.

Tim, triumphant, called William back.

'Got it!' he said. 'They were both the same.' Melanie and Sadie Marsh had both been blood group A. The medical records the school still held confirmed it.

'And the mother?'

'I'm afraid we don't know that,' said Tim, though a visit to the local doctor might be worth a shot. William was somewhat deflated, his theory already disproved. But Tim was prepared to squander more time, so he let him. A few more phonecalls and he found the family doctor. Who was cautiously willing to talk to him in confidence.

'Shocking tragedy,' he said, tut-tutting, and was persuaded to check through his records at Tim's request. It could hardly make any difference now and the police hadn't even thought to ask. While Robert Marsh had removed himself from the scene.

Tim rang William back, now also subdued.

'Group O,' he said. 'The most common of them all.'

Which left them apparently back at square one. William began to despair.

'I thought we were there,' he told Luisa the following day as they sat together at the playground watching Morwenna. The seedy stranger was loitering under the trees; William realised how long it had been since he'd seen him.

'What are you looking at?' asked Luisa, glancing round.

'That guy over there in the raggedy overcoat.'

She raised her eyebrows enquiringly and William started to laugh.

'It's nothing really. I suppose I just don't much like the cut of his jib. There's something definitely sinister about him. He always seems to be hanging around the kids.'

William looked for the two little boys and there they were, playing on the slide. There seemed to be no one parental around, no adult to whom it looked as if they belonged. And yet they seemed perfectly at ease. William made a sudden decision; too many bad things had been happening.

'Stay here,' he said to Luisa. 'I won't be long.' And strode across the grass to confront the man.

Just as he was approaching him, the man saw William coming. He checked his watch as if he were suddenly late and hurriedly walked away. William gave up. There was nothing he could say. He was simply being an interfering busybody. But he didn't like it and intended to stay on his case. And next time he had the chance, he would confront him.

'No good,' he said to Luisa, 'the bastard's scarpered.'

She wanted an explanation so he gave one. Luisa's eyes softened; what a gem of a man he was. She reached for his hand and squeezed it in empathy.

'You know something,' she told him, gazing deep into his eyes. 'You are quite the most decent man I have ever met.'

32

That night, when he couldn't sleep, William had a sudden flash of intuition. Just because the Marshes appeared not to fit, did not automatically mean that his theory was dud. He went upstairs and sought inspiration from his geological map. The pale blue circle was irrefutably there, witness to some sort of pattern. He grabbed a scrap of rough paper and jotted down notes. The Marshes, the schoolboys and then the bank manager. It shouldn't be too difficult to track each one of them down and accurately test his theory about blood. He knew in his bones that he had a point, refused to be deflected.

Luckily he had made his peace with Tim, whom he called as early as he dared, dimly remembering that the lad lived in rented accommodation.

'Sorry to disturb you . . .' But Tim was already up and running. His mind, it turned out, had been following similar lines. They conferred, agreed and Tim offered to do the legwork. He had, after all, the credentials to pull it off.

'I am the press, remember,' he said self-importantly. In a position to flash his card to open all doors. William, visualising the intensity on the young face, agreed to defer to the pro and let him rip. Tim's very youth and enthusiasm often made him feel tired. He chuckled as he returned upstairs to check if Morwenna was awake. All his former enthusiasm was creeping back. He would crack this case if it was the last thing that he did. And after that, maybe, go out and look for a job.

The week had gone by in a flash; there wasn't a lot of time left. William, content to leave Tim on the case, fretted about how to get to see Luisa again. He couldn't just hang around like a lovelorn schoolboy. Faint heart, as the old saw went, never won fair lady. And yet he was a married man and she a virtuous woman. How did they handle such tricky matters these days? He hadn't a clue. He thought of consulting Polly Graham but wasn't entirely sure how much he could trust her. Had heard too much of her cackling repartee to risk becoming the butt of her mordant wit. And then, coincidentally, she called.

'I am having a fund-raising bash for the local Conservatives,' she said. 'My place, tomorrow night. I am sorry it's so last minute but . . .' William laughed; he really didn't mind. Had never been too proud to act as a stopgap. Was used to standing in as a substitute male. Besides, in his dull little social life, it might make a pleasant diversion. Even though he was a staunch Lib Dem, and always had been. As Polly, had she been more on the ball, might have known. He booked a babysitter and checked that he had a clean shirt. Mrs P, purely out of the goodness of her heart, efficiently shone his shoes.

'Going out, then?' she asked, with approval. To her mind, he had drawn the short straw.

'Just to a charity do round the corner, with friends.' Amazing how guilty he felt.

'Do you good,' she said approvingly. Time he got up off his bum and had some fun. She wouldn't even blame him if he got off with somebody else. That snotty madam certainly had it coming. Forever swanning around and neglecting him. To Mrs P's conservative mind, it simply wasn't on.

Guest of honour was the local MP, Harvey Greenslade. William, who had encountered him before, disliked the man on sight. All the things that were wrong with the Tories in one supercilious package, with a loud, commanding voice like a brigadier's. He had just arrived with his entourage when William sauntered in, and was working the room methodically, shaking hands.

'William!' said Polly, clasping him round the neck and dragging him over reluctantly to be presented. Greenslade had soft, carefully manicured hands and a cold stare aimed just to the left of William's ear. Constantly on the lookout for someone who might be of use. The sort of obsequious charm that was quite insincere. William uttered a platitude before disengaging his hand. His inclination was to wipe his palm, but he succeeded in restraining himself. Instead, suddenly realising just how peckish he was, he headed downstairs to the buffet in the kitchen. This was where he felt most at his ease, scene of Polly's numerous coffee mornings.

The spacious room was filling up with local residents, many of whom he knew. He nodded and smiled as he loaded his plate, then headed into a corner to join some old chums.

'Didn't expect to run into you here,' said Oliver, an affable Kensington solicitor whose friendly, bespectacled wife had just been made a QC.

William grinned. 'You're right, it's not really my scene. But Polly's a mate and I owe her a favour or two.' Which must sound a tad ungracious considering the spread she'd laid on. Polly, who loved to show off her home, was ever the consummate hostess, though her dreary husband, the insurance broker, as usual was nowhere to be seen.

'No Edwina?' asked the QC wife.

William shook his head. 'Off on one of her foreign jaunts,' he explained. The woman looked sympathetic, had always had a bit of a soft spot for William. And was mildly suspicious of any woman who insisted on putting her own career first. She had managed to juggle her recent elevation by waiting until the children were grown and fled. She asked if he were working again and William laughed and confessed with his customary candour.

'Nobody wants me,' he said, which was not quite the truth.

They chatted on for a while, acknowledging other neighbours. And then, as he glanced around the room,

333

William was suddenly struck dumb. He glimpsed a recent arrival and froze. At the foot of the stairs, which he'd just descended, was a thin-faced man with wispy hair and a jacket that had seen better days. With a sharp intake of breath and muttered apology, William shuffled around for a clearer view. It was him, the bloke from the park, and he still looked shifty. He was standing alone and isolated, nervously clutching a drink. William made a swift decision and started to elbow his way through the crowd. Now was the ideal time for some sort of a showdown, if only to clear the air. But the surge round the buffet impeded his progress. By the time he had managed to work his way through, his quarry was gone.

Dumping his half-empty plate on a table, William shot rapidly up the stairs. The hallway was packed and the front door wide open. Harvey Greenslade was starting his speech.

'Order, now, order,' shouted one of his pimply retinue, and slowly the voluble babble began to abate. Greenslade, affectedly donning a pair of gold pince-nez, began to declaim ponderously and at considerable length. William, helplessly pinned at the rear of the room, frantically looked around for the seedy man. Who seemed no longer to be even in the room; in fact, to have vanished without trace. At last, after what seemed interminable hours, Greenslade got to the crux of things and exhorted his loyal followers to give generously. After heavy applause, the crush eventually eased and William was able to grab Polly and yank her aside.

'Who was that man?' he asked urgently, pointing into thin air. 'The balding one with the rundown look. If you'll pardon the description.'

Polly looked puzzled. 'Not anyone I know. Perhaps he tagged along with the Greenslade party.'

Perhaps, or then, perhaps not. He didn't look much like a Tory. But whatever the truth, he was clearly no longer there. William combed each floor of the house to make sure. He must have been some sort of gatecrasher, though it did seem unlikely. William, suddenly bored and dispirited, made his excuses and slunk off home.

The message light was flashing. Tim, sounding very hyped up. He had checked with Mrs Hargreaves and, bless her, she'd come up trumps. Her husband's blood group had been AB negative. It looked as if William's latest theory might not be quite so hare-brained after all.

'Luisa,' said William breathlessly, as they sat together on a bench beneath the trees. Edwina was due home at the end of the week and he still hadn't found the right words. She turned on him misty, dark, soulful eyes and he took her impulsively into his arms, breathing the lemony essence of her hair. 'Oh, my darling,' he murmured, quite carried away, then kissed her very hard and with genuine feeling.

'William,' said Luisa, responding in like manner. Then they both recoiled and stared at each other in shock. In all the years he had been with Edwina, William had not so much as glanced at anyone else. Not with more than just gallant approval. Most certainly, never with lust. And now this sloe-eyed stranger had crept up and stolen his heart in what seemed like a matter of mere seconds. He still didn't really understand it. Except that she did wonders for his dented self-esteem. He was sick of being kicked around by the harpy he had married. Luisa appeared to look up to him, to treat him with appropriate respect.

They sat in silence, lost in each other's eyes, and Luisa fiddled nervously with her hair. It was clear, from her sudden loss of composure, that she was every bit as shaken up as he was. From what he'd gathered from their various furtive meetings, he knew her to be a woman of iron principle. Despite the aura of desolation that seemed to engulf her life, it wasn't her style, he was sure of it, to steal another woman's husband. She was far too proud. He reached for both her hands and gently kissed the palms, then kissed her again, more fervently, on the mouth.

'I've wanted to do that from the moment I first saw you.'

'I know. I have felt the same.'

William's heart was thumping out of control and his blood was rushing in his ears with ecstasy. *She loves me!* He could hardly get his head around the notion, a woman this chic and composed. She took him seriously, admired the man he was. Was looking at him now with yearning and love. But where did they go from here? He had to decide; time was fast running out and he still didn't know.

He couldn't just turn his back and walk away from all he had worked so hard to achieve with Edwina. The marriage might be heading towards the rocks but he still wasn't totally sure if he wanted to jump ship.

A small, chubby hand was plonked on his knee and there was a breathless Morwenna. She'd been out there in the meadow, looking for buttercups, and her face was streaked with mud and bright golden pollen. Saved by the bell, he released his pent-up breath and began to see the humour of the situation.

'Come here, poppet.' He fished out his handkerchief and lovingly wiped her face. He could not imagine a more effective passion killer than a lively two-year-old perpetually in attendance. Luisa, luckily, found it amusing too. As usual, their minds were working in full accord. She scooped up the child in a massive bear hug and buried her face in the silky hair, breathing in the fragrance of her skin.

'Babies always smell like vanilla,' she said. 'I wonder why that is.'

'Purity,' said William. 'They are not yet polluted. We might all learn a lesson or two from them.'

They walked, hands linked all three of them, back to where reality set in, and William wished the moment might be frozen in time. To stroll on through eternity with these two female creatures he loved, not to have to make a decision or come crashing down from cloud nine. But that, alas, was impossible. Edwina would shortly be home. They stood in the entrance to Holland Park and he dared once more to take her in his arms.

'We are going to have to talk,' he said, 'as soon as it can be arranged.' Without the watching presence of Morwenna. He was still no closer to knowing what he should do. Predominant in his mind right now was that he couldn't bear the thought of letting her go.

'What can we do?' Her eyes were tragic. 'There can't be any future. You're not free.'

And then, quite simply, she turned and walked away. And William watched her go with a breaking heart.

The news from Tim was encouraging. Pilkington's blood group, too, was a perfect match. It was starting to look as if William might be right and someone specifically targeting that particular blood group. But why? Until they had that figured, it was still inconclusive.

'Blood transfusions. Think along those lines. Assuming they all were donors, which we'll check, that might be the catalyst that unites them.'

Tim wasn't with him. William explained. 'Seems the murderer must have an axe to grind.'

'So we're looking for someone with blood type AB negative?'

'Slightly better odds than a needle in a haystack. Remember the little we already know. That only three per cent of people share that group.' Still, it was hard to see how they ought to proceed. First William put in a call to Aisha for help.

He found himself reluctant to visit the surgery. All of a sudden he was bashful of facing Luisa. Until he knew in

338

his heart for certain exactly what he wanted, it wasn't fair to batter her emotions any more. Away from her, with his sanity partially restored, he saw in stark detail the truth of their situation. There was nothing he could offer her, not while he was a kept man. And he would not risk destroying the marriage and forfeiting the child. He had acted too impetuously. The day of reckoning had arrived. His wife was on her way back; he would have to come clean.

Aisha was her usual friendly self, intrigued to know the background to his inquiries.

'I'll explain some time, I promise,' he said. But felt that, right now, it was somehow bad luck if too many knew what he was up to. Tim and Luisa, those were the people he trusted. Not even Mrs P would be part of this little cabal.

'What happens,' he asked, 'to the blood that is donated? Where does it actually go once it's been taken?'

'To various blood banks around the country. To be stored for use whenever needed.'

'And do they keep any documentation of the names and identities of the donors?'

'Indeed. It's all on computer at the transfusion centre. Can be accessed at any time by an authorised person.'

Slowly, slowly it was starting to come together. And where would the probable centre be, he wanted to know.

'Bristol, almost certainly,' said Aisha promptly. 'They have closed down many of the others. That's the main one.'

* * *

'What we really need now,' said Tim brightly, 'is another murder on which to test our facts.' Everything seemed to be falling into place. They could scarcely believe how well they'd done.

'Since he appears to be closing in,' said William grimly, 'my guess is that the next one will be here in London.'

33

Josephine was in the front garden, pruning the roses, when Harvey eventually appeared. He had sleeked back his thick greying hair with his silver-backed brushes and fixed his heavy silk tie into a perfect old-fashioned knot. His suit was classic, his grooming immaculate; his cologne had the sharp tang of lime. He had even clipped his nostril hairs and flossed his teeth till the gums bled. Turning his head from side to side in front of the triptych mirror, he sucked in his stomach and checked his breath, then popped a strong mint in his mouth to be doubly sure. Now that he was so much in the public eye, it paid to take no chances.

'Off to the House?' she asked innocently, strolling over to the car. Harvey let down the electronic window; he hated it when she enquired but she was his wife. He had been with Jo Jo now for twenty-two years. The world saw them as the ideal couple.

'There's a three-line whip at eleven,' he said, 'so I'll probably stay up there overnight.' Jo Jo smiled without any sign of rancour. As patient, long-suffering helpmeets went, she was, beyond question, the tops.

'Poor you,' she said, without a trace of irony. 'It's shocking just how hard they make you work.' No longer the pale beauty she had been when they first met, she had nevertheless handled the interim years with grace. Still slim as a girl with skin like a wild rose, she had surreptitiously desiccated from within. From across a room, with her colourless curly hair, she still possessed the appeal of her debutante days. Only when approached more closely, and the slightly fixed stare of her eyes became apparent, was it noticeable that she might not be quite as stable as she seemed. Twenty-two years of marriage to Harvey had certainly taken their toll. Deprived of the children she had always longed for, she had sunk herself into her public role. Wife to an increasingly eminent politician with leadership possibilities looming large. Life for the gentle and charming Josephine Greenslade ought to have been a dream but was not.

'What time tomorrow will you be back, dear?' She was more than resigned to his absences.

'Not certain. I'll have to let you know.' Since they'd moved back to London from the peace of the Cotswolds, life had assumed a frenetic patina she still hadn't quite got to grips with. But it wasn't in Jo Jo's nature to make a fuss. She was still quite in awe of the brilliant man who had picked her, and content, more or less, to remain in his shadow. No matter how lonely it often was.

'Don't go exhausting yourself, then,' she said, pecking him on the cheek. 'Remember we have the constituency dinner on Thursday as well as the Strasbourg trip at the weekend.' She did make a marvellous social secretary, not that he actually needed one. He had four staff members to back him up here and a couple more besides in Westminster. But he humoured his wife by allowing her to meddle, provided it didn't intrude. It was, after all, her family home they now lived in, her inheritance on which his whole career was based. When the lure of politics had decreed that he should marry, shrewd Harvey Greenslade had chosen both wisely and well. Josephine Hamilton was pure cut glass. It suited all his purposes to cherish her.

Her father, Sir Douglas Hamilton, had been the sitting member until his untimely death in the street from a stroke. Strings had been pulled and Harvey shoe-horned in, released from the sleepy backwater that had so much bored him. This was certainly more like it, the safest Tory seat in the whole country. They had been out of office quite long enough; he had strong expectations of the June election.

A couple of committees and his morning's work was done. Harvey took a leisurely lunch at the Tate, then indulged himself by wandering through the Turners, which always made him feel a better man. By three he was done, still with time on his hands, so he grabbed a taxi to William IV Street and the private drinking club he had long frequented. If his luck was in, who knew what might transpire? His libido lately had been feeling pretty frisky.

He kept this side of his life from Jo Jo, though occasionally wondered how much she actually guessed. What was never referred to could do no harm. They remained punctiliously courteous towards each other. There was always the risk that the press might cotton on, but that only added to the thrill of these adventures. Provided he maintained an uxorious public persona, Harvey reckoned smugly that he was smarter than any of them. They would have to run very fast indeed if they wanted to trip him up.

He returned to the Westminster flat at five for a nap and a shower before dinner. He was taking his constituency chairman to the Garrick for a contingency powwow on the election. If they got it right – and he thought they probably would – by June he might well be in the Cabinet. And after that, the sky was surely the limit. Harvey relished the thought of so much power. He had come a considerable way in the last two decades, since his days as a very flash advertising man, and was steadily re-inventing himself. The move to Campden Hill Square was opportune – when his mother-in-law, poor old dear, went into a home – and represented the acme of all his social cravings. Next stop Downing Street if the election went their way. Harvey Greenslade was riding high, a very self-confident man.

He had chosen this block for its high-tech security as much as the division bell proximity. He could cross the road in a matter of minutes without ever having to inconvenience himself. Not for him all those tedious wasted hours, hanging around in the House, simply waiting to vote. That was a mug's game, and Harvey was by no means a mug but a vertically aimed projectile, accelerating fast.

'Evening, Jones,' he said to the security man, surrounded in his cubicle by his flickering bank of screens.

'Evening, sir,' said the black man deferentially. He'd been trained as a prison guard before pulling out this plum. He slid off his stool to press the lift button and stood there, respect incarnate, until it arrived. He secretly didn't much care for the man, found him overbearing and a bully, but had learned early on the way to keep him sweet. Grovel, grovel, grovel, like an old-fashioned Uncle Tom, and always be on hand with a smile and a cheery word.

'Weather's a little brighter,' he said as the lift doors started to close. 'Seems like we may yet be getting a glimpse of spring.'

He was still on the late shift when Harvey returned after midnight, having done his electoral duty by the whips. The Garrick dinner had been entirely satisfactory and they'd toasted their certain success with a series of brandies. Then he'd said goodnight to the stuffy constituency chairman and walked on into Soho for dessert. The bad thing about politics was the unremitting dullness. He felt he was more than due some recreation.

'Oh, by the way,' he said casually now to Jones, 'I'm expecting a bit of company later. Send them up.'

'Right, sir,' said Jones, his ebony face impassive. He was used to Harvey Greenslade's erratic life.

Once the lift doors had clanged shut, he returned to reading his paper, with one eye cocked on the bank of security screens. Very little amiss ever went on here; the nights were usually long and uneventful. The building was as fortified as MI5. Not the most exciting of jobs but certainly very well paid. Cushy, too, in this airless, well-heated building. Certainly compared to the prison service. Jones was careful never to step out of line. He'd not find a gravy train like this again.

When the doorbell rang and he buzzed in the caller, he was startled to see a motorcycle courier. He glanced at the clock, almost ten to one. Surely they didn't normally work this late? The courier still had his visor down and was clutching an official-looking box. Jones leaned forward to take it from his hands but the man firmly shook his head. It had to be handed direct to Mr Greenslade. Parliamentary top security and all that.

'You want me to call him now?' asked Jones, amazed. The courier simply nodded silently. *Well, on your head be it* . . . He clicked on the connection and was further surprised when Greenslade told him to send the fellow up.

After that, with the couple of beers he'd had, Jones found it hard to keep his eyes from closing. Curtis would shortly be relieving him. Tonight it had seemed a very long shift. He nodded off in the comfort of his den and actually never saw the visitor leave. Though, of course, that would not go down on his records. Whatever the cameras might say.

Curtis, the other security guard, was on duty when the PPS arrived. Robin was a pleasant young man, fresh-faced and engagingly enthusiastic. Always treated the staff as equals, in politics an invaluable plus.

'How is he this morning?' he asked breezily as he walked by, arms as usual laden with government papers. Greenslade was famed for his very uncertain temper. Among the denizens of Westminster, he was not a popular man.

'Haven't actually seen him today. He hasn't yet been down.' Unusual, now he thought of it, for Greenslade was a regular early riser.

'Must be sleeping it off,' said Robin with a knowing grin.

When he failed to gain admittance, Robin used his own key and was startled to see that the bedroom door was still closed. Ten to ten and a mountain of work to be got through. He hesitated disturbing him; wasn't quite sure what he should do. In the end he returned, rather lamely, to the lobby to consult the security guard.

'It seems he isn't even up yet,' he said. 'And I really don't want to be the one to disturb him. Would you mind ringing him, to warn him that I'm here, and I'll go across the street for a quick cup of coffee.'

Curtis dutifully dialled the number, which simply rang and rang. 'Are you sure he's actually in there?' he asked and the PPS shook his head.

'He said he was staying up last night because of the three-line whip. Maybe he changed his mind and went home to Kensington.' Why he needed these two fancy London addresses was something the young man could never comprehend. But if Greenslade had gone home to Campden Hill Square, he would surely have let him know by now. And be back here in time for this morning's regular briefing.

'The bedroom door's closed. I didn't like to wake him.' They looked at each other for a moment's mute understanding. Then: 'Better get back up there, I suppose, and take a proper look.'

The blinds were down and the room in absolute darkness, but Robin could just make out someone on the bed. He coughed rather loudly and rattled around, but still the figure didn't move.

'Sir?' he whispered enquiringly, before daring to switch on the light. 'Christ!' he said then at his normal volume. And belted back downstairs to fetch the guard.

Harvey Greenslade was handcuffed to the bed, wearing nothing but a laced-up leather mask. The quilt was rolled back and the sheets drenched with blood. The smell in the over-heated room was appalling. Curtis efficiently felt for a pulse but the body was already stone cold. He must have been in this state for a matter of hours. The question was: how had the murderer gained access? And where had he vanished to after the deed had been done?

348

Robin went to unlace the mask but Curtis was professional enough to stop him.

'Wait, don't touch him. You could destroy valuable evidence. We must call the cops and do it the proper way.'

'But the press . . .' wailed Robin, imagining the headlines and his boss splashed in lurid detail across the front pages. The man was a jerk and he'd never been able to like him but, still, there was a limit to what he deserved. And the wife was nice. At the thought of her, Robin felt himself on the brink of tears. Someone would have to break the news. He had a nasty feeling he knew who that would be.

Curtis stuck to his guns. He was a pro.

'I don't give a shit about the press,' he said. 'It has to be done by the book.' Which first meant covering his own delicate hide. He couldn't be seen to have been on duty when it happened. As long as it could be pinned down to Jones's shift, then he might still be in the clear. And at least they would have the surveillance tapes of anyone coming or going.

This time the police came out in full force, sirens screaming, the works. No more shoving it under the carpet; this was the metropolis, the victim a public figure. Within minutes of Curtis's call they arrived, five big men all squashed into the lobby with mobiles, forensic kit, even a sniffer dog. They followed Curtis grimly up to the flat, with Robin trailing ineffectually in their wake. They all grouped round the grisly scene on the bed and the pathologist took his time examining the corpse. Dead at least six hours, was the pronouncement. And then the officer in charge proceeded to unlace the hood.

Greenslade's face was contorted in a grimace which might have started as pleasure but rapidly changed to pain. The leather had constricted him so his cheeks were purple and puffy. His eyes had turned bright scarlet by whatever it was that had been done. As the lacing was loosened and the hood fell away, the group round the bed watched in horror. Robin, by now, was feeling distinctly queasy. He wasn't at all sure that he was up to it. This was far worse than anything he'd imagined but, then, he'd led a relatively sheltered life.

The lacing finally parted, the leather fell away, and Greenslade's head, propped up on a pile of pillows, lolled forward and practically came off. The knife had gone into his throat so deeply that only the tendons and spinal cord were holding it all together. In addition to which, he'd been slashed from throat to groin, as effectively gutted as a fish. Robin's head began to swim and he made it to the bathroom just in time. As he knelt with his head over the lavatory bowl, his thoughts were full of the delicate Josephine Greenslade. And how she would ever survive a trauma like this.

34

Edwina was home from Canada, seemingly still subdued, though William, for the first time, scarcely noticed. Too much else right now was going on in his life for him to care about her selfish mood fluctuations. She had had her chance and blown it royally. One of these days he intended to have it all out. Meanwhile his principal preoccupation was worrying about the Greenslade murder. The publicity was splattered across all the front pages. At last they'd got the message and were taking action.

He cursed himself, as he had so many times, for having been such a reckless fool as to get himself noticed in the first place. If it hadn't been for that *Argus* article, he would not have been glimpsed on television. With the name of the street, as well as the house number, prominently displayed. And even though Greenslade had actually been killed in Westminster, the world now knew exactly where he had lived. Just around the corner, in Campden Hill Square, far too close to Hillgate Place for comfort. If only William had kept his sleuthing to himself, he would be that much better able to sleep at night. He had allowed conceit to stand in the way of cool reason, thus setting himself – and his family – up as prime targets. The more they found out about this ruthless killer, that much more horrendous it became.

The obvious thing now would be to take it all to the police and throw himself and his family under their protection. Yet William still hesitated, uncertain if this were wise. What if they simply screwed up as they had before? He kept closely in touch with the valiant Tim, still doing sterling research, tracking down the families of the victims. He'd established already that several were regular donors. They were also turning out AB negative as well. The problem now was to link them in some way, for which he needed access to the records. Again, of course, the police might be able to assist them, though they'd more likely take it all away and shut out William and Tim. Which William wasn't prepared to allow, not at this late stage. They had come so far, done so much research, he was still determined to crack it himself.

The Scotland Yard crime squad were giving the two security men a thorough going over. They worked in alternating eight-hour shifts, during which each was solely responsible for the building's safety. Jones, suppressing the fact that he might have nodded off, assured them categorically he'd seen nothing out of the ordinary. Only a couple of tenants, both of them Labour MPs, returning late after voting in the House. Plus a motorcycle courier delivering an urgent package, whom he'd sent straight up to Mr Greenslade, as directed. They replayed the surveillance tapes and studied them, frame by frame, and there indeed was the messenger entering the lobby. Dressed entirely in black leather and still wearing his helmet with the opaque visor down.

'Aren't you supposed to insist they remove their headgear?' asked one of the crime squad. 'So you can check them out? Like in the banks.'

Jones thought rapidly and warily scratched his head, uncertain of the appropriate reply. It was something he hadn't encountered before though, now he came to think of it, they were right. Best tread carefully or he'd find himself out on his ear. And he with young children still at school.

'Don't really know,' he said, after a cautious pause. 'This one certainly seemed in a bit of a hurry. And Mr Greenslade was expecting him. Had said to send him straight up.' Assuming, of course, it was the courier he had meant. But no one else had visited him that night. The two men studying the tapes exclaimed and the rest of them crowded round.

'What happened to the courier? He seems never to have reappeared.'

'Is there a back entrance?' Jones shook his head. Not one out of range of the bank of cameras. Perhaps there was a missing tape. Again Jones shook his head; they were all in careful sequence, numbered with date and time. The system was pretty effective.

'So where the hell did he get to? You must know. You surely had to let him out at some point.'

Jones began to panic. Didn't know what to say. Could hardly admit that he might just have nodded off. He pointed out that it was right at the end of his shift. Probably Curtis had been the one to see the man leave.

'All right,' said the head honcho wearily. 'We'll come back to you again later.' Give you a second chance, was what he meant. They still had Curtis to interview. Perhaps he would prove a slightly more lucid witness. But they drew a blank with him, too, though he couldn't have been more obliging. He'd started his vigil a little after one and seen no one at all until dawn. The graveyard shift was usually pretty dead with only the arrival of the cleaners making any diversion.

'About what time would that be?' asked a policeman. They were contracted in from an outside cleaning firm.

'Four-ish,' said Curtis, efficiently checking his clip-board. 'They work at night so as not to disturb the residents.' He fast-forwarded the tape and suddenly there they were, a group of chattering overalled women being let into the lobby.

'Stop right there,' commanded a senior officer and they all peered more closely at the group. Five of them, look-ing pretty much the same, small and olive-skinned, quite obviously foreign. Cypriots or something like that, all of them interchangeable.

'Don't know what this country would do without its illegal immigrants,' remarked one of the crime squad

cynically. 'Paid, no doubt, in backhanders without needing to bother about tax or insurance like the rest of us.'
They rewound the tape and watched it through again, the
women dispersing to their designated areas.

'How long are they usually here?'

'About a couple of hours. See,' he said, fast-forwarding
again. 'Ten past six and they're leaving.' Each of the women
was now carrying a large bin bag, tied at the top in a
knot. They surged through the doorway and into a waiting van, faintly discernible through the smoked glass.

'And that was all that happened last night?'

He nodded. Till Robin arrived. Yet somehow upstairs
a man had been violently butchered. And they hadn't the
least idea how it could have been done.

'Perhaps it was a neighbour,' suggested one of the crime
squad flippantly. The place, after all, was swarming with
Labour MPs.

'Unlikely,' said his boss, ignoring the levity. Though
word throughout the building had it that Greenslade
hadn't exactly been flavour of the month.

He knew he shouldn't do it, it would only be unfair, but
his need to see Luisa became insupportable. Despite his
firm resolution to leave her alone while he thought, he
fretted for her unbelievably, worse than he ever could
have guessed. Not only on a sexual level, she had also
turned into a friend. He missed her calm and pragmatic
approach, would have liked to have had her take on what
he should do. He knew that if he contacted her, he'd be

potentially endangering her life, but needed her logical and intelligent understanding to help him work things out. Going to the police was not enough. He couldn't guarantee they'd understand. And it was far too late to involve Edwina who, anyway, had problems of her own. Also, he ached to make love to Luisa. Was sick like a schoolboy in the throes of first love.

Mrs P picked up on it fast, as she would. 'You all right?' she asked him more than once, cocking a shrewd eye on his obvious suffering. Whatever had been going on was clearly beginning to take its toll. And just as the missus had come home. She hoped he might confide in her but William wasn't playing. Murder was one thing, in the public domain, but this entirely private.

'Just thinking about the murder,' he lied. 'It being on our doorstep this time round.'

'Oo yes,' said Mrs P with immediate relish, back on her favourite topic. 'You knew him, didn't you?' Sorting through her pail. She lapped up any titbit concerning celebrity.

'Met him a couple of times. Didn't like him. Far too smooth and phoney for my taste. I'm not surprised that they bumped him off. The best sort of Tory is a dead one.' But for once he couldn't get her to rise. She was far more fly than she appeared. Whatever was bothering him was even closer to home. He'd never succeed in pulling the wool over her eyes.

He was wondering whether he dared call the surgery when he had the most amazing piece of luck. He was standing in the Tesco checkout queue, his mind a million miles away, when she tapped him lightly on the shoulder.

'Luisa! How marvellous!' He kissed her cheek, longing to crush her to his chest and ravish her on the spot. 'I was thinking of you. Where can we go to talk?' He was hoping she might invite him to her home. Luisa, looking as unworldly as a convent girl, appeared to give the matter serious thought. Either she was leading him on or else she was too high-principled to read his mind correctly. Whatever, he found her innocence irresistible and felt he might spontaneously combust. They landed up in a seedy café halfway up the Earls Court Road. The surroundings were abysmal but neither of them cared; all they wanted was the chance to be together. He'd left Morwenna with the doting Mrs P. The weather was turning bad again and she had the beginnings of a cough. It felt good, just occasionally, to have her off his hands. He found all that full-time vigilance exhausting.

Luisa, he thought when he came to study her, looked slightly drawn, perhaps even thinner. Her usually glossy hair was flat and dull, the area round her mouth a little pinched. Wordlessly, he took her hand and raised it to his lips. She asked politely if Edwina were safely home and he curtly told her that she was. All he could think of, as he gazed into her eyes, was the ache of deprivation he felt in both heart and groin.

'How've you been?' he asked gently, and she shook her head with emotion, fumbling in her handbag for a tissue. As bad as that? Hope rose wildly in his chest and he stumbled on with what he was trying to say.

'I've missed you too. Unimaginably. Hadn't really understood till now exactly how much I care.' Edwina might be back in body but her mind was clearly still preoccupied elsewhere. They'd hardly even had a proper conversation. The difference was he was now immune. The pain had gone, it no longer hurt. The focus of his life was sitting right here. He picked up her hand and tenderly kissed the palm and she made no attempt to resist him but left it there.

'Is there somewhere we could go and really be together?' Her home, a rented room, even a hotel. Luisa mutely shook her head, her eyes two pools of misty sorrow. Whatever it was restraining her, he knew that he mustn't try to force her. Had already been far more uncontrolled than he ought. Something in her real life was obviously holding her back and only time would allow her to work it through. He tried to swing the conversation back by telling her more about the Greenslade case. As if she would care, but at least it made a diversion. They both needed space and time in which to think.

'It seems,' he said, 'that our killer is closing in. I'll be fascinated to see where he strikes next.'

Colour returned slowly to Luisa's wan cheeks and she started to breathe more normally. William released her hand and stirred his tea. He needed to get a grip on his overwrought emotions. 'Tell me one thing,' he asked her boldly. 'Do I stand a chance in the end of ever seducing you?'

There, it was out, and she didn't pull away but smiled with amusement and laid her hand on his cheek. 'Everything comes to he who waits,' she said. And that was as good as he was going to get, at least for the time being. One thing he could be thankful for, she hadn't entirely rejected him out of hand.

She had obviously paid close attention to the case, seemed to know almost as much about it as he did. 'Have you come up with any new theories?' she asked and he told her that was part of the basic problem. He outlined briefly Tim's progress with research and said they were making strides with the blood group theory. Luisa seemed fascinated and asked a lot of questions. She hadn't known AB negative was so rare.

'Only three per cent of the population.'

'Wow! I'm just an ordinary Blood Group O myself.'

'There's nothing at all ordinary about you, my dear.' And this time he did dare to kiss her on the mouth.

'Behave,' she admonished, pushing him away. There were people in the café who were staring. 'Why do you suppose he is coming after you?'

'I would have thought that obvious,' said William in darkened mood. 'After that bloody interview I gave.'

'Do take care,' she said with growing concern. 'I simply couldn't bear it if anything happened to you.'

'Bless you.' He kissed her again with fervour and this time she didn't resist. 'But you don't need to worry. I'm thinking of doing the right thing and taking what I know to Scotland Yard. Tim and I are a little out of our depth. It's time, I think, that we 'fessed up to the authorities.'

She seemed relieved, then said she had to go. But agreed to meet him again whenever he wanted. At least, on the romantic front, he seemed to be making strides. As he walked her back through Holland Park, his heart was really singing.

But he still wasn't sure about going to the police.

On an impulse, he stopped off at Polly's house in case she could throw some light on the Greenslade case. He found her pottering in the conservatory, delighted at an excuse for an early drink.

'Shocking, isn't it?' she said with salacious glee as she poured a couple of massive dry martinis. 'Poor Jo Jo doesn't know what has hit her. I can't imagine what on earth she's going to do.'

'Do the police have any idea who might have done it?'

Polly shook her head. 'Not that they're divulging, at least. I assume it was one of his casual pick-ups. Off the record, the bastard had it coming.'

William was intrigued. 'Do tell.'

'Well,' said Polly, with ill-concealed enjoyment. 'It wasn't exactly Clapham Common but I never really thought him entirely straight.'

'Didn't know him that well. Only encountered him twice. Though he did seem a bit of a slimy toad.' He remembered the handshake and the cold, hard eyes, the habit of looking past you as he talked.

360

'He hated women in that typically British way. Despised them all and constantly slighted his wife.'

'So why on earth did she marry him?' asked William ingenuously. It couldn't have been for the money, since that was hers.

'Loved him, I guess. Women do silly things. And he certainly was dead handsome in his youth.'

He asked if she knew whether Greenslade had been a blood donor.

'I would think so,' she said, 'he was always a public do-gooder. It's just the sort of thing he would make a big show of. Man of the people, future leader, setting a good example wherever he could. Even though his private life was dreck.' She pulled a face.

They gossiped on and she poured him the other half. Until, reluctantly, he told her he had to go. Edwina would be home in a couple of hours and he still had the supper to prepare. Plus bathing the child and getting her up to bed. As he walked the few yards to his own front door, he thought about Harvey Greenslade. Not a nice man but no one deserved to be murdered. Definitely not as horrendously as that.

35

The trip hadn't exactly been an unqualified success, though Edwina had no intention of letting William know that. He seemed strangely altered, which alarmed her slightly, polite yet at the same time unnervingly remote. She was so accustomed to his staid old ways, hadn't properly focused on him in months. After the four hectic days of the trade fair, they had taken a helicopter ride to Victoria, where Gareth, pulling out all the stops, had booked them a suite in a vast old-fashioned hotel looking straight out across the harbour where whales could occasionally be sighted. They had so much space it was laughable, balconies on each of the bedrooms and a dining room with a full set of high-backed chairs. Even a kitchen and separate laundry room. She dared not ask how much it all was costing.

'We could live here,' she said, and for a moment the idea took hold. No one would ever be likely to track them down. They could start another life together, free of this terrible mess. But the lack of response in Gareth struck a chill. And, in any case, sooner or later they would have to go home and face the music. Only not quite yet. Three more days of this fantasy life with the hope that he'd finally let her into his heart. At least give some indication of how he felt.

At the fair they'd both projected their customary laughing confidence and Gareth had been very evidently proud of how she looked. They had networked and partied as energetically as they could and stayed up each night far too late. The radiation between them had never been more intense, but now they'd decamped to damp and breezy Victoria, she felt that heat ebbing away. She wasn't quite sure what he wanted from her. Perhaps just a murky office fling. Which was why she was feeling so despondent now. Edwina was not accustomed to being slighted.

The share price was still wavering; they weren't yet out of the rough. And dotcom companies were crashing all about them. Bean counter Barry was still tight-lipped; the extravagance of the West Coast trip had not improved his mood. Still, they were the main shareholders, Gareth and herself, so ultimately the buck stopped entirely with them. They seemed to have stirred up a lot of potential business. Barry just hoped that, when the dust did finally settle, firm orders would prove it all to have been worthwhile. Otherwise they still risked losing the lot which, to Edwina at least, meant everything she'd got.

She had asked him if he loved her and he'd fed her the usual pap, but only when in the throes of passionate sex. At mealtimes or out in public he rarely even touched her, and the bite of his caustic wit had a new feral edge.

On more than one occasion he had reduced her almost to tears. He appeared to enjoy humiliating her and simply shrugged it off. Occasionally she caught him talking furtively on his mobile but he always ended the call when he knew she was there. So altogether, not a happy time. She even found herself feeling slightly homesick.

William, on the other hand, was on an incredible high, for everything suddenly seemed to be coming together. He had real hopes now of a future of sorts with Luisa, reckoned it could be just a matter of time. The thought of destroying his marriage was still far too painful to consider, but the love he now felt for the diffident Sicilian was something that could not be denied. She was well worth the wait, of that he was convinced and, in any case, he seemed to be losing Edwina. Whatever was going on in her complicated mind, she appeared no longer to want to share with him. Which was all right with William, since now he couldn't care less. Provided, of course, he could hold on to Morwenna.

And then Tim rang with some really excellent news. He had finally succeeded in tracking down Robert Marsh.

'He's been away. On an expedition to Peru. Wanted to turn his back on his terrible sorrow.'

But now he was safely returned to Northampton, attempting to pick up the shards of his shattered life. And, to Tim's amazement, had even agreed to talk. He suddenly wanted to get things off his chest. And do whatever he could to help catch the murderer.

'Where does he stand now with the police?' asked William. Presumably he was no longer on bail if they'd allowed him out of the country.

'He's a free man,' said Tim, 'because of his DNA. Though very embittered by the way it's all been mishandled. The fact they appear to have totally botched up.'

'But he'll talk to you?'

'Actually welcomes it. In fact, has a burning desire to back us up.'

Which was truly satisfying after all the disheartening months. William thought once again how glad he was that he'd renewed his trust in the estimable Tim.

Meanwhile, in the metropolis, much was still being made of the Greenslade murder. Dirt was being dredged up about his private life and the implications were that it had been an accident waiting to happen. Ancient rivals with scores to settle kept popping up out of the woodwork. And wretched Mrs Greenslade, so Polly reported, had gone into the Priory to recover. William, however, still privately stuck to his guns. The facts all fitted his blood group theory; even the vicinity was right. They were looking at a time several years ago, if they followed the trail from the murder of Aunt Jane. At which point the Greenslades were living just outside Kemble, bang in the centre of William's target zone. If he had given blood, which was still being ascertained, he fitted the victims' profile absolutely. Which was more than just coincidence, of that William was convinced. This was just the biggest fish so far to surface.

'Probably I should have gone to the police,' he told Luisa, 'but I just couldn't bear it if they fucked things up again.' And once they'd got their hands on all his data, he knew they were more than likely to have slammed the door in his face. That was petty bureaucracy; he wasn't prepared to risk it. Not when he might just be reeling the murderer in.

She was sympathetic, had total belief in his logic. Admired him for being such an honest and upright man. They were endeavouring to meet now on an almost daily basis and Morwenna was quite ecstatic at so many treats. They had done the Natural History Museum and also Kensington Palace and now he was wondering if they dared go further afield. Edwina seemed sunk in a gloom of such despondency, he no longer really cared if the child spilled the beans. Edwina was used to him hanging around with Polly, turned up her nose at what she termed her 'feather-brained bimbo set'. Which wasn't entirely fair, but he didn't bother to argue. At least, if she despised them, she was unlikely to get possessive and Luisa could very easily be one of them.

Tim, it transpired, had certainly struck gold when he doggedly continued to follow up Robert Marsh. The man still looked ragged, with cheekbones like chiselled flint, and his hair was far more ashen than in the photographs. He had aged a good ten years in as many months but had finally turned the stopcock on his emotions. What had happened was now history; he'd the rest of his life for regret. Right now the only thing he wanted was action.

The house, Tim noted, was more or less shut up, with the blinds on some of the rooms still firmly closed. The garden was a wilderness and the swing beginning to rust. The light had surely gone out of his life the day his family died. He showed Tim into the spacious kitchen where dishes were piled in the sink. The table was littered with surveys and reports; he had moved his centre of operations to this room.

'I can't face the rest of the house,' he confessed. 'Would you like me to make us some coffee?'

Tim, obligingly, helped him tidy up, sensing the male camaraderie was breaking the ice. He had to tread as delicately as possible, knowing this territory to be a potential minefield. So he cheerfully sluiced plates and stacked them in the rack, then took a cloth and efficiently wiped down the worktops. An appealing room, he noticed with appreciation. How much nicer it would have been with a woman's touch. Bit by bit he gained Robert Marsh's trust and then they settled down for a proper talk.

Edwina, meantime, was anxiously studying the Dow Jones, occasionally ringing her father for moral support. If things failed to work out, there was not a lot more she could do. Except, perhaps, to pray or bet on the horses. She had done all she could and given it her best. That single fact she knew was indisputable.

'What does William say?' asked Arnold Fairchild, hardly

bothering to disguise the fact that he considered his son-in-law a wimp.

'He is very supportive,' said Edwina hurriedly, unwilling to admit they were barely speaking these days. She still wasn't sure how she'd managed to achieve it, but everything in her life was an unholy mess.

She came home early and started preparing supper, a sort of expiation of her sins. What she needed now more than anything was William's arms around her and the old unconditional love she had always relied on. What she got was an empty house and echoing silence. Whatever it was they got up to, they weren't home yet. Edwina peeled potatoes and put on an oxtail stew, then ran upstairs on a whim to wash her hair. Something was badly wrong and she suddenly knew it. She found herself shaking with cold apprehension until she heard the sound of his key in the lock.

'Hi there!' she called, with as much levity as she could muster, flitting down the stairs in her velour housecoat. William, arms full of shopping, merely gaped. His wife had become a virtual stranger in her own house. Morwenna, ignoring her, wailed to be released, then ran into the playroom to turn on the telly. They were, Edwina saw, a quite separate entity, complete and perfectly functional, sufficient unto themselves.

'You're home early. Anything wrong?' As he unpacked meat and groceries, there wasn't a hint of sarcasm.

'Just thought it long overdue that we spent some time together.' She flung her arms impulsively about his neck and kissed him, surprising them both. 'Don't worry about supper. I've got a stew in the oven.' And some extra special burgundy in the wine rack. William, slightly baffled, managed to disentangle himself then popped upstairs to his study to sort out his head. *Now* what was she up to? He was filled with instant suspicion. When Edwina played the little woman there was definitely something amiss.

The meal was great and he the first to say so, as he mopped up succulent gravy with fresh French bread. 'You've used Guinness,' he said approvingly and she laughed at his expertise. There had been a time, when they first got together, when he hadn't even known how to boil an egg.

'I can still do it when I try. I know I've been neglecting you lately.' This was the moment that she ought to have come clean, but somehow she sensed he wasn't listening.

'There's a thing about Hitler on later tonight,' he said. 'The first of a three-part series. I think I'll watch it. No need for you to stay up,' he added, starting to clear away the plates. 'Treat yourself to an early night. I am quite sure you richly deserve it.'

And then, perhaps mercifully, the telephone rang. And Edwina never got to say her bit. She finished clearing up, while William talked to Tim, realising too late that they hadn't even touched the salad.

Tim was positively jubilant. Marsh had really delivered. Had fallen in with their theory and given it substance. The best part of all was his blood group was AB negative,

369

which suggested he'd been the prime target, though not in a straightforward way.

'His feeling is that somebody wanted to hurt him. And achieved that in the most vicious way by knocking off his wife and little daughters.'

'Has he any idea who that might have been?'

'None whatsoever. He is totally in the dark.'

'And no one with a motive comes to mind?'

'Not that he can think of. I believe him.'

The two sat and thought in communicative silence, relieved to know that they'd been on the right track.

'And he's definitely a donor?'

'Yes, he was clear about that. Gives blood regularly because of his rare group and always to the same blood bank, which ought to help.'

'Can we access the files, do you suppose?' William was suddenly getting hopeful.

Tim was less confident. 'I'm not too sure about that.' Even his magic press card might not prevail. The time had come when they needed the police, but both continued to be sceptical of the results. If they hadn't listened then, why should things have changed? Except that they now had Robert Marsh as their trump card.

It was Marsh, indeed, who ultimately came to their rescue with his detailed knowledge of how the transfusion service worked.

'Blood is taken and stored in many centres until it is actually needed,' he said.

'Is it mixed together, according to blood group?' Tim asked him.

'Yes, so that it sort of becomes anonymous.'

'And who gets to use it?' The notebook was out, pencil poised. Suddenly doors were magically starting to open. At last some explanation of their conundrum. William's instincts had been accurate all along.

'Any hospital or accident centre who needs it suddenly. In the case of real catastrophe the emergency services are called in. Blood is often transported from several different blood banks. It all depends on the immediacy of the circumstances.'

'And, presumably, also the rarity of the blood group.'

'Quite so.'

'So,' said Tim triumphantly, talking again to William. 'All I need to do now is go back through the newspaper files and look for major accidents in the vicinity. Which might have needed a large transfusion of blood.'

Like rail crashes, motorway pile-ups. William was less sure. 'It's a huge area for you to cover as well as a long stretch of time.' Already five years since Jane Fairchild's death. It seemed an impossible task but Tim remained cocky.

'Leave it to me,' he told William confidently. 'Remember I have friends and inside connections.'

Luisa shyly shared William's optimism when he poured it all out to her next day. They had daringly risked an afternoon cinema visit while Morwenna was safely stowed with

Polly's brood. They sat entwined at the back of the local fleapit, sunk in old-fashioned armchairs, lost in their private world. Only a handful of pensioners were grouped in the front few rows. Otherwise they had the place to themselves. It was some old Spanish movie he'd been chasing for several years, but neither was very involved in what was happening on the screen. It took him back to his teenage days, the thrilling, breathless furtiveness of it all. The close proximity, the fumbling, the thwarted desire. Right now he had never felt quite so sexually charged.

'I love you,' he found himself murmuring, as he breathed in the essence of her hair and felt her move instinctively closer in his embrace.

'I know,' she responded, in a voice he could only just hear.

And then he kissed her, lingeringly and long, not knowing that by that simple exchange he was irrevocably sealing their fate.

36

It was over, *finito*; the chips were finally down. Overnight fast.bucks.com had well and truly crashed. The share price had dropped by a hundred and twelve per cent and Edwina and Gareth's paper fortune had effectively shrivelled into ashes. All was lost. They would have to shut up shop and let the staff go. And then crawl grovellingly back to the financiers to explain just how badly they'd screwed up. She wept over the telephone to her father but all he could do was make soothing sounds. She had known all along it was a gamble, he reminded her. Now she must be a good, brave girl and learn how to ride the storm. One thing she was thankful for, she had not allowed him to invest. She remembered Gareth's wheedling suggestion and was glad she had stood her ground. Her parents' money was safe; that, at least, was something. Not that Arnold Fairchild would ever have been so unwise as to speculate recklessly on something dreamed up by his daughter. He was adept at handing out free advice but far too canny to take a punt himself. Which was how he had held on to his affluence, she now realised. Another bitter lesson learned from life.

Now she had to go home and face William, and tell him she had casually bankrupted them. She knew that the house would almost certainly have to go, though, beyond that, didn't dare conjecture. She had managed to raise half a million in loans and now the day of reckoning was upon her. Her father seemed confident she would make it all back in the end. She only wished she could share his positive attitude. First, however, there was Gareth to contend with. He was in it every bit as deeply as she was. She refused to be the one to shoulder all the blame, even though she felt she'd contributed most of the hard slog.

The team were standing around looking pale and grim, faced with the prospect of sudden unemployment. At a time when the whole industry was notably in trouble and bright young things, like they were, two a penny. But Edwina, right now, could not spare them much sympathy. She was far too shocked to consider what she had done.

'It's your bloody fault!' she screamed at Gareth. 'You haven't been putting in the hours.'

Gareth, remarkably as suave and composed as ever, merely raised one quizzical eyebrow and defused her.

'And whose idea was it in the first place?' he reminded her, buffing his nails languidly on his sleeve.

'But I did most of the work,' she said. And you took advantage of it, you sod.

'We both went into it with eyes wide open. We knew all along what a risk we were taking.'

'But it could have worked out, I know it could. If only we had made a bit more effort.'

'Meaning me, I suppose?' His demeanour was faintly mocking and now a bitter smile quirked the corners of his mouth. He was utterly vile, she could see that plainly now, and had only ever been toying with her for amusement.

'You know I've worked my butt off,' she said fiercely, aware that their raised voices could be heard. If only he would comfort her, would share his own apprehension. But he was as cold and withdrawn as she'd ever seen him, as if she were nothing more than just one of his cast-offs, way past her sell-by date. Suddenly he started to grin and she turned to see what he was finding so funny. The disdainful Portia was lolling at her desk, making no attempt to disguise the fact she was listening. Edwina wanted to spit at her. Instead she just legged it back to her work station. It was insufferable the way he was failing to support her. Knowing what a disaster this was for her.

Suddenly all she wanted was to be at home, safe in their cosy kitchen with her husband and child. She'd neglected them both unforgivably all these months but now would do her utmost to make amends. William would sort things out, she knew that for certain. Had never once let her down in all these years. She told the team she was going home and went off in search of a taxi. She couldn't really afford one any more but the thought of public transport was too depressing.

* * *

The house was full of activity, with Mrs P running a load. She was singing along to Radio 2 while Morwenna sat crayoning at the table.

'Mummy,' she said as Edwina burst in, as though she hadn't expected to see her. She did have a point; it was only half past eleven and lately she hadn't been home much, even at night.

'Something wrong, pet?' Mrs P shouted over the music, not even deigning to turn the volume down. Well, soon she'd be getting her marching orders, thought Edwina with grim satisfaction. The woman was far too brazen for her liking, treating the house as though it were her own.

'Turn that racket off,' she barked, then looked around for William. Just when she needed him most he wasn't there.

'Where's my husband?'

Mrs P simply shrugged. 'I think he just stepped out for a breath of air.' Wearing his good sports jacket and a hint of aftershave. He hadn't said but she hardly needed to ask; *she* hadn't come down in the last shower, no way. She was glad Edwina had caught him out, too. The bitch had had it coming all these years.

'D'you want a cuppa?' she asked compliantly, automatically switching on the kettle. Edwina haughtily shook her head and stomped upstairs to her bedroom. Meanwhile Morwenna seemed totally unfazed. Just went on quietly with her colouring.

* * *

He was home by lunchtime, seeming a touch distracted and not at all his usual equable self. She didn't ask why – she didn't dare – but greeted him more breezily than she felt. He was taken aback to find Edwina there and listened fairly stoically as she poured out all her woes. Pale sunshine at last was filtering through the storm clouds so they took a bottle of wine out on to the patio and sat together on the old wooden bench they had lugged home so enthusiastically from the garden centre. Eons ago, or so it seemed, and now their world was crashing about their ears. Edwina badly wanted to cry as she looked around their small patch, knowing they would soon have to give it up and all because of her. She painstakingly went through every detail and William listened impassively. He showed little sign of emotion, which was odd. When at last she finished, he just continued to stare into space, then said he would make them a sandwich for their lunch.

'We'll just have to cope,' was his only comment. He had never much bothered about material things.

What she craved more than anything was the comfort of his arms, but the love he gave so lavishly to Morwenna no longer seemed to be forthcoming to her. Not that, in her heart, she could hold it against him. Considering how unfaithful she had been, she no longer deserved it or him. If he knew about Gareth, he might turn and walk away and nobody in the world could possibly blame him. If only they could start all over again but William still seemed so remote. She bit back her sorrow and tried to act normal.

She had to continue to put on a brave face, if only for the child.

Worse was to follow, at least from Edwina's viewpoint. When she returned to the office early the next morning, she found her colleagues buzzing with salacious gossip. Gareth had gone, they told her triumphantly. Had cleared his desk and walked out.

"Bye, you suckers,' he had said, by way of farewell. 'I'm off to start a brand new life in the sun. Hope you survive.' Just like that and he'd meant it too. She went through all his drawers and they were empty.

'Where's Portia?' she asked sharply, too stricken to cover up, and complicitous glances passed among the group.

'Gone with him,' said one of them, bolder than the rest, and Edwina saw in their eyes how much they knew. 'Her father has a place in the South of France.'

She fled to the ladies and had a good cry, then walked on down the many flights in order to avoid using the lift. She dared not be seen till she'd regained some composure, would not be made the office laughing stock.

She sat miserably in a wine bar, wanting only to curl up and die. All she had ever striven for was now completely ruined and she wasn't entirely certain she could survive. She had really loved him and thought he'd loved her too, had never known such intensity in their lovemaking. She thought of Rome and their recent time in Vancouver, then put her head on the table and openly wept. He had left her for Portia, the trust fund babe, presumably to start a new affluent life. He would doubtless marry her, he was getting on, and Portia couldn't be more than half his age. And rich. At least, she thought as she scrubbed at her swollen eyes, she had finally hit rock bottom. Things couldn't get any worse, which was some consolation.

She was wrong.

William had his own sorted life and Edwina didn't like to impinge. She had to admit that he coped remarkably well with both running the house efficiently and Morwenna. Even Mrs P had a clearly defined role in their lives. The mornings she came were filled with bustling activity. Sitting in the playroom, trying to read to the child, Edwina could hear the babble of conversation as they matily cleared things away. They were still on about the murders and some crackpot new theory of his. He wouldn't have time for playing the sleuth once they put the house on the market. And Mrs P would have to go too, the sooner the better as far as Edwina was concerned. Morwenna was growing restless; the book was a little too advanced. Since the weather was better, she decided to take her out. Fresh air would do them both good.

'We're off to the playground,' she said, poking her nose round the door. 'Care to join us?'

William shook his head. He had other, more important, things on his mind. And if she took the child, he'd be able to escape and try to sort out a problem of his own. 'Maybe I'll join you later,' he said. 'I have one or two small errands I must run first.'

* * *

He was frantic to see Luisa, trapped like a rat in a cage by his errant wife. He was so used to having all his time to himself, he couldn't abide her unexpected intrusion. In some ways the crash of her business suited his purposes, for an all-round upheaval might help him to sort out his head. Yet he also couldn't bear the thought of hitting her while she was down, so would have to postpone any major confrontation for a while. He was sympathetic, just couldn't be bothered to show it, for Edwina had had things her own way for far too long. If only Luisa would understand; he was cautiously confident that she might. So long as she knew that his feelings were real, she was decent enough not to want to put herself first. But she did deserve an explanation. He would hang around the surgery till she emerged.

Just thinking of Luisa gave William a warm glow. In a very short time she had grown such a part of his life. His heart began to flutter as he headed towards Holland Park. He felt like a foolish lovesick swain, more alive than he had been in ages. Edwina's disaster meant he'd have to get a job, so at least, once again, he'd have money of his own. Talk about silver linings. How they'd sort out the future he didn't know. Provided it didn't upset Morwenna, it was really more or less in the lap of the gods.

He wandered up and down outside the surgery, not liking to disturb her by going in. She took her work very seriously and the room was open plan. When he'd tried it once before, she'd been obviously embarrassed, so he

380

hoped that today she was on the morning shift. Being here reminded him of Aisha and the help she'd given him on the blood group front. He ought to go down to Cambridge and talk to Tim, felt that just lately he hadn't been pulling his weight. The news reports on the Greenslade affair continued to dominate the headlines. The murder of such a prominent figure, especially in such sleazy circumstances, had finally caught the public's full attention. So now the police were suddenly on the job. He still privately hoped he would get to the killer first.

By 12.15 Luisa still hadn't appeared, so he ventured to stick his nose round the surgery door. He caught the eye of the receptionist, who grinned when she saw him skulking.

'She's not in this morning,' she called to him. 'Try again after lunch.'

He grinned and nodded, feeling a bit of an ass. Was he making too much of a spectacle of himself? They must all consider him a frightful twerp. He hoped it didn't discomfort Luisa too much. If he walked very briskly he could catch up with his girls and treat them both to a pizza to save having to cook.

Edwina was slumped despondently on a bench beside the playground, engrossed in the *Financial Times*. Seeing the words in stark, cold print made her dotcom disaster seem even worse. Now the world would know what a failure she was, after all the years she had confidently swanned around. She hoped they wouldn't despise her too much, that her father would continue to respect her. Gareth, in his accustomed way, had jumped ship just in time. No doubt Portia's father would see him all right, unless he detected what a fake the man really was. He had always used women and now she could see why. She ground her teeth to keep back the tears and bleakly wondered how on earth they were going to cope.

A shadow fell across her. William. 'Hi!' he said, looking considerably more cheerful. The sun was shining, the gardens were full of blossom. Perhaps there could be a happy ending after all, as long as he never found out about the affair.

'I was reading the obits,' she said, bravely trying to smile. At least they were in good company. A hundred other new dotcoms had also failed.

William sat down beside her and glanced at the paper. 'I thought we'd all go for a pizza,' he said. He could see she was suffering, wanted badly to make her feel better. Felt terrible treachery at the way he'd been carrying on. He glanced around him. Today the park was quiet. Everyone else at work, of course. Those of them who had jobs.

'Where's Morwenna?' he said, the alert custodian, looking around the playground for his child.

'Over there on the swings,' said Edwina vaguely, chewing a hangnail abstractedly as she read.

William stood up and turned a half-circle. For once the playground was completely devoid of children. Even with this milder weather, the wigwams were uninhabited.

While the swings hung listless and forlorn like the one in the Marsh front garden. Neglected like unwanted toys. Deserted.

There was no sign anywhere of Morwenna. She had gone.

37

'You bloody incompetent!' William shrieked at her, virtually choking on his panic. 'You've only gone and let some pervert steal our kid!' For a moment he thought he might actually die of rage, could feel his veins bursting in his temples. Edwina looked up from her paper and peered around.

'What are you on about? She's over there playing.' Only, of course, she wasn't. 'Calm down,' she said, beginning to take control. 'All that's happened is she's simply wandered off.' Men could be so obtuse at times, though it wasn't at all like William to lose his cool. William, still shaking, suppressed an urge to throttle her. He should never have allowed her to take Morwenna out on her own if this was the measure of her responsibility. No wonder she'd turned out such a lousy mother, suited only for a high-flying business career. Now, not even that.

Edwina folded her paper carefully, stashed it in the stroller and stood up. She was more upset than she cared to let on but didn't want William to see.

'You go that way,' she said, pointing towards the Round

Pond, 'and I'll just check on the Bayswater Road.' Heaven forbid, let her please not have wandered into traffic. 'We'll meet back here in, say, fifteen minutes. One of us will have found her by then. Little beast.' She even managed a half-smile. The terrible twos, as they were always reminding her. Morwenna, despite her angelic appearance, at times could be a holy terror.

William, gasping, ran shouting across the grass in the direction of the palace. He stopped and cross-examined the few people he encountered, but no one remembered seeing a little girl. The swans – she'd probably gone to look for them. He ought to have thought of that immediately. His heartbeat slowly regulated itself and he moved at a less frantic pace. That would be it, she'd be down at the edge of the water. Provided she hadn't fallen in; panic resurged. Oh God, he would never let her out of his sight again. He blamed it all upon his guilty conscience. If he hadn't gone looking for Luisa this wouldn't have happened. They'd have been here together, a secure family unit, and she would have still been happily playing in the playground, under proper parental supervision.

A police car approached him across the grass, alerted by his obvious agitation.

'My daughter,' he told them when they wound down the window. 'She seems to have wandered away.'

'How long's she been missing?' But William didn't know. It might have been as much as half an hour. The policeman switched on his radio and alerted his colleagues around the park.

'We'll find her, sir. Don't you worry about that. A two-year-old can't have gone far.'

At their suggestion, William got into the back of the car and sat tensely watching for Morwenna as they drove. First, they made a slow circuit of the pond, then swept back in a wider arc to where he had last seen Edwina. Who was back at the bench with the empty stroller, her face now a picture of dread.

'No success?'

'None at all.' At least there had been no traffic accident reported.

'So what do we do now?'

'Come back with us to the station. And file a proper report while we organise a search.' William was loath to leave the park; suppose she came toddling back and found her mother not there. But the officers convinced him that their procedure was best. The sooner they made it official, the safer she'd be. William caught a glance pass between them which caused his spirits to dive, but he didn't, if only for Edwina's sake, want to show the extent of his alarm. His beloved Morwenna, the most precious thing in his life, vanished like that in just a matter of minutes. One look at Edwina's pale stricken face helped put a muzzle on his anger. It was her daughter too and though undoubtedly her fault, that must make it all the more upsetting. And after she'd just been through so much at work. He squeezed her hand and she gave him a grateful look. At least the ice between them appeared to be thawing. They needed to pull together now if only to remain sane.

'I'm sorry,' she whispered, with tears in her eyes, so he pulled her gently into his arms and held her.

'We'll need a recent photograph,' said the desk sergeant when they got there. He seemed so matter of fact that William's nerves steadied. If the police could take it so much in their stride, then it wasn't the end of the world. She could be already at home, they said, and he remembered, with relief, Mrs P.

'Mind if I use your phone?' he asked, then held his breath as he dialled. Please, please, please . . . but the answer was a blank. There wasn't yet any sign of her in Hillgate Place.

'Poor little mite,' said Mrs P, appalled. 'Do you want me to come over there and help you search?'

No, he told her, best to wait there at the house just in case there was any news. Edwina had her mobile so they could keep in touch and of course the police were monitoring the whole operation. And then he took a great gulp of air and reassured the agonised Edwina.

'They'll find her,' he said. 'I promise you that.' But his heart knew he couldn't be certain. And that was what really scared him the most. More than anything that had happened so far.

It was late afternoon by the time they finally got home and valiant Mrs P was still holding the fort.

'Any news?' she cried anxiously when they walked in the door, then saw from their stricken faces that there was not. All she could do was wordlessly brew them some tea then, for once, have the sense to make herself scarce.

'Call me any time you need me,' she whispered in William's ear and even went so far as to hug Edwina. Edwina had turned into a walking zombie whose teeth were audibly chattering with shock. William suggested she should go upstairs and lie down but she said that until the baby was found, there was no point. She couldn't close her eyes, might never do so again. What had happened was vastly more terrible even than the crash. That had been only money, this her beloved child. If anything awful had happened to her, how could she possibly live with herself?

'It's entirely my fault,' she chanted, over and over, and all William could do to ease her pain was hold her. The police had put all their routines into action and the news was now spreading throughout the metropolis. Scotland Yard detectives had come on to the case and the whole of the London police force was on red alert. So this was what it took, thought William bitterly, to galvanise them into any sort of real action. One tiny child, momentarily mislaid, whereas out there, all these months, roamed a ruthless killer. He didn't come out and say so but the chill in his heart grew worse. For some of these officers had come from the Greenslade case.

So the time had finally come to spill the beans, and this he did, at length, to the DI. It took a couple of hours but they weren't going anywhere else and, because of his shattering loss, the man was sympathetic. And after a

ittle while, called in one of his aides and instructed him
o check facts and take copious notes. At last William
had stumbled on a policeman with a brain who wasn't
dismissing his theories as foolish waffle.

'So you think your daughter's loss might be connected?'
he said eventually and William mutely nodded his head
n pain. It might sound far-fetched but they had to consider
every angle and he was, after all, a potential target since
he'd unwittingly appeared on television. Especially as
Greenslade had lived just around the corner and the loca-
ion of the murders appeared to be closing in.

'Any idea who you think might be responsible?'

'None at all,' said William with absolute truth. All he
could see was a strongly developing pattern with a killer
who moved on relentlessly stealthy feet.

'It's a game of Look Behind You,' he said. You never
could tell when you were safe.

'And why the child?'

'He has done it before.' The little Marsh daughters, the
Hargreaves boys. Aunt Jane's dog, the yoga teacher's cat.
He seemed to be going vindictively for the helpless and
the weak. For whatever reason, they didn't yet know, but
it looked like retribution. William felt faint.

'So what does he want from you?' asked the DI.

'Revenge,' said William simply, suddenly seeing it. He
had meddled where he ought not to have done and now
was receiving his comeuppance. Rough justice, maybe,
but it fit the pattern. And this particular murderer had no
mercy.

'But if he's got her,' said Edwina, aghast, 'why has he not yet made himself known?' No ransom note, no threatening demands. Nothing to let them know that he held Morwenna.

'He will do,' said the DI grimly. 'It can only be a question of time.'

By the following morning there was still no news, so the whole thing was handed to the media. In a matter of hours, Morwenna's picture was splashed across the press and plans were afoot for a television appeal, with Edwina appearing live on *Crimewatch*. It seemed awfully drastic in such a short space of time but at least the police were finally doing their stuff. Even Arnold Fairchild detached himself from the shadows and offered a fat reward to find his grandchild. William spent many hours closeted with Scotland Yard, explaining in detail his theories about the blood groups. And Tim was summoned from Cambridge to join them, with the results of all the assiduous research he'd been doing.

The DI seemed impressed. He lit another cigarette and thoughtfully stroked his chin.

'If what you need now,' he told them, 'is access to the blood banks, I think the police computer can do the trick.'

And so it seemed they were finally on their way. If it weren't for the loss of Morwenna, they'd be exultant. Edwina was steadily holding her own, comforted by a WPC, while her parents hovered and tried to do what they could. At least disaster was unifying. For the first time in what seemed like ages, they were all pulling on the same side.

And all the time William was secretly longing for Luisa. He knew it was bad, disloyal to Edwina, and somehow trivialised the horror of Morwenna's disappearance. Yet he ached for her to comfort him, to pour out his darkest fears, to share with her the agony of this terrible night of the soul. He wondered if she'd seen the news coverage, assumed she had, it was pretty comprehensive. Worried about her own reactions to it, too. She had lately become so attached to the child, had already had to endure the tragic loss of her own. And Luisa was so fragile, he hoped she'd be able to cope. Thought about phoning the surgery yet couldn't quite bring himself to do so. Some stupid superstition told him that if he was able to resist her, Morwenna was that much more likely to be found. There; and he who'd been brought up with no religion. Soon he'd be praying to Saint Anthony or touching wood. It seemed he was, quite simply, going mad. And all because he had coveted another woman.

Instead he turned his attention to Edwina and tried, by both words and deeds, to make amends. It was not her fault she'd been raised such a headstrong woman, encouraged to do what she liked in pursuit of success. She couldn't help it either if she fundamentally lacked maternal feelings. Some people found it hard to love. Edwina was one of those. He tried to salve his guilt by putting himself out for her, persuaded her it had not been entirely her fault. The sainthood that her friends admired now cloaked him to the full while all the time concealing a treacherous heart.

In his blackest moments, when he couldn't sleep, he made a pact with the God he didn't believe in. If Morwenna could only be restored to him, safe and unharmed, he'd be prepared to forgo Luisa and try instead to make his marriage work. The prospect, on either front, was bleak, but the child was of prime importance. So he didn't phone her or try to seek her out, just gritted his teeth and, yes, prayed.

'Please,' begged Edwina tragically that night, appearing, white and gaunt, on television. 'Don't hurt my baby. Help us to get her back.' Then put her head in her hands and openly cried.

She'd been gone five days and still there had been no sighting. Nor had anyone emerged to claim the reward. William and Edwina existed like ghostly spectres while Mrs P rallied around making pots of tea. The Fairchilds, unable to bear the strain, had withdrawn to the heights of Highgate while the press continued to bay at the Hillgate Place door.

'Tell them to go away,' moaned Edwina but William pointed out that they needed them there. Morwenna's disappearance had become a national issue, had forced the police to exert themselves as well. If anything could flush her out, it was this sort of public attention. With time, he knew, their interest would wane as other hotter stories took her place. And then where would they be, without the cavalry?

One early evening he joined a park patrol, painstakingly revisiting an endless circuitous route. They stopped and questioned everyone they encountered, repeatedly asking the same monotonous question. Have you seen this child? Many of the people they stopped were commuters who regularly took this detour home. All were attentive and sympathetic but none came up with anything that was helpful. For all the information they could glean, she might have been spirited away. William glanced at the statue of Peter Pan and tried to close his mind to romantic theories.

They were returning dejectedly along the bumpy track, back to the place where Morwenna had last been seen, when William's practised eye was caught by a motionless figure, standing inside a clump of trees, practically out of sight. That particular standpoint had a clear view of the playground and something about the figure rang instant bells. Of course. How could he ever have been so stupid? The fear and anxiety of the past few days had clearly affected his mind. He banged urgently on the glass partition and told the police driver to stop. Then flung himself out while the vehicle was still moving and set off in crazed pursuit.

This time there was no escaping William, who caught him by the throat in frenzied rage. 'What have you done to her?' he screamed hysterically, shaking the man like a terrier with a rat. The two policemen caught up with him and tore them both apart.

'Arrest this man!' shrieked William, beside himself. 'He's a disgusting pervert, always hanging around the kids.' The seedy stranger looked bewildered and afraid but made no attempt at all to get away. His clothes were shabby and his nose still red and chapped. He looked a very sorry specimen indeed.

'Your name, sir?' asked the senior policeman, officiously flipping open his notebook.

'What am I supposed to have done?' asked the man quietly, calmer and more self-possessed than William would have expected. Did he think he was going to brazen it out? Clearly he had no shame.

'That we'll establish back at the station. First please identify yourself.'

Gregory Hill, he told them, still looking furtive, and was bundled into the car without further ado.

'What's going on?' he asked William anxiously, but William, sitting beside him, still as a rock, refused to answer or even look at him. If the slippery bastard tried to wriggle out now, he'd not be responsible for his actions. The blatant gall of it, just standing there in full sight. But at least they had finally caught themselves a suspect.

38

With the help of the police laboratory and some official intervention, Tim was well on the way to cracking the enigma. William, he knew, was currently too spaced out to put his mind to helping, or even care. They had apprehended a suspect, that was all he'd been able to ascertain. Tim was determined to get there first for the sake of his future career. Now they had open access to the Blood Transfusion Centre in Bristol, they were able, without too much effort, to check out the names. And all the murder victims they'd been tracking were recorded as having, at one time or another, given blood. In addition to which, they all shared the same blood group. The ultra rare AB negative. If Morwenna were not still missing, it would be cause for cautious optimism. As it was, Tim just stuck assiduously to the case. With hard facts in hand, he was able to return to the clippings files and search for any news story that seemed to match the criteria.

Gregory Hill, it transpired, was a writer of children's books. When asked for his credentials, he reeled off an impressive list, including the vastly successful *Cobbleywobs* series (Morwenna's favourite) which had recently won him a prestigious BAFTA award. William continued suspicious but the desk sergeant did a complete about turn and treated the famous author with unctuous respect. So what was he doing then, lurking in the park? It still didn't alter the facts. Hill looked slightly uncomfortable and fidgeted a little. He went there for inspiration, he explained, and the spirit of Peter Pan. Writing alone all day was a solitary business. He needed at times to get out and stretch his legs.

But the playground, pressed William, while the sergeant merely listened. Why was he so fixated on the kids? Hill turned incredibly honest blue eyes to him and confessed that he did have a personal interest there, too.

'They're my sons,' he said, 'and I'm not allowed to see them.' There had recently been a particularly ugly divorce. At first William didn't believe him but he appeared to be sincere. And by now the sergeant was practically licking his hand. After all had been sorted out and Hill had obliged him with an autograph, the charge sheet was torn up and he was permitted to go. With apologies from the sergeant for having detained him in the first place, but in delicate cases, like a missing child, he'd understand they had to be extra vigilant. Et cetera, et cetera. William, somewhat disgruntledly, left too.

'I am sorry about your daughter,' said Hill awkwardly, proffering his hand. 'I can imagine the sort of agony you must be going through. After all, I've been in a similar mess myself.' Though not, of course, life-threatening. He appeared to bear no malice at William's accusation, was keen to know if there was any way in which he could help. William, softening, accepted that he was all he said, then, remembering his presence at Polly's party, asked how he came to be there. Now Hill did look a trifle uncomfortable and William's suspicions returned. That party had preceded the murder of Harvey Greenslade. The kiddibook writer's was the one face that didn't fit.

'I gatecrashed,' Hill told him honestly, after a pause. 'Something, I have to confess, I do quite a lot. I tell you, being a writer's a lonely occupation, which often leads to rampant cabin fever.' Especially now that he'd lost his family and home. William sympathised. He wasn't even employed at all yet sometimes found the role of house husband confining, to say the least. They parted congenially and agreed there were no hard feelings and William trudged wearily home. Back to square one, he realised with a leaden heart, with still not a clue as to where his baby had gone.

And now his longing for Luisa surpassed all boundaries. He had made a pact with himself to forget her but found that it couldn't be kept. She had grown so very dear to him in the few months he had known her that an endless vista of life apart was more than he could bear. Certainly not at a time like this, when his heart was cracked open and raw, despite what noble resolutions he might once have had. As it was, she must think he had abandoned her entirely or surely by now she'd have been in touch. She had grown to dote upon Morwenna, as she had on her own precious child, and since the abduction still dominated the news, there was small chance she wasn't aware of it. It might be disloyal to Edwina but he also felt he had a duty to explain. Most of all, an irresistible urge to see her and seek strength from her calmness and support. He was, after all, only human. And he loved her.

And so he broke his self-imposed rule and slipped out one morning to call her at the surgery. The receptionist, sounding surprised, said she wasn't there, had quit the job without warning a week before. William was shattered; this was not what he'd expected, had assumed that his well-publicised suffering would mean she would stick around. He sought in vain for something coherent to say, then humbly asked for her home number. No, said the receptionist, she hadn't been on the phone. And had never even told them where she lived. Somewhere off the Portobello Road was all she had ever admitted to. None of them had got to know her enough to have visited. William was pulverised as he wandered dejectedly home, bereft of his very last bastion of support. He was still half crazed at the loss of his daughter and Edwina was practically out of her mind with grief. Without Luisa's steadying influence, he wasn't at all sure that he could cope.

There was a message in Mrs P's flamboyant scrawl for him to contact Tim at the Cambridge number. William was in no mood for talking to anyone but dialled it just the same, with a shaking hand. All he really wanted to do was run upstairs and hide but Edwina was there ahead of him, working through her grief. And, indeed, the call turned out to be well worth it, for Tim had more excellent news. His dogged research appeared at last to have paid off. Working systematically backwards from the date of Jane Fairchild's murder, he had come up with a handful of major disasters roughly within the catchment area William had circled on his map. By merging the two sets of statistics, he had pinpointed things even more precisely. So that, after hours of headache-inducing scrutiny, he had come up with a list of just five news items spread out over a period of several years. One of which, the most dramatic, concerned a fatal car crash on the A303, when a family named Urquhart had been totally wiped out. Almost exactly thirteen years ago.

'What happened to the other car?'

'The driver miraculously survived, but only just. It was one of those fancy foreign jobs which more or less imploded on impact. They had to scrape him from the wreckage and air-lift him to hospital.'

'Was he given blood?'

'A total transfusion. That's what initially caught my eye.'

'And his blood group?'

'Haven't yet found that out but the police are on the job. All I've established so far from the cuttings is that his passenger, unbelievably, walked away unharmed. Didn't even hang around to see if the driver survived. The coroner diplomatically attributed it to shock.'

'And do you know anything about the driver?'

'One Enzo Perrotti, an Italian from Milan. Over here working in the motor industry, based in Milton Keynes.'

William was hugely impressed; his spirits suddenly lifted. 'So what are you hanging around for, boy? Get out there and go find him.' Despite his gloom, he was suddenly fired up. If this man, Perrotti, were still around, he might well hold the key to the whole affair. For starters, he'd allegedly been responsible for the deaths of five members of one family. A terrible burden of guilt to have to carry, irrespective of where the blame might actually lie. Leading, very possibly, to someone's desire for atonement. He was, after all, the sole survivor of the crash, apart from the one who had casually walked away.

'Will do,' said Tim importantly. 'Am taking the day off right now. Over and out.' He was clearly enjoying himself enormously, thrilled to be in his natural element as sleuth. It was some comfort to William to know he could rely on such a capable pair of hands. Then he slumped back into despondency over Luisa. And, of course, the loss of Morwenna.

For now a truly dreadful suspicion was creeping into his mind, one he tried hard to suppress yet couldn't shake off. It seemed an unlikely coincidence that they'd vanished at precisely the same time. Morwenna and now Luisa, apparently into thin air. Maybe, just possibly, they were somewhere safe together, though his mind shied off wondering why. He couldn't talk to Edwina about it since

400

she didn't even know of Luisa's existence, and hesitated to take it to the police. First he would try to locate her on his own, at least until he found evidence to implicate her. But where to start looking? He was totally in the dark. All he'd ever known about her private life was the same as the receptionist had said. Somewhere in the vicinity of the Portobello Road, that was all she had ever let him know. And he, blind fool, had not given it a thought, despite his attempts to get her to take him there. The only possible clues lay in the surgery and that was when he remembered the doctor, Aisha. He rang and asked if they could talk and she readily agreed to meet him that day for a drink.

When it came to the point, there was no beating about the bush. Morwenna's safety was far too important for William even to think of playing games. He did see a spark in Aisha's eyes of something a little like disappointment. But he was in no mood for flirtation, and now quite immune to her charm. He needed to find Luisa, and fast. He begged Aisha to help him.

She was thoughtful as she sipped her cider, running through everything she knew.

'She wasn't exactly forthcoming,' she said. 'Pleasant enough and efficient at her job, yet at the same time pretty reserved. I tried once or twice to pal up with her but she had a habit of politely backing off.'

William knew precisely what she meant, as if one misplaced word might make her run. He had put it down to a natural timidity but now an awful idea was starting to form. What, when it came to it, did he actually know about her except that she was alone and intrinsically sad? She had hinted at some sort of darkness in her past and there was, of course, the lost child. But beyond that, he realised, he scarcely even knew her. Looking back, it seemed that he had done most of the talking.

'She was certainly a good listener,' said Aisha. 'I often thought she was wasted in that job.'

'What exactly did she do?'

'Just filing and clerical work. She was a whiz on the computer, we were lucky to have found her. I can't imagine how we're going to manage.'

Nor me, screamed a voice in the void that was William's brain, but he made a gargantuan effort to shut it up. Not now, he told himself grimly. All that mattered was recovering the child before anything worse could happen to her. And, whatever the circumstances, this might turn out to be a lead.

'We would normally keep some record at the surgery,' said Aisha. 'But for some reason she always insisted on payment in cash. No P45 nor even Schedule D. Pin money, I assumed, since she never appeared hard up. A cultured woman in a foreign land, doing part-time work mainly as a hobby. With perhaps a well-heeled partner in the background to pay the real bills. I wish now I had been a little more intrusive.'

'You must tell the police,' she urged but William was reluctant to betray Luisa. There had to be some sort of

402

straightforward explanation. If only she would turn up and prove him right.

'You're crazy!' said Aisha when he finally filled her in. 'If you don't act immediately, you could be risking your daughter's life.'

Which brought him down to earth with a mighty bang. For a while he'd been off with the fairies again. He must be losing his grip. Aisha was right, of course she was, and he couldn't afford to waste another second. It might mean having to confess all to Edwina but that, right now, was the least of his concerns.

He left his beer untouched. Aisha said she would go with him to the police station.

There was not a great deal more the police could do, short of a house-to-house search. It could be arranged but would take a lot of time, which realistically they really didn't have. Aisha returned to the surgery while William trudged back home, stopping impulsively at the café on the corner for a shot of much-needed caffeine.

'How's your little girl today?' asked the lumpy-thighed waitress brightly. William stared at her dully; what planet had she been inhabiting all week? She swabbed down the table with a dubious-looking cloth, then poured him a frothy cappuccino. 'Only she seemed a little fretful when I saw her the other day. Could it be she's having trouble with her teeth? Her nanny was being quite strict with her, practically dragging her along. Poor little mite.'

403

William stared blankly as it slowly sank in, then the blood started hammering in his ears.

'When exactly was this?' he asked, with a sudden jolt of hope.

'Tuesday,' she said immediately, not even having to think.

'And the nanny?' She had to be making it up. It couldn't turn out this easy.

'The foreign lady.' She looked a little puzzled. Surely he knew that already; what was he like? 'I must say, I was surprised not to see you with them for a change. A right little threesome you've become.'

'Where was this?' William asked carefully, ready to kill if she failed him.

'Right across the road,' she said, pointing towards McDonald's. In that great forbidding tower block that dominated Notting Hill Gate. The one he was always complaining about because it ruined the skyline.

'Thanks,' he said, not even touching his coffee. 'Do me a favour, please, and call the police.'

It was a great grey concrete atrocity, built in the frugal sixties, which should, by rights, have been dynamited years ago. Rows of identical balconies on storey upon storey of depressing flats, all with nasty identical net curtains and trays of withering plants. William had passed it endlessly; it was straight across the road from Hillgate Street. He crossed and stood on the pavement outside, not certain what he should do. The panel of bells by the entrance gave nothing away. Numbers only, no names attached, in a futile attempt at security. He knew he should probably wait for the police but couldn't control his frenzied excitement. He had to get in there right away, would kick down every door until he found her. Instead he settled for pressing random bells until at last, miraculously, someone answered.

'I've come to collect my daughter,' he said, trying hard to keep the anxiety out of his voice, 'but seem to have forgotten the flat number. A two-year-old with a Dutch doll bob.'

'Eighth floor,' said the disembodied voice. And obligingly buzzed him in.

The lift smelled strongly of urine and was lavishly embellished with graffiti. William took it up to the top floor, then stood in the empty corridor, silently pondering. Eight identical doors led off a dank and fetid passage. It was like a nightmare gameshow in which he had only one shot. He dared not risk alerting her until he was ready to strike. But the place seemed deserted and silent as the grave. He didn't have any idea what his next step should be.

And then he heard, quite distinctly, the sound of plaintive crying and recognised immediately whose it was. He crept along the concrete floor, listening at each door. Then made his choice and urgently rang the bell.

'Luisa!' he commanded. 'Open up!'

39

Enzo Perrotti's blood group was AB negative, though he wasn't listed as ever having been a donor. At the time of the accident he'd been airlifted to hospital in Salisbury but from that point on the trail had gone pretty cold. His horrendous injuries were detailed in his medical notes, including the fact that he'd been given a total transfusion. He had stayed there, critically ill, for eight weeks, after which, miraculously cured, he had been discharged. There it all was, in black and white, but Tim was keen to discover a whole lot more. He wangled an introduction to a senior consultant who passed him on to the matron of the hospital. At first she was reluctant to talk but changed when she saw his impressive authorisation. Having been so sluggish in the early days, the police were now falling over themselves to help. The Greenslade case remained unsolved though they did now admit there could be a possible link.

She was big and bosomy in crisp blue and white, and grudgingly offered Tim a cup of tea. She had been at the hospital eighteen years and well remembered that horrific fatal carcrash.

'The children were the worst,' she said. 'Practically smashed to pieces, poor little things. They brought them here but there wasn't a thing we could do. Killed on impact, both of them, which was, I suppose, a blessing.' She shuddered as she recalled the scene and it all came flooding back. The grandmother had gone straight through the windscreen, her head still just hanging on by threads.

'What exactly happened?' asked Tim, who had read the coroner's report.

She shrugged. 'A genuine accident, as far as I'm aware. That particular stretch of road is notoriously dangerous.'

'Do you remember your patient, Enzo Perrotti?'

'Indeed I do. He was here with us eight weeks.' She had looked up his file on receipt of Tim's urgent phonecall and now had the medical details off by heart. 'It's amazing he survived at all; practically every bone in his body was shattered. They threaded him together on wire like a dinosaur. I have never seen anything so bizarre.'

'Do you still have news of him now? Where he went after he was discharged?'

She pursed her lips and shook her head. 'The only address we ever had for him was in Milton Keynes. But remember, that was thirteen years ago. He might well have moved on by now.'

Tim laughed before he could stop himself. 'Certainly if he has any discrimination.' Then, conscious of her disapproval, adopted a graver expression.

'Do you recall if he had visitors? Nearest and dearest, that sort of thing?'

'I do remember that his English was near perfect and, even at his most poorly, the charm of the man.' Her eyes grew thoughtful; she was looking back and a small, sad smile touched the corners of her mouth. 'Even as ill as he was, he hated to be any trouble, but all my nurses adored him. He could do no wrong. After a while his wife turned up, flew in from Italy unexpectedly. I remember wondering why she hadn't come at once. And what he was doing living here without her.'

Marina Perrotti. It was all here in his notes. A regal woman who was totally controlled. She had the style and elegance of an Italian with real money. And graciously tipped the nursing staff as if in a five-star hotel. Having established to her satisfaction that he wasn't about to die she had done the unexpected and gone home.

'Leaving him here alone?'

'So it would seem.' She would never get used to the public, their odd little ways.

'When he finally left here, he certainly broke a few hearts. He really was a charmer, like a film star.'

That was about all she could tell him so Tim said his thanks and got out. Thirteen years was a long time for tracking someone's peregrinations but his next stop would have to be Milton Keynes.

When she finally opened the door and he saw her face, his instinct was to grab her and not let go. Gone was the fleeting beauty who had captivated him from the start. Here was a gaunt and ravaged woman with staring black coals for eyes. In a week she had aged ten years. He was appalled. They looked at each other in frozen silence until a thrilled Morwenna distracted him.

'*Daddy!*' she shrieked, and he instinctively stepped forward, ready to scoop her up in his arms and console her.

'Get back!' snapped Luisa threateningly, stopping him short in his tracks. At which point he saw the hostility in her eyes and withdrew. The room was stark and under-furnished with only the barest necessities. The carpet was fraying and disgustingly stained, the furniture gathered from a tip. Morwenna, his darling, was seated in a playpen with some sort of harness confining her. Beside her on the floor was a pile of glossy new toys, but the teddy she was cradling looked chewed and decidedly defunct, the relic of some other child's pathetic past.

'You don't understand,' said Luisa, interpreting his thoughts. And the truth was that, no, he most definitely did not.

Milton Keynes was better than Tim had imagined, though created with an accountant's flair rather than any archi-tect's. It was like so much of contemporary middle Britain, impersonal and entirely without charm. But organised and well laid out and, presumably, cost-effective. Cedar Court was one of a mass of identical red brick develop-ments, conveniently situated for both shopping and public transport. Tim took a quick look round the neat little grid before boldly ringing the Perrotti bell. There was no answer. Now why was that not a surprise?

'Can I help you?' asked the woman next door, popping out to water her geraniums. It was warm and bright, a real sun trap. She had tomato plants trained up the wall.

'Nice here,' said Tim, at his most effusive. 'You seem to have everything on tap.'

'Good for the shops,' she agreed cheerily, 'and only two minutes from the station.' *Though I wouldn't want to live here*, thought Tim, but left it diplomatically unsaid.

'I am looking for a family called Perrotti,' he said, making a point of scrutinising his notes. 'Do you happen to know if they still live here?'

'She does,' said the neighbour, 'though she's very seldom here. Been travelling a lot in the past few years.'

'And him?'

She looked up from her watering with surprise. '*Enzo* Perrotti? Why, he's dead.'

Morwenna appeared to be perfectly well cared for, if a little over emotional at suddenly seeing her dad. She fought to reach him from the confines of her pen but Luisa ordered her sharply to be still. All around the room were scattered open suitcases, each in various stages of being packed. One appeared to contain nothing but little girl's clothes, each item lovingly wrapped in tissue paper.

'Going somewhere?' asked William, folding his arms. The child was safe, that was really all that mattered. The comforting could come later once he had got her home. Now there were questions to which he needed answers.

'Back to Sicily,' said Luisa calmly. 'It is time to let my mother see her grandchild.'

William mentally gaped yet kept his cool. The necessary explanations could come later. In the distance he dimly heard the sound of approaching sirens; the waitress had done as bid and summoned the law. He didn't want to alert Luisa, needed to keep the dialogue flowing. Something was badly askew but he didn't know what.

'Tell me,' he said, at his most persuasive, making another dive to pick up Morwenna. But Luisa, lighter-footed, got there first. She grabbed the child and clasped her tight then stepped purposefully back towards the balcony. The door was wide open with the curtains blowing wild. The screech of the police sirens had suddenly ceased.

'One more step,' she said, 'and she goes over the edge.' And he saw from her manic eyes that she really meant it. Something quite dreadful had happened to Luisa but now was not the moment for idle chat.

William backed away again and leaned against the front door. His heart was hammering in his chest but he wouldn't allow her to prevail. Provided he kept his cool and talked her through it, the police would shortly be here to back him up. He could now hear distant voices and shouting in the street so started to talk loudly and rapidly to distract her.

'That's not necessary. Please put her down.' One false movement and he sensed she'd be true to her word. Morwenna, fortunately, thought it was all a great game, and giggled with pleasure as she hugged Luisa's neck.

'I mean it. Don't move.' She backed up against the balcony rail while William fought his panic and tried to stay calm.

'Tell me,' he said again, placatingly. 'You are obviously in some sort of trouble. Please let me help.'

'Dead?' said Tim, astonished. 'When would that be?'

'Oh, ages ago,' said the woman. 'And shortly after, the little girl too. It was a truly terrible tragedy. I tell you, I thought it would finish her off and indeed it very nearly did. She was in the hospital herself for a year. And when she came home she was strangely altered, tougher somehow and withdrawn. Well, she would be, I suppose, after something that dreadful. She had always been so light-hearted and full of fun. And vain, you never saw anything like it.'

'Do you mind me asking what he died of?' said Tim.

'Don't really know,' said the woman. 'Some sort of blood disorder that he passed on to the baby. He was gone in about a year from the diagnosis.'

Bells began to jangle in Tim's brain. Piece by piece the puzzle was solving itself.

'I had to do it,' she volunteered after a while. 'They had destroyed my happiness, but most of all murdered my baby. All I could do was attempt to settle the score. Why should any of them get off entirely scot free?'

Her cheeks were now slightly flushed with indignation

and he saw again, fleetingly, a shadow of her passing beauty. He noticed now how much thinner she had grown; she was really little more than skin and bone. His heart began to go out to her, though her words froze the blood in his veins. If she meant what he rather thought she did, then she was a dangerous killer. But also the woman he had loved, an impossible dilemma.

'What are you trying to tell me?' he asked, watching her hands tighten about Morwenna.

'That it was me all the time, doing all those murders, trying to seek some justice for what I had lost.' She started to cry with great gulping sobs but still stayed exactly where she was. William heard furtive movements in the corridor outside, a voice talking quietly into a radio. Then someone rapped smartly on the door and he heard the jangle of keys. They were coming in, but she had still got Morwenna and he knew now for absolute certain that she meant what she'd said.

'Hold on a moment,' he told her and opened the door. Four policemen and a WPC were crowded together outside, one of them holding a bunch of skeleton keys.

'Stay back!' he said urgently. 'I think I can talk her through it. And she's standing out there on the balcony, holding my child.'

The leading policeman assessed the situation then gave him a silent nod.

'We'll be here,' he muttered, indicating his radio. 'We'll get access to the next-door flats and surround her from outside.'

William closed the door and resumed his stance. If only he could persuade her to put down Morwenna.

'She must be awfully heavy for you,' he said hopefully, holding out his arms, but Luisa fiercely shook her head and clasped the child even tighter. William took a couple of deep breaths, surprised to find his voice still nearly normal. He used the tone that he always took with her, soft, sympathetic and affectionate. He was only too aware that one false move could blow it and that she was holding his universe in her arms.

'What exactly did they do?' he asked her, prepared to listen for as long as it took. His only consolation was that Morwenna was sucking her thumb.

The extent of his injuries had meant a complete blood transfusion. Involving, because his blood group was rare, unexpected complications. The transfusion centre had sent out an SOS and they'd borrowed from other blood banks in the area. It was nobody's fault, just the emergency services in extremis. They had saved his life but then later he died, from virulent Hepatitis C. The year was 1988, before they were able to check out these things. They were just unfortunate, so the hospital said. But she had taken it harder than she might have.

'It was her only kiddie,' said the woman, suddenly emotional. 'And he and she were so totally in love, it warmed your heart just to see them. Things hadn't been easy for them in the past. She never actually said so, but I could sense it. I think he was an exile from his family

414

in Milan. She obviously worshipped the ground he trod. She had wanted a baby all these years, then he passed on this terrible infection.'

There were tears in her eyes and Tim squeezed her hand. But inside he was positively shouting.

'One of those donors killed him. I never found out which one. But I vowed, when Adriana died too, that I was going to seek revenge.' She turned to him beseechingly. 'Can you imagine how badly I felt?'

All too easily, he wanted to reply, watching her shift the weight of his darling child. She was growing emotional and had to be watched. On either side he could hear the stealthy scrape of marksmen getting into position.

'After the rest cure I needed something to do. If only to keep myself from going stir crazy. I have always been good on computers, so applied for a job at the hospital, where I found that annexing the records was a piece of cake.' She smiled as if remembering quite how easy it had been. 'And after that, it all fell into place.'

William was stunned, his brain in total shock. The more she talked, the lovelier she became.

'And had you no mercy?' he found himself whispering.

'Why should I? What did they care? Look what they'd done to me. They ought to have been more responsible in the first place with all those good works they notched up.'

From the hospital she had moved on to the blood transfusion centre, cloaking herself in her natural reserve so that nobody ever even noticed her. It gave her something to fill her time and kept her adrenalin flowing. When the killings started, she got carried away. Most of the rest he already knew.

'You were very clever to work it all out. I have always admired a man with a superlative brain.' Her smile had grown gentle and the intensity was gone from her eyes. At this moment she'd reverted to the woman he'd thought he had loved.

'Why did you come to London?' he asked, fascinated despite himself. She shifted the sleeping Morwenna in her arms and gave him a provocative look.

'After you. What did you think? It was obvious, I'd have thought. You were the joker in the pack. I knew I had to stop you.'

The beat of William's heart grew stronger. So he hadn't been wrong after all. He took a long pause before asking the next question, aware of exactly what it might set off.

'But you didn't,' he said softly. 'Why was that?'

'I think you know the answer to that question.' And there they stood, only yards apart though light years in practical terms.

'It's still not too late.' He was taking a massive gamble but, sadly, she shook her head.

'The game ended,' she said throatily, 'when I realised I had fallen in love with you. I always thought I was a one man woman; it turns out I was wrong.' And this time the tears on her cheeks were the genuine thing.

From the adjoining balcony came the sound of a loud-hailer; the waiting police had finally run out of patience.

'Luisa Salvoni. Put down the child and raise your hands above your head. And then walk forward through the door. We've got you covered on all sides. Give yourself up.'

The smile she gave him was bitter sweet as slowly she shook her head.

'Never,' she whispered, and handed him Morwenna.

Then hoisted herself over the balcony rail and stepped off into space.

40

She was out in the garden, mowing the lawn, when he finally got home. The traffic on the motorway had been nose to tail for the last half-hour because of disruptive roadworks outside Oxford. Still, he was here now, breathing the purer air, and he stood and watched her silently for a while before announcing himself. The extra weight really suited her, made her softer and more fulfilled, and he liked the way she had cut her hair, framing her face in long tendrils. Morwenna, now a mature nearly four, was following her docilely with a broom, sweeping up the grass cuttings into neat piles. Together they were a picture of tranquillity. Emotion rose in his throat and threatened to choke him. He still found himself on the brink of tears on the most unlikely occasions. The shrink had said it would pass eventually, all part of the process of healing. He had to work his way through it in his own good time.

'All right, sweetie?' she called, noticing him as she turned, and he strode across the grass to give her a kiss.

'You shouldn't be doing that,' he protested, wresting

the mower from her hands. 'Have some sense, for good-ness' sake. In your condition.'

'I'm not an invalid,' said Edwina calmly. 'It won't do the baby any harm.' But he tossed aside his jacket and finished the last few rows while she went into the cottage to pour him a drink.

'Good day?' she asked when they were seated under the trees, watching Morwenna romping with her puppy. That terrifying experience appeared to have left her unscathed. It was amazing just how resilient toddlers could be.

'Pretty hectic. Though I mustn't complain.' Teaching in Oxford was keeping him on his toes.

'Well, we've baked some brownies and a Victoria sponge and made you a very special supper.' Her skin was glow-ing from being outdoors so much. He had never, since they met, known her look better.

'You know, pregnancy really suits you. Perhaps we should have a few more.'

'Whoa!' she said in mock alarm. 'Let's get this one sorted out first.'

When they sold the house, they had moved down here and pumped new life into Aunt Jane's cottage. They had packed away her knick-knacks and stowed them in the attic until, some time at a future date, Morwenna would be old enough to respect them. She and that ebullient puppy; the cottage looked like a scene of carnage. But they'd grown to love it, despite the lack of space, and were living very contentedly in their reduced circumstances.

* * *

419

Everything had changed in just a year and the biggest excitement of all was, of course, the baby. Edwina could not believe she could be so happy, with all thoughts of Gareth completely banished and gone. She did feel a pang when she read about his marriage but even that had really been only passing. They deserved each other, he and the supercilious Portia. She bet he would munch his way through her money like the weevil he was. And then, in all probability, move on. It seemed to be the pattern of his life. When she thought how close she had come to wrecking everything, she closed her eyes and shuddered. All that had happened had somehow been for the good, though she hoped never to have to go through anything like it again. The near loss of Morwenna had driven her right to the edge, but William had valiantly stood by her and they'd pulled through.

She looked at him fondly now as he frowned over the evening paper, and liked the distinction of his newly greying hair. It suited him, made him look more mature by adding a touch of gravitas he had formerly lacked. Each of them had been to hell and back and still hadn't talked it through. Her mother had insisted that they both have a spot of therapy but only William had bothered to stay the course. Edwina was far too impatient and self-assured. And all the curing she'd needed had been the baby. When it came to the crunch, she'd stayed quiet about Gareth, and there wasn't any point in reviving it now. Sue, when she came to visit, occasionally asked about him, and Edwina was pleased to assure her it was all in the past.

'I was a total idiot,' she freely admitted. 'Risking my marriage in that way.' But fate had generously given her a second shot and now she was playing strictly by the rules. And she loved this idyllic, rural life, found she didn't miss the city one bit. She had even revived Aunt Jane's bric-à-brac stall, though now the proceeds went towards curing breast cancer.

She occasionally popped up to town for a spot of shopping and still met up with the other two girls for lunch. Life for Sue continued much the same but Meryl was visibly tenser and more neurotic. Still hadn't succeeded in catching herself a man, was starting to date unsuitably and reply to lonely hearts ads.

'It's all right for you,' she grumbled to Edwina. 'You always manage to come out smelling of roses.' It was amazing to see how their marriage had stabilised and all because of the abduction of Morwenna.

William found teaching in Oxford a real challenge, though more exhausting than he ever would have imagined. Caring for a toddler had had its share of stress but not in the league of a bunch of bright undergrads. They certainly kept him on his toes and he sometimes found it hard to stay one jump ahead. But that was what made him so content, the feeling that his brain was being stretched. He sometimes came home too tired for even the crossword which hugely amused Edwina.

What had happened with Luisa was something he'd succeeded in blocking out, except occasionally in the dead of night when exhaustion kept him lying there awake. He still found it hard to believe she had been a killer, that shy, gentle creature who had managed to touch his heart. Now he understood why she had refused to get involved – she was carrying Hepatitis C and hadn't wanted to infect him. Which meant that her feelings towards him must have been genuine. Though he dared not allow his memory to go there, because it still hurt so much . . .

Edwina occasionally asked him about those horrible final moments, but the memory of Luisa's falling body was more than he could bear. Why it had had to happen that way he still didn't quite understand. Though the police had told him he was lucky to be alive, since she'd been on his trail all those weeks. Instead of Greenslade it might well have been him; they had found her list in the flat in Milton Keynes.

'Something must have happened to cause her to change her mind,' said the DI. William said nothing. What would be the point? He hadn't even confided in Tim when the case had been finally wound up. Some things would always remain sacred in his heart. Especially the memory of Luisa.

FAMILY REUNION

Carol Smith

As her eightieth birthday approaches, Odile Annesley, who has been living alone in France for forty years, contacts her scattered grandchildren to give them details of her will. The five granddaughters see it as the perfect opportunity for a family get-together abroad. Solid Clemency, the perfect wife and mother; London property dealer, Madeleine; Paris dress designer, Elodie; academic Canadian, Isabelle; poor, deprived Cherie, the misfit. And Harry, the golden boy. Each has grown up in their own world but, like all families, the shared characteristics are there. Then the killing starts, the secrets spill and it is clear that one of them is very different indeed . . . .

UNFINISHED BUSINESS

Carol Smith

The brutal murder of golden girl, Jinx McLennan, early one Sunday in her exclusive Kensington house, shocks the neighbours and triggers a police inquiry that delves deeply into her colourful past. Single, childless, Jinx nevertheless had it all – brains, popularity, her own successful business, plus a wide-ranging network of lovers and friends. Closest of all were her own small design team, the surrogate family who've been with her from the start: devoted, long-suffering Dottie and her artist husband, Sam; gentle, reliable Ambrose, the team's backbone; Wayne, the zany trainee with the outrageous lifestyle; and Serafina, hot on the fast track, who wants everything Jinx had, but now. Plus millionare genius, Damien Rudge, the goose who lays their golden eggs. The trail goes cold until, in a shock revelation, it turns out to be a case of mistaken identity. The wrong person has been murdered. Out there somewhere is still a crazed killer with unfinished business who will have to kill again.

Other bestselling Time Warner titles available by mail: